*Praise for*
The Songbird of Hope Hill

"In *The Songbird of Hope Hill,* Kim Sawyer has penned an unforgettable story of God's grace and redemption. Birdie's and Ephraim's love story is a parable for the love God has for us. You'll be thinking of these characters long after you've turned the last page. I know I still am."
—KATHLEEN Y'BARBO, *Publishers Weekly* bestselling author of *The Black Midnight* and *The Bayou Nouvelle Brides*

"Kim Vogel Sawyer blends affecting atmosphere, complex circumstances, challenging conflicts, and rewarding resolution in her latest historical novel, *The Songbird of Hope Hill.* In Birdie Clarkson, Sawyer has created that character we all yearn to comfort—the sinner who desperately craves love for her broken, humbled heart. One can't help but to cheer for Birdie in her brave willingness to step forward into peace and freedom. This book satisfies our longing to experience again the kind of forgiveness and divine justice that only Jesus can grant."
—TRISH PERRY, author of *The Guy I'm Not Dating*

"What a precious story of God's grace and redemption! Kim Vogel Sawyer writes with poignant precision, weaving stories with depth that draw in her readers. *The Songbird of Hope Hill* had my full attention from its absorbing start to its tender finish, leaving me teary-eyed—and longing for a sequel. Splendid!"
—SHARLENE MACLAREN, author of twenty-three novels

"*The Songbird of Hope Hill* held my heart from the first page. Set in Texas in 1895, this touching story is about Birdie Clarkson, a good girl who was forced to make bad decisions, and Ephraim Overly, the son of a minister and his wife who want to save fallen women. That task proves to be a tough one, and secrets from the past haunt these characters like an ever-blowing prairie wind. Fans of Francine Rivers's *Redeeming Love* should enjoy this story of redemption and one young woman's need to find grace and forgiveness."

—LENORA WORTH, author of *Disappearance in Pinecraft*

"Kim Vogel Sawyer's *The Songbird of Hope Hill* illustrates that no matter how often or how far we fall, God is always there to help us back up. Truly nothing—nothing—can separate us from the love of God."

—JULIANNA DEERING, author of
the Drew Farthering Mystery series

# The Songbird of Hope Hill

## Other Novels by Kim Vogel Sawyer

*Beneath a Prairie Moon*

*Bringing Maggie Home*

*Echoes of Mercy*

*Grace and the Preacher*

*The Grace That Leads Us Home*

*Just As I Am*

*Guide Me Home*

*The Librarian of Boone's Hollow*

*Return to Boone's Hollow*

*Room for Hope*

*Still My Forever*

*The Tapestry of Grace*

*Through the Deep Waters*

*What Once Was Lost*

*When Grace Sings*

*When Love Returns*

*When Mercy Rains*

# The Songbird of
# Hope Hill

A Novel

KIM VOGEL SAWYER

WATERBROOK

All Scripture quotations are taken from the King James Version.

A WaterBrook Trade Paperback Original

Copyright © 2024 by Kim Vogel Sawyer

Published in the United States by WaterBrook, an imprint of Random House, a division of Penguin Random House LLC.

WATERBROOK and colophon are registered trademarks of Penguin Random House LLC.

LIBRARY OF CONGRESS CATALOGING-IN-PUBLICATION DATA

Names: Sawyer, Kim Vogel, author.
Title: The songbird of Hope Hill : a novel / Kim Vogel Sawyer.
Description: First edition. | [Colorado Springs] : WaterBrook, 2024.
Identifiers: LCCN 2023039955 | ISBN 9780593600818 (trade paperback ; acid-free paper) | ISBN 9780593600825 (ebook)
Subjects: LCGFT: Christian fiction. | Novels.
Classification: LCC PS3619.A97 S683 2024 | DDC 813/.6—dc23/eng/20230913
LC record is available at https://lccn.loc.gov/2023039955

Printed in the United States of America on acid-free paper

waterbrookmultnomah.com

2 4 6 8 9 7 5 3 1

First Edition

*Book design by Virginia Norey*
*Bird on branch art by Pagina/stock.adobe.com*

For Eileen.

You told me to write a story that says there are no lost causes in heaven's eyes. You believed it and showed it in the way you loved.

I miss you, my friend!

For the scripture saith, Whosoever believeth on him shall not be ashamed.

—Romans 10:11

# The Songbird of Hope Hill

# Chapter One

Early February 1895
Outskirts of Tulsey, Texas
Birdie Clarkson

"Girls? Girls! Hour to open!"

Miz Holland's grating call roused Birdie from a restless sleep. She stretched, and the ropes holding her hay-stuffed mattress squawked. She rubbed her eyes. When she'd gone to sleep eight hours ago, bright noonday sun was trying to sneak past the edges of the fringed window shade. Now those slivers of light were gone as nighttime cloaked the landscape. Her room was as dark as a tomb. Fitting, since what she did here made her feel dead inside.

She sat up and blinked several times, trying to discern the location of her bedside lamp. She didn't dare break another one. The cost of replacement was too high. Slowly, she reached toward an hourglass-shaped object. Her palm encountered the cool glass globe of her lamp. She skimmed her fingers downward to the base, located the little tin of matches, and struck one on the flint. The flare pierced her eyes, and she squinted. She raised the globe, lit the wick, and put out the match's flame with a puff of breath. Seated on the edge of her lumpy mattress, she stared at the lamp's flickering glow and gathered the courage to rise. Dress. Go downstairs.

The other girls at Lida's Palace didn't bother lighting a lamp upon rising. They dressed in the dark. Birdie hadn't been here long enough to learn the trick. But as soon as she'd donned her "work gown" and brushed her brown waves that Miz Holland called her crowning glory, she would extinguish her lamp. Partly to save the oil, for which she was expected to pay. Mostly because she had no desire to see her mirrored reflection attired in the bawdy costume . . . nor anything else that took place in this small room.

Noises—the patter of feet on floorboards, the creak of drawers or wardrobe doors opening and then snapping closed, a dull thud followed by a muffled curse—filtered through the thin walls separating her room from the others in the old hotel. Miz Holland's girls were readying themselves to receive the evening's visitors. To earn her keep, Birdie must do the same.

Pulling in a breath of fortification through her flared nostrils, she trudged to the corner and removed her gauzy, emerald-green, lace-embellished gown from its hook. Her stomach churned as she slipped her arms into the thin fabric sleeves. How many men would come tonight? How many would choose her? Since she was so new, she hadn't yet become anyone's favorite. Some of the girls bragged about the number of men who favored them over the others. Birdie had no desire to win such a contest. Then again, a girl's popularity secured her continued sanctuary in Lida's Palace. Would she be cast out if she couldn't be, as Miz Holland put it, more friendly?

Birdie inwardly shuddered. She wouldn't be here at all if hunger hadn't driven her a week ago to knock on the door of her mama's old school friend's home and request a piece of bread or a bowl of soup.

In her mind's eye, she saw the woman's scowl change to recognition and then to a conniving smile as she appraised Birdie from her wind-tangled hair to the scuffed toes of her dusty shoes. Birdie experienced again the trepidation that had tiptoed through her at Miz Holland's sly assessment. Why hadn't she run away? If only she'd run away . . .

*Bang! Bang! Bang!*

The angry thuds on the door made her jerk. Her thumb caught in the delicate lace at the cuff of her right sleeve and tore it. Groaning in regret, she hurried to the door, frantically tying her sash as she went. She flung her door open and discovered Minerva, the oldest of the girls residing at Lida's Palace, standing in the hall with her fists on her hips.

Minerva tossed her head, fluttering the feathers she'd woven into her fiery red braid. "Lida ain't gonna hold breakfast for you. She says come now." She twisted her lips in a sneer. "Look at you. You ain't even combed your hair yet." Her gaze dropped to the loop of lace dangling against Birdie's wrist. "An' it looks like you got a little repair work to do." Her eyes glinted with humor. "Some fella get a little eager last night?"

Birdie's face flamed. She shook her head. "No. I—"

Minerva rolled her eyes. "'Course not. Why would he? Spindly thing like you ain't got nothin' worth buyin'."

Birdie pressed her chin to her shoulder and closed her eyes. If only it were true. Maybe Miz Holland would kick her out. But then how would she pay for travel to Kansas City, where Papa's sister lived? Birdie still remembered standing with her aunt at Papa's graveside six years ago, asking, "What will I do now? How will I go on without my father?"

Aunt Sally had put her arm around Birdie and pulled her close. "Dear girl, your earthly father's gone, but you still have a heavenly Father. He'll never leave you. You can lean on Him." She'd then taken Birdie by the shoulders. "What do you think about coming to Kansas with me? You can finish your schooling and work with me in my dress shop. Maybe your mama will send you, if we ask."

From the time she was little, Birdie had been handy with a needle. She could be a good helper for her aunt. Returning to a house where no kindhearted papa would sing songs with her or kiss her good night held no appeal. But when Birdie asked for money for the trip to Kansas, Mama threw a tantrum and called her selfish. So Birdie had stayed. Until the day Mama left.

Fifteen dollars and eighty-five cents. That's what the station clerk at the depot said she needed to buy a train ticket from Tulsey to Kansas City. How many nights would it take to earn such a sum? And would Aunt Sally even welcome her, now that she'd—

Minerva's derisive huff pulled Birdie from her thoughts. The girl flounced toward the staircase, feathers gently waving, and called over her shoulder, "If you're wantin' breakfast, better hurry up before Olga eats it all. That one sure can't be called *spindly*." Her laughter rang.

Birdie folded her arms across her aching chest and hung her head, shame weighting her. Hunger had driven her here. She'd hardly eaten a bite since she arrived. She didn't want breakfast. She just wanted . . . out.

If only Papa hadn't died. Then—

*You still have a heavenly Father. You can lean on Him.* Aunt Sally's sweet words whispered through Birdie's heart. Even though Birdie's parents hadn't attended church regularly, Papa had sung songs about God, who Aunt Sally called the heavenly Father. Birdie wished she could call Him her own. But if there was a Father in heaven, He'd surely turned His back on her the minute she crossed the threshold of Lida's Palace.

The growl of wagon wheels on the hardpacked dirt driveway sneaked past the uninsulated walls. She broke out in a cold sweat. Customers were coming.

### Ephraim Overly

The old Bradford Hotel hunkered against the gray backdrop of evening like a giant cyclops. A cyclops, because only the front-

door window—oval, with a border of leaded-glass diamonds—
was backlit by lamplight. That glow, as soft as the first rays of
dawn peeking over the horizon, was meant to draw a fellow in,
make him feel welcome. Gooseflesh prickled Ephraim's arms.
Now the hotel was a business called Lida's Palace. And he'd
been to places similar to it with his father often enough to know
this was no palace.

Beside him on the wagon seat, Father leaned forward and
rubbed his palms together. "It seems we're ahead of the crowd
tonight."

Ephraim glanced up and down the hitching rail running the
full width of the building. Not a single wagon or saddled horse
waited in front. "That's good," he said.

Father gave a stiff nod. "It is very good." He pointed. "Make a
half circle and park at the end of the porch, facing the road.
If anyone else arrives while we're inside, our wagon won't be
blocked, and—if necessary—we'll be able to make a hasty departure."

Considering their visit to Lida's Palace a month ago, and the
resulting mayhem when they left, Ephraim approved Father's
suggestion. It had taken a week for the painful knot on his head
from a well-aimed rock to disappear. "Yes, sir." He made a wide
turn in the yard, the wheels stirring little swirls of fine dust that
quickly whisked away on the evening breeze. "Whoa . . ." The
pair of sorrel geldings drew to a halt, snorting, and Ephraim set
the brake.

Father's jaw was set at a determined angle, his shoulders
square. The shadow thrown by his hat's wide, flat brim hid
his expression, but Ephraim didn't need to see him to know
Father's eyes held a glint of fervor. The same glint that always
appeared before he did battle.

Father slapped his knees and stood. "Come with me,
Ephraim."

Ephraim gave a start. "But, Father, I—" He gulped. "I never go in." Nor did he want to. He received enough ridicule and rejection as a result of his father's frequent visits to houses of ill repute.

Father put his hand on Ephraim's shoulder. "Come with me."

When Father used his firm tone, Ephraim—although a grown man of twenty-six years—automatically obeyed. He hopped down from the wagon and trailed Father to the porch steps. Climbed the three risers. Trod to the door that led to iniquity.

Father grasped the doorknob and entered without knocking. Ephraim hesitated outside the threshold, his limbs quivering. "Son . . ." Father's low-toned, simple command propelled Ephraim into the entry as the door clicked shut behind him.

Beneath his feet, scuffed penny-sized tiles still bore the name THE BRADFORD in black against white. His heart wrenched. If only it were still a hotel. Why did places like Lida's Palace flourish when he and his parents prayed so diligently for the despicable business to end? He'd pondered the question many times over the past years, but he still had no answer.

A middle-aged woman in a ruffled red ball gown, her lips painted the same bright color as the sheeny fabric of her frock, sashayed across the faded carpet of the hotel parlor and stopped in front of Father. Her kohl-lined eyes narrowed. "You again?"

Behind her, at least a dozen young women lounged on sofas and chairs. All wore face paint similar to the older woman's, but their clothing was unsuitable for public display. Ephraim didn't know where to look, so he settled his gaze on the floor tiles.

"Yes, I am here again, Lida." Father's booming voice filled the room. "But tonight you have no 'hounds' to sic on me or my son."

Lida chuckled, the sound almost sinister. "Oh, they'll be along soon enough, Reverend Overly. No preacher's ever preached a sermon good enough to keep 'em away." She paced back and forth in front of Father, her skirts rustling with the movement. "An' no preachin' has ever convinced any of my girls to leave me. They're taken care of here. Fed. Housed. Treated good. Out there?" She came to a stop, but the shadow of her waving hand came near Ephraim's toes. "Folks stick their noses in the air an' snub 'em. Won't give 'em the time of day. Why would they want to leave this warm home for cold rejection?"

Full laughter rolled, and Ephraim glanced at Lida's smug face before turning his focus to the floor again. "But go ahead, Isaiah. Give 'em your best sermon. It'll do me good to see 'em ignore you the way your *fine Christian folks*"—she made the phrase sound like a curse—"snub them."

Sweat tickled Ephraim's neck. He shrugged within his jacket, but the gesture did nothing to remove the uncomfortable weight of guilt her words inspired. *Thou shalt love thy neighbour as thyself.* He'd been taught Jesus' admonition from his earliest memories. Churchgoers were surely familiar with the biblical instruction. But how many truly followed it? In truth, he struggled to love those who frequented establishments like Lida's and, equally so, the holier-than-thou people who mocked his father's ministry.

Father looped his hand through Ephraim's elbow and escorted him to the center of the room. "Ladies, this is my son."

Lida snorted.

"He can verify," Father went on in his strong, ever-confident voice, "everything of which I am about to tell you. What I will say is truth. Full truth, not manipulation or twisted truth, as you just heard from the mouth of your so-called benefactor."

What was Father doing? He'd never involved Ephraim in this way before. Ephraim's gaze unwillingly traveled across the prostitutes' faces. All but one stared directly at him. Some seemed bored, others scornful. One, with feathers woven into her thick red braid, gave him a brash appraisal that made him want to hide behind Father. *Love thy neighbour.* Did Jesus ask the impossible? Ephraim looked aside.

"Certainly here you are housed and fed," Father said, "but you have no freedom. Freedom is found in a relationship with God through His Son, Jesus Christ, who absolves all who ask from every sin."

Ephraim had heard his father preach on salvation and the forgiveness of sin so many times, he could have recited the lines along with him. While Father shared the biblical account about Jesus assuring the woman who'd been caught in adultery that she could assume a new life, free of the dark blot of sinful choices, Ephraim silently prayed that these lost, broken young women who were loved by God would make a new choice this day to leave this place where men purchased their bodies and battered their souls.

"Come with me today. Come to Hope Hill, a safe haven, where you will receive an education. My dear wife, Ophelia, will teach you skills and help you find places of honest employment. You will earn a fair wage and needn't sacrifice something to strangers that is meant to be shared as an expression of love to a devoted husband. Come with me now!" Father released Ephraim's arm and held his hands wide in invitation. "A new life awaits. Who will come?"

Silence filled the room, save the steady *tick-tick* from a stately grandfather clock in the corner and the occasional chirp from a yellow bird flitting from rod to rod in a dented cage in front of the fully draped windows.

Ephraim held his breath, hoping some would rise, would come, as Father had bidden them. As he'd prayed they would. The girls, with the exception of a slip of a girl who sat with her chin pressed to her shoulder, her face nearly hidden by a veil of wavy dark hair, shifted in their seats and seemed to look anywhere in the room except at Father.

Lida, smirking, sidled near. She slowly clapped in mock applause. "That was some fiery sermon, Isaiah, but like I told you, my girls ain't interested in what y'all's peddling. They're happy right where they are."

"Happy?" Father blasted the word. "Not a one of these girls are happy, Lida, and neither are you. You're helpless and afraid and guilt-ridden, and you think you're trapped. But what I told them applies to you, too. Come. Learn a new way of life. Find true joy, Lida. Jesus loves you, and—"

Lida turned her back on Father, waving her arms at the girls the way a hen flaps its wings at its chicks. "Upstairs, all of you! Stay there until I call you."

The girls stood, giving one another uncertain looks. Whispering, shoulders hunched as if expecting blows to fall, they inched toward the staircase.

Father walked alongside them. "You don't have to go upstairs. You have another choice. You have a chance for freedom. You can walk out the door."

Lida moved step by step with Father, shaking her head and murmuring, "Up those stairs away from this religious fanatic. Up, girls, up."

One by one, they mounted the stairs, none of them even glancing at Father. He grasped the turned finial on the newel post with one hand and held the other toward the girls. "Walk out the door into a new life, ladies!" Father's tone turned pleading, and Ephraim prayed for the girls to pay heed. "Come with us now. Come."

Lida released a little gasp and hurried to the door. She peered out, then turned with a triumphant smile. "Customers comin'.

Your time's up, *Reverend*. Better scat before my hounds are on you."

Ephraim looked, too. A wagon with two men on its seat and a horse with a rider were turning in at the end of the half-mile-long drive. Ephraim rubbed the spot where the rock had struck him. "Father?"

Father turned one more imploring gaze toward the girls. "Doesn't anyone want to leave this life of pain for true peace and freedom?"

The last girl—the very thin one who'd never raised her face during Father's impassioned sermon—stopped. She turned around, her pale hands holding her robe closed at her throat and her wide eyes shifting from Father to Lida to Father again. "I . . ." She swallowed. "I do."

# Chapter Two

Ephraim

Ephraim pulled in a breath of surprise—God had answered his prayer with a yes!

"And I, too." The call came from somewhere on the upstairs landing. A girl with uncombed blond hair pushed her way through the group gathered at the top of the staircase. She linked arms with the dark-haired girl and the two of them pattered to the bottom. She cast a side-eye glance at Lida. "C-can I come, too?"

"All are welcome at Hope Hill." Father boomed the reply so loudly his voice echoed from the tall stamped-tin ceiling. Then he stepped between the girls, took each by an elbow, and hurried them out the door.

Ephraim stumbled behind them, his body quaking in both gratitude and worry. Two souls rescued! A cause for celebration! But Lida followed close behind him, spewing vile words at Father. The approaching customers could cause trouble. He and Father needed to get the girls away before Lida convinced the men to help her take them back. Father never raised a hand in violence. The meek shall inherit the earth, he preached, and he lived the belief. If the men resorted to brute force, they would lose these girls. Unless God intervened.

*God, our Shield and Defender, protect them. And us.*

Ephraim climbed onto the driver's seat while Father ushered the girls to the back of the revival wagon. There was no gate to remove since Ephraim had taken it off before leaving for the evening, but Father struggled with the attached fold-down step. Apparently, the iron workings needed to be greased again. Why hadn't Ephraim checked that when he removed the gate? *Hurry, hurry,* his thoughts begged.

"Who do you think you are, Isaiah Overly?" Lida stood at the end of the porch and shook her fist at Father. "You've got no right to steal my merchandise!"

Ephraim cringed. Such a horrible way to refer to human beings, created in the image of God Himself. How many times had the girls who lived under Lida's roof heard themselves referred to in such a callous manner? How long would it take them to overcome the idea that they were commodities to be sold? How long would it take Father to get them into the wagon?

Lida stomped her foot against the porch floor, anger blazing her cheeks the same bold color of her dress. "Ain't you stole enough from me already? Now you'd take my very livelihood?"

The step clanked into position, and Ephraim heaved a sigh of relief. Father offered his hand, and neither girl hesitated in accepting his help. The gesture cheered Ephraim. Some small element of trust must still linger in their trampled souls. The two climbed into the wagon and sat side by side on one of the benches.

Father climbed into the back, too, and gave the girls one of Mother's quilts. Even wrapped in the quilt, the girls shivered. The evening was mild, so the tremble was from trepidation, not cold. Ephraim understood. He quivered from head to toe.

Father aimed a frown in Ephraim's direction. "Let's go."

Ephraim turned forward and gave the reins a snap. The horses strained against the rigging, and the wagon jerked into motion toward the road. Ephraim fixed his eyes on the coming men. He and Father hadn't rescued any girls on their last visit to Lida's and still they were attacked. Considering their two passengers in the wagon, the men had a bigger reason to set upon them tonight.

He sent another desperate plea for safety—his, Father's, and the girls'—toward the star-speckled heavens.

"Go then! See if I care!" Lida's strident voice pierced the night air. "There'll be other girls comin' to replace 'em. There always are. 'Cause the world is full o' men like—"

"Hurry the horses, Ephraim." Father spoke over whatever else Lida said. "We need to get these young ladies home."

"Yes, sir." He flicked the reins and called, "Get up, now, Red and Rusty." The horses obediently broke into a perfectly matched trot.

Their wagon drew alongside the man riding horseback. Ephraim's pulse pounded against his throat at twice the speed of the horses' hooves against the ground. The man glanced over, expressionless, and returned his attention toward Lida's Palace. Then Ephraim's wagon met the approaching one. Neither its driver nor the passenger glanced his way.

Ephraim's heart swelled in joy and wonder. A miracle. Surely he'd just witnessed a miracle. "Two prayers answered in one night," he said on a note of praise. "God is raining down His blessings." He aimed a smile over his shoulder, then gave a start. Where were his passengers?

Father emerged from beneath one bench. The girls scooted from beneath the second. No wonder the men hadn't paid Ephraim any mind. They'd thought he was alone. So not a miracle after all. But wasn't it miraculous that two girls had chosen to leave Lida's Palace? Although Father had rescued dozens of girls over the years from other brothels in the central part of the vast state of Texas, until tonight, none had come from Lida's. The evening's rescue was cause for celebration.

He silently apologized to the Lord for his moment of doubt, then thanked Him again for prompting these two to leave their former life behind. As his parents had taught him, he also prayed for the one he viewed as an enemy, Lida Holland. Mother always said those who victimized others were likely victims at one time, too, and deserved compassion. Father was the preacher, but Mother had the most Christlike spirit Ephraim knew.

As he ended his prayer, one of the brothel owner's comments roared through his memory.

*"Ain't you stole enough from me already?"*

The choice of words, and the venom behind them, raised a multitude of questions in Ephraim's mind. Maybe when they got home, and the girls were safe in the room Mother had readied in hope of it being used, he would ask Father what Lida meant. He yawned, the long day and the tension of the last hour overwhelming him at once. Or perhaps he'd ask tomorrow, when they were both rested.

He sent another look over his shoulder. Father sat with arms folded, eyes closed, head bobbing with the wagon's rocking motion. But both girls were wide-eyed and alert, gazes flicking here and there. Were they watching for pursuers, or had they been locked up so long they'd forgotten the width and breadth of the open expanse and were marveling at the Texas countryside?

One of the wheels hit a rock, and the wagon jolted. Ephraim turned his attention to the moonlit road again, but an image of the new rescues lingered in his mind. He had witnessed enough girls adjusting to life outside of brothels to know that these two would need time to accept and appropriately handle their newfound freedom. They'd need patience and prayer and the kind of healing only God Himself could give.

He yawned again, his eyes scrunching closed with its force. Their new life would start tomorrow, within the bounds of Hope Hill. An hour's drive was still ahead of them. He hoped he could stay awake long enough to get them safely home.

Birdie

Mrs. Overly, the kind-faced woman who'd escorted Birdie and Olga to an upstairs sleeping room in the huge house the preacher called Hope Hill, offered a gentle smile to both girls. "Good night. Sleep well."

"Good night, ma'am. Thank you," Birdie said. Olga only nodded.

Mrs. Overly clicked the door closed behind her. The gentle *pat-pat* of her footsteps faded away, and then silence fell upon the room. Birdie released a long, slow breath. She sank against the down-filled pillow, finally daring to believe she was free of service in Lida's Palace. And to be in such a grand home! When the wagon had turned onto the lane leading to a two-story house with a turret pointing toward the stars on one corner and a spindled balcony above a porch larger than the entire house in which Birdie had grown up, she'd nearly lost her ability to breathe.

She closed her eyes and pictured again the candles winking in the front windows. Tiny flickers of welcome. A delightful shiver rattled through her frame. Under the soft moonlight, Hope Hill was . . . beautiful. And Mrs. Overly said it was her new home. Mrs. Overly also instructed them to sleep, but Birdie had spent most of the day sleeping. Even though the bed was comfortable, the fresh sheets inviting, she was too awake to sleep. Or was she in fact sleeping and this place was only a dream?

She popped her eyes open and squinted around the shadowy room at the unfamiliar wallpaper, furnishings, and pair of uncovered windows allowing a view of the star-speckled sky. No, this was not Lida's Palace. She sighed, a smile tugging at the corners of her lips.

Suddenly Olga tossed her covers aside and bounded from the mattress. She darted around the iron footboard of Birdie's bed and popped the doors open on the wardrobe centered between the windows. She pawed through the items inside, muttering under her breath.

Although Birdie and Olga were wide awake after having slept most of the day, everyone else who resided here needed their rest. She and Olga should at least be quiet. "What are you doing?" Birdie whispered.

Olga huffed. "Looking for a bigger nightgown."

Birdie cringed at how loud Olga's voice seemed. She sat up, too, and lit the lamp on the stand between the beds. Maybe if Olga found what she needed, she'd get back in bed and be quiet. She carried the lamp to the wardrobe and held it so the light flowed across the garments hanging on hooks inside the large piece of furniture.

"*Danke*," Olga said. She grabbed a plain cotton nightgown from a hook and draped it across her front. "Does it look to fit me?"

Birdie took a step back and scanned the gown. Its simplicity was a welcome change from the clothes they'd been forced to wear at Lida's. She nodded.

Olga slapped the wardrobe doors closed and tossed the gown across the foot of Birdie's bed. She wrestled the gown she'd been given by Mrs. Overly over her head. Birdie looked aside, not wanting to invade Olga's privacy, but kept the lamp gripped in front of her so Olga could see what she was doing.

Gazing at the velvety sky outside the window, she listened to soft grunts, the swish of cotton fabric, and finally a relieved sigh. Was Olga dressed again? She peeked from the corner of her eye and encountered Olga's broad grin.

"You are a funny one."

Birdie frowned. "Funny? Why?"

Olga grabbed the nightgown she'd discarded and tossed it

on the floor near the door on her way back to the bed she'd been assigned. "So shy, staring out a window at nothing while I change clothes." She sat on the edge of the mattress and smoothed the new nightgown over her knees. "You never shared a room with sisters while growing up, *ja*?"

"I was my parents' only child." At least, the only child who'd lived past infancy. Mama and Papa had buried three baby boys before Birdie's arrival. Papa said that was why Mama held herself aloof from Birdie—out of fear of giving her heart and then having it broken again. But Birdie wasn't so sure about that. She eased around the bed and put the lamp on the table again. She slipped between the sheets, but didn't extinguish the lamp. Clearly, neither of them were going to sleep. "Did you have a lot of sisters?"

Olga held up four fingers. "Two older, two younger. And also four brothers. Not a moment by myself, ever, when I was a girl." She sighed and sent a searching look from ceiling to floor and corner to corner. "And we girls all shared a room half the size of this one. So crowded. I always hated feeling all crammed in." She grabbed handfuls of fabric at her waist and tugged, frowning at the cloth. "Soon this will be too small, too." She licked her lips and lifted her gaze to Birdie. "They will send me packing when it is."

Birdie angled her head. Hadn't the preacher said all were welcome at Hope Hill? "Why would they?"

Olga snorted. "Shy and naïve, too. How you came to be one of Lida's girls is a puzzle." She leaned forward slightly. "There is a baby growing inside me, Birdie. That is why I came tonight. Lida knew. Last week she told me I would have to go when I got too big to fit in my work clothes." She flapped her hand at the basket in the corner, where the two of them had deposited their clothes from Miz Holland. "Another month, maybe, and I would bust the seams." She sat up and gazed toward the window, her expression wistful. "The preacher coming tonight almost makes me think God planned it."

*God planned it* . . . Birdie's heart fluttered.

Olga snorted again and looked down. "Pretty *dämlich*, ja? Thinking that a *Gott in Himmel* would bother with the likes of you and me?"

The little flutter fizzled and died. Olga was probably right. "If the preacher hadn't come, what would you have done?"

Olga fiddled with the buttons at the bodice of her gown. "What others like me do when a babe is coming. Visit someone who can . . ." Her chin rose, and her eyes glittered with unshed tears. "I didn't want to. Why hurt the poor little thing? It did nothing wrong. But I've had no other home except Lida's since I was fifteen and my papa caught me kissing Sam Baldwin in our barn. He called me bad names and told me to leave. But I guess he was right about me, ja? After all . . ." She caressed her stomach, blinking hard, and shrugged. "If I got rid of it, Lida would let me come back. So . . . that's what I would have done."

Birdie stared at Olga's unsmiling face for several seconds, uncertain what to say or do. But feelings of gratitude overwhelmed her, and she blurted in a rush, "Then I'm glad the preacher came tonight. I'm glad you decided to leave Lida's. And I'm glad—" Should she talk of such personal things with someone she hardly knew? But Olga had been honest with her. She would be honest, too. "I'm glad you and your baby are safe."

Olga slid her palms from her belly to the quilt. She sighed. "For now we are. But I won't call this baby mine. I didn't want to get rid of it, but I won't keep it, either." She shuddered, and her eyes went steely. "I will stay here as long as I can hide it. So that means you must keep my secret. Do you hear me, Birdie?"

Birdie nodded automatically. "I won't tell."

"Good." Olga flopped sideways on the bed, pulling up her

knees. "If God loves the way the preacher said He does, then He will take this baby away from me. We will both be better off." She rolled over, turning her back to Birdie. "Put out the lamp. We might as well try to sleep."

Birdie did as Olga asked, but she couldn't sleep. Olga had called her naïve, but Birdie knew how babies were made. She laid her hands on her flat belly and stared at the plaster ceiling, imagining God somewhere far beyond her view. Might she have a baby growing inside her? She borrowed Olga's statement and whispered to the quiet room, "If God loves the way the preacher said He does . . . there won't be one in me."

# Chapter Three

Ophelia Overly

A t half past ten in the morning, Ophelia braced herself for the laborious climb to the second floor where the most recent arrivals were still sleeping. She wasn't surprised when they'd not responded to the morning wake-up chimes. They didn't yet know the chimes' purpose, and they were accustomed to sleeping during the day and working at night. But now they must adjust to a different schedule.

Behind the closed pocket doors to the right of the staircase, Ephraim played the music room's grand piano while the girls sang a fairly new song, "Lead On, O King Eternal." All the rescued residents at Hope Hill participated in music lessons with Ephraim. Singing together, the same way King David had instructed the Israelites centuries ago, bonded people and gave them a common purpose. Such a wise man, her Isaiah, to have Ephraim form the girls into a choir that helped lead worship at revival meetings. How could anyone criticize a group that sang praise to the heavenly Father?

" 'Lead on, O King eternal; we follow, not with fears, for gladness breaks like morning where'er your face appears . . . ' "

The soul-stirring words bolstered Ophelia as she climbed the risers one by one. Eighteen steps in all, a wearying journey. At the top, she paused until the pounding in her chest calmed, and then she followed the faded carpet runner past open doors in the wide, seemingly endless hallway to the single closed door at the very end on the left-hand side.

She knocked, listened for a moment, then knocked again. "Olga? Birdie?" Ophelia cracked the door open and peeked inside. Two quilt-covered lumps lay motionless on the feather mattresses. A rumpled nightgown puddled on the floor next to the door, out of place in the otherwise tidy room. Ophelia frowned at it for a moment, puzzled as to its presence, then picked it up and put it in the woven basket meant to hold soiled laundry. As she straightened, someone snuffled, and a bed frame creaked. At least one of the girls was awake.

Ophelia turned to face the beds and discovered the smaller of the two new arrivals, the one named Birdie, sitting up and blinking blearily. Ophelia smiled. "Good morning," she said in a normal tone. The second girl hadn't awakened yet, but she needed to rise. No sense in whispering. "You slept through breakfast. Now we're approaching noon, so it's nearly dinner-time. Time to—"

"What is that?" Birdie leaned in the direction of the doorway and tipped her head.

Ophelia drew back, confused. Then she realized the girls' voices from the floor below had increased in volume. The lovely blend crept all the way up the stairs, down the hallway, and into the bedroom. She chuckled lightly. "That is our choir. A captivating sound, don't you agree?"

The girl's amber-colored eyes widened. "You have a choir?"

Ophelia crossed to Birdie's bed and rested her hands on the footboard's white-painted top rail. "Indeed. All our residents participate." With the exception of little Ellie, of course. Ophelia's heart twisted. But maybe someday? "My son, Ephraim, is a gifted musician. He accompanies and directs the choir. They will be finished by the time you are dressed and downstairs, and they don't practice on Saturday or Sunday. But you and Olga will be a part of it starting next week."

Birdie clasped the quilt to her throat as if cradling it. Such a strange reaction. Ophelia offered a concerned frown. "Is something troubling you?"

Birdie shook her head, but her teary eyes and quivering chin indicated otherwise.

"Are you sure?"

Birdie gulped, and she opened her mouth as if to reply.

Olga abruptly sat up. She bounced a glare from Birdie to Ophelia. "Why are you in here?" The query growled out in a sleep-rasped tone.

"Waking you for the day." Ophelia chose a no-nonsense approach, past interactions with newcomers guiding her. "As I just told Birdie, it's nearly dinnertime, so please rise, dress, and come downstairs."

Olga groaned and flopped against her pillows.

Ophelia hid a smile. "I don't know if you recall everything I told you last night. As a reminder, the room next to the staircase is our bathing room. You'll find towels in the cupboard next to the washstand and a tin of tooth powder on the stand. I had Myra—you'll meet her at dinner—put fresh water in the pitcher for you, so you may wash your faces and brush your teeth." She turned toward the bureau next to the door. "There are undergarments, as well as stockings, hair pins, combs, and toothbrushes in the drawers." How difficult it must be to arrive at a place with nothing more than the clothes on one's back. These girls were truly starting over. Thanks to gracious donors, at least she and Isaiah could offer brand-new items for the girls' fresh start.

She crossed to the wardrobe and opened the doors. "Please choose whichever dresses you like."

Olga propped herself up on one elbow, her other hand pressed against her stomach, and scowled in the direction of the wardrobe. "What size are they? The nightgown you gave me to wear was too tight."

Ah, that explained the one Ophelia found on the floor.

"If these dresses are too *schmal*, do you have other ones?"

Although Olga's tone was sharp, Ophelia sensed embarrassment rather than aggravation behind the query. She offered the girl an assuring smile. "Indeed, we do. If none of these are suitable, we will go up to the attic together and search through the trunks." She prayed the climb to the attic wouldn't be necessary. Ascending the steep risers of the narrow staircase taxed her, and descending made her dizzy. "But there is a nice assortment here in a variety of sizes, so I trust you'll find one that fits, just as you did with the nightgown."

She moved to the door and paused with her hand on the porcelain knob. "After you've washed the sleep from your eyes and dressed for the day, please go to the study. It's across from the dining room on the south side of the downstairs hallway. Reverend Overly has a few things to discuss with you concerning your new home."

Olga and Birdie exchanged glances—Olga with an arched brow and twisted lips, Birdie with rapidly blinking, uncertain eyes. Ophelia had seen both looks before. Some of the girls balked at the rules. A few had even left immediately after hearing the requirements for living at Hope Hill. Ophelia sent up a silent prayer that neither Olga nor Birdie would choose to return to their former lives. Such a lifestyle would wear them out before they were middle age, and they would spend every day being used rather than cherished. God wanted so much more for them than endless mistreatment. Isaiah preached it, and Ophelia believed it with her whole heart.

She offered one more smile. "Welcome again, girls. We are so happy to have you here, and we truly pray you soon come to think of Hope Hill as your home."

Birdie

The moment Mrs. Overly closed the door behind her, Olga leaped from her bed. "Never mind washing my face or brushing my teeth. I need to find something to wear and visit the outhouse."

Birdie needed it, too, but she could wait her turn. On bare feet, she padded to the door. "I'll go make use of the washbowl and let you dress in private." Olga was already searching through a drawer and didn't answer. Birdie left the room.

Last night, they'd not been given a chance to examine their surroundings. With everyone else downstairs already, Birdie felt free to explore. She moved down the hallway slowly, peeking into each of the other sleeping rooms as she went. Each room had a wardrobe, a bureau, a basket, a chair, and two beds draped with quilts and topped with a pair of pillows. Although the items were similar to those in the room she'd been given to share with Olga, the varied wall coverings and quilts gave each room a unique personality. She smiled, savoring the homeyness. Then she gave a start, awareness dawning. None of the many tall, eight-pane windows wore curtains or shades. In her short time at Miz Holland's place, she'd forgotten the joy and warmth of sunlight flooding a room.

She reached the washroom's door, but she remained in the hallway and gazed at the beams of yellow slanting from the open doorways onto the carpet runner. The sight was almost magical. But as she looked more closely, her smile faltered. The sunlight revealed faded patches on the rose-designed carpet. She skimmed her fingers across the blooms on the floral wall coverings. They, too, were muted, and zigzag creases in the paper showed where the plaster beneath had cracked.

Sadness nibbled at her. The house had seemed so grand in the evening shadows. This morning's bright view exposed a house as worn and weary in appearance as Lida's Palace. She inwardly shuddered. Then she gave herself a little shake. What had Reverend Overly called Hope Hill? She searched her memory and found the words—*a safe haven*. She remembered Mrs. Overly's kind welcome and generosity in providing for her needs. Maybe this house wasn't new and shiny, but neither was Birdie. And here she wouldn't be forced to do what Lida made her do. Reverend Overly had said so, and deep inside, she believed him. His eyes were kind, like Papa's.

Olga, wearing a brown and yellow plaid dress, her blond hair in an untidy braid, charged past her and clattered down the stairs. Birdie gave herself a little push into motion. Reverend Overly was waiting. As she entered the washroom, her stomach growled, and she came to a halt. Hungry? She was *hungry*? Her stomach hadn't panged in request for food since her first night at Lida's Palace. Already Hope Hill was bringing change.

She hurried through her wash, donned the first dress she pulled from the wardrobe, and then descended the stairs. She walked down the hallway that divided the house in half toward the back door, aware of activity in each room but not pausing to examine what was taking place. A rock-paved path split thirty paces from the house, and Birdie turned left toward the large, white-painted outhouse that Mrs. Overly had pointed out before escorting Olga and Birdie to their room last night. The unpainted smaller one on the right, the woman had explained, was for Reverend Overly and their son, Ephraim. Ephraim, the one who'd stood uncertainly beside his father in Lida's parlor, who'd driven the wagon that carried her to freedom, who—Birdie now knew—played piano.

Not until she'd heard the notes float into her room that morning had she realized how much she missed music. After Papa died, there was no music in Birdie's life. Mama didn't sing—she grumbled. There was a canary at Lida's Palace, but it never sang—it barely chirped. The tiny bit of melody she'd heard upon waking at Hope Hill ministered to her in ways she didn't know she needed. And Mrs. Overly said she and Olga would be part of a choir. Singing. Every Monday through Friday. Would Reverend Overly tell her more about the choir during their meeting?

Eagerness propelled her across the yard and into the house. She made use of the washbowl next to the door, and then followed Mrs. Overly's instructions for locating the study. Olga was already there, sitting in one of a pair of matching padded armchairs in front of a massive desk. A tall and slender girl wearing a full apron over her dark blue dress was applying a feather duster to the books on the floor-to-ceiling shelves lining the back wall. Reverend Overly sat behind the desk, rocking gently in a glossy wooden chair.

Birdie tapped lightly on the doorframe. "Excuse me? May I come in?"

The reverend glanced over, and a smile formed on his mustached face. He held one hand toward her, his gray-blue eyes warm and welcoming. "Of course you may, Miss Clarkson. Take the seat there next to Miss Mueller, and let us become better acquainted."

Birdie sat and assumed Olga's same pose, ankles crossed and hands clasped in her lap.

Reverend Overly shifted his attention to the other girl. "Miss Kearney?"

The young woman turned around and gripped the duster the way a bride held a bouquet. "Yes, sir?"

"Please complete your cleaning after dinner."

"Yes, sir." She departed, flicking a curious glance at Olga and Birdie as she went.

The reverend perched a pair of spectacles onto his nose, dipped his pen into an inkpot next to a pad of paper, and poised his hand above the pad. "Now, then, Miss Clarkson, let's start with you. Your full name, please?"

Such a simple question, but Birdie wasn't sure how to answer. "Um . . . my given name is Elizabeth Lillian Clarkson." She watched him scratch the combination of her grandmothers' names, bestowed on her at birth, onto the page. She might be starting a new life here, but there was one thing she didn't want to leave behind—the name her dear papa chose when she was still a baby. "But I am always called Birdie." Mama said it was because she was so scrawny, but Papa said it was because, like the first birdsong of spring, she brought great joy. She liked Papa's explanation better. "I . . . I prefer it, please."

Reverend Overly's head bobbed in a nod, and he added "Birdie" behind her name. "And where are your parents, Miss Clarkson?"

Another difficult-to-answer question. Birdie squirmed. "My father is buried in the Waco cemetery. He died when I was almost twelve. My mother . . ." She cringed. How could she admit it to a preacher? But, then, this preacher knew where Birdie had been, so maybe Mama's story wouldn't shock him. She pulled in a breath, gathering courage. "She ran off with a drummer and I don't know where she is." The remainder of her breath wheezed out behind the admission.

She sensed Olga gaping at her, but she didn't look. She kept her gaze fixed on the pad of paper and Reverend Overly's hand holding the pen. The man wrote what she'd said, and then lifted his head and met her gaze.

"How old are you, Miss Clarkson?"

Finally. An easy question. "I'll be eighteen in June, on the twenty-third."

He nodded and recorded her birthday. "And what grade in school have you completed?"

She would have finished her eleventh year of school if Mama

hadn't left or if she'd gone to Aunt Sally. Should she tell Reverend Overly so? She considered his question and decided to give a simple answer. "I completed tenth grade."

He made a note on the page, turned to a fresh sheet, then asked Olga the same questions. Birdie listened, intrigued by Olga's loss of her mother a year before Birdie lost Papa. She already knew that Olga's father had kicked her out and that's why she was at Lida's Palace, but she'd thought the other girl was years older. She and Olga were only a few months apart in age. But Olga was far behind in education. She hadn't gone to school beyond grade four.

Reverend Overly wrote Olga's answers, then set his pen aside. He peered directly at Olga. "Each morning from eight until ten o'clock, Mrs. Overly teaches a variety of subjects in the dining room. Our girls who have received fewer than eight years of education are required to attend."

Olga folded her arms. "I can read and write. And cipher, too."

The reverend nodded. "That's a good start, and very beneficial. But you will have greater opportunities in life if you know more than rudimentary skills. So, Miss Mueller, beginning Monday morning, you will join Ellie, Miss Allen, Miss Jacks, Miss Brown, Miss Flores, and Miss Shelley for personal tutoring and advancement."

Olga set her lips in a stubborn line.

So did Reverend Overly. "Now . . . let us discuss the other day-to-day expectations for our residents."

# Chapter Four

### Ephraim

Ephraim's heart went out to the new girls seated across from him at the dining room table. His parents had been involved in ministry the majority of his life, so sharing a table with a cast of ever-changing people was commonplace. Eventually, these two would adjust, too. But this first meal at a table crowded with strangers in an unfamiliar room echoing with the clanks of silverware on plates, chatter, and laughter must seem overwhelming.

Before Father had asked the blessing for the meal, Mother introduced the newcomers to the other residents, from Iris, the eldest of the girls at twenty-three, to little Ellie, who'd been born in an upstairs bedroom at Hope Hill six years ago. Mother called the girls by their names, but Father always addressed them using their surnames and the title "Miss." When Ephraim spoke to them directly, he followed formality, as well. But he couldn't help thinking of them by their first names.

From his place wedged in at Father's right at the head of the table, he had a view of every person gathered. His gaze circled the group, briefly lighting on Harriet, Myra, Alberta, Iris, Bernice, Ellie on her tall stool next to Mother, Mathilda, Lucretia, Reva, Gladys, and finally Olga and Birdie. Other than Ellie, who never contributed to conversation, the residents were enjoying their time of fellowship and refreshment. Birdie and Olga ate and glanced around, but neither spoke a word. Not even to each other.

Again, sympathy twined through him, but he didn't try to catch the eyes of either girl and offer an encouraging smile. Unfortunately, such a kind effort could create discomfort. Or it might encourage something else. Mother and Father had both repeatedly warned him about remaining professional, even impersonal, lest his actions be misinterpreted. Not that his parents viewed the residents as unworthy of affection. Far from it, or they wouldn't seek to rescue them. But seeking a relationship with a man could distract them from seeking a relationship with the One who could restore them from the inside out. Ephraim would never interfere with his father's Spirit-given call to teach these girls to love and serve the Lord Jesus Christ.

When everyone had finished their meal, Mother and Lucretia went to the kitchen and returned a few moments later carrying trays of berry bowls filled with dried plum pudding. Ephraim's mouth watered. Most of the plums gathered from trees near the creek a quarter mile behind the house were used for jelly, with only a few dried for future use. Mother must have chosen to make a special dessert to welcome their new arrivals. Lucretia served the new girls first, and Olga's eyes widened when the rose-colored glass bowl was placed in front of her.

Although one of their meal rules was to wait until everyone was served before eating, no one objected when Olga snatched up her spoon and dipped in. At the first bite, she closed her eyes and inhaled, as if trying to escape into the flavor and scent of the pudding. Then she leaned over the bowl. Even before Mother and Lucretia had returned to their own seats, Olga had consumed every bit of her serving of pudding.

She sat up, glanced around, and pink flooded her cheeks. She laid the spoon next to the empty bowl, wiped her mouth with her napkin, and pushed away from the table. "Excuse me." She fled the room, and everyone else, still seated, stared after her.

Birdie half rose from her chair, one thin hand reaching out as if hopeful to catch Olga and draw her back.

Mother put her empty tray on the sideboard and started toward the doorway.

"Ophelia?" Father said, his voice firm yet kind.

Mother stopped and turned back.

"I think perhaps Miss Mueller would appreciate a few minutes of solitude to collect herself. Why not sit down and enjoy the delightful dessert you made?"

Mother pursed her lips in indecision, but after a few seconds she nodded and returned to her chair. Little Ellie leaned sideways and rested her cheek against Mother's shoulder. Mother gave the child a kiss on the top of her ever-tousled red-gold curls, then picked up Ellie's spoon and placed it into her hand. As she did so, Birdie slowly lowered herself onto her seat.

Birdie stirred her dessert, her head low, as everyone else ate the fruited pudding, quiet at first, but slowly regaining the jollity expressed prior to Olga's departure. Ephraim frequently glanced at Birdie while enjoying his dessert. Birdie and Olga had come from the same brothel, but he didn't presume that meant they were friends. Father had rescued pairs of girls from houses of ill repute at other times, and more often than not, there was animosity between them, the sad result of competing for the attentions of the customers. But Birdie continually looked toward the doorway, concern glimmering in her pale-brown eyes.

He didn't see the hardened edges so prevalent with most of their rescues on this girl. How could she still possess a tender soul after what had been done to her? When the girls rose and began carrying their dishes to the kitchen, Ephraim followed Birdie with his gaze. Although not instructed, she gathered Olga's abandoned dishes with her own. He found himself intrigued by her hesitant yet graceful motions and her perceived desire to be helpful.

Father's hand descended on Ephraim's wrist. He quickly shifted his focus. "Yes, sir?"

"The wind is picking up. Are you scheduled to play the organ for Zeke Cooper's burial tomorrow?"

Thoughts of Birdie whisked away with the reminder of the rancher's unexpected passing. Ephraim had liked the old man who lived on the property next to Hope Hill, had considered him a friend. He'd chosen to play "Shall We Gather at the River," a hymn the rancher often whistled as he went about his chores. "Yes, sir, I am."

"Then perhaps you should put the top on the wagon. It will keep the dust from settling in the keys and buttons of the organ while you drive to the cemetery."

The suggestion was a wise one. Of course. Father was always wise. But Ephraim suspected Father had an ulterior reason for suggesting it now, and heat ignited the back of his neck. He'd paid too much attention to Miss Birdie Clarkson. He stood, gathering his dishes as he did so. "I'll go as soon as I put my dishes and things in the wash basin."

Father took the items from Ephraim's hands. "I'll see to the dishes. You"—he glanced at the kitchen doorway where Birdie stood in a pose that screamed of uncertainty, her head low and to the side, almost touching her shoulder with her chin—"go."

Ephraim swallowed the words of encouragement he longed to offer to the young woman and left.


Birdie


According to the instructions Reverend Overly had given, the girls were to spend the two hours after dinner engaged in various chores or skills-building. But worry sent Birdie past the parlor, where several girls had gathered with baskets of mending, up the stairs to the room she'd been given to share with Olga. The door was closed, and the sound of weeping on the other side of it nearly broke Birdie's heart.

Even though it was her room, too, she gave a light knock before entering. She left the door open and crossed to Olga's bed, where the girl lay curled on her side, her face pressed into her pillow. Birdie sat on the edge of the bed next to Olga's knees and touched her shoulder.

"Olga?"

Olga shrugged, dislodging Birdie's hand. "Leave me alone."

*"Leave me alone!"* Mama's voice seemed to blare in Birdie's ears, making her wince. She'd always scuttled away when Mama demanded it, but she couldn't bring herself to leave Olga. Olga needed someone, and Birdie needed someone to need her.

"I won't. Not until you tell me why you're crying."

Olga covered her face with her bent arm. "Must you be so *störrisch?*"

Birdie frowned. "What is 'store-ish'?"

A snort emerged from behind Olga's elbow. She sat up and rubbed her fingers under her nose. "What you are. Stubborn. Should you not be learning stitching right now?"

"I already know how to stitch." Were the girls who lived at Hope Hill paid for the work they did here? At Lida's, Reverend Overly had mentioned earning a wage, but during this morning's meeting he'd only spoken of chores, classes, Bible study, choir, and behavioral expectations. When would she earn the money needed to go to Aunt Sally's? She pushed the thought aside and focused again on Olga. "What happened to upset you? Why did you run off?"

Olga lowered her head and toyed with the buttons on her bodice. "It was the *pluma-moos.*"

Birdie wished she spoke German. She had no idea what Olga meant.

"I haven't had it since the Christmas before my *mutter* died. She always made it for us as a treat. When I tasted it, I . . ."

Then Birdie understood—pluma-moos was plum pudding.

Olga swallowed. Her head still low, she peered at Birdie through her mussy fringe of bangs. "I remembered being little. And safe. And . . . clean." Suddenly she bounced from the bed, nearly knocking Birdie aside. "I cannot stay here."

Birdie stood. "Why not?"

Olga paced the room, wringing her hands. "You heard what Reverend Overly said. All the rules. The cooking and cleaning and studying and singing"—

Birdie's heart caught.

—"and . . . and being *good*." She came to a stop and glared at Birdie. "I am not *good*, Birdie. This baby in my belly proves it. And once they know, they . . . they'll . . ." She shook her head and began pacing again. "*Nein*, I cannot stay."

"But where will you go? Not to . . ." She couldn't bring herself to mention Lida's Palace or the person who could make babies leave a mother's womb.

"I don't know."

Olga's uncertainty unexpectedly cheered Birdie. "Then stay until you know."

Olga planted both palms on the slight bulge of her belly. "How much time do you think I have? Wouldn't it be better if—"

"Birdie?"

Birdie spun toward the doorway.

Mrs. Overly stood there, perspiration dotting her flushed, serious face. "You're needed in the parlor, dear. Go on down and join the others." Although the woman spoke kindly, Birdie saw a hint of stubbornness—store-ishness?—in her expression.

Birdie weakly gestured to Olga. "But—"

"Go now."

The older woman's firm insistence garnered Birdie's obedience. As she passed Mrs. Overly, she dared to whisper, "Convince her to stay."

The woman offered a warm smile and touched Birdie's sleeve. Birdie left, and Mrs. Overly closed the door behind her.

Nearly a half hour later, both Olga and Mrs. Overly joined the group in the parlor. Olga picked up an apron, needle, and thread, and went to work as if she hadn't run from the dining room in tears. Birdie hoped to learn what Mrs. Overly said to Olga, but Olga didn't bring it up, and Birdie didn't ask. But Olga stayed that night, and the next.

Early Sunday morning, they all climbed into the wagon that had carried her away from Lida's Palace. The Overlys' son, Ephraim, drove them to Tulsey and parked the wagon in front of a huge redbrick church. Reverend Overly unfolded the metal step and helped each of them alight. Birdie trembled from head to toe, though she couldn't determine the cause. Nervousness? Excitement to attend a real church service again, the way she had with Papa when she was very small? Worry that she might encounter one of the men who'd visited Lida's? Maybe all of it. She fell in line with the other girls and entered the sanctuary.

The reverberating notes from a massive pipe organ filled the room and raised joy in Birdie's heart. The beauty of stained glass windows in mosaic patterns, glossy beams arching overhead, and brass sconces lining the walls ignited a sense of wonder. Something deep inside her began to yearn, but for what? She couldn't define the feeling any more than she could understand the continued tremble rattling her frame.

Reverend Overly, holding little Ellie's hand, led their group up the center aisle. He stopped at the end of a long, empty bench near the front and gestured his son in first. Mrs. Overly followed, and then residents of Hope Hill slid in until the pew was full. Reverend Overly stepped to the next pew, and the remaining girls, including Birdie and Olga, took a place on it.

Birdie listened to the organist and allowed her gaze to wander from corner to corner of the large sanctuary, exploring her surroundings and also the faces of gathered worshippers. To her relief, none looked familiar. She inwardly berated herself. Would men who attended such a beautiful church visit a place like Lida's Palace? Relief settled her tremors. But then she realized a number of people seemed focused on her and the other girls. Their expressions—stern, sour, disapproving—raised gooseflesh on her arms beneath the lovely dress she'd donned that morning.

They knew. Because she was with Reverend Overly, they knew.

She hadn't understood what Olga meant when she'd told Birdie that Friday's dessert took her back to when she was still clean, but now she did. A shame greater than the vast enjoyment she'd taken in the richly colored glass windows and glorious organ music claimed her. Though she was no longer one of Lida's girls, the disgraceful stain of her time there remained. Not even this nice dress hid it. These fine people saw what she was—what she would now always be—and they knew she didn't belong in this place of purity and beauty.

She sat in misery all through the singing and preaching, staring at the cross on the wall behind the minister's wooden stand until the service ended. She refused to glance left or right as they filed out to the wagon and climbed in. The other girls, even Olga, chatted with one another on the hour-long ride to Hope Hill, but Birdie couldn't join in. The condemning faces under the roof of the beautiful church building were imprinted on her memory. She would carry them forever, the same way she carried the memory of what she'd endured under Lida's roof.

Not clean. Not good. Olga's descriptions fit too well. She wouldn't be able to shed those titles until she left Tulsey. She couldn't leave Tulsey without money for train fare. As soon as they finished their dinner, she would speak to Reverend Overly. She would ask him about earning the honest wage he'd mentioned the night he came to Lida's Palace. She would save her money and go to Kansas City where no one knew her or what she'd done. And she hoped that somehow Aunt Sally wouldn't see beneath her surface to the stain within.

# Chapter Five

Ophelia

After a cold dinner of sandwiches—their standard fare on Sundays to allow as much rest as possible—Ophelia and the two kitchen helpers for the week, Alberta and Mathilda, rinsed and stacked the dishes for washing after supper. She sent the girls off to relax, then fetched a lap quilt and went to the wicker rocker on the front porch, her favorite place on the entire property.

She settled into the chair, draped the quilt over her legs, and gently rocked. Having spent her childhood in Massachusetts, where snow and frigid temperatures were common this time of year, she appreciated the milder weather of central Texas. She also relished the quiet of Sunday afternoons at Hope Hill. These hours of rest bolstered her and renewed her spirit, giving her the reserve she needed to work the remainder of the week.

Isaiah was napping in their bedroom, Ephraim had gone to his small cottage behind the main house to read, and the girls were enjoying their free afternoon in whatever way they chose. Isaiah believed the adage about idle hands being the devil's workshop, so the household schedule didn't allow for idle time. But he also believed that even the Lord Himself rested after His week of creating, and they should follow His example. She chuckled to herself. When the Lord crafted Isaiah, He must have been showing off. Her dear husband was such a dedicated soul, determined to leave the world a better place than the way he'd found it.

On the rolling expanse of still winter-brown grass stretching toward the road in front of the house, Ellie sat cross-legged with her arm draped over their shaggy black-and-white border collie, Ted. Such a gentle dog, despite being trained to guard the property. Ophelia observed the pair, concern about the little girl mingling with affection for the animal. A movement at the edge of the house caught her eye, and she shifted her gaze in that direction. One of their newest arrivals, Birdie, wandered from the edge of the house. Ophelia watched her cross the grounds toward Ellie.

Ted stood, assuming his protective stance, and Birdie hesitated. Then she stretched out her hand. Ted sniffed it, his fluffy tail gave a quick wag, and he hunkered next to Ellie again. Ophelia couldn't resist a nod of approval. Ted had rightly read the young woman's character. Ophelia saw her as a harmless, gentle soul, too.

Birdie crouched down. Although Ophelia couldn't hear what she was saying given the distance between them, she took note of Birdie's smile and moving lips. No doubt trying to engage Ellie in conversation. Unconsciously, she leaned forward a bit. Might the child respond to someone new and kind? She sat tense, hopeful, inwardly praying. After a few moments, Birdie rose and started toward the house.

Ophelia slumped against the chair's back, sighing. Would the Lord never answer her prayers for the child?

Birdie climbed the porch steps and then paused several feet away. "Am I disturbing you?"

Ophelia gestured to the bench beneath the windows. "Not at all. Please join me."

As Birdie seated herself, she looked across the lawn. "Ellie is a very pretty little girl."

Ophelia shifted her attention to the child, too. Her red-gold spiraling curls glistened under the sun, and even though Ellie sat with her back to the house, Ophelia saw the child's delicate features and unique blue-green irises in her mind's eye. "Yes, that she is."

"Is she your little girl?"

Ophelia chuckled softly, turning to Birdie. "That's a more complicated question to answer than you might think. She was born right here at Hope Hill. Although I helped her enter the world and have helped care for her ever since, I did not give birth to her. She is not a child of my womb, but she is a child of my heart."

"A child of your heart . . ." A small smile lifted the corners of Birdie's usually somber lips. "I like that." Then her frown returned. "What happened to her mother?"

Ophelia closed her eyes for a moment, pain stabbing. "I don't know." She opened her eyes and met Birdie's curious yet compassionate gaze. "When Ellie was not quite two years old, we awoke one morning to the realization Ellie's mother had left during the night. We searched for her, even had the authorities in Tulsey send out telegrams to neighboring communities in hope of locating her, but no one reported a sighting. She's never returned, although I pray she will someday." Ophelia again focused on Ellie. "Just as I pray our little girl will find her voice."

Birdie released a little gasp. "I thought she was too shy to talk to me. But she is mute?"

Still gazing at the child, Ophelia considered her answer. "The doctors don't believe so. When she was a baby, she cried. As a toddler, she babbled. Physically, she has the ability to speak. But ever since the inconsolable weeping of her first day without her mother, she hasn't made a sound." Ophelia turned to Birdie and witnessed tears glimmering in the girl's eyes. Her heart warmed toward this newcomer. "Isaiah, Ephraim, and I pray daily for Ellie to use her voice and share what she's thinking and feeling so we can help her. While we wait, we love her."

Birdie nodded slowly, her expression thoughtful. Then she gave a little jolt. Her eyes went wide. "You said Ellie was born here. Was her mother . . . ?" Pink splashed the girl's cheeks.

Ophelia understood. "She was rescued from a brothel in Belton." Women and babies who'd resided with her and Isaiah over the past years flooded Ophelia's memories. "Several of the women who left the brothels did so because they were expecting a child and didn't wish to deliver in such a place. We've also housed women who found themselves in a family way without the benefit of a husband. Society shuns them, but we welcome them and see to their needs. Whether former prostitutes or not, we help them find respectable jobs that allow them to care for their children, if they decide to raise the baby themselves."

"What happens to the babies if the mothers don't raise them themselves?" Birdie's voice quavered, and she gripped her hands against her rib cage as if trying to hold herself together.

Was Birdie expecting? If so, she was very early in the pregnancy. Unlike Olga, whose changing form and ravenous appetite hinted at a growing babe. Not that Olga had yet admitted such. If Birdie knew about Olga's situation, her concern might be for her friend's future. Or perhaps she was fearful about her own. Either way, Ophelia smiled, hoping to assure the young woman. "There is an asylum for orphans and abandoned children in Austin. The director there finds good homes for the babies. Thus, they are well cared for." She leaned forward and gave Birdie's clenched hands a gentle squeeze. The girl's tense pose relaxed. Gratified, Ophelia settled in her chair again. "All women in need are welcome at Hope Hill, Birdie, regardless of the reason for the need."

A pinch in her chest reminded Ophelia of her own need. She sent up a silent prayer for healing. Isaiah could not continue this ministry alone. Too many would speculate about illicit goings-on if a single man ran a home to rescue and rehabilitate fallen women. The Lord knew this. The Lord also knew the importance of this work. She trusted Him to do what was best to ensure Hope Hill's doors would stay open to those many deemed the least of these. But she also wished He would act swiftly. She feared she didn't have time to waste.


Birdie


Birdie considered running to her room and telling Olga she wouldn't be sent away when the Overlys learned about her coming baby. But she paused. She might not get another chance to speak to either of the directors on her own until next Sunday. The question burning on her tongue needed a reply.

Mrs. Overly had leaned fully against her chair's curved backrest and closed her eyes, but Birdie didn't think she was sleeping. Only resting. She cleared her throat. The woman's eyes opened.

Birdie drew a breath. "Ma'am, there's something I need to know."

Mrs. Overly offered a gentle nod. "Of course. What is it?"

"When the reverend spoke to us at"—her face flamed just thinking about that shameful place—"Lida's Palace, he said if we came here, we would earn a wage. That's why I left. To earn money without having to . . . you know." She angled her face away, unwilling to witness disapproval in the woman's eyes. "I need money. For a train ticket." She risked a glance. Not a hint of disgust colored Mrs. Overly's expression. Slowly, she met her gaze. "My papa's sister lives in Kansas City. I want to go to her."

Mrs. Overly's fine eyebrows rose. "This is good, Birdie, that you have a relative you trust. Do you have her address? We could write to her and make arrangements with her for your travel."

Birdie frowned. "Do you mean we would ask Aunt Sally to buy the ticket?"

"Yes, that would be the eventual request." Mrs. Overly rocked the chair, her gaze unwavering.

Birdie remembered Mama calling her selfish for expecting someone else to fund her trip. She was already soiled. She shouldn't be selfish, too. She needed to buy the ticket herself.

"Our first query, however," Mrs. Overly went on before Birdie could speak, "would be to ascertain your aunt is willing to receive you. It wouldn't be wise to send you so far away without assurance that a safe home is available to you."

Birdie's frame went cold. Aunt Sally was what Papa had called a godly woman. She probably went to church every Sunday, the same as the people who'd filled the pews in the big, beautiful building in Tulsey she'd visited that morning. She couldn't bear it if Aunt Sally looked at her the way those people had. What would it take to erase the filthy stain of her past choices? Whatever it was, she had to do it. And she would start by earning the ticket herself. The unselfish act would help redeem her.

She'd left behind what little she'd earned at Lida's Palace. The girls' earnings were kept in jars on a shelf in Miz Holland's kitchen. Birdie would never see that money again. And maybe it was best. It was tainted money. She wanted to earn, as Reverend Overly had put it, an honest wage.

Birdie stood. "I don't want to contact Aunt Sally until I have enough money to buy a ticket myself. She shouldn't have to pay my way. When do I get paid for the work I do here?"

Mrs. Overly rose, too, and took Birdie's hands. "My dear, we don't pay our girls to live and serve here. When you've finished the training we provide and take a job somewhere else, you'll earn a wage. I'm sorry you misunderstood Isaiah's statement."

Birdie was sorry, too. "How long do you think it will be before I am allowed to seek a job somewhere else?"

Mrs. Overly released Birdie's hands. "That is dependent on your diligence. When Isaiah is assured you have the necessary skills to see to your own financial needs, he will begin making inquiries of local businesses who are willing to give our girls a chance at a better life." She cupped Birdie's cheek, a touch so motherly and sweet, tears threatened. "The Lord has a good plan for your life, Birdie, as He does for every soul ever born. While you are here and learning, listen for His voice. Open your heart to His leading. You've encountered a rough spot in your life's journey, but you needn't stay there. Better things await. Those better things can take time to discover, but they are worth the wait when we trust the One who loves us most."

Her hand drifted away, but her sweet smile remained. "I am trusting Him to work His perfect will for the future of every person here at Hope Hill. Will you trust Him, Birdie?"

Birdie contemplated Mrs. Overly's question. She'd thought some of the things Reverend Overly had asked were difficult to answer, but this question felt impossible. She'd trusted Papa, but he'd died. She'd never really trusted Mama because she didn't think Mama liked her very much. She'd trusted Miz Holland to help her when Mama went away, but that woman's "help" was hurtful. She'd come here, trusting she'd receive the money needed to go to Kansas, but now that wasn't true, either.

Could she trust a God she didn't know and had never seen when she couldn't trust the people she did know? The only answer that formed on her tongue would disappoint this kind woman. Birdie entered the house, as silent as little Ellie.

# Chapter Six

Ephraim

Monday morning, Ephraim laid a sheet of music on each chair in the music room. He had spent much of Sunday painstakingly copying the soprano and alto lines of "I'll Live for Him," a hymn Father had requested for the upcoming Friday revival in Speegleville. Then he fetched two copies of sheet music for some familiar hymns from the file cabinet tucked beneath one of the octagon-shaped room's many windows. The new arrivals would need those as well.

Ephraim wasn't concerned about the hymns "Come Home, Poor Sinner" and "I Stood Outside the Gate." The girls had performed those selections more than a dozen times. This week, he intended to focus on "I'll Live for Him," a newer hymn.

The chorus played in his mind as he retrieved two more folding chairs from the closet and added them to the half-circle arrangement. *I'll live for Him who died for me, how happy then my life shall be!* Ephraim had been taught at a young age to live for Jesus. His parents modeled dedication in the way they served souls society rejected. Hope Hill was their third refuge for fallen women. They'd been run out of the cities of Waco and Gatesville by angry citizens who opposed their ministry. Of the places he'd lived, he liked Hope Hill the best. Its location almost three miles outside of Tulsey meant they could avoid constant scrutiny. The rolling, open landscape around the large, old home offered an element of peace. But it also left him lonely and isolated from others his age. Except for the residents, with whom he wasn't supposed to socialize.

. . . *how happy then my life shall be!*

The phrase from the hymn taunted him. He was living for Jesus, using his talents to honor God, just as his parents had taught him. Just as his parents daily modeled. They seemed happy. But was he?

The mantel clock chimed the hour, rescuing him from his troubled thoughts. He crossed to the pocket doors and slid them open on their squeaky rails. The girls filed in and took their seats, sopranos to his left, altos to his right. The two new ones, Birdie and Olga, remained in the doorway.

Ephraim gestured them into the room with a sweep of his arm. "Come in, come in."

They entered, but stood uncertainly just inside the doors.

Ephraim pasted a warm yet not too friendly smile on his face. Maybe he should consider becoming a stage actor. So often he felt he was playing a role rather than being himself. "Welcome to your first rehearsal with the Hope Hill Choir. As soon as you tell me what parts you sing, melody or harmony, we'll find an appropriate placement for you."

Olga shrugged. "I sing low notes. But I don't know if they're melody or harmony."

Ephraim escorted her to the piano and, standing in front of the keyboard, played the opening line for "Amazing Grace" with his right hand only. He angled a look at Olga. "I played the soprano and alto together. The lower notes are the alto line—the harmony. Is that what you sing?"

The girl shrugged again, folding her arms over her chest. "Ja, I think so."

Ephraim sat on the bench and positioned his fingers above the keys. "Let's try this. I'll play the alto line by itself. Tell me if it seems familiar." He plinked out the notes, his gaze on Olga's unsmiling face. When he finished, he said, "Is that your part?"

"I'm not sure."

Nor was Ephraim, but he couldn't use up their whole practice time figuring it out. A wiser choice was to assign Olga a part. He pointed to the empty chair at the end of the alto line. "Let's start with you here, next to Miss Schulte." Harriet Schulte was a strong alto. "Listen to what she sings and sing it, too. All right?"

Olga nodded and sat.

Satisfied he'd solved the problem, he turned to Birdie. "Do you know what part you sing, or would you like me to play the notes again?"

"I sing the melody line."

Ephraim secretly delighted at her confident reply. For the first time since their paths crossed, she didn't seem afraid of her own shadow. And adding one of each part to the choir would continue its balance. "Very good," he said, and he meant it. He indicated the open chair at the soprano end and smiled at Birdie. "This will be your spot, beside Miss Long." He waited until she sat next to Gladys, then moved to the piano. "All right, ladies, let's warm up our voices. Scale of C."

He played the notes and sang along with the simple exercise, using "la" in place of words on each ascending and then descending note. A sweet, pure tone carried over the others—a voice he hadn't heard before today. Was it Olga's or Birdie's?

He peered over the top of the piano, skimming the entire line of faces. "Very nice, ladies. Let's do it again, but say 'lo' this time." He tipped his ear toward the group as he played the notes, listening instead of singing. The pleasant sound seemed to come from the soprano half of the group. So it was Birdie. A grin tugged at his cheek. Birdie . . . the songbird. How appropriate.

Keeping his observation to himself, he moved on to another vocal exercise, utilizing the higher ranges. By now, even the other girls were sending awed glances in Birdie's direction. She, however, seemed unaware of the attention. Her amber-eyed gaze was aimed straight ahead, a sweet curve fixed on her rosy lips.

Ephraim worked his way up the keys. She matched pitches to high C with apparent ease. Had she received musical training at some point, or was this a natural talent—a gift? He wanted to ask, but not in front of the others. If he singled her out, he might intimidate her into silence. He would share his discovery with Mother and allow her to probe Birdie's background. In the meantime, they had a new song to learn.

"I believe that's enough." He rose and rounded the piano, then stood in front of them with his hands in his trouser pockets. "I put a new piece of music out today—it's titled 'I'll Live for Him.' Let's start with it."

As he always did when presenting a new song, he began by playing it through on the piano. Those who could read the notes followed along on their sheet music. The others listened, their expressions attentive. Then he played the melody line by itself, inviting the sopranos to sing. The altos received the same singular focus. When he believed both groups were familiar with their parts, he combined them, listening closely for places where they might need some additional attention.

The first half hour passed quickly, with full focus given to the new song. He dedicated the second half to reviewing Father's standard hymns. The entire time, he thrilled at Birdie's sweet, pure voice matching each note with perfection. He'd had the privilege of attending the university in Georgetown, where he participated in the choir and studied music education, and he believed he'd been exposed to some wonderful vocalists. But Birdie's voice rivaled them all. How had someone of her young age developed such a talent?

At fifty-five minutes past the hour, Ephraim closed the cover on the keys and stood. "Very good practice, ladies." He wished he could add that they sounded exceptional today, thanks to the addition of Birdie's phenomenal voice. She seemed to need encouragement. But he would likely hurt the others' feelings if he said something in front of everyone. He would tell Mother, and she could pass along the compliment to Birdie when she queried about the girl's musical background. "Please be prepared to focus predominantly on the new song this week in preparation for our performance in Speegleville on Friday."

"Another revival?" Iris blasted the query.

Ephraim raised his eyebrows at the young woman. If Mother or Father were in the room, she wouldn't speak so snidely. Her doing so sent a message of disrespect toward him and his parents, and his defenses rose. He rounded the piano, his gaze fixed on Iris's face. "Yes, Miss Brown, another revival. Another opportunity for people to hear and respond to the gospel message." With effort, he assumed a calm, even tone. He borrowed the points that Father often presented when seeking support for Hope Hill's mission. "Another opportunity for people to recommit to true faith after a period of indifference. Another opportunity to invite people to cast aside judgmental attitudes and love the way Jesus calls us to love." Not to mention another opportunity to raise funds for the furtherance of this place of refuge.

While he spoke, Iris squirmed in her chair. When he finished, she glanced at the girls seated on either side of her, then hung her head.

Remorse struck him. He'd humiliated her. Hadn't her dignity been trampled enough by outsiders? Hope Hill was supposed to be a place of healing. *Love thy neighbour as thyself* . . . He released a sigh. "Miss Brown, my intention was to point out, mostly for the benefit of our newest arrivals, the reasons we lead revivals. I apologize if you feel I was scolding you. Will you forgive me?"

Slowly, Iris raised her head, but she looked past Ephraim, her expression sullen. "I'm on meal preparation duty. Excuse me." She darted to the pocket doors, screeched one open, and disappeared beyond the tall, paneled door.

Whispers broke out among the girls. Ephraim cleared his throat, and the hushed exchanges stilled. "You are dismissed."

The girls departed, some in pairs, others alone, until only Mathilda remained. She approached Ephraim, a sly smile twitching. "Mr. Overly, I can tell you why Iris is upset. And it ain't 'cause you scolded her."

Ephraim always distanced himself from the girls' occasional disagreements, allowing Mother or Father to lead the squabblers to peace or at least to a place of compromise. But guilt nibbled at him. Had he allowed his earlier introspection about his purpose here to color his response to Iris? It might help him restore peace between him and Iris if he understood her reasons for posing the question the way she had. "Please explain, Miss Weaver."

"She likes you."

Ephraim held his hand up. "Now, I don't think—"

Mathilda giggled. "I ain't lyin'. Her an' me, we room together. She talks about you every night before we drift off to sleep, about what you were wearin' that day or what she thought about somethin' you said. Oh, she's right fond of you. An' you payin' extra attention to the new girl durin' practice got her feathers all ruffled up."

Ephraim scowled. "Extra attention . . . to which new girl?"

Mathilda tilted her head and smirked. "You know who I mean." She tossed her brown ponytail over her shoulder, grinning. "She does sing real pretty. I can see why you'd perk up around her, seein' as how you like music, too. But Iris likely didn't see it that way. She thought you was payin' attention to her for"—she lowered her voice to a whisper—"personal reasons."

He inwardly cringed. He *was* impressed with Birdie's voice. He wouldn't deny it. But how had he alerted the girls to his fascination? And did his feelings extend beyond her ability to sing?

Time to end this conversation. For more reasons than one. "Come, Miss Weaver, music class is finished for the day. You have duties awaiting." He ushered her to the door, ignoring the knowing grin she aimed at him as she left. He slid the door closed behind her and flipped the latch. Alone in the room, he crossed to the piano and sat on the round stool. He ran his hand through his hair, blowing out a breath.

According to Mathilda, Iris liked him. In truth, the declaration wasn't a surprise. Iris had given hints—offering him an extra dessert, lingering after music practice to ask questions, taking the end of the bench in the wagon closest to the driver's seat and engaging him in conversation when the group drove to town or to revival locations. He'd been intentionally polite but not unduly friendly. Most likely, her infatuation had more to do with him being the only available male within arm's reach than him, specifically. Such had been the case for many girls from the time he was old enough to sprout chin whiskers.

At times, loneliness tempted him to respond. He'd confessed his wants to Mother, and he remembered her wise counsel. *"These girls need to find their joy and fulfillment in a relationship with Jesus, just as you do, my son. Keep Him central in your life and He will give you the desires of your heart."* Mother also told him that she and Father prayed daily for the Lord to lead Ephraim to the woman meant to be his wife. But how would God answer those prayers when Ephraim was only with his parents and the women they rescued?

He wished he'd found his intended when he was in college.

Then he'd have a helpmeet serving with him, the way his parents did. What did Father laughingly say when Ephraim expressed "I wish" thoughts? He rasped the remembered Scottish proverb, "If wishes were horses, beggars would ride."

Wishing wouldn't bring him a wife. Wishing wouldn't remove this unsettledness in the center of his soul. Wishing wouldn't fix anything. According to his parents, good Christians didn't wish, they prayed.

Without conscious thought, he folded back the cover, placed his fingers on the keys, and began to play. The words filled his mind, and he added his voice to the music. "'O what peace we often forfeit, O what needless pain we bear, all because we do not carry everything to God in prayer!'"

He played and sang every verse of "What a Friend We Have in Jesus." Then he played it again, his voice silent, as the words played in his memory. Certain phrases—*Have we trials and temptations? Do thy friends despise, forsake thee? Take it to the Lord in prayer*—pinched his heart. He held the final note for several seconds, then lifted his finger and listened to the sound fade. He bowed his head. *Lord—*

Someone rattled the pocket door. "Mr. Overly? Mr. Overly!" The panicked voice on the other side of the door brought Ephraim to his feet so abruptly he banged his knees on the piano. Wincing, he scrambled over and released the latch. He slid the door open.

Harriet grabbed his sleeve. "Come quick. It's your mama. She fell down and we can't wake her up."

# Chapter Seven

## Ophelia

Ophelia was aware of being carried. By an angel? Was she being taken to heaven? Oh, to see Jesus! But she wanted to say goodbye to Isaiah first. She squirmed, groaning in her attempt to open her eyes.

"Shhh."

The deep voice—almost musical in its delivery—soothed her. Then her body sank into something soft and welcoming. A cloud, perhaps? Or was she now cradled in her Savior's arms? She had to know. She forced her eyes open, and disappointment struck so hard, tears swam.

She was in her bedroom, on her bed, with Ephraim leaning over her. "Oh. It's you."

His tense brow relaxed, and a relieved smile formed. "Yes, Mother, it's me." His warm hand cupped her cheek. "Do you know what happened?"

She searched her memory for what she'd been doing before the angel—no, Ephraim—laid her on her bed. Ah, yes, fetching pickled cabbage for their dinner. She recalled climbing the cellar stairs with the crock bowl in her arms, turning to place it on the worktable, experiencing a sharp pain in her shoulder, and . . . nothing else.

"Did I break the bowl?"

Ephraim released a strained chuckle. "Don't worry about that. We have other bowls."

Bernice and Lucretia, both with tears staining their faces, crowded into her line of vision. Bernice said, "You gave us a terrible scare, Mrs. Overly, falling to the floor like a rag doll. Are you all right?"

She certainly wasn't. She'd had spells before, times when she couldn't catch her breath or pain gripped her shoulder or back, but she'd not fainted until today. The illness was advancing. She held her hand to the trembling young women. "I'm fine, girls. Don't worry. Please finish dinner preparations without me. You can do it." With reluctance, they stepped away from the bed and left the room. She shifted her bleary focus to her son. "You may go, too. I just need a little rest."

Ephraim sat on the edge of the bed, his jaw jutting as determinedly as Isaiah's did when he marched out the door for another rescue. "You need a doctor, but Father took the team and wagon to Speegleville to finalize the details for Friday's event. He won't be home until late." Worry shone in his blue eyes. "We should invest in a saddle horse for emergencies such as this. It isn't wise to leave us all stranded out here."

Ophelia tried to laugh, but a cough emerged instead. "Son, you forget we have a Protector who is mightier than a saddle horse. God is always with us."

"Well, He didn't prevent you from fainting." Ephraim's tone turned sharp, and he turned his face aside, his chin quivering.

She was so weary. Sleep beckoned. But this recent episode could mean her time was nearing its end. A loving mother prepared her children. She had to tell him. "Son?" She waited until he looked at her again. "'Ashes to ashes, dust to dust' . . . this is said at graveside services, yes?"

Ephraim nodded, his face growing pale.

"Our bodies do not last forever. If they did, we'd never go to heaven, so I am glad for—" Pain twinged between her shoulder blades. She closed her eyes until it passed. She wheezed out her held breath and met her son's gaze again. "—the temporary nature of physical life. That's not to say I'm eager to leave you and your father, but I won't resist when the time comes. And the time, Ephraim . . ." His dear face blurred, tears distorting her vision. "It draws nigh."

Ephraim shook his head. "Mother, you can't know that."

"But I do." Oh, how she wanted to rest. But she would see to Ephraim first. "My father, and his father before him, suffered the same malady. It's a weakness of the heart. My grandfather only lived to forty-eight years, my father to fifty-two. I'm a year older than Grandpa was when he went to his reward. I've known since I was a young girl that my heart would give out before I reached old age."

Ephraim growled in his throat. "It isn't fair."

Ophelia attempted a soft laugh, but it sounded more like a strangled sob. "I won't argue the statement. Few things in life are fair. None of the girls who have come and gone over the years would claim to have been treated fairly. Yet God promises to restore what the locusts have eaten. He redeems, Ephraim." Her eyelids slid down, their weightiness overwhelming her. "I know, because He gave me you even after . . . after . . ."

Talking was too hard. Her lips went slack. Her eyes closed.

"Mother?" Ephraim's voice seemed very far away.

She sighed and slipped into nothingness.

### Birdie

Birdie was scooping the remains of the shattered pottery and shreds of sauerkraut into a dustpan when Ephraim burst into the kitchen. The wildness in his eyes brought her to her feet, and she braced herself for bad news.

"Girls, my mother—Mrs. Overly, I mean—needs a doctor. I'm

going to run to the Cooper ranch and borrow a horse, then ride
into town."

Relief sagged Birdie's knees. The kind woman was still alive.
Birdie gripped the edge of the counter to keep herself upright
and longed for something to say to comfort the distraught son.
She saw in his eyes the same fear she'd experienced when Papa
collapsed after being kicked in the belly by a mule. Papa had
died. She didn't want Mrs. Overly to die, too.

Iris darted to him, wringing her apron skirt in her hands.
"But it's two miles to the Coopers', then another mile into town.
You'll be gone for hours. What will we do if something happens
while you're away?"

"You'll do what my mother would have you do." Ephraim
spoke evenly, but his entire frame trembled, and his hands
balled into fists. "You have your duties. Carry on just as you
would if both Mother and Father were standing nearby. Do it
heartily, as unto the Lord." He scanned the room, frowning.
"Where is Ellie?"

Harriet waved her hand in the direction of the back door.
"She ran outside when the bowl crashed to the floor an' Mrs.
Overly fell, too. She's probably hiding in the barn with Ted."

Ephraim sighed. "She's probably happier with the dog than
she would be with us. Let her be for now, but someone should
check on her in an hour if she hasn't returned to the house."

Birdie had to do something to help. She raised her hand. "I'll
do it."

"Thank you." He glanced around again, as if trying to gain
his bearings. "Lucretia, please go in and sit with Mrs. Overly.
She shouldn't be alone if . . . if . . ."

Lucretia shook her head. "You don't have to say it. I'll go."
She scuttled around him and out the door.

Iris placed her hands on his jacket lapels. "I'll see to everything, Ephraim. You go now and fetch the doc."

"Yes. I'm going." Ephraim caught the young woman's wrists and gently set her away from him. "Everyone, be safe." He strode out.

Iris put her hands on her hips and set her head at a saucy angle. "You heard him. I'm in charge."

Mathilda huffed. "He didn't say nothin' of the kind. He said for us to do what Mrs. Overly would have us do, and that means you're to be stirrin' the soup."

Iris glared at her roommate for a moment, but then she sashayed to the stove and snatched up a wooden spoon. "I don't know why I'm bothering. None of us will be able to eat a bite until he's back with the doctor, but I reckon the least we can do is what Mrs. Overly would ask." Suddenly the girl's stiff shoulders seemed to wilt. "She's a good person. She don't deserve . . ."

Olga slunk from the corner where she'd hunkered against the fireplace ever since Mrs. Overly's collapse. "W-what do you think will happen to all of us if Mrs. Overly dies?"

Myra wheeled on her, her eyes spitting fire. "Don't say such a thing!"

Iris peeked over her shoulder. "I don't like thinking of it, either, but it could happen. She looked so . . . gray." She slapped the spoon onto the stove and turned around. "If she dies, this place'll close. Reverend Overly comes and goes all the time. Mrs. Overly's the one who sees to us. We might as well be thinking about where we'll go if she does"—she gulped—"die."

Birdie's heart beat hard and fast. They were all grown-ups, yet they were all fearful and worried. How much more must little Ellie, who didn't have the words to express herself, be feeling? She'd told Ephraim she would seek out the child later, but she couldn't wait. She headed for the door.

"Where are you going?" Iris called after her.

Unwilling to engage in an argument, she left without answering. The wind slapped the door into its frame and plastered her skirt to her front. Its force hindered her progress. How would Ephraim run against such wind? She wished she knew how to pray. She'd ask God to give him strength and help him reach the doctor in time. She trudged across the dry, brittle grass, her head low to protect her face from blowing dirt. As she neared the barn door, a sharp yip greeted her.

"It's all right, Ted," she called. She entered the cool, dark space, relieved to be out of the wind. She blinked rapidly, scanning the shadowy interior. In the far corner, beneath a warped built-in counter cluttered with various tools, was Ted's white face. A small shape huddled next to him. Her heart twisted in sympathy.

Birdie hurried across the hay-speckled, hard ground and knelt in front of the child. "Ellie, aren't you lonely out here by yourself? Why don't you come into the house with me? It might make you feel better to be with us."

Ellie wrapped her arms around Ted's neck and buried her face in his furry ruff. The dog panted but made no effort to move.

Birdie gave the dog's ears a quick scratch. "Ted's a good friend, I know, but he can't fix your dinner for you. Aren't you hungry by now?" She watched Ellie, waiting for the little girl to look up. "We're having beans with ham. And biscuits." But no sauerkraut. "Doesn't that sound good? Maybe . . ." Should she offer? She didn't know whether Ted was ever allowed in the house. But these were unique circumstances. "Ted can lay beside you while you eat. Then, if you drop a little something, he'll clean it right up."

Ellie shifted her head and peeked at Birdie with one eye.

Birdie hid a smile. "I bet Ted's hungry. He'd probably really like some beans and ham."

Ellie's thin arms dropped from the dog's neck. Birdie backed up, and Ellie scooted from beneath the table. Ted rose and came with her, his tongue lolling and bright black eyes following the child's every move.

Birdie brushed the bits of hay from Ellie's dress, then extended her hand. To her surprise and delight, Ellie took hold. Together, they headed for the yard with Ted trotting alongside Ellie.

"I'm glad you decided to come in." The wind was behind her now, tossing her hair over her face. Ellie's bobbed spirals waved wildly, too. Birdie reminded herself to brush Ellie's hair later. "Ephraim was worried about you. It will make him happy to know you're safe in the house with the rest of us."

Ellie squinted upward, her nose crinkling.

"Ephraim isn't here right now, though." Maybe it was foolish to carry on a one-sided conversation, yet she couldn't deny it also felt good to talk openly with the child, the way she'd seen Mrs. Overly do. "He went to the Cooper ranch for a horse. He's going after the doctor."

The child's forehead puckered. She pawed the air with her free hand, and Ted tucked his head under her palm.

Birdie squeezed the little hand she held. "The doctor is coming to check on Mrs. Overly. She's resting now. But after we eat, we'll let you peek in on her. Will that make you feel better?"

A huge sigh heaved from the little girl.

Birdie took the response as a yes. She smiled and brushed Ellie's knuckles against her own skirt. "Good. In we go." She opened the door and ushered Ellie and Ted inside. The dog paused at the threshold and looked up at Birdie. Birdie was certain she glimpsed gratitude in his pointed face, and she couldn't resist delivering one more quick ear scratch.

She made use of the washstand next to the door and helped Ellie wash her hands. Then she trailed Ellie and Ted down the hallway to the dining room opening. Plates, bowls, and cutlery were neatly laid out, except in front of the chairs where Mr. and

Mrs. Overly and Ephraim usually sat. Ellie headed for her stool, but her gaze fell on the empty space in front of Mrs. Overly's chair. Her eyes welled.

Alberta entered the dining room, carrying a soup tureen. She set it at the end of the table, then crouched in front of Ellie. "Don't worry, Ellie. I'll be in my place, and I'll make sure your napkin's tucked in good, same as Mrs. Overly would do. All right?"

Ellie hung her head, and Alberta gave her a hug. Then she yelped and stepped back. "What's Ted doing in here?"

The dog sat on his haunches and panted, his mouth wide in what Birdie read as a satisfied smile.

Birdie hurried over. "Is it all right? It will make Ellie feel better to have Ted close by."

Alberta scowled at the dog, then shifted her attention to Ellie. Her scowl faded. She put her hand on the child's tangled mop of curls. "Of course it will. Ellie, you climb up on your stool. I'll let everybody know we've got an extra visitor at our table today." Then she looked at Birdie. "Go to the kitchen. Olga needs your help with . . . something."

# Chapter Eight

Birdie

B irdie entered the kitchen, and Gladys caught her arm. "Olga went all to pieces, wailing and asking what'll we do, what'll we do, over and over like she didn't know anything else to say. Way she was acting, made me think she'd gone out of her mind. Iris told her to go to her room if she wanted to throw a fit. She went up right before you came in."

Concern filled Birdie. Was such an upset dangerous to Olga's baby? "I'll go see to her." She turned toward the hallway opening.

Iris splashed ham and beans from the pot into a tureen. She snorted under her breath. "Olga ought to be ashamed of how she's acting. Don't we have enough to worry about, with Mrs. Overly sick in her bed and us not having any protection if somebody decides to pay an ugly visit?"

Birdie paused and sent Iris a sharp look. "Ugly visit? What do you mean?"

Alberta came back into the kitchen. She crossed to the stove and snatched the ladle out of Iris's hand. "That won't happen here. Stop trying to stir up trouble."

Iris stepped aside, then crossed her arms and glowered. "The only thing I was stirring is soup. And if ugly visitors ran Reverend and Mrs. Overly out of towns before, it could happen again. Especially if people find out she's sick and he ain't here."

Mathilda paused in transferring plump biscuits from the

baking sheet to a linen-lined basket. "How would they know? Who'd tell?"

Iris rolled her eyes. "People ain't stupid, Mathilda. When Ephraim comes riding into town on a borrowed horse, people will know he didn't have his own wagon to use, which means the reverend's gone off with it. And as soon as Ephraim goes into the doctor's office, people will know something's wrong out here."

"They won't know it's Mrs. Overly, though." Mathilda chewed her lower lip.

"It won't matter!" Iris threw her arms wide. "All they have to know is there's no fit man on the place to defend us." She pushed past Birdie. "I'm going up to the balcony to keep watch. If I see somebody comin', I'll warn everyone." She hurried off.

Mathilda stared after her, mouth hanging open. Then she laughed and shook her head. "If a gang of men who want to run us off shows up, no warnin' is gonna make any difference. Besides, Iris is tetched in the head if she thinks I believe she's goin' up to watch for an angry mob. She's watchin' for Ephraim so she can run down an' be sittin' at his mama's bedside when the doctor gets here. She's always showin' off for him."

Birdie didn't care about Iris. She cared about Mrs. Overly, little Ellie, and Olga. She couldn't do anything for Mrs. Overly. She'd already seen to Ellie, who was fine in the dining room with her faithful Ted close by. Now she should check on Olga. She inched in the direction of the hallway. "I'm going to see if Olga's better. If she's not ready to come down, go ahead and eat without us."

Mathilda crinkled her nose. "We ain't supposed to eat until everybody's at the table. Reverend Overly says so." Then she sighed. "But I reckon this day's so mixed up, nobody's gonna care." She picked up the basket. "Go on, Birdie. I hope Olga's all over her fit by now."

Birdie half ran through the house and up the stairs. At least if Olga's *fit*, as Mathilda called it, was still happening, the doctor could look in on her when he finished with Mrs. Overly. The thought comforted her, and her feet automatically slowed to a walk as she made her way down the long hallway to their bedroom.

Olga was curled on her bed, staring out the window. She glanced over when Birdie came in. She grimaced and rolled to her side to face the wall. "I'm fine now." Her voice came out strong, lending credence to the words.

Birdie crossed to the foot of the bed and leaned sideways to make eye contact. "Then come downstairs and have your dinner."

"Eat without me."

"Nein." Birdie deliberately borrowed Olga's word for denial. "Not eating isn't good for you." She hesitated. Should she say it? Yes, she should. "Or your baby."

Olga sighed and flopped onto her back. "Then bring me a tray. I can't go down there. Not after I . . . I . . ." She covered her eyes with her bent arm.

Birdie rounded the end of the bed and sat on the edge of the mattress. "After you . . . what? Got scared?" Olga didn't move her arm, but she nodded behind it. Birdie squeezed Olga's knee. "Everyone was scared. Scared for Mrs. Overly. Scared for Ephraim. Scared for us, too. You weren't the only one."

Olga slapped her arm onto the mattress and scowled at Birdie. "But no one else fell apart. I've never done that before. Iris said to stop acting like a maniac. A maniac, Birdie! Do you know what that is?"

Of course Birdie knew. She squeezed Olga's knee again. "You aren't a maniac. You just got overwhelmed. Don't listen to Iris. She doesn't know anything."

Olga released a guttural laugh. "Oh, I think she does."

"But she doesn't know *everything*. And she might be bossy, but she isn't the boss." Birdie remembered something her papa told her when she came home, heartsore over mistreatment by the school bully. "She can't make you feel foolish unless you let her." Birdie took hold of Olga's arm and pulled it away from her face. "Listen to me, Olga. You were scared for Mrs. Overly and you showed it. I call that being compassionate, not being a maniac."

Olga stared into Birdie's face for several seconds, her expression unreadable. Then she sighed and angled her gaze at the window again. "You're nice to say all that and try to make me feel better. But you might as well know . . . I wasn't scared for Mrs. Overly as much as I was scared for me."

Birdie tipped her head. "Why?"

Olga peeked at Birdie from the corner of her eye. Tears swam, making her blue irises shine. "Only yesterday, Mrs. Overly told me I could stay here until my baby is born. When I said I didn't want it, she said she knew people who would find it a good home. I thought my troubles were over." One tear broke loose of Olga's lower lashes and rolled down her cheek. "But if she dies, Iris is right. This place will close down. Where will I go then? What will I do? What will any of us do?"

Birdie couldn't answer, because she didn't know. But she did know one thing. "Not eating won't fix it. So come downstairs. Have your dinner. I'm sure Reverend Overly will have some ideas when he's back from his trip this afternoon. Until then, let's do what Ephraim said—the things Mrs. Overly would have us do."

"Eating dinner and doing chores won't fix it, either."

Olga's despair made Birdie's heart ache. Mostly because she was right. "I know, but if we're busy, we won't think about our troubles so much. Come on." She stood and held out her hand. "Let's go down with the others, all right?"

Olga pulled in a big breath and whooshed it out. She took Birdie's hand. "All right."

## Ephraim

While the doctor spent time with Mother, Ephraim paced up and down the hallway. Ellie walked beside him, and Ted stayed close to her. It was a tight fit, the three of them abreast. Especially when one of them had a furry, swinging tail. Ephraim came close to putting the dog outside. Father certainly wouldn't approve Ted's presence in the house. But the animal had a calming effect on the child and, surprisingly, on Ephraim, too. He was in charge in Father's absence. Until Father's return, Ted could stay inside with them.

Ephraim's ears picked up snippets of conversations from various places in the house—the girls, going about their usual duties, as he'd requested. They used quieter voices than usual, but at least they were talking to one another. One small piece of normalcy in an otherwise very upsetting day.

Thank goodness he'd stayed here instead of accompanying Father to Speegleville. He'd wanted to examine the organ at the Speegleville church and familiarize himself with its workings. Every instrument had its own quirks, he'd learned over the years of travel to various churches, and it was best to discover them before playing for an audience. Besides, he still hadn't found a moment alone to address the odd statement Lida Holland had made as he and Father drove away with Birdie and Olga in the back of their wagon last Thursday. He'd hoped to ask about it when the two of them were away from the house, alone on the road with no ears to overhear. But he lost his chance when Father instructed him to remain at Hope Hill and drove off without him.

The brothel owner's venomous query—"*Ain't you stole enough from me already?*"—echoed through his memory again. Father had never rescued a woman from Lida's Palace previously, so what could he have taken from her? Something of value, considering her hateful tone as she delivered the taunt. From childhood, Ephraim had always been fairly imaginative. But even his imagination couldn't conjure a reason for such a bold accusation. No matter the reason, appeasing his curiosity paled in comparison to his gratitude for being here when Mother needed him. And before he retired to his cottage tonight, he would address with his father the wisdom of purchasing a saddle horse.

The door to his parents' bedroom opened, and the doctor emerged.

Ephraim leaned down to Ellie. "Take Ted with you and find Lucretia." Uncertainty flickered in the little girl's blue-green eyes. He delivered a gentle nudge between her shoulder blades. "Go on now." Ellie scrunched her lips into a deep frown, but she turned and trotted off, her hand on Ted's ruff. Ephraim turned to Dr. Paddock. "How is she?"

"For now?" The older man ran his fingers through his steel-gray hair, pushing the strands away from his broad forehead. "She's stable. But still frail. It was a significant episode."

Ephraim's hands began to tremble. He shoved them into his trouser pockets. "Her heart?"

The doctor nodded. "I left a list of suggestions on the stand beside her bed. Following them will help protect the weakened muscle in the future."

"The future . . ." Hope stuttered his pulse. "So she isn't in imminent danger of . . . ?" He couldn't bring himself to add the word *dying*.

A sad smile formed beneath the doctor's thick mustache. "The time of anyone's homegoing is in the hands of the Maker, Ephraim. I can't predict how many days, months, or even years remain for her. All I know is she suffered an attack of angina pectoris, and one attack usually leads to another until a massive one stops the heart for good."

Just as she'd said happened to her father and grandfather. Pain stabbed Ephraim's chest with such intensity he wondered if such a fate awaited him, too.

"In the meantime," the doctor continued, "rest is good medicine. I gave her a powder to ease her discomfort. She'll likely sleep until morning, and that's exactly what's best right now." Dr. Paddock placed his hand on Ephraim's shoulder. "I know you want to stay close to her. I'll tie the horse you borrowed from the Coopers to the back of my buggy and return it to their ranch on my way to town."

Ephraim sighed in gratitude. "Thank you, sir. I appreciate it. Is it all right if Father stops by your office and pays you for your call the next time he's in Tulsey?"

"That will be fine." His hand slid away and he took a backward step. "Be sure and review the list I made and see that she follows it. It's not a cure, but it will help."

Ephraim thanked him again and saw him to the door. Then he darted to the bedroom and let himself in. As the doctor had said, Mother was asleep. She looked so peaceful. If he hadn't picked her still form up off the floor himself, he'd never know she'd suffered a serious attack. He tiptoed to the stand and picked up the list. It took some time to decipher the doctor's messy pencil scratchings, but he didn't see anything that might make Mother balk. Except not going up and down stairs. Ellie's bedroom was on the second floor. Every night, Mother went up and read to the child before tucking her into bed. Neither would want to end the practice.

"Mr. Overly?"

The hesitant whisper came from the other side of the door. Ephraim laid the paper on the stand and crossed to the door in two long strides. Lucretia waited in the hallway. She glanced past him, her forehead puckered in worry, as he stepped from the room with his finger on his lips in silent instruction. He lowered his hand and mouthed "thank you" for her remaining quiet. Rest was good medicine, the doctor said, and he wanted his mother to get the rest she needed.

"Is she gonna be all right?" Lucretia whispered, wringing her hands at her waist.

Ephraim didn't have a good answer for the girl. He shrugged, then closed the door and guided her a few feet up the hallway. "Did you need something?"

"No, but Ellie does." She gestured to the end of the hallway.

Ellie sat on the floor against the wall. She'd pulled up her knees, folded her arms on top of them, and buried her face in her bent elbow. Sympathy stung him. The child's pose painted a picture of despondency. If he was still Ellie's age, he might sit the same way.

"It ain't like she'll call out and disturb your mama." Sadness tinged Lucretia's tone. "So can you take her in and let her peek at Mrs. Overly? It's been a hard day on all of us, but most especially on Ellie."

Things would be even harder for Ellie if Mother didn't recover. He pushed the unpleasant thought aside and gave Lucretia a nod. "I'll take her in now."

# Chapter Nine

Ephraim

The midday's wind had blown itself out by suppertime, so Ephraim chose to watch for Father from Mother's rocking chair on the porch. Ted waited with him. Ellie hadn't been happy about putting the dog outside again, but Father would be upset enough about Mother's condition. There was no sense in adding to his angst by letting him find Ted where he didn't belong. Just as dusk was falling, much later than Ephraim had expected, their revival wagon rolled onto the yard. He trotted down the stairs and ran out to meet it.

Father drew the team to a halt and set the brake. "What's the matter?" He scanned the grounds, as if seeking calamity.

Ephraim informed him about Mother's collapse, shared the details concerning the doctor's visit, and made his request to purchase a saddle horse. Father listened attentively, almost impassively, but his gloved hands rhythmically squeezed and relaxed on the reins, giving mute testimony of inner turmoil. When Ephraim finished speaking, Father released a heavy sigh.

"I've known since my earliest acquaintanceship with dear Ophelia that this day would come." He chuckled softly. "Have I ever told you that she initially refused my courtship, stating it would be unfair for me to bind myself to a woman who would likely leave me a widower?"

No, he hadn't. Maybe if he had, today's events wouldn't have been such a shock.

"Your mother is the most unselfish person I know. I told her then if I only had a short time with her, it would be a greater blessing than I deserved. My life has been the richer because I have Ophelia Marker Overly as my partner in love, in life, and in ministry."

A knot formed in Ephraim's throat. Part sorrow for his parents, part anger at them for not preparing him for the likelihood of this day. But maybe they'd done it to protect him. Living under a cloud of constant worry was no way to live.

Father lifted his face to the pinkish-gray sky where a half-moon glowed bright and stars winked from horizon to horizon. "Since our first days together, she and I have prayed for the Lord's healing if it be His will, and for His strength and comfort if not. The Lord will do what He deems best. Blessed be the name of the Lord." His chin quivered, and his eyes slid shut.

Ephraim's chest went tight, making it painful to draw a breath. He'd witnessed his parents' faithfulness through trials and heartaches and outright persecution. Father's expression of trust didn't surprise him. But neither did it encourage him. And that concerned him. Perhaps his trust wasn't as firmly grounded as theirs was.

"Father?" He waited until his father looked at him. He'd planned to ask which of them would assume the nighttime practice of reading to Ellie and tucking her into bed, but a different question emerged. "What did Lida Holland mean when she said you'd stolen enough from her?"

Father's face drained of color so quickly, Ephraim feared he was suffering an attack of angina pectoris, too. Father's fingers wrapped tight on the reins. He stared downward, seemingly at Ephraim, but Ephraim sensed he didn't really see him.

Ephraim tipped his head. "Father?"

Father gave a little jolt. "Son." The title grated out, as if Father's throat had closed up. "Lida Holland is a bitter woman. She has reasons to be, but even so . . ." He angled his face skyward again. He remained still and silent for several seconds. Then he nodded, shifted on the seat, and fixed his gaze on Ephraim's. "I didn't steal from her. And that is all I can say." He climbed down from the wagon seat and gripped Ephraim by his upper arms. "There will be much for us to discuss, plans we need to make, changes to anticipate. And we will have that conversation in the morning, after I've spent time in prayer."

Ephraim hadn't expected otherwise. Father never proceeded until he asked the Lord for direction and wisdom. Suddenly Father pulled Ephraim to him in a hug, even guiding his head into the curve of his neck with his cupped hand. Startled, Ephraim stood stiffly within his father's embrace. He couldn't recall the last time he'd been held that way. Father's lips pressed against the crown of his head, and then Father released him.

"Please see to the team." He spoke in a normal tone as he strode toward the house. "I need to check on your mother."

Ephraim did as Father requested, performing the familiar task without conscious thought. When the horses were in their stalls, he headed for his cottage. Midway up the path, he thought about little Ellie. She'd stared forlornly at Mother when he'd taken her into his parents' bedroom, her little hands reaching toward her but not touching her. She'd given him a look of betrayal when he put Ted outside. Although she had no words, her eyes spoke volumes. Would one of the girls read the meaning behind her pleading gaze and take Mother's place for the bedtime routine?

The child's sad eyes haunted him. He couldn't let her go to bed on her own, without a kind word, a bedtime story, and a prayer. He turned on his heel and headed for the house. He entered by the back door and stopped just inside, shocked by the silence. The daily schedule called for bedtime preparation at nine o'clock, following Father's evening devotion in the parlor, with all quiet by nine-thirty.

He peeked into the kitchen and squinted at the wall clock above the worktable. The clock hands indicated eight-thirty. But not a soul was around. He listened closely, straining for noises indicating someone was still awake. No voices. No creaking floorboards. Apparently, they'd all turned in early.

If Ellie was already in bed, he shouldn't disturb her. He reached for the doorknob, intending to let himself out, but a low-toned voice caught his attention. Someone was still awake. He moved down the hallway, peering through the shadows. As he reached his parents' bedroom door, he realized the sound came from within. He angled his head toward the door. Yes, Father was talking. To Mother? If so, she was awake. He could inquire about Ellie.

He raised his hand to lightly knock, but before his knuckles connected with the paneled door, he heard Father say, "Forgive me, Lord, and guide me."

Ephraim lowered his hand. Father was praying. He shouldn't intrude. Slowly, he turned in the direction of the back door.

"Give me the right words if he needs to know. Silence me if he doesn't."

The anguish behind the request froze Ephraim in place. The prayer continued, but Father's voice became an indistinguishable murmur. Ephraim gave himself a little jerk that set his feet in motion toward the door. Guilt smote him for eavesdropping. At the same time, curiosity gripped him.

Of whom was Father speaking? Could it be Ephraim? His parents had kept secret the seriousness of Mother's condition. Were they withholding other important information from him? His mouth went dry, and he forced a painful swallow. Discovering Mother's health condition had been shock and sorrow enough for his lifetime. Did he really want to know what other secret Father might be harboring?

Birdie

The morning after Mrs. Overly's fainting spell, everyone except Mrs. Overly gathered for breakfast at seven o'clock. Birdie, Reva, and Gladys were on cooking duty. They served grits and toasted biscuits with jam, which Mrs. Overly had designated for Tuesday's breakfast. After they ate, Reverend Overly shared the doctor's instructions for his wife's care. Though Birdie had only known the woman a short time, she'd already grown fond of her. Based on the concerned, attentive faces around the table, the other girls felt the same.

When the reverend laid aside the paper the doctor left behind, Lucretia said, "Whatever we can do to make things easier on her, we'll do it."

The other girls nodded or added their agreement, and Birdie nodded, too. The appreciative, approving smile Reverend Overly cast over the group further ignited her intention to be as helpful as possible. A niggle of guilt stabbed her conscience. Was she being helpful for Mrs. Overly's sake, or to prove to the reverend she was ready to take a paying job? She didn't want to be selfish, but at the same time, she didn't want Mrs. Overly's illness to delay her travel to Kansas City and Aunt Sally.

Reverend Overly was speaking again. She forced herself to pay attention.

"Until Mrs. Overly recovers, Ephraim will assume responsibility for shopping and trading for food supplies." The reverend placed his hand on Ephraim's shoulder, the way Birdie imagined a king might place a mantle of leadership on a knight's shoulders. "For the remainder of this week, he will serve as teacher in the classroom. I have complete confidence in Ephraim's ability to oversee instruction. Of course, it is my hope"—he aimed an almost impish grin at his son—"and Ephraim's, as well, that this will be a temporary duty and Mrs. Overly will be rested enough to resume teaching by next Monday."

Olga made a face. "Could we put off classes until Mrs. Overly is better?"

Reverend Overly gave a firm shake of his head, lowering his hand to the table and weaving his fingers together. "Mrs. Overly would be distressed if schoolwork is waylaid. We must not cause her undue angst. Thus, we will honor her by studying and continuing to learn."

Olga sighed. "Yes, sir."

"Mrs. Overly has established a rotating, equitable schedule." He continued in the authoritative tone that had convinced Birdie to leave Miz Holland's place. "We will continue to follow it, and we will do so heartily, as . . ." He arched a brow.

"As unto the Lord," several of the girls and Ephraim chorused.

Birdie and Olga echoed the vow.

Reverend Overly offered another approving smile.

Iris set her head at a regal angle. "I suppose, with Mrs. Overly limited to this floor of the house, you'll appoint one of us to oversee upstairs chores." She wound the dark blond curl that always fell alongside her cheek around her finger. "I would be happy to inspect the rooms for cleanliness and report to you."

Mathilda snickered, and a few of the girls rolled their eyes. Birdie glanced at Olga, who was staring at Iris with a scowl marring her face.

Reverend Overly cleared his throat. "I appreciate your willingness to be extra diligent, Miss Brown, but Mrs. Overly and I have agreed upon hiring a housekeeper. We ask that you all add your prayers to ours that the Lord leads us to His choice for this important role in our household. Of course, the change will require some other changes, which will affect at least two of you." His gaze traveled the length of the table and rested on little

Ellie. "A housekeeper will want her own room as part of payment. Ellie's room is the largest of the bedrooms upstairs, which is why it's where we've generally housed the women who delivered a baby and needed peace and solitude to adjust to motherhood."

Olga fidgeted in her chair, lightly bumping Birdie with her elbow.

"Since we don't anticipate needing it for that purpose immediately," he went on, still focused on the little curly-haired girl sitting quiet on her stool, "we will move Ellie in with one of you and give that room to the housekeeper, whomever she might be."

A conniving smile appeared on Iris's face. "Ellie can move in with me."

Mathilda sat up. "Don't you mean in with *us*?"

Iris shrugged. "You can share with Lucretia. She doesn't have a roommate."

Several mild protests arose.

Reverend Overly waved his hands. "Mrs. Overly and I have already decided to put Ellie in with Miss Jacks."

Iris huffed. "But—"

The reverend shifted his attention to Iris. "As you said, Miss Jacks currently rooms alone. It makes sense to have Ellie join her. The fewer people disrupted, the better." His firm tone must have cowed Iris into silence, because she slumped back in her chair and hung her head. He sent his gaze around the table again. "But we won't make the change until it's necessary. There's no way of knowing how long it will take to locate someone who's willing to join our ministry. So we will leave things as they are for now, and each of you will be responsible for maintaining order and cleanliness in your living spaces."

He removed his watch from the little pocket in his vest and examined the timepiece. "I see it's a few minutes past eight o'clock. We are late for our studies. Those of you who are taking classes, please go with Ephraim now." Ephraim and several of the girls, including Olga and Ellie, rose and left the room. "Those on cleanup duty, please see to your chores. If anyone needs me, I will be at my wife's bedside or in my study." He strode from the room.

Birdie pushed away from the table, as did the remaining girls, and everyone moved on to the duties indicated on the assignment chart in the kitchen. At ten o'clock, just as they had yesterday, they gathered in the parlor for their music time. Ephraim seemed a bit subdued compared to the day before, but Birdie enjoyed every minute of joining her voice with the others in song.

She particularly enjoyed learning, "Come Home, Poor Sinner." Although somber in tune, some of the words seemed to give a personal message. The call to come home and no longer roam was exactly what she longed to do. More specifically, to find a home where she was loved the way Papa had loved her, a home of warmth and welcome. She envisioned that home with Aunt Sally, who was so much like her dear papa.

As much as Mrs. Overly's unexpected illness pained her, it also offered an opportunity. She would work hard, sing well, be cooperative and uncomplaining. She would prove to Reverend Overly that she was no longer the girl who'd worked for Miz Holland, but was a new, better, worthy version, ready to earn a decent wage.

The entire day, in whatever task she performed, from dusting the baseboards and furniture to helping with meal preparation and cleanup, she worked heartily. The way Reverend and Mrs. Overly expected.

When supper was finished and Reverend Overly had dismissed them from the table, she gathered up her dishes.

"Miss Clarkson?" Reverend Overly turned a somber look in Birdie's direction. "I would appreciate a few words with you."

Birdie stood with her hands full, unsure what to do. "Now? Or . . ." She glanced at the items she held.

"Leave them. Miss Long will take them. Follow me."

# Chapter Ten

Birdie

Reverend Overly paused at his study door and gestured her to a chair. She hurried in and sat. He crossed to his desk, leaving the door open behind them. She was heartened by the open door. Anyone walking by could overhear whatever he intended to say. Surely, if she'd done something wrong, he would protect her privacy. Maybe he wanted to tell her he'd found a job for her already. The brief worry that had gripped her at his request for a meeting whisked away, and eagerness replaced it.

"Miss Clarkson, my son tells me you have a lovely singing voice. 'A rare gift' were his exact words."

She stared at him, her mouth falling open. The idea that Ephraim had spoken about her to his father created a flutter in the center of her chest. "He . . . he said that?"

"Indeed he did." The man rocked his chair. "He thought perhaps you'd received training at a music conservatory."

She shook her head, still reeling. "No, sir. Never. I . . . I . . ." She swallowed. "I don't know what to say." She also didn't know why the reverend had shared Ephraim's compliment. "Um . . . thank you?"

He chuckled softly. "You're welcome. I'm glad that Ephraim's assessment has pleased you." He drew in a deep breath. "And it leads me to make a request."

The flutter changed to a quick-paced pound. She licked her dry lips. "W-what is that, sir?"

He sat forward, resting his elbows on the desktop she'd wiped clear of dust earlier that day. "If you recall, Ephraim was gone this past Saturday attending a funeral. He attends many funerals at the request of grieving families. They hire him to play their departed loved one's favorite hymns or a hymn of his choosing at the graveside."

Birdie raised her eyebrows, intrigued. She knew he played the piano, because he accompanied the choir. But a person couldn't take a piano to a cemetery. Maybe he was like Papa, who had played the harmonica. Or her childhood neighbor, who'd played a fiddle. She'd always enjoyed listening to their tunes. "What does he play?"

"The organ."

The gleaming pipes of the organ in the Tulsey church filled her mind's eye. She gasped. "At cemeteries? How?"

A smile twitched, bringing out a pair of dimples that gave the usually serious man a boyish appearance. "He has a traveling organ, not much larger than the table there beneath the window."

She looked at the table, taking note of its size and shape. "I see," she said, although she still didn't understand how an instrument that made such a majestic sound could be so small.

"As I said," Reverend Overly continued, drawing Birdie's attention to him, "the families hire him, and they pay a fee for his service. Ephraim has often wished to take the choir with him. Hearing the words to hymns might bring greater comfort to the families. But we haven't done so because many of our girls would lose time dedicated to study. We're quite intent that every girl receives an adequate education for their own betterment."

Suddenly Birdie thought she knew why the reverend had called her for this meeting. "I completed ten grades already, so if I sang at the gravesides, it would only take me away from chores."

His nod confirmed she'd guessed correctly.

Her thoughts tumbled onward. The families paid Ephraim. If the families paid her, too, she could save the money for a train ticket. The idea of singing all by herself in front of an audience made her feel a little queasy, but she wanted to earn a decent wage. What would be more decent than comforting heartbroken families with song?

The reverend sat back in his chair and linked his fingers over his vest front. "Each of the girls who reside at Hope Hill contribute toward the general expenses by making goods to sell."

The seeming change in topic startled her. "You mean the aprons and such?"

"Indeed, I do. Mrs. Overly told me your stitching is excellent, and that you are quite diligent to form the most perfect designs with the colored threads."

Birdie absorbed the approval glowing in his gray-blue eyes. Papa had beamed at her that way when she brought home good reports from school or did well in her chores. She basked in the warmth of his praise. "Thank you, sir."

"You're welcome. I know you're already contributing with your stitchwork, but what do you think about hiring out as a soloist for funerals? Are you open to such a venture?"

Disappointment niggled. She wouldn't be allowed to keep the money she earned from singing. But the thought of comforting grieving families appealed to her. She'd so needed comfort when Papa died. "Yes, sir. I think I could do it."

His smile broadened. "Wonderful! You're an answer to prayer, Miss Clarkson."

She raised her eyebrows. "I am? How?"

"If we're to hire a full-time housekeeper, we have need of bringing in some additional funds. Only this morning Ophelia and I asked the Lord to show us a way to afford a housekeeper. Not an hour later Ephraim divulged your God-given talent. He and I prayed together that if it was God's will for you to sing at funerals, you would agree." Suddenly he sobered. He leaned forward, his intense gaze fixed on hers. "Quite often our Lord doesn't answer quickly. When He does, I know He has a blessing in store. I am grateful to you, Miss Clarkson, and I also look forward to how God will bless you as you utilize your gift to comfort grief-stricken families and support the respite Mrs. Overly requires."

How could she think of a train ticket when Mrs. Overly had such a need for rest? She swallowed the last bit of disappointment she'd experienced. If she could help Mrs. Overly and comfort grieving families, then no one would see her as selfish.

He planted his palms on the desktop and pushed himself upright. "I won't take any more of your leisure time, except to say . . ." He rounded the desk and gripped her hand between his. "Thank you."

Birdie exited the study and nearly collided with Olga. Olga grabbed her hand and pulled her into the empty dining room. "What did he want with you?"

Birdie repeated what Reverend Overly had told her, including what he'd said about God blessing her for using her voice to comfort families. Her heart fluttered. Would the blessing be the money she needed to go to Aunt Sally?

Olga nudged her. "Birdie? You stopped talking and then seemed to drift away somewhere. Are you all right?"

Birdie gathered her scattered thoughts. "I am. I was only wondering . . . about God . . . and His blessings."

Olga laughed.

Birdie frowned. "What's funny?"

Olga's eyes twinkled. "Less than a week we have been here and you already believe in God's blessings. The preacher is a miracle worker."

Unexpectedly, tears threatened. "You don't believe that God blesses people?"

Olga chortled, her frame shaking with her merriment. "Ja, I believe God blesses people like Mrs. Overly. He proved it by sending you here to sing and bring in money. But what do you get for it?"

The satisfaction of helping. Singing again after holding songs inside because Papa wasn't there to sing with her. Getting to spend time with Ephraim. The last one gave her an inward jolt. She wouldn't share any of those reasons—those blessings—with Olga. The girl would only laugh at her again. She shrugged.

All humor faded from Olga's eyes, and resolve replaced it. "My pa always said God helps those who help themselves. If you want blessings, Birdie, you have to reach out and grab them." She glanced into the hallway, then leaned close. "If it was me going to those funerals, when I got paid, I would put some of the money in my pocket and keep it. You earned it. You shouldn't have to share all of it."

Birdie gaped at her roommate. "But Mrs. Overly—"

Olga gave a little swish with her hand, the way someone shooed away a fly. "If God is real, He will take care of Mrs. Overly without your help. If He's so powerful, He shouldn't need us at all, ja?"

Birdie pressed her chin to her shoulder, a feeble attempt to hide from Olga's question.

A chime sounded—the call to evening devotions.

Birdie heaved out a relieved sigh. She wouldn't have to answer Olga now. Maybe by bedtime, Olga would forget she'd even asked the question. She followed the other girl down the hallway to the parlor. As she settled into a chair, an unpleasant idea formed in the back of her mind. She'd stayed with Mama instead of going to Kansas because Mama said she needed her. But Mama had only wanted her for chores. She'd gone into Miz Holland's house because she was told she'd be fed and cared for. Then the woman had used her for her own gain. Had Reverend

Overly told her she would be blessed in order to trick her into earning money with her voice? Did he really care about her, or was he like Miz Holland after all, only wanting the money she could make?

### Ephraim

Ephraim guided the horses to the smoothest parts of the road leading to Speegleville. The wagon's wood-framed cover, in place to protect their best clothes from dust, made the conveyance top-heavy. If a wheel dropped into a deep groove or hole, the wagon could topple. He shuddered, considering the possible injuries to his passengers.

The day was beautiful—sunny and mild with only a light breeze stirring the dried grasses that covered the landscape as far as he could see. Despite the ideal travel conditions, he wasn't happy about being on the road. He'd wanted to cancel the Speegleville revival. Or at least cancel the choir's participation. Not that the girls weren't ready. They sounded better than ever with Birdie singing lead soprano. They'd worked hard and memorized the new song, and he knew they would impress the attendees. But he didn't like leaving Mother behind with only Ellie and the widow Cooper for company. If not for Mother's insistence that she would wither from guilt if her illness prevented people from hearing the good news of Jesus' saving grace, Ephraim would have refused to ready the wagon, help the girls board, and take up the reins.

Father sat on the seat beside Ephraim. The girls filled the benches in the wagon, their soft chatter a steady hum accompanying the grate of the wheels and the gentle *clop-clop* of horses' hooves on the road. For most of their drive, Father's eyes had remained closed. But not in sleep. Ephraim knew from experi-

888888888

8888888888

888888888

ence he was praying. Petitioning the Holy Spirit to guide his words. For the hearts of the attendees to be open to receiving the free gift of salvation offered by Jesus. For Ephraim and the choir to lean on Christ's strength and not rely on their own humble abilities. For whatever else the Lord laid on his heart. Today, he was probably also praying for Mother to be awake when they returned, eager to hear how many people made professions of faith.

Suddenly Father's arm shot out, his finger pointing. "There's the sign for Speegleville. Turn left on the first road past the sign. The church is situated on the southern edge of town—the first building we'll come upon."

The girls' chatter ceased with Father's announcement. As Ephraim had taught them to do, they began singing scales to ready their voices for the performance. Ephraim listened while watching for the turn, easily picking out Birdie's pure tone from the others. Such a difference a single voice made. Was there a lesson hiding in his observation? He should ponder it more deeply when the revival was over.

The wagon lurched, and he grimaced. "Easy, Red and Rusty," he called, and the horses slowed. This road on which Father had directed him was more a path than an actual road, wide enough for only a single wagon. He hoped no one approached from the opposite direction, or he'd have to drive the team into the uneven patch of thick grass where mounds of dirt marked the locations of prairie dog holes. A horse could break a leg stepping into one of those holes.

They topped a gentle rise, and he spotted a weathered clapboard structure ahead. It had no bell tower, stained glass windows, or even a cover of whitewash, but it must be the church because it was the first building on the road. Ephraim sent his father a puzzled look. "Is that where we're going?"

Father was smiling, his eyes aglow with familiar fervor. "It is.

And look, there are already two wagons. People are hungry to hear the gospel, Ephraim. The Lord be praised."

Ephraim nodded in reply, then guided the horses to the side of the unpretentious building. Double doors at the top of a set of crooked wooden steps were propped open with sizable rocks. As he parked, a small boy appeared in the opening. The boy pattered down the steps, squinted at the wagon for several seconds, then dashed back inside. Ephraim heard him shout, "Preacher's here!" He stifled a groan. If people were already inside, he wouldn't have an opportunity to test the organ before playing "Lead On, O King Eternal" as a prelude. He'd have to rely on the Spirit going before him and preparing his fingers and feet for this particular instrument.

Father clambered over the edge of the wagon and hopped down. He set off for the building. Ephraim went to the back and unfolded the metal step for the girls. One by one they descended, until the entire choir stood in formation on the trampled dead grass.

Iris made a sour face. "That's the saddest-looking church I've ever seen. I hope we didn't come here for nothing."

Ephraim gave the response Father would if he heard the remark. "If only one soul is saved, it will be worth our effort to come."

Iris fiddled with the ruffle of lace at her collar and fell silent.

"All right," Ephraim said, scanning the group with his gaze, "we'll open the revival with 'I Stood Outside the Gate,' then return to our seats while the reverend preaches. When he signals us, we'll go to the front and sing 'Come Home, Poor Sinner.' If responses go long, we may need to sing it twice. Watch me for direction."

Iris huffed, swiping her brow with the back of her hand. "We know all this, Ephraim. We've sung dozens of times already."

But apparently none of the messages had yet reached Iris's

heart. At least, he saw no evidence of the Spirit gentling her. Mother would say he needed to pray harder for Iris. Right now, though, he needed to pray for himself—for patience. He forced a smile. "Yes, *you* know the routine, Miss Brown, but this is a first performance for Miss Clarkson and Miss Mueller. They will feel more confident if they receive these instructions." Iris rolled her eyes, and he pretended not to notice. He addressed the entire group again. "When the reverend has welcomed the new Christians into the fold, then we will sing 'I'll Live for Him.'" He pulled in a deep, steadying breath. "Any questions?"

Olga raised her hand.

"Miss Mueller?"

"Can we go in now? I've been watching. Lots of folks are already inside. There might not be any seats left if we wait much longer, and I would rather not stand the whole time."

Ephraim glanced over his shoulder. People were pouring across the yard and entering the building. This was fixing to be a stirring revival.

*Go before us, Lord, and let Your Spirit have its way.* The prayer formed automatically, and he couldn't help but be bolstered by it. Maybe the Spirit was already working in him.

He nodded at Olga. "You're right. Come along, ladies." He led them to the church.

# Chapter Eleven

## Birdie

Birdie sat on the edge of the backless bench, enthralled. She'd known Reverend Overly was persuasive. He had convinced her and Olga and all the other choir girls to leave the brothels and come to Hope Hill. She knew he was familiar with God's Word, because every morning and evening since their arrival, he'd read from his large, worn Bible and shared the meaning of the verses. But his presentation in this simple sanctuary, empty of the beauty that had captured her at the Tulsey church, tugged at her in ways she'd never experienced before.

People filled the benches behind her, so crowded that children had to sit on their parents' laps. Many of the adults also strained forward. Did they, like her, feel a magnetic pull drawing them from their seats to the dais with Reverend Overly?

"This woman . . . this woman . . ." The reverend held his Bible aloft and pointed to a section on the page. "Her entire life was bound up in sinful choices. Rejected by the other women in her town, she wouldn't even draw water in the early morning hours before the blistering heat of the sun parched her lips so she needn't face their scorn. She hoped to hide."

Birdie swallowed a little gasp. How often had she tried to hide by turning her face away from whatever frightened or hurt her? She hid from Mama's harsh treatment. She hid from the pain of losing Papa. She hid from the ugliness she was forced to endure at Miz Holland's place. Hiding was lonely. Her heart went out to this unknown woman.

"But Jesus saw her."

Birdie's pulse stuttered into double beats. Did Jesus see her, too, even when she tried to hide? *Oh, please, no . . .*

"And when He looked at her, He didn't only see a woman bound by sin. Oh, no. He saw a woman in need of a Savior. And He knew if she received the Savior, she would be washed clean!" He swept his hand in a grand gesture, his eyes ablaze. "Her grievous sins gone! Sent so far away it was as if they had never occurred! God would flood her soul with His own Spirit and this woman . . . this needy, broken, ostracized woman"—his voice gained strength with each description—"would be a new creature, transformed from the inside out!"

Reverend Overly's form went blurry. Stifling a grunt of impatience, Birdie swished her fingers across her eyes and erased the moisture distorting her vision. She wanted to see the certainty in his expression that Jesus could make such a difference.

Suddenly the reverend turned and smiled at the choir girls scrunched together on a single front-row bench. "Did not these young women sing beautifully for you?"

Assents rose from every corner of the room. Birdie's cheeks warmed at the praise.

"They blessed us, yes?"

Louder approval and a spattering of applause provided the reply.

"One would never guess that these lovely young women, whose voices shared a beautiful message of truth, were once like this woman whom Jesus met at Jacob's well. Unwilling to venture out. Abandoned by ones who'd claimed to love them. Shunned by others who didn't understand the choices they'd made."

The tears returned, and Birdie blinked hard. She hadn't expected to have her personal history laid bare before strangers. A part of her wanted to jump up and run out of the building, but another part of her longed to hear again the reverend's claim that this woman was transformed from the inside out. She wanted to know how it had happened for the woman at Jacob's well. She wanted to know how it could happen for her.

Reverend Overly held one hand toward the choir, but aimed his flushed face beyond them to the listening audience. "The same Jesus who redeemed the woman at the well has rescued these women from their prisons of iniquity. The same Jesus who convinced them to leave behind their pasts for a brighter future is waiting to receive you, too. There is no one too young or too old for salvation to reach. There is no sin too heinous that it can't be forgiven. There—"

"Hold up there, Preacher." A man near the front on the opposite side of the aisle bolted to his feet. He balled his hands on his hips and glowered at the reverend. "What you just said . . . no sin too heinous—"

"That it can't be forgiven," Reverend Overly boomed, his voice rattling the rafters.

The man shook his head. "You're wrong. 'Cause some sins, they're just too big to be forgot."

Reverend Overly placed his Bible on the wooden stand on the dais and moved to the edge of the platform. "Talk to me, brother. What sins do you carry that you're afraid are too big for God to forgive?"

The man's face splotched red behind his dark whiskers. "They ain't my sins. They're the ones those gals over there carry for sellin' themselves." He turned his angry glare on the choir.

Birdie's blood ran cold. Her body jerked backward, her elbows connecting with Gladys and Olga. Gladys huffed and elbowed her back, but Birdie welcomed the sharp jab. Maybe it would knock loose the awful weight of shame that had fallen over her.

The man growled low in his throat, and he pointed at the

reverend. "Can't believe you brung people like that into God's house."

Murmurs—some nervous, some approving—rolled through the sanctuary. Reverend Overly raised both hands, his expression pleading. "Folks, let's not allow anger to take hold here. Jesus came to seek and save the lost. The Spirit is drawing some of you to come to Him. It's His desire that none—*none!*—be left outside heaven's gate. Have a seat, brother, and let me finish."

The man remained ramrod straight, his jaw thrust in an angry angle. "How 'bout you tell these fine folks about some different places in the Bible, towns by the name o' Sodom an' Gomorrah. Tell 'em what happened there. How holy fire rained down on 'em."

The reverend shook his head, sadness furrowing his brow. "God's judgment indeed fell there, but that fire rained down because they wouldn't repent and change their ways. Their story should be a cautionary one for all of us who have yet to repent of our sins and give our lives to the Lord."

The man turned his back on Reverend Overly and sent his glower across the congregation. "Do you hear what he's sayin'? Maybe he thinks we ought to just leave all them houses of iniquity alone. Let the goin's-on in those places continue. Well, I think they need a little fire an' brimstone. I say they ought to be burned to the ground!"

Another man closer to the back of the sanctuary stood. "Dan, none of us came to hear your blather. Sit down an' let the preacher talk."

The man named Dan snorted. "Why? He's spoutin' about sin, but he don't do anything to make it stop." He turned, a snarl curling his lips. "You said these gals over here come from the brothels. You get 'em out?"

Reverend Overly lifted his chin. "I invited them. The Spirit prompted them to heed my invitation. I take no credit for their choices."

Dan folded his arms. "I'd heard tell about how you visit the brothels an' ask the girls to come live at your house instead. Some folks think you're a saint for it. Others say you're castin' your pearls before swine."

Birdie had never heard the phrase about pearls and swine before, but she knew which this man considered her. She tucked her chin tight against her shoulder and closed her eyes.

"And what do you think, Brother Dan?" Reverend Overly spoke quietly, thoughtfully, even gently. Even so, his question sent a shudder through Birdie's frame.

"I'll tell you what I think, Reverend Overly." Birdie kept her eyes shut, but she heard the derision in Dan's voice. She didn't need to see him to know his face matched those she couldn't forget from the other church. "I think if you really are God's servant, an' if you really want to make a difference, you'll take a torch instead o' *talk* to every brothel you visit."

Scuffling noises brought Birdie's eyes open. Two men had grabbed Dan, and the pair were wrestling him up the aisle. Olga caught hold of Birdie's arm and pulled her from her seat. She huddled with the other choir girls in the front corner of the sanctuary and watched the men force Dan out of the church. The men closed the doors behind him and turned the lock.

Fists pounded on the door, but the two fellows sauntered up the aisle and returned to their benches as if nothing of worth had occurred. The taller of the pair, still standing, swished his palms together. "That Dan, he causes a ruckus any time brothels are mentioned. He's had a burr under his saddle about them places for years. Rumor has it his baby sister works in one up near Dallas. I think he only come here hopin' you'd say somethin' that'd give him an excuse to let loose." He gave a nod. "Go ahead now, Preacher. Get on with your sermon." He sat.

For several seconds, the reverend stood with his eyes closed, so still and unmoving Birdie wondered if he'd ceased to breathe. His eyes popped open, and he turned his gaze toward the choir. "Ladies, come sing. I think the message you'll deliver in song will be better than anything I could say right now." He stepped down from the dais and crossed to the bench they'd vacated when the squabble broke out.

Ephraim hurried to the organ, sending them a silent message with his raised brows and barely discernible nod. Birdie stepped up on the platform with the others. Once in position, she linked her hands behind her back and stared past the audience to the wall behind them, the way Ephraim had instructed. The notes from the organ, powerful in the small, closed space, seemed to vibrate through her chest as she sang along with the others.

"'Come Home, poor sinner; why longer roam, thy Savior's calling, "Come home, come home!"'"

Midway through the chorus following the first verse, Reverend Overly stood and faced the congregation. He thundered over the choir members' voices, "Are you ready to cast off your burden of sin? Then come now. Come home to Jesus."

Ephraim played, the girls sang, but no one left their benches. They sang the second verse, the chorus, then began verse three. "'Oh, come to Jesus, do not delay . . .'"

A woman from the end of the third bench rose and went to the preacher. They tipped their bowed heads together, and the woman's sobs nearly drowned out the choir's chorus. She stepped away from the reverend and knelt at a low bench in front of the dais. Her knees had barely touched the floorboards when two more—another woman and an elderly man—came up and moved straight to the kneeling bench.

"'Jesus is pleading; He's interceding,'" the girls sang, and a middle-aged man joined those in the front. Three more came forward during the chorus, then another while they sang the fifth and final verse.

Between quiet exchanges with each of the people kneeling at the front, Reverend Overly addressed the congregation, inviting others to come and be redeemed. Ephraim continued playing. The girls kept singing. People kept coming. That strange tug Birdie had experienced before the angry man interrupted pulled at her again. But she remained rooted on the stage and sang. And sang. And sang.

At least twenty people crowded the front area before Reverend Overly raised both hands high. Ephraim's fingers slowed on the keys, and the last note echoed for several seconds before fading away. He remained on the organ stool, though, so the choir stayed in position.

Reverend Overly invited all who'd come to the front to stand. Birdie couldn't resist peeking at them. Reverend Overly had said they'd be new. She wasn't sure what she expected, but she was surprised. Even disappointed. They seemed unchanged except for tear-stained cheeks and watery eyes. He went down the line, shaking each of their hands in turn. He welcomed them one by one to the family of God, calling them "brother" or "sister" in his resounding voice.

Unconsciously, Birdie swayed in their direction, as if someone had tossed a rope around her and was trying to draw her near. With effort, she kept her feet firmly planted. They still had a song to sing.

When the reverend reached the end of the line, he turned a smile on those still seated. "The decision to receive Christ as Savior isn't limited to revival meetings or even to being in a church building. His invitation is open every minute of every day. His ears never close to the sound of a sinner's voice calling out in repentance." He held his hand toward the benches.

"Those whose names are now written in the Lamb's Book of Life, go ahead and sit. Listen while the choir shares another song with us. Let their words be your commitment to remain true to the One in whom you entrusted yourself this evening."

They sang the closing hymn and then, with Bernice leading them, trailed directly from the platform down the aisle. Some of the folks sitting at the ends of the benches smiled or offered words of thanks or praise as they passed by. A few averted their faces, as if embarrassed to look upon these women who'd once worked in such lowly places. Birdie couldn't hide, so she kept her face aimed straight ahead and tried to focus on the back of Olga's head. Still, she saw too much from the corner of her eye.

A man at the back unlocked and opened the doors for them, and they spilled into the yard. They gathered in a little group near the wagon with Ephraim. Ephraim scanned the grounds, his brows pulled into a V of worry. Birdie looked around, too, afraid Dan was still nearby and waiting to accost them. But the yard was empty save the many wagons and horses.

Ephraim blew out a breath that seemed to erase his tension. A smile formed, and he sent it across the girls. "You did very well this evening, ladies. I'm proud of all of you."

Mathilda tittered. "I was afraid there'd be a fight. That man . . . Dan . . ." She shuddered. "I hope to never see the likes of him again."

Many of the girls added their agreement, and Birdie couldn't help but nod, too.

Ephraim's smile faded. "Yes. His behavior was deplorable and could very well have trampled the good the Lord wanted to accomplish tonight. But, I confess, I agree with some of what he said."

". . . *some sins, they're just too big to be forgot.*" Dan's snarling comment stung her anew. Did Ephraim believe it, too? A knot lodged in her throat.

"Ah, the Spirit was with us tonight!" Reverend Overly, beaming, strode up and flung his arm across Ephraim's shoulders. "Nineteen souls saved and two recommitments to the Lord! Nearly one-third of the number gathered responded to the Savior's call! I've been invited to return in early summer for a group baptism." He laughed, the sound bubbling with delight, and he ushered the group to the rear of the wagon. "We'll all come, and you ladies can regale them with song again. Perhaps 'Lead On, O King Eternal'—yes, Ephraim? But for now, let's get home and share this good news with Mrs. Overly."

# Chapter Twelve

## Ophelia

Ophelia stroked Ellie's silky curls. The child had fallen asleep with her head in Ophelia's lap over an hour ago. She continued to sleep soundly even though Isaiah's joyful voice nearly rattled the windows as he shared the successful outcome of the Speegleville revival. When he paused for a breath, Ophelia lifted her hand toward him and said, "Please stop shouting, dear one. The heavens are already rejoicing. You needn't inform the Lord and His hosts."

Isaiah laughed and dropped into the chair closest to the end of the sofa where Ophelia sat. He took her hand between his and raised it to his lips, then cradled it on the arm of the sofa. "Ah, Ophelia . . ." He spoke in a near whisper. "When the Spirit moves, I am so blessed." Abruptly he stood and reached for Ellie. "Let me carry her up and put her to bed. Then we can go, too."

Lucretia had offered to take Ellie to her bed when she and the other girls went up upon their return. But Ophelia hadn't been ready to release the child. She'd spent so many hours closed in her room over the past week, she was hungry for time with the dear little girl. It was late—past eleven o'clock—but Ophelia wasn't yet ready for sleep. She glanced across the parlor at Ephraim. He'd sat quiet and introspective throughout his father's boisterous recital. She sensed he had things to say, too. She would stay up and listen.

She smiled at Isaiah, cupping her hand on Ellie's small shoulder. "I had a long nap this afternoon and am not sleepy yet. You go ahead. I'll have Ephraim take her up soon."

Isaiah straightened and yawned. "Very well. But not too late, my dear, yes?" He pecked a kiss on her lips, then on Ellie's temple, and left the room.

Ophelia listened until the soft *click* of their door latch signaled he'd turned in. She faced her son. "What is troubling you, Ephraim?"

He gave a start. "What makes you think something is troubling me?"

She chuckled softly. "Perhaps the way you've held your head in your hand since you slunk into that chair."

He immediately sat up, his hand dropping away from his jaw. "I'm only tired. It's been a long day."

She arched one brow. "Is it tiredness carving the lines between your eyes?" She slowly shook her head, examining his worried face. "I think it's something more. Am I right?"

He sat scowling for several seconds, chewing the corner of his lip, and finally he sighed. "You're right, Mother. There is something . . . burdening me."

"Tell me."

He leaned forward, propping his elbows on his widespread knees. A wavy lock of his hair fell across his forehead and rested on the bridge of his glasses. She toyed with one of Ellie's soft curls in lieu of smoothing his hair into place. A grown man didn't need such a ministration from his mother. "Father didn't tell you everything about the revival." His voice rasped, as if speaking pained him. "In the middle of his sermon, a man confronted him."

Ophelia listened, various emotions playing through her while Ephraim told her the things the interloper had said and done. The man's attitude didn't surprise her. She and Isaiah had faced much opposition over the years, some acts uglier than others. But apparently they hadn't prepared Ephraim as well as they'd believed for him to be so affected by the interruption.

"I can't stop thinking about his comment about God's holy fire descending." Ephraim's brows pinched together. "Everything about prostitution is destructive. The women in the brothels . . . none choose such work out of desire but out of desperation. Then, once they've sold themselves, they lose all sense of self-worth. They become trapped in a so-called job that demeans them." The muscles in his jaw tightened, lines of anguish marring his forehead. "The men who frequent brothels engage in depravity, sullying an act God intended to be holy between a husband and wife." His gaze drifted to little Ellie. "It results in unwanted conceptions, babies born under a cloud of shame." He looked into Ophelia's eyes again, and the pain lurking in his blue irises pierced her. "Nothing good comes of it, Mother."

Ellie stirred, screwing her face into an adorable grimace. Ophelia automatically smoothed the child's hair and murmured, "Shhh . . ." Ellie curled more tightly into a ball and quieted. Ophelia continued gently stroking her red-gold curls for a few minutes, gathering her thoughts and praying for guidance in how to respond. One comment stood out strongly in her mind and begged rebuttal.

"Ephraim, you are correct about the destruction prostitution brings. But no matter how a child is conceived, the child is innocent of wrongdoing. A child's conception never takes God by surprise. He loves every soul, regardless of how humble its beginning. Thus, the child needn't hide beneath a covering of shame. Every child is a blessing, not a burden." She stared into his eyes as she spoke, inwardly begging, *Listen to me, Ephraim. Hear me. Believe me.*

Ephraim sat up, flinging his arms wide. "I know you're right,

Mother. But Dan is also right. What you and Father are doing, rescuing a few women at a time, isn't enough. It will never be enough." His expression hardened. "Every brothel should be burned to the ground."

Ellie squeaked and her eyes popped open. She shifted her head and looked at Ophelia, surprise registering in her eyes. She sat up and stared around blearily.

Ophelia caught the child's chin and tipped her face to hers. "Yes, you fell asleep in the parlor. Were you dreaming? I hope it was a pleasant one." She waited, hoping, but Ellie only blinked in reply. Ophelia lowered her hand. "Are you ready to go up to your bed now? Remember, I can't go up with you"—oh, how she bemoaned her wretched heart that stole precious moments with this little girl—"but you can go up by yourself. Or . . ." She glanced at Ephraim. "Ephraim can carry you."

At once, Ellie held out her arms to Ephraim.

A sad smile appeared on his lips. He stood, crossed the short distance between them, and lifted the little girl onto his hip. She wrapped her arms around his neck and laid her head on his shoulder. Ephraim's expression softened, and he planted a kiss in the same spot Isaiah had kissed earlier. He nodded. "A blessing, not a burden."

Was he speaking to Ellie, to Ophelia, or to himself? It didn't matter. He spoke with the assurance of truth. Her prayer had been answered. *Help him remember, Lord.*

He turned his weary gaze on Ophelia. "Good night, Mother. Sleep well."

"Thank you, Ephraim. You, too." She watched him move to the staircase and ascend the risers, his strong arms locked protectively around the little girl. Love swelled within her, creating a sweet ache, and she whispered, "I love you both, children of my heart." Then she extinguished the lamps and joined her sleeping husband.

### Ephraim

The morning after the Speegleville revival, Ephraim removed the cover from the wagon and loaded the bed with bushel baskets of canned jelly, embroidered handkerchiefs, and hand-sewn aprons. Usually, Mother did the trading for foodstuffs with the mercantile in Tulsey, but until Father was convinced she was recovered enough for the drive to town, Ephraim would take care of it. He hoped he would garner as favorable trades as Mother always did.

As he was hitching the horses into their rigging, Mathilda, Reva, and Birdie entered the barn. Mathilda carried a handled basket on her arm. She brought it to Ephraim. "Your mama wants you to give this to the doctor to thank him for his fine care."

Ephraim peeked inside. Two loaves of fresh-baked bread and a single jar of their precious apple butter were nestled in its bottom. "Does she mean this as his payment?" Father had given him a fifty-cent piece to cover the doctor's fee.

Mathilda shook her head. "She said it's a gift."

Ephraim whistled through his teeth. "And a fine one, at that." He took the basket and put it on the floorboard beneath the driver's seat. He turned and found all three girls still standing there. "Did you need something else?"

Reva giggled. "We're to go along, too, and help with the trading. Mrs. Overly said so."

If Mother said so, then Ephraim wouldn't argue. Besides, he welcomed company for the drive. The girls' presence might keep him from dwelling on the unpleasant thoughts that interrupted his sleep last night. "All right, then. Let's go."

He helped the girls into the back, then folded up the step and slid the gate into place. He didn't want anything, including the girls, rattling out the back during the drive.

The girls chatted as the wagon carried them across the rolling prairie, but Ephraim mostly listened. Temptation to contribute pulled as hard as the horses against their riggings. Wouldn't it be enjoyable to ask questions and get to know them better? He'd almost forgotten the pleasure of engaging in a lengthy conversation that didn't involve giving instruction about a piece of music. But his long-standing practice of holding himself aloof wouldn't allow him to relax. He drove directly to the mercantile and parked in front. He helped the girls out, gave them each one of the lighter baskets, and picked up the one filled with jars of jelly himself.

As they entered the store, Mathilda sidled up alongside him. "Mr. Overly, if you want to do your other errands while we shop, it's all right. Reva and me have both helped your ma enough times to know what to ask for."

Ephraim paused, considering her offer. He didn't want to be accused of shirking his responsibilities, but if the girls shopped while he ran the other errands, they'd be able to return to Hope Hill sooner and get the food items put away well before suppertime. The plan made sense.

"All right." He placed his basket on the counter. "How long do you think you'll need?"

She glanced around the store. "Quite a few customers here, so . . . maybe three-quarters of an hour?"

He nodded. "I'll be back in less than an hour. Wait for me on the porch if I run a little late."

The doctor was out on a call, but Ephraim gave the payment and the things from the basket to the man's wife. She thanked him, then touched his sleeve. "You'll likely get a request to use your organ at the cemetery early next week. A man new to town with a whole passel of youngsters lost his wife. Feel real bad for them, and most especially those children who'll have to go on without their mama."

Ephraim didn't even know yet who had died, but his heart automatically swelled in sympathy for those left behind. How would he bear it when his mother took her final breath? He gave a nod and swallowed. "If they would be comforted by my being there, I'm willing."

She patted his arm. "Thank you, Ephraim. You're a fine young man." She led him to the door and saw him out.

He drove to Browning's Livery, putting aside the sad news of loss in favor of something happier—Father's approval about purchasing an alternate means of transportation. Father had given Ephraim all the offering received at the revival as well as the money from the tin in his office. The amount wasn't huge, but they'd prayed together at breakfast for favor. If they were meant to have a saddle horse, Father insisted, God would provide it.

Ephraim held to a fragile hope as he queried the owner, Mr. Browning, about available saddle horses.

"I got several good ones," Mr. Browning said, scratching his whiskered chin, "but not a one for what you're offerin'. I hate to disappoint you, but I doubt you'll find a saddle-broke horse with enough good years left in him to be worthwhile for less'n a hundred dollars." He shrugged. "You ain't even got half that."

Ephraim cringed. He'd never felt poor. He'd always had a roof over his head and decent clothes to wear, and he had never gone hungry. But at that moment, he felt like a beggar. He fingered the coins in his pocket, wishing they would multiply like the loaves and fishes in the Bible story. "If you hear about a horse for sale for what I have to spend, would you get word to me?" Ephraim never divulged personal information, but worry compelled him to add, "We had an emergency earlier this week and needed the doctor for my mother. My father had taken the wagon for the day, so I had no way to get to town and fetch help.

It's important we find a reliable horse in case we have need again."

Mr. Browning's face scrunched up in concern. "Is your ma doin' better now?"

She'd never be completely well. The thought pained Ephraim. He swallowed. "She's better," he said.

"Glad to hear it. Your ma's a good woman. Oh, some might criticize her for sharin' her home with *soiled doves*"—he pursed his lips as if he'd tasted something sour—"but I follow what the Good Book says about doin' unto others. I wouldn't want nobody speakin' ill of me or mine, so I keep my mouth shut about other folks' doings. I don't mind tellin' you, though, your ma's got a heart of gold."

A mixture of pride and sorrow gripped Ephraim. Mr. Browning was right. Mother did so much good. Why didn't God heal her heart so she could continue pouring out on downtrodden and broken souls?

The man clapped him on the shoulder. "I'll keep my ears open about a horse an' let you know if somethin' comes up."

"Thank you." Ephraim left the livery. He'd hoped to leave with a saddle horse tied to the back of his wagon. Discouragement weighed on him. Relying on what folks put in the offering plate at revivals or donations from benefactors offered no real security. If he took a job teaching music in a school, he'd have a steady salary. But if he taught full-time, he wouldn't be able to perform his caretaking duties at Hope Hill, lead the choir at Father's revivals, or otherwise assist in his parents' ministry.

*"I'll live for Him who died for me, how happy then my life shall be!"*

Why did those words taunt him so?

He shoved the song's lyrics from his mind and climbed onto the driver's seat. "Come on, boys," he called to the horses, "let's fetch our supplies and the girls and go home."

He rounded the corner to the main street and aimed the horses in the direction of the mercantile. Up ahead, a small crowd had gathered in front of the building. Some of the spectators stood in the street, forcing him to stop the wagon several yards from the store. The cluster of people reminded him of how the girls had gathered around when Mother collapsed. Had someone fallen ill or gotten injured?

Ephraim set the brake, then stood and peered over the tops of people's heads. He leaned this way and that, seeking a better view, and two women parted. He received a glimpse of what held everyone's attention. His heart nearly exploded from his chest. He leaped over the edge of the wagon and made a dash for the mercantile porch.

# Chapter Thirteen

Birdie

Birdie backed herself against the mercantile's lapped siding. A useless move. She couldn't escape Lida Holland's tirade. The woman advanced on her, leaning so close, her foul breath filled Birdie's nostrils.

More than a dozen people stood around, watching and listening. Reva and Mathilda had scuttled to the opposite side of their many bundles of goods, abandoning Birdie to face the furious woman alone. Birdie didn't blame them. She didn't expect anyone to intervene. Why should they? After what she'd done at Lida's Palace, she deserved to be verbally attacked on a public street. *Some sins, they're just too big to be forgot.* She only wished Miz Holland would finish and leave so she could escape to Hope Hill and hide.

Suddenly Ephraim broke through the crowd and pushed himself between Birdie and Miz Holland, forcing the woman backward a few feet. "Girls, get in the wagon." He barked the order, his voice as harsh as Miz Holland's when she'd accused Birdie of ungratefulness.

Birdie scrambled around the pile of packages. The girls linked arms and turned in the direction of the wagon, but the crowd blocked their way. They stood beside the pile of food stores, clinging to each other and quaking.

"Lida Holland, you're drunk." Ephraim's voice rang as loudly as Reverend Overly's, sending a chill through Birdie's frame. "Go home and sleep it off."

Miz Holland sneered. "I've still got my senses. That gal owes me. I took her in, an' right away she busted a brand-new lamp at my place. It cost me dear. You an' your papa stole off with her before she squared her account."

Ephraim's cheeks blazed red, and his jaw muscles tightened. "If I square her account," he said through clenched teeth, "will you promise to leave her alone from now on?"

The woman angled her head and peered at Ephraim through slitted eyes. "Sure. I promise. I'll leave *her* alone once I get my due."

The strange emphasis on a single word sent another chill up Birdie's spine.

Ephraim's hand slid into his trouser pocket. "How much?"

Miz Holland laughed. She thrust her hand out, palm up. "Four dollars an' two bits."

The color drained from Ephraim's face. "F-four dollars—"

"An' two bits." She bounced her hand. "C'mon, pay up. Or send her back to me until she gives me her due."

Someone in the crowd hollered, "I wouldn't pay a penny over the two bits, Ephraim," and several people laughed. Birdie shrank back, wishing the curtain of shame could render her invisible.

Ephraim's Adam's apple bobbed in a swallow. He pulled out a handful of change from his pocket and counted out several coins. He dropped them into Miz Holland's palm. She curled her fingers around them and tossed her head, her smile triumphant. "You kept your word. I'll keep mine. Birdie's yours now." Then her expression hardened, and she shook the fist holding the money at Ephraim. "But you tell your pa this don't come close to settlin' what *he* owes me." She whirled past him, bumping him with her shoulder as she went, and flounced into the mercantile.

Ephraim turned to the crowd with a fierce glower. "Show's

over, folks. Go on about your business," he said in a voice as powerful as his father's.

A few guffaws blasted, but the people ambled off in various directions. As they left, Ephraim seemed to wilt. He crossed to the girls, his heels dragging and his shoulders slumped. He looked as weary as if he'd just finished a wrestling match. The way Birdie felt.

He stopped in front of them and his gaze lit on Birdie. "Are you all right?"

Mathilda wrung her hands. "I am now. That lady scared me."

"Me, too." Reva shivered. "I thought she was gonna drag Birdie away."

Ephraim nodded, his blue eyes still pinned on Birdie. "She's gone. There's no need to be frightened now."

She wasn't afraid anymore, but shouldn't she be relieved? Grateful? Even joyful? He'd paid her debt and secured her freedom forever from Miz Holland's clutches. But the only thing she felt was guilt. She blurted, "Why did you give her the money? I'm not . . ." She couldn't bring herself to add *worth it,* but the words hung in the air like a bad stench.

Ephraim glanced through the mercantile's plate glass window, a scowl puckering his brow. "You're not beholden to her anymore. That's all that matters." He gave a little jolt, then bent down and picked up a crate. "Let's load our goods and get out of here."

Birdie scooped up a basket, and Mathilda and Reva did the same. They followed Ephraim to the wagon. Working together, they loaded everything in two trips, and then Ephraim helped Mathilda and Reva into the bed. Birdie came last, and when he reached for her elbow, she drew back, staring at his broad hand. Why had he given Miz Holland so much money if he believed, as Dan did, that the sins she'd committed were too vile to forget?

"Birdie?"

She looked up and met his puzzled gaze. "Why did you pay her?" She needed to hear him say she was worth the money spent. She was worthy of being free of her past.

He grimaced. "I probably shouldn't have. Father will likely berate me for not asking proof of the cost of the lamp you broke." His eyebrows, a shade darker than his light-brown hair, tipped together. "Was she truthful? Did you break a lamp?"

She turned her head aside, her chest aching. "I did. A real pretty one with a hand-painted globe. But I don't know if it cost so much to replace. I only know she said I had to"—she gulped—"work off the debt."

"Well, that's done now." Ephraim gave her shoulder a soft pat. "Come on. Let's go."

She allowed him to help her into the wagon. She watched him put the gate into place and stride around to the driver's seat, hoping he might glance her way and smile or say something to assure her. He flicked the reins and made a clicking noise with his tongue on his teeth. The horses strained into motion.

Reva shot her a meaningful look. "I bet you're eager to be home."

Home . . . a beautiful word. Birdie nodded. She couldn't get away from Tulsey and Miz Holland quickly enough. But when they reached Hope Hill and Reverend Overly found out what Ephraim had done to secure her freedom, what would he say to her? A rock of dread settled in her belly. Maybe she wasn't in a hurry, after all.


## Ephraim

At supper Saturday evening, Father announced they would have their own church service in the morning in the parlor. Ephraim wasn't surprised. Often, Father led a private worship service the Sunday after a revival since the travel wore everyone out. But Ephraim suspected this time Father wanted to avoid encountering any of the folks who'd witnessed Lida Holland's attack on Birdie earlier that day.

He inwardly cringed, reliving the humiliation of addressing the brothel owner on the public street. Folks would jabber about the event for days. They'd likely embellish it, too, turning the verbal exchange into a fistfight and increasing the sum of money Ephraim had given her to a ridiculous amount. Not that what he'd paid wasn't ridiculous. More than four dollars for a lamp in a brothel? He'd been taken for a fool, but Father agreed he'd had no choice. And, Father had said on a sigh of relief, now they needn't worry about the woman bothering Birdie ever again. If she kept her word. Ephraim wasn't sure he trusted her, but what choice did he have?

"As I'm sure you've all heard by now," Father was continuing, his mug of coffee nestled between his palms, "an unpleasant situation arose when three of our girls and Ephraim were in town this morning."

Ephraim sent a quick peek at the girls involved. Reva and Mathilda seemed to puff up with importance, but if Birdie shrank down any further in her chair, she'd slip off and land under the table.

"It's over now, and there's no sense in addressing it." When Father used his firmest tone, Ephraim knew he meant it. He would never again mention Lida Holland's attack nor the amount of money paid to her. "I would rather focus on a need of which Ephraim was made aware. A family in town has suffered a tragic loss with the death of the mother. The father is now left to raise several children on his own. He will need prayer support, and I would like to take time now to lift this man in prayer. Please bow your heads."

Ephraim followed Father's instruction, but no prayer for the widower and his children formed in his mind. He couldn't stop thinking about Mother and wondering what would happen when a final attack took her home. Would the ministry his parents started crumble? If so, where would the girls go? What of Ellie, who was Mother's little shadow? Who would care for her? Instead of praying for the family in town, he found himself praying for Father, for the girls, for Ellie, even for himself.

*"I'll live for Him who died for me . . ."* The hymn's phrase intruded upon his prayer. Mother had lived unselfishly every day of her life, everything done for God and His glory. She deserved to be healthy and able to continue her calling. The bitter taste of bile filled his throat. Mother's malady was unfair, and he told God so.

"Amen," Father intoned. A chorus of amens echoed.

Ephraim raised his head and discovered Father's intense gaze on him. Had he accidentally prayed aloud? Or had Father somehow read his thoughts? He squirmed in his seat.

The girls rose and began clearing the table. Ephraim quickly stood, too, intending to go to the music room and play piano. Music always cleared his head and cheered him.

"Ephraim and Miss Clarkson." Father spoke over the clatter of cleanup. "I would like to briefly speak with you in the study. Please follow me."

Ephraim pushed in his chair and waited until Birdie rounded the table. He gestured her ahead of him, and they trailed Father across the hall to the study. Father stood beside the door until they entered, and then he closed the door and crossed to his desk. He smiled as he settled into his chair. "Come. Sit. Let's discuss tomorrow's time of worship."

Ephraim escorted Birdie to the chairs. She quickly sat in the one closest to the door and laid her hands in her lap. He took the second chair and crossed his legs, propping his ankle on his knee. For reasons he couldn't understand, nervousness gripped him. He bounced his foot to distract himself from the odd feeling. "Do you have a preference on which hymns we'll sing?"

Father nodded. "Since Dr. Paddock has probably told the grieving family in Tulsey about you, you should be prepared to attend the graveside service. Ephraim, you're accustomed to playing, but this will be Miss Clarkson's first time to join you. She will feel more confident if she's had an opportunity to sing alone before she stands in front of a crowd. So, Miss Clarkson, I would like you to sing 'Come Home, Poor Sinner' for us tomorrow morning as a practice for the funeral."

Birdie briefly tipped her face toward her shoulder in what was becoming a familiar gesture. Ephraim's heart went out to her. She was nervous, too. He said, "Isn't that an unusual song for a burial?"

"Unusual, perhaps, but not inappropriate." Father gave a firm nod, as if agreeing with his own assessment. "If the woman was a believer, she's gone home. There will likely be unbelievers attending. They need to hear the message it provides."

Birdie looked across the desk at Father, her chin quivering. "I know I said I would help if I could, but now I'm not sure. Will it be . . . unseemly for me to sing for folks?"

Father rocked in his chair. "Unseemly in what way?"

She glanced at Ephraim, and her cheeks bloomed rosy pink. "Because of where I lived before coming here."

Father sat forward, his chair's springs popping. "Nonsense. You must do as the apostle Paul advised the believers in Philippi, 'forgetting those things which are behind, and reaching forth unto those things which are before.'" He frowned. "Can you change what's already been?"

Misery crumpled her face. She shook her head.

"Then what good does it do to dwell on it?" Fervor glinted in his eyes, but his tone was more encouraging than forceful. "You must press forward, as the apostle did, striving for his high calling in Jesus Christ. You have a calling, Birdie, as does every soul ever conceived."

Ephraim's foot slipped to the floor. Suddenly the message didn't seem for Birdie alone.

"God has gifted you with the voice of an angel. An angel!" Father sat up straight and lifted both hands in the air. "You must use it for His glory. Do you understand?"

Birdie's chest rose and fell with her rapid breathing. "How can He use someone like me? I'm . . ." Her chin angled to her shoulder, and her eyes closed.

"Miss Clarkson, look at me."

Slowly, Birdie lifted her head and turned in Father's direction.

Father pinned his eyes on her face. "No more of that self-defeating talk."

Birdie licked her lips and blinked rapidly.

"If you don't want to sing because you feel unprepared, Ephraim will practice with you." Father leaned closer by increments as he spoke, his gaze unwavering and his usually booming voice soft yet riveting. "If you're nervous to stand alone in front of an audience, Mrs. Overly and I will pray for you and encourage you. But from this moment forward, there will be no mention of what used to be." Tenderness flooded his eyes. "You may not use past mistakes as an excuse to ignore the pathway God prepared for you from the beginning of time. Do you understand, Miss Clarkson?"

Birdie stared unblinking at Father. She nodded.

"Good." Father pushed himself upright. "Now, you two, go practice. I have a sermon to prepare for tomorrow."

She scuttled out, and Ephraim followed on surprisingly quivery legs.

# Chapter Fourteen

Birdie

W as she really doing this?

The morning breeze tossed the wavy wisps of hair falling from her temples and tickled her cheeks. The scent of woodsmoke drifted from a chimney somewhere beyond her sight, teasing her nose. A pair of birds, chirping their aggravation at being disturbed by the wagon's passing, swooped from a tangle of brush beside the road. The sun beamed like a beacon in the sky, making her grateful for the shade of her bonnet. All these sensory details convinced her the moment was real, not a dream. Even so, she struggled with believing it was all true. She was riding beside Ephraim and Mrs. Overly to the cemetery where she would sing to comfort a grieving family.

Her stomach rolled, and she pressed her hands against her middle. "I think I'm going to be sick."

Mrs. Overly put her arm around Birdie's shoulder. "Ephraim, stop the team."

Ephraim pulled the reins, and the horses snorted to a halt. He leaned past his mother and gave Birdie a worried frown. "Do you want to get down?"

She wanted to turn the wagon around and go back to Hope Hill. She wanted to ask if they thought any of the people who'd witnessed Miz Holland's verbal attack or any of the church people would be at the cemetery. But Reverend Overly had commanded her not to speak of the past, and she didn't know how to ask without mentioning past events. She squeaked out, "I don't know."

"You aren't sick, Miss Clarkson. You're experiencing a touch of stage fright." Ephraim's brow remained furrowed in concern, but his voice held confidence. "You need to breathe. Pull a full breath in through your nose and release it slowly through your mouth. Go ahead."

"I'll do it, too," Mrs. Overly said.

Birdie stared into the woman's face and imitated her, drawing in air until her lungs felt ready to burst, then letting it ease out. After the third release, she let her hands droop into her lap.

Ephraim smiled hopefully at her. "Did it help?"

Focusing on breathing had pulled her attention from the queasiness in her stomach. Since she wasn't thinking about feeling sick, she didn't feel sick anymore. She nodded.

"Good." He sounded as relieved as she felt. "Every performer experiences stage fright. It's nothing to be ashamed of. Would you like to know the secret to overcoming stage fright?"

She leaned forward slightly, eager. "Yes. What is it?"

His grin turned impish. "You already know. Because you did it. Breathe deeply. The deep breaths calm your racing pulse. When your pulse is calm, your voice will function as it's intended. That's why I have the choir take a big breath before they start to sing. It works."

What he said made sense. But he'd forgotten something. "In the choir, I'm not singing by myself." She'd nearly fainted from nervousness yesterday morning, singing in front of the other girls and the Overlys. Would it not be worse today, in front of people who might know what Reverend Overly said should be forgotten? Misery rolled through her. God might forget, but she couldn't, and none of those people would, either. Why pretend otherwise? "Today it's only me."

"It doesn't matter." He sounded so sure of himself. "You'll see if you give it a chance."

She wanted to believe him. She chewed her lip, uncertainty making her stomach whirl again.

"I have an idea." Mrs. Overly tapped the dimple in her chin with her finger, her expression thoughtful. "The family is expecting you both, so we shouldn't disappoint them. Today you will sing, Birdie, while Ephraim plays. But if it's too hard for you—if you still feel sick after you've finished—we will never ask you to sing on your own at a funeral again. Does that seem reasonable?"

Birdie still wanted to go back to Hope Hill. But not fulfilling a commitment was a selfish act. She had to see it through. Knowing she wouldn't be forced to endure this fear again eased her nervousness. "Yes, ma'am. Thank you."

Mrs. Overly faced forward. "All right, Ephraim, you are a witness to our agreement. Let's go."

There were very few people gathered near the mound of freshly turned earth at the southeast corner of the cemetery, and Birdie had no difficulty picking out the grieving father. He held a small boy, and four children of various ages surrounded him, each clinging to his sleeve or the hem of his coat. Birdie's eyes welled in sympathy for them.

Ephraim drew the wagon as close to the group as possible without parking on a grave. Mrs. Overly and Birdie stayed on the seat while he took the smallest organ Birdie had ever seen from the back and carried it toward the group. Then he helped the two women down, retrieved a small stool from the bed, and escorted them across the trampled grass to the gravesite.

Birdie practiced deep breaths while the minister read from his Bible and spoke. She was aware of his soothing tone, but she missed his actual words, her attention on the poor motherless

children. If she knew how to pray, she would pray for their aching souls. If she lived to be a hundred, she'd never forget the
agony of standing beside Papa's grave, knowing he would never
come home again. But how could she think about herself when
faced with others' deep sadness? She didn't know how to pray,
but she did know how to sing. The desire to comfort them rose
above her nervousness.

The preacher closed his Bible. "Now Mr. Overly and his soloist will bless us with a song."

Ephraim sat on the little stool and pumped the organ's foot
pedals. His fingers touched the keys, and the opening notes
poured from the instrument in an amazingly pure tone. Birdie
drew in a full breath, lifted her eyes to the single cloud floating
high overhead, and, to her surprise, the melody effortlessly
poured from her lips. Although her knees quivered from beginning to end beneath the skirts of her nicest dress, her voice remained strong and steady. Ephraim's advice had carried her
through. Or was God bolstering her because she was doing
what He'd planned for her to do?

The thought straightened her spine, and she finished the
final note an octave higher than the composer wrote it. The
organ wheezed into silence, and Birdie bowed her head, grateful
that she was done, but even more so that she'd finished the
task.

She, Ephraim, and Mrs. Overly remained beside the grave
while the minister closed with a prayer of comfort for the departed woman's family. After his "amen," he spoke briefly with
the father. He bent down and delivered a quiet word to each
of the children save the youngest, who'd fallen asleep in his father's arms. Then he strode across the grass to Ephraim and
shook his hand.

"Thank you for ministering to the family." He turned to
Birdie. "And thank you, too, young lady. You delivered a pre-

cious gift today." He slipped his hand inside his suit coat and brought out an envelope, which he gave to Ephraim. "I pray this will compensate you for your time."

Ephraim took the envelope and passed it to Mrs. Overly. Then he shook the preacher's hand again. "Thank you. We will pray for the family."

The preacher gave a somber nod, and he angled his face toward the father and children. The man had gone down on one knee, and the children all leaned in, resting their cheeks against his bent frame. "The Lord giveth and the Lord taketh away. Blessed be His name," he choked out. "But sometimes I wish I understood His ways. Mr. Fischer moved his family here from New Mexico Territory for a fresh start when their oldest son was killed by bandits, only to lose his wife and newborn baby in childbirth at the end of their journey."

Birdie thought her heart might break at the sad situation.

Mrs. Overly shook her head, sighing. "So much sorrow at once. Will they stay in Tulsey, or go back to their former home?"

The preacher shrugged. "My understanding is there is no other family, so what would he go back to? He spent every penny buying a plot of ground to grow cotton. I'm sure they'll stay, but I don't know how he'll manage on his own. As you can see, the children are quite young." Then he drew in a breath, the way Birdie had to calm her nerves. "But as the Word tells us, God gives strength to the weary and increases the power of the weak. We must hold to this promise and trust it for Mr. Fischer." He returned to the family.

Mrs. Overly linked arms with Birdie and pulled her close. She whispered, "Ephraim needs to load the organ. This will take him a few minutes. Let's give the Fischers some privacy." She guided Birdie several yards away.

Birdie didn't mind turning her back on the grieving family. She feared the image of their sadness would be burned into her memory for the rest of her life. She ached especially for the children. The oldest of the group, a girl, was probably about the age Birdie had been when Papa died. At least it seemed the children were loved by their remaining parent, and they had each other. Mama had never been affectionate with Birdie, but after Papa died, she distanced herself even more. With no siblings of her own, Birdie had been lonely.

She gave herself an internal shake. Hadn't Reverend Overly told her not to look back? She'd never understand Mama's strange coldness toward her only child. Thinking about it only made her sad. It was best to look forward. To when she had the money to board the train and go to Aunt Sally. When she would be loved again. A smile tugged at her lips, and a sigh eased from her throat.

Mrs. Overly gave her a pensive look. "What are you thinking?"

"About my aunt." Birdie spoke softly. She didn't want to disturb the Fischer family. "And how glad I am that she is waiting for me. I might have lost my father and mother, but I'm not alone, because I have Aunt Sally."

Mrs. Overly gave Birdie a quick hug. "I'm glad for you, too, dear. I know you're eager to make your way to Kansas City."

Yes, she was. "When do you think Reverend Overly will let me take a paying job?" Birdie clapped her hand over her mouth. Why hadn't she thought of this before? She slid her hand to her throat. "Before I can earn money for a train ticket, I need to pay back what Ephraim gave to Miz Holland." She'd spent two miserable weeks at Lida's Palace and hadn't earned enough to pay for the broken lamp. How long would it take to earn that sum on top of what she needed for a ticket?

Mrs. Overly cupped Birdie's cheek with her warm palm. "Dear girl, do not worry about what was given for your release. The debt is paid. Your safety is secured. That's all that matters."

Birdie stared, open-mouthed, for several seconds, processing the woman's statement. What had she done to deserve such kindness? Why did these people do what they did for girls like her?

She stepped free of the tender touch. "Ma'am, how did you and Reverend Overly come to rescue people like me? I don't know anyone else who would bother. Why do you?"

Mrs. Overly smiled so sweetly, it created an ache in the center of Birdie's chest. "That is a very long story, dear Birdie, but the shortened version is simply that Isaiah became convicted of the need more than twenty years ago in a very personal way." She slipped her hand through Birdie's elbow and guided her toward the wagon. "He believed the Lord had called him to the task, and he was determined to make a positive difference in the world, one young woman at a time. Our first attempt to save a young woman failed dismally, but Isaiah refused to let it discourage him. And over the years, despite the challenges and obstacles thrown in our way, the Lord has blessed him—and me!—with many more successes than failures."

She tipped her head and touched temples with Birdie. "You are already a success, Birdie."

Birdie came to a stumbling halt, shocked. "Me? How?"

Mrs. Overly laughed lightly. "Why, you're already pouring yourself out on others. Do you know how rare it is for someone who's been badly hurt to care about someone else's needs?" Tenderness crept into her eyes again, touching Birdie in a lovely way. "I know today was hard for you, but you sang anyway. You blessed the Fischer family, and you blessed me with your obedience. Isaiah will be so proud of you, and—may I say it?—your papa would be proud, too."

If Ephraim hadn't strode up at that moment, Birdie would have thrown herself into Mrs. Overly's arms and wept. Worry lines knit Ephraim's brow. "You look tired, Mother."

"Perhaps I am," she said.

He offered his arm, and she took hold. "Then let's get you home." The three of them moved in unison across the uneven ground. "When we get there, I must remember to talk to Father about a request Mr. Fischer made. It's possible we can help him more than only providing music for his wife's funeral."

Birdie's ears perked up. Mrs. Overly's praise still rang in her heart. If there was another way to, as the woman had put it, pour herself out, she was ready.

Mrs. Overly looked up at her son. "What is the request, Ephraim?"

"Wait until we're on the road." He bobbed his head toward the Fischers, who were still sitting around the grave as if attending a picnic.

They reached the wagon, and he helped her onto the seat, then assisted Birdie. He trotted around the team, giving each rust-colored horse a quick rub as he went, and clambered up. The seat bounced as he settled himself. He released the brake and flicked the reins. When he'd guided the horses out of the cemetery, he turned a hopeful look on his mother.

"I overheard Mr. Fischer ask the preacher if he knew of anyone who would be willing to come to his house each day to clean and cook and see to the youngest children while the older ones are in school." He sighed, shaking his head. "Otherwise, he said, his biggest girl will have to drop out of school and care for her brothers and sister. He'd rather she received an education."

"A wise father," Mrs. Overly said. "Are you thinking one of our girls would be a good help for Mr. Fischer?"

Birdie held her breath. She was ready to earn the decent wage, but would Reverend Overly believe she was ready? Her thoughts begged, *Pick me! Pick me!*

Ephraim tugged on the right rein, and the horses obediently pulled the wagon into a curve. "Don't some of them come from large families? If they've had the responsibility of seeing to younger siblings, they'd likely be ready for such a responsibility."

Birdie's hopes sank. She had no experience in helping with children. But she knew who did. She shifted eagerly on the seat. "I know who could do it. And she speaks German, too, just like the Fischers."

Mrs. Overly tipped her face in Birdie's direction. "Are you thinking of Olga?"

"Yes, ma'am." She couldn't help smiling. Olga would be a perfect fit.

Mrs. Overly shook her head and took Birdie's hand. "Isaiah won't allow Olga to hire out until she's finished her studies. He's very firm about the importance of an education, and I agree with him." She squeezed Birdie's hand and released it. She turned to Ephraim again. "I believe Alberta, Lucretia, and Harriet came from large families. Lucretia hasn't quite completed her eighth-year coursework, but the other two have. I will ask Isaiah about the possibility of Alberta or Harriet helping the Fischers."

Birdie tapped Mrs. Overly on the arm. "Ma'am? When you speak to the reverend about one of the other girls working for Mr. Fischer, would you also ask about me? I'm ready"—she gulped, reining in her eagerness—"to start earning a wage."

# Chapter Fifteen

## Ophelia

Because Ophelia had accompanied Ephraim and Birdie to the cemetery, the girls had spent their usual morning classroom time in chores and skills-learning. So that afternoon, although she longed for a nap, she gathered the students in the dining room and instructed them to open their various books. Tiredness sagged her frame, but her heart exulted. How she loved teaching. For as far back as she could remember, it was what she wanted to be—a teacher.

When Isaiah shared his desire to rescue women who'd fallen into prostitution, she'd been certain her own dreams must be put aside in favor of his. She'd come to a place of peace with it, believing fully in Isaiah's ministry. But as it turned out, her teaching ability proved beneficial. Their combined desires served a greater purpose. God always knew best.

She paused at Ellie's spot at the table and examined the child's arithmetic paper. Out of the seven single-digit addition problems on the page, only one was incorrect. Ophelia leaned down and whispered in Ellie's ear, "Look again at problem number four."

Ellie stared at the paper. She flicked her fingers upward one by one, scrunching her nose in concentration. Then she snatched up her pencil, drew a line through the answer and wrote a new one. She looked up at Ophelia, a question in her eyes.

Ophelia patted the child's shoulder. "That's correct. Well done."

The little girl beamed and turned her attention back to the page.

Ophelia moved on around the table, offering encouragement, further instruction, or correction as needed. A slight twinge in her right shoulder brought her up short. She pressed the spot, breathing deeply the way Ephraim had told Birdie to do, and waited for either the discomfort to pass or a deeper pain to take hold. While she waited, she prayed it would pass. She wasn't ready to go yet. There was still much to do. Isaiah needed her. They were two halves of a whole, serving in tandem. The Lord knew this. He must have a plan.

The twinge eased, and she sent up a silent thank-You. Then a second prayer formed without effort. *Don't let my death mean death for Isaiah's ministry of rescue and restoration. These girls need Your hope and healing. Raise up a Gideon to take my place.*

Peace settled on her as gently as down. A sigh eased from her throat—one of trust and contentment. She continued around the table.

After the evening devotion, which Isaiah based on the encouragement found in Psalm 118:14–16, she read a short story to Ellie and then sent her upstairs with Lucretia. Although she mourned not being able to tuck Ellie into bed herself, she was grateful for the young woman's willingness to help tend to the child. Ellie needed to bond more fully with Lucretia if the two were to share a room after a housekeeper moved in. Isaiah hadn't yet advertised for one. He insisted, and she agreed, that they needed a bit more money in their tin bank before hiring someone. But she trusted the Lord to provide for and guide them. Just as she trusted the Lord to give Isaiah discernment about assisting Mr. Fischer with his need.

As Isaiah readied himself for bed and Ophelia brushed out her hair, she watched him in the mirror. The moment he pulled back the covers, she spoke. "Before we sleep, there's something we need to discuss."

He frowned at her. "Now? It's been a long day for you. You need rest."

She placed her brush on the table and turned on her stool. "And I will rest, as soon as we've finished our conversation."

He came around the bed and sat on its end, his knees nearly touching hers. He rested his hands on his nightshirt-covered thighs and fixed his gaze on her face. "All right, then. I'm listening."

His intense focus pleased her. And somewhat amused her. Isaiah gave everything, even a conversation at bedtime with his wife, his full heart. Such a different man he was from his father, who took rather than gave. But she didn't want to think about Luther Overly tonight.

She repeated what Ephraim had told her about Mr. Fischer's request for someone to care for his children during the school hours. She suggested that either Alberta or Harriet had the necessary abilities for the job. As she spoke, Isaiah's eyebrows moved in silent reaction, proving he listened to every word. When she'd finished, she asked, "What do you think?"

"I want to pray about it first."

She smiled her approval.

"And I want to visit Mr. Fischer, to assess his moral character. I won't send one of our girls to a household where they might be molested or otherwise mistreated."

She placed her hand over his. "Nor would I want you to, no matter what salary he might offer. But I will tell you, based on what I witnessed at the gravesite, he seems a tender, dedicated father."

"That speaks well of him." Isaiah moved his hand slightly, lacing his fingers with hers. "If I deem his home is a safe place of employment, then it could be a blessing to him for one of our girls to serve as caretaker for his children, as well as a fresh beginning for the girl."

"I agree," Ophelia said.

"Good." He braced himself to rise. "Then let us—"

Ophelia gave his hand a tug. "There's one more thing."

He remained seated, but his slight scowl communicated he preferred that the time for talk was done and she should rest.

She nodded in silent understanding. "I'll be succinct. Birdie Clarkson also requested her release to a job site. She says she is ready."

Isaiah's forehead scrunched into a frown. "She could be right."

Ophelia drew back in surprise at his uncertain response. The girl had schooling. She also possessed a skill that would serve her well and a family member with whom she could live. Why didn't Isaiah enthusiastically agree? "Yet you hold apprehension?"

Isaiah sighed. "I do."

Ophelia leaned toward him. "Why?"

He took her face in his broad hands. "It's late and I see the weariness in your eyes. You need your rest. Please, let this topic go for now."

Curiosity niggled, but he was right about the late hour. She needed sleep. She tilted her face, pressing her cheek more firmly into the warmth of his palm. "All right, Isaiah."

He sighed heavily. He drew her close and kissed her lips. Then he helped her rise. "Thank you. We can talk more tomorrow."

She sent him a weary yet teasing grin. "Indeed we will."

Birdie

After Birdie sang at the cemetery for the Fischer family, music time at Hope Hill changed. Ephraim began having her stand a few feet in front of the choir when they practiced. She sang with the choir, but felt isolated from it. She didn't like the change, and she didn't like the way some of the girls changed toward her. Iris, especially. Iris had never been overtly friendly, but now she used a snippy tone each time she spoke to Birdie, and she made cutting comments to the other girls in Birdie's hearing.

After a few days of suffering their censure in silence, she found the courage to ask Ephraim why she had to stand in front. He said he wanted her to build confidence in singing by herself. His explanation made sense, so she asked him to share his reason with the other girls. To her relief, he addressed the group on Friday morning at the beginning of their singing time. Birdie hoped the girls would understand and return to the camaraderie she'd enjoyed.

As they left the music room when practice was over, Iris sidled up next to Birdie and nudged her with her elbow. A light nudge, almost teasing. Birdie offered a hesitant smile. Had Ephraim's explanation put out Iris's fire of resentment?

Iris whispered in her ear, "Can't fight your own battles? You have to get Ephraim on your side? No one likes a complainer, Birdie." She flounced off, her nose in the air.

Birdie hadn't been excited to see her name under "window washing" on the chores list for the week, but after Iris's stinging remarks, she welcomed the solitary duty. She'd have time to gather her dignity. She filled a bucket with water, withdrew several rags from the basket in the pantry, and went to the front porch.

She soaked a rag in the water and lifted it to the window. On the other side, Mrs. Overly and Ellie sat on the parlor sofa. Mrs.

Overly was reading to the little girl. They looked so sweet and cozy together. If she hadn't known the child was born to someone else, she would think Mrs. Overly was Ellie's mother. She doubted a real mother would love Ellie more. Mrs. Overly was such a kind woman. And a trustworthy one. She had talked to Reverend Overly about releasing Birdie to take a job, just as she'd promised, and Reverend Overly promised Birdie he would send a query letter to Aunt Sally. As soon as Birdie could remember the address.

She stifled a groan, parts of the past the reverend told her to leave behind flooding her memory. After Papa died, she and Mama stayed in Waco only another two or three months. Then their landlord said they had to go. He'd taken several pieces of furniture in exchange for the rent, but he grew tired of bartering and wanted money, so Mama packed up their few remaining belongings and the two of them moved to Tulsey, where Mama had grown up.

Birdie recalled how sad she was when the landlord carried out Papa's bureau. Birdie had wanted one of Papa's handkerchiefs because they still smelled like him. Mama told her to stop being a baby about a square of rumpled cotton and shooed the man out of the house. She still mourned its loss. But not until the reverend asked for Aunt Sally's address did Birdie remember what else was in the handkerchief drawer—the letters Aunt Sally had sent over the years.

If Birdie had been allowed to retrieve a handkerchief, she probably would have taken the letters that meant so much to Papa, too. But Mama's unreasonable denial back then now delayed Birdie from being able to leave Tulsey and go to Kansas. Why had Mama always been so disagreeable?

Birdie moved to the second pane and bent to dip her rag in the water. She released a squeak of surprise. Ted sat next to the bucket, his tongue lolling and bright eyes aimed at Birdie. She laughed and draped the rag over the edge of the bucket. "You scamp, you startled me." He stood, poking his nose closer. She ran her hands through his ruff the way she'd seen Ellie do. The dog's presence cheered her after Iris's chilly treatment. "You're such a good boy, Ted. Would you like to help me finish the windows?"

His furry tail swished, and then he lay flat, resting his chin on his front paws. His dark eyes remained fixed on Birdie.

She couldn't hold back another laugh. "You don't need words to tell me what you think about washing windows. And . . ." She sneaked a quick look around, not wanting anyone to overhear and accuse her of complaining. "I don't blame you. It's not much fun."

The dog whined and wiggled his backside. Then, quick as a striking snake, he leapt up and whirled toward the porch steps. He bared his teeth, the fur at his neck rising like a porcupine's quills.

Birdie looked, but no one was there. She touched the dog's head. "What's the matter, Ted? What scared you?"

He growled, his stance threatening. Gooseflesh broke out over her arms. Birdie inched sideways until she stood behind the dog, searching the grounds. She didn't spot anything that would cause the animal alarm, yet he was clearly bothered. Did he see something she couldn't see? The idea unnerved her. Maybe she should go inside and alert Reverend Overly.

As suddenly as the dog shifted into an aggressive stance, he relaxed. His ruff smoothed, his tongue lolled out the side of his mouth, and he sat on his haunches and looked up at her with his doggy smile in place.

Birdie put her hands on her hips and shook her head at the animal. "Ted, that wasn't nice. Were you putting on a show for me? If so, please don't do that again. You scared me."

He whined and raised one paw to her, clearly a bid for forgiveness. She dropped to her knees and took his paw. "All right. I harbor no ill feelings." He lunged forward and swiped her cheek with his warm, velvety tongue. She laughed and wiped her face. "If you want to wash something, how about helping with the windows, hm?"

The dog barked twice and dashed off the porch. He raced around the turret side of the house and disappeared from view.

She called after him, "Some help you are!" Still chuckling, she took the rag from the bucket and moved to the next windowpane. Before she applied the rag to the pane, a bell rang, signaling everyone to wash up for dinner. She dropped the rag into the bucket and left the items under the window so they'd be ready for her to finish the task after dinner.

As she headed to the house, she pondered the dog's behavior. She should tell Reverend or Mrs. Overly about Ted's sudden change in demeanor. Then Iris's hissing accusation repeated itself in her memory. She shook her head. She didn't know a lot about dogs. Maybe his actions hadn't been so odd, after all. She would keep the information to herself. She wouldn't give the other girl another reason to criticize her.

# Chapter Sixteen

## Ephraim

At the close of the Sunday morning service in Tulsey, Father strode up the aisle to the minister. Mother, holding Ellie by the hand, ushered the girls to their waiting wagon. Ephraim deliberately waited until the group was out the doors before following. He needed some distance between himself and Iris. The young woman's flirtation had always made him uncomfortable, but this past week she'd increased her eyelash fluttering, "accidental" brushes against his arm, and secretive smiles that weren't secret to anyone, including Birdie.

Which was another troubling thought. Why did he care so much about Birdie seeing Iris's romantic advances? He should be more worried about Father's or Mother's notice and disapproval. Yet his greatest concern was offending Birdie Clarkson. Ever since he'd dived between her and Lida Holland, he'd battled the urge to protect her. Which would only create greater issues between her and the other girls. He needed to rein in his feelings toward the girl. Some distance might help.

He stepped from the tower portico into the late February sunshine. He slapped his hat into place, mostly to shield his eyes, and headed for the wagon, but a burst of lighthearted laughter captured his attention and brought him to a halt. He turned toward the sound and located a trio of young men engaging two young ladies in conversation near the street. The smiles, the relaxed stances, the ease they seemed to possess with one another's company brought a rush of longing. The only time he'd been as carefree as they appeared were the years he spent in college, away from Father and Mother and their ministry that made him a pariah to people who objected to the company they kept.

So many of his classmates had met the ones with whom they wanted to spend the rest of their lives. But, despite his desire to find his life partner, Ephraim had made a conscious effort to avoid such thoughts. Mother fully supported Father's ministry, but Mother was exceptionally compassionate. He'd never met another woman who he believed would be willing to share her life with a dozen former prostitutes. If he wanted a family of his own, he'd need to leave Hope Hill. But where would he go? What would he do? And could he in good conscience abandon his parents when they relied on his help?

One of the young men angled his head in Ephraim's direction and their gazes met. A smirk curled the fellow's lips, and he poked his nearest buddy with his elbow. The second one looked, too, then the pair snickered.

Ephraim turned his back on another burst of laughter, this one taunting rather than lighthearted, and lengthened his stride to reach the wagon as quickly as possible without running. Someone stepped into his pathway, bringing him to an abrupt halt. He started to walk around the man, but the fellow put out his hand. Ephraim recognized Mr. Browning from the livery.

The man laughed, and the tone helped chase away the memory of the young men's sniggering. "I'm glad I caught you before you left. You asked me to let you know about saddle horses for sale. Are you still interested?"

Ephraim would cheerfully accept some good news. "Yes, I am. Have you located one?"

The man scratched his cheek where his razor had nicked the skin. "Well, I heard a rumor that the owner of Lida's Palace"—

Ephraim's entire frame flashed hot and then ice cold.

—"is fixing to sell off a pair of horses she got in trade for . . ." His face blotched red. He glanced around, then shrugged. "Don't reckon I gotta tell you what for."

Ephraim nodded. He already knew.

Mr. Browning harrumphed. "Way I heard it, she'll entertain most any offer just to keep from having to buy more feed. Decent folks ain't interested in adding to her coffers, so she won't likely get many takers. But it'd be a way for your pa to buy a fairly good horse for a low price."

The man probably didn't intend to intimate his father wasn't a decent person and therefore had no compunction about doing business with the brothel owner. Even so, his choice of words rankled. Ephraim tamped down the defensive reply forming on his tongue and forced a smile instead. "Thank you, Mr. Browning. I'll let Father know and allow him to decide whether or not to pursue . . . it."

"Good. Good." Mr. Browning tipped his hat and took a backward step. "You enjoy the rest of your day now, Ephraim. So long."

Ephraim turned again toward the wagon. One of the girls must have folded down the step. Father was still missing, but the girls and Mother had all climbed aboard. Iris sat at the front end of the bench behind the driver's seat with her elbow resting on the seatback, just as she'd done on the drive to church. He'd felt like she was trying to wear a hole in the back of his good suit coat with her constant rubbing against him.

A low groan rumbled in his throat. What was he going to do about that girl? An arm slid across his shoulders, and he turned with a start. When had Father joined him?

Father sent a knowing look in the direction of the wagon, then raised his brows at Ephraim. "Will the ride be more comfortable for you if I drive us home?"

Ephraim swallowed a chuckle. How did Father know what Ephraim was thinking? "It might."

Father chortled, too, nodding. "Then consider it done." He lowered his arm and slid his hand into his trouser pocket. "I'm sorry I kept you all waiting. I wanted to make sure the reverend agreed with my assessment of Arthur Fischer's character before contacting the widower about hiring one of our girls."

"And did he?"

"He did." Great satisfaction underscored Father's simple statement.

Ephraim pushed his hands into his pockets and rocked on his heels. "So which girl have you chosen to work for him?"

Father glanced toward the wagon. "Miss Schulte expressed the most interest, but I believe Miss Kearney will be a better fit for the family. She's a year older than Miss Schulte, and she's grown a great deal in compassion and patience during her time with us." He raised one eyebrow. "Do you remember her first few days?"

Ephraim had only been back from college for two weeks when Alberta moved in, rescued from a horrendous situation in Leroy. She'd been so argumentative, combatant, and devious, he'd considered taking another year of schooling to avoid being under the same roof with her. Of all the girls he'd encountered during his parents' time of ministry, she'd been one of the worst. "I remember," he said.

Father's expression softened. "Her change is proof of what God's love can do. When we give ourselves over to Him, He redeems and restores."

Ephraim remembered Mother's claim the night of her attack that God promised to restore what the locusts had eaten. He'd seen the truth of it time and again in these girls' lives. Could it happen for someone as hardened as Lida Holland? He gave a little jolt. "Oh! Mr. Browning told me about a pair of available horses." He repeated everything the livery owner had shared, observing Father's expression as he spoke. Although Father often seemed able to read Ephraim, Ephraim received no hint of Father's thoughts.

"Well . . ." Father smoothed his mustache with his finger. "If Miss Kearney is to go to the Fischer's homestead each day, she'll need a means of travel. A saddle horse would take her there and back faster than the wagon, and she wouldn't need you or me to spend hours each day transporting her." He sighed. "I'll pray about it." Suddenly he stared past Ephraim, his eyes glazing, as if he were seeing into the future. Or the past? "I've prayed for years for God to soften Lida's heart. The hurtful things she does are from a place of deep pain, betrayal, and bitterness. I know our God redeems, but—"

He fell silent so quickly, it was as if an invisible hand clamped over his mouth. He sent a side-eye glance at Ephraim and chuckled, the sound sheepish. "Your mother is likely wondering what we're doing over here, talking instead of taking everyone home to eat." He placed his hand on Ephraim's back and urged him into motion. "Climb in the back and sit with your mother. I'll drive us home."

After eating a cold dinner, Ephraim went to his cottage. He kept the funeral organ in his small sitting room, and most Sunday afternoons he practiced the songs he intended to teach the girls during the week. But this day, he had no desire to play. The realization saddened him. He changed out of his church clothes into work clothes even though he knew he wouldn't do any manual labor on the property. Not on a Sunday. But taking a walk wasn't labor. Maybe Ted would enjoy accompanying him. He hadn't checked the back fence line since before Christmas. He could check for rails that might need to be repaired or replaced.

He sauntered to the barn, where the border collie liked to

sleep during the hottest hours of the day. As he approached the barn, he heard someone talking. A female voice, soft and melodious. His heart gave a leap. Was Birdie in there with Ted?

The large sliding door was half open, allowing him easy entrance. He blinked a few times, letting his eyes adjust from bright sunshine to gray shadows, and his gaze located not only Birdie, but Ellie, too, both petting the dog. He cleared his throat, and all three looked his way.

Ellie rose from her crouched position and ran to him, concern etched into her little face. She grabbed his hand and pulled him across the floor to Ted. She knelt, giving his hand a yank, and Ephraim dropped to his knees next to her. He glanced at Birdie, but her worried gaze was on the little girl.

Ellie's fingers parted the thick black fur on Ted's shoulder, and she gave him a pleading look. Ephraim examined the spot Ellie had exposed, and he frowned. Was the dog injured? He gently moved Ellie's hand and probed the spot. Ted whimpered, and Ephraim stroked the animal's head in apology.

He'd get no explanation from Ellie, so he addressed Birdie. "Do you know what happened?"

Birdie pulled Ellie to her side and shook her head. "I have no idea. Ellie brought me out and showed me. I almost didn't see it. His dark fur hid the bloodstain. But something hurt him. It's a fairly long scratch, and it looks deep. Might he have gotten caught in the Coopers' fence? Or maybe an animal attacked him?"

Ellie leaned forward and rested her cheek on Ted's back.

"Ellie, sit up, please," Ephraim said. "I want to look closer at the wound, and you're in my way."

The child shot him a glare, but she sat up and snuggled close to Birdie. Ephraim took his time parting Ted's fur and exploring the wound. He didn't believe it was a scratch from the neighbor's barbed wire fence. The dog's thick coat would protect him from the barbs. Nor was it a bite. It looked as if a bullet had grazed his skin.

He sat back on his heels and aimed a smile at Ellie. "You're a good friend to Ted, Ellie, to let us know that he got hurt. I'd like to doctor him. Will you help?"

Her big eyes screamed agreement.

"Good. Please go to the house and ask one of the girls for the first-aid kit from the pantry." He hoped she'd be able to make clear what she wanted. The pantry shelves overflowed with various items. "Everything we need to help Ted is in the kit."

Ellie jumped up and ran from the barn.

Ephraim watched her go. When he was certain she wouldn't overhear, he faced Birdie. "I don't want Ellie to know this because it would frighten her too much, but I think someone tried to shoot Ted."

Birdie gaped at him with her hand at her throat. "W-what? Who would want to hurt Ted?"

Ephraim set his lips in a grim line. "Someone who wanted to sneak onto the property."

Her throat convulsed. "Ephraim, on Friday when I was washing the parlor windows, Ted was with me on the porch. Suddenly he growled and acted very strange. He looked so fierce, like he was ready to attack, but there wasn't anyone around."

"What time was this?"

She rolled her eyes upward for a moment, as if seeking the answer. "Before dinner. The hand-washing bell rang just after he jumped off the porch and ran around the side of the house."

He tilted his head. "How can you be sure there wasn't anyone there? You couldn't see behind the house from the porch."

Fear glimmered in her eyes. "Oh, my. Someone could have been there." Her face drained of color. "Do you think he was watching me, or only snooping around?"

The protectiveness he'd experienced before filled him. He

reached over Ted's prone form and took her hand. "I doubt it has anything to do with you, specifically. In the past, people who opposed Father's ministry made unannounced visits and caused mischief." They'd been free of such shenanigans at Hope Hill, though. Until now. He forced an encouraging smile and squeezed her hand. "Please don't worry."

She clung to him. "But what if—" The sound of pounding feet intruded. She jerked backward, pulling her hand free of his grasp.

Ephraim stood and faced the door. Ellie raced into the barn, followed closely by Iris. Somehow Ellie had made clear what she needed, because Iris carried the basket of bandages and medicines Mother kept for emergencies. Ephraim marveled at the accomplishment. She was a clever child.

Ellie ran straight to Ted and flopped down next to him. Iris's gaze lit on Birdie, and her feet momentarily slowed. Her eyes narrowed. She hurried the last few feet and thrust the basket at Ephraim but kept her glare fixed on Birdie.

Ephraim took the basket. He knelt by the dog. "I'll need someone to hold his fur out of the way." Birdie was stroking Ellie's hair, completely focused on the child, so he looked up at Iris. "Would you help me?"

Iris abruptly shifted her attention to Ephraim. A conniving smile curled her lips. She knelt beside him so close her skirt draped over his knee and their hips bumped. Her nearness unnerved him, and his hands trembled, but he did the best he could to clean and bandage the wound. When he finished, he stood and moved away from Iris. "Thank you," he managed through gritted teeth.

She rose slowly, picking up the basket as she stood. "You're welcome." She spoke in a sugary, singsong voice that somehow still spat venom. She peeked at Birdie from the corner of her eye. "The dog's cared for. Are we all going in now?"

Birdie leaned down and whispered something in Ellie's ear. The little girl stood. She aimed a look of sorrow at Ted, but she took Birdie's hand and the two of them left the barn. Iris followed them, her skirts swaying with her saunter. She sent frequent glances over her shoulder at Ephraim as she went.

He waited until they'd been gone for several minutes before covering Ted with a burlap sack and heading for the house. He hated to deliver bad news on their day of rest, but Father and Mother needed to know about the dog's injury. And about Birdie's experience. If someone was out to cause harm at Hope Hill, they should take extra precautions.

# Chapter Seventeen

## Ophelia

Ophelia angled the brim of her bonnet to better block the sun. At an hour past noon, it was almost directly overhead. A bonnet could suffice and she needn't use a parasol. A blessing, because holding it aloft even in a slight breeze depleted her strength. Today's occasional gusts would likely carry it out of her hands. Isaiah must have considered such when he chose the time of day for their trek to Lida's Palace to look at the horses Mr. Browning mentioned to Ephraim.

She angled her gaze at her husband. He appeared so somber sitting straight up on the driver's seat of their wagon, reins woven between his gloved fingers, his hat brim settled low on his forehead. Very seldom did the two of them set out alone. It should be a pleasant outing with much conversation. But he stared straight ahead, his chin jutting, voice silent, seemingly oblivious to anything but the road unfolding before them.

Although Isaiah might not see levity in their mission, Ophelia stifled a chortle. "Isaiah, dear, you needn't wear your battle face. We aren't marching to war. As you pointed out this morning, it's unlikely Lida will be awake at this time of day." She had come along for propriety's sake in case Lida or one of the women who resided with her was up and came out to see what they were doing.

A tiny grunt left his throat. "I wasn't thinking about encountering Lida. I'm accustomed to her antagonistic attitude toward me and have learned to ignore it."

"And forgive it?" Ophelia asked the question softly, almost a whisper. She wasn't sure she wanted Isaiah to hear. Maybe it wasn't fair to ask.

Isaiah's stiff shoulders wilted. "How can I not forgive and forget when I tell our girls how freedom is found when they forgive themselves and their former abusers and lay aside their pasts? Only a few days ago I talked to Miss Clarkson about forgetting what was behind and reaching for what's ahead. I would be a hypocrite to expect more of them than I do of myself. Truthfully, this ongoing feud with Lida helps me empathize with how difficult forgiving and forgetting can be for our girls."

She placed her hand on his knee. They'd prayed for so long for God to break through the brothel owner's wall of bitter regret and lead her to freedom. Would Ophelia see the prayer answered on this side of heaven? Selfishly, she hoped so. She wanted to witness the woman's redemption. For all their sakes. "If you aren't worrying about how Lida might react to our presence, why are you so quiet?"

"I can't set aside the thought that someone came onto our property and shot Ted." Isaiah sighed. "If we didn't need a horse so badly, I wouldn't have left Hope Hill today."

Ophelia shuddered. "I hope it was only a hunter's stray bullet. Ephraim did say a section of our fence had fallen down, which could invite someone to hunt rabbits or foxes on our land."

"Maybe." Isaiah didn't sound convinced. "We've had to uproot ourselves twice already because our girls were no longer safe in our home. I thought when God settled us here, we'd found our permanent location. Did it not seem providential that the big house was available? Everything about it was perfect. So many rooms, enough to shelter more girls than we'd been able to rescue before. And back near Tulsey where our ministry started, where our son was born, where we had a chance to . . ."

Pain and confusion laced his tone. Isaiah had always been the strong one, the positive one, the one who encouraged her to trust God and not give in to fear or discouragement. The situation with Ted had rattled him more deeply than she'd realized.

She scooted close and hugged his elbow to her ribs. "It was providential, Isaiah. It *is* providential. God moved us here for His good purposes. You've faithfully followed Him every step of your adult life thus far. Please don't doubt Him now."

Isaiah fell silent. He looked ahead, but was he watching the road, or had he slipped somewhere inside himself? Perhaps to the past he'd claimed he should forget? She watched the road ahead, too. They were near the turn to the old Bradford Hotel. She would nudge him if it seemed he intended to drive past it. In the meantime, she should savor this peaceful time alone on the prairie with Isaiah away from the hubbub of their blessedly full house.

A dust devil danced across the road. A chipmunk scampered on top of a large, flat rock and stood on its hind feet for a moment, then darted for shade. A hawk floated overhead in a lazy circle, its wings spread wide. She searched the landscape for the hawk's shadow, and she smiled when she spotted its tiny form moving on the ground.

"I don't doubt Him, Ophelia," Isaiah suddenly said as if no time had passed since her plea.

She quickly turned her attention on his somber profile.

"But I do sometimes doubt myself."

Her heart ached for him. How many girls had they rescued from the clutches of despair? How many were now engaged in honest jobs or married to men who loved and cherished them? The Lord had been so good to them. They could count dozens

of successes. But the one who meant the most to Isaiah remained trapped. He would never rest until the first woman he'd
tried to rescue was no longer tangled in the web of prostitution.
And only God knew when that day would come.

Nothing she said would comfort him, so she didn't speak.
She rested her head on his shoulder and prayed for God to comfort her dear one and restore his confidence. Ophelia whole-
heartedly believed it was God's will for every soul to find its
completeness in a relationship with its Creator. Didn't the Bible
say God sent His Son to seek and save the lost? The poor woman
was so very, very lost. Isaiah would never be completely content
until she'd found the freedom in which he lived and preached.
A little sigh emerged as she finished her prayer, *Whatever it takes,
dear Father, will You grant him the desire of his heart?*

They reached the long lane leading to the old hotel. Isaiah
pulled the reins, leaning slightly with the turn, and Ophelia was
forced to sit up. He drove the wagon past the hotel to the small
animal shelter set well behind the building. "Whoa, Red and
Rusty." The obedient horses stopped. He set the brake, then
shifted on the seat and faced her. "Do you want to get down and
see the horses, too?"

She knew nothing about horses, but she wanted to be with
him every chance she had left. "Yes."

He climbed down, then reached for her. Her feet met the
ground, but his hands lingered on her waist. A soft smile tipped
up the corners of his mustache and his eyes grew moist. "It's
good to have this time with you, all to ourselves."

She rested her cheek against his chest, grateful that he'd set
aside his worries long enough to savor this rare alone time. "I
love you, Isaiah."

"And I you, Ophelia." His lips brushed the top of her head.
He took her hand and turned toward the shelter. "Let's go take
a look at these animals and see if we want to make an offer."

They drew near the three-sided shed. A black horse with a pair of white stockings and a star on its forehead stood at the far end. A ratty-looking rope dangled from its neck. A cream-colored horse with a white mane rested on a thin bed of dirty hay beneath the wood-shingled roof.

Ophelia stopped at the structure's edge. The smell of manure assaulted her nose. How long had it been since someone raked out the soiled hay? Lida wasn't caring very well for these poor creatures. Then another scent sneaked in, and she frowned. "Isaiah, do you smell cigar smoke?"

He sniffed the air. "It's faint, but I think you're right." He shook his head. "It's pretty foolish to smoke near a wooden structure. Especially with this hay scattered around. I hope whoever does it is very careful when they put the cigar out." He released her hand and crossed to the resting horse. "Hello there." The animal unfolded its legs and stood. It stuck its muzzle against Isaiah's neck and snuffled. Isaiah laughed and drew back. He rubbed the animal's jaw and shot a grin at Ophelia. "This one's friendly."

She smiled, too, enjoying her husband's smile. "And very handsome."

He moved in a zigzag path toward the second horse, his attention aimed at his boots. The black horse huffed air through its flared nostrils. Isaiah stopped a few feet away. "What's wrong, fella? Am I making you nervous?"

The horse raised its head and snorted, its black, tangled mane bouncing. It danced itself into the corner.

Isaiah stepped free of the enclosure into the full sunshine and strode to Ophelia. He stood with his hands on his hips and faced the shelter opening. "They're both healthy-looking animals with no visible injuries, although both could benefit from a brushing. By just looking at them, I can't determine whether they'd accept a saddle and rider, but at least I've confirmed for myself there are two horses that seem in good condition. I wish there was some way of knowing how much she's asking for them."

Ophelia squinted up at him. "Are you interested in both? The black one seems skittish. I'd be afraid to let one of the girls ride him. And Ellie loves to play in the barn. Might he be a danger to her?"

"Skittish, yes," Isaiah said, "but he didn't try to bite or kick at me. I think he's just nervous. Maybe from the cigar smoke. Horses don't care for the smell of smoke. It would be interesting to see if he behaved differently in a secure, clean structure."

"Nothing's ever good enough for you Overlys, ain't that right, Isaiah?"

The drawling voice carried from the other side of their wagon. Isaiah jerked toward the sound, and Ophelia turned, too. The quick movement brought a touch of dizziness, and she took hold of Isaiah's elbow with both hands.

Lida Holland ambled around the wagon's rear and leaned against a back wheel. She wore a gown over a nightdress, and her feet were bare. The informal clothing, her uncombed hair, and the kohl smudges under her eyes indicated she'd been roused from bed. "What're you doin', sneaking around out here?"

Isaiah shifted his gaze in the direction of the shelter. "We didn't intend to sneak. We were told you had some horses for sale, and we came to look them over."

"That so?" She tossed her head, then coughed into her hand. "Can't believe you'd be willing to pay for 'em, seeing as how you're so practiced at just taking what you want."

Ophelia felt Isaiah's muscles go taut. She released his arm and took one small step in the woman's direction. "Good afternoon, Lida. It's been a while since we met. Do you remember me?"

Lida's eyes narrowed to slits, like a snake's. She gave Ophelia a slow examination, and a crooked smile twisted her lips. "I do. You look a little punier than I remember, though."

Ophelia forced a soft laugh. "It's been a few years. Time tends to bring change."

Lida raised one eyebrow. "For some, I reckon." She flipped a thick hank of hair behind her shoulder. "I heard talk that you'd been sick. Sorry to hear it."

She didn't sound sorry, but Ophelia decided to respond to the words instead of the tone. "Thank you. I hope you've been well."

Lida released a very unladylike huff and pushed away from the wheel. "How 'bout we drop the small talk. This ain't no church tea." She sauntered toward them, staggering slightly. "Are you really wanting these animals?"

Isaiah moved beside Ophelia, and she slipped her hand in the bend of his elbow. He set his feet wide and pushed his other hand into his trouser pocket. "I'm interested in them. If they are saddle horses."

Lida stopped a few feet from them and squinted against the sun. "The fellas who left 'em rode in on 'em. But they ain't been sat on even once since I got stuck taking them in trade."

Isaiah shifted in place. Ophelia wished she could toss a quilt around Lida's shoulders. She shouldn't be in broad daylight in front of a man while attired in such sheer clothing. She sensed Lida enjoyed making Isaiah squirm, though.

Isaiah turned his face in the direction of the horses. "Would you mind if I tried riding one? To ascertain they're still willing to accept a rider?"

Concern rose in Ophelia's chest. Isaiah hadn't ridden a horse since the first years of their marriage, almost thirty years ago. She squeezed his arm. "Not without a saddle, Isaiah, please?"

Lida folded her arms over her chest. "Got two saddles there

in the shed, under those blankets. Probably pretty mouse chewed by now, but I don't reckon that'll matter much."

"All right." Isaiah shrugged out of his jacket and handed it to Ophelia. "I'll give the milky one there a try."


## Ephraim

Father and Mother had told everyone at dinner they were going on a necessary errand and asked them to pray for God's favor. Father also instructed the girls to go about their assigned duties and to serve supper at the usual hour of six o'clock. He and Mother intended to be back well before then. Ephraim alone knew where his folks were going and why. He held little confidence that Lida Holland would strike any kind of reasonable deal with Father. The woman had demanded over four dollars to replace a lamp. She'd probably ask twice the usual price for any horse in her possession, no matter what Mr. Browning said.

Just before they left, Father took Ephraim aside and asked him to remain near the house until their return. Although Father didn't mention it, Ephraim knew he was to keep watch for any suspicious activity on the property. So he spent the afternoon outside, pulling out all the dead growth from the flower beds around the house and raking up the abundance of tiny branches snipped from the trees by ever-present pesky squirrels.

Being outdoors gave him a much-needed break from Iris's attention. But he hated leaving Birdie inside with the others and no supervision. Iris curtailed her jealousy-induced condescension toward Birdie around Mother and Father, although she didn't seem to mind letting Ephraim witness it. She might have thought her treatment would dampen Ephraim's opinion of Birdie, but it had the opposite effect. With every snooty look, every snippy comment, Ephraim's protectiveness grew toward the girl who sang, as Father had put it, like an angel.

Under other circumstances, he would likely pursue a relationship with Birdie. He liked so many things about her. Her love for music, of course, intrigued him, but more than that, she was kind to everyone, especially little Ellie. She never shirked a duty no matter how menial. Iris gave her many opportunities to engage in verbal spats, but to Ephraim's knowledge, she refrained from rising to the bait. Was it kindness or patience that let her stand silent against Iris's mistreatment? Whichever, he admired her restraint. He'd be a liar if he didn't admit he found her physically attractive. Her trim form, wavy dark hair, and sweet face were appealing.

But a relationship with Birdie wasn't possible. She was one of Hope Hill's girls, forbidden even as a friend by his parents' rules. And she was determined to leave as soon as possible. She had no other family than her aunt in Kansas City. As much as he liked her, he couldn't be selfish enough to ask her to stay in Tulsey. Besides, in Tulsey, she would always be seen as one of Lida's girls. Or as one of Reverend Overly's girls, which, for some people, was just as repulsive. In Kansas City, she could be Birdie. Just Birdie. It was better for her.

The wagon rolled up the lane an hour before supper. Ephraim paused in raking and cupped his hand over his eyes. Was a horse tied to the back of the wagon? He blinked twice, and shock straightened his spine. There was! He dropped the rake and ran out to meet the wagon. He went straight to the horse. The poor thing was filthy, but dirt couldn't hide its beauty. God had blessed them beyond Ephraim's expectations. He sent up a prayer of gratitude as he ran his hand from the animal's neck to its withers, whistling through his teeth.

He trotted to the edge of the wagon and smiled up at his

parents. "What an incredible animal. I can hardly believe she sold it to you for what we had."

Father and Mother exchanged a wary look. Mother said, "Well . . . not quite."

Ephraim's elation floundered. "What do you mean?"

Mother's expression turned sheepish. "She wanted seventy-five dollars. But she took our forty-two as a down payment and let us take him home with us. If we don't pay the balance by the end of March, we have to return him. And we sacrifice what we already gave her."

Ephraim growled under his breath. The horse was worth more than the asking price, but Lida had to know they wouldn't be able to raise that much money in five weeks' time. So much for his thinking God had blessed them. They'd done no more than temporarily rent a horse for three times what should be charged.

He clenched his fists. "She's a thief. A conniving, immoral thief."

Mother's face paled. "Ephraim, don't speak of her that way. Don't speak of anyone that way. As long as people draw breath, there is hope for redemption. We should pray for her."

Ephraim bit down on the end of his tongue until he knew he could speak in a respectful tone. "We have prayed for her, Mother. We've prayed for her and for every brothel owner in every state and territory of this country. For as long as I can remember, we've prayed. But has it done any good?" He choked out a bitter laugh. "They'll never change. The only way to stop them is to do what that fellow Dan said—burn them to the ground."

He untied the rope from the wagon and led the new horse toward the barn. "C'mon, boy. I'm going to untangle that pretty mane of yours and brush the dirt from your hide." The horse wouldn't be here for long, but while it was his, he'd give it better care than Lida had.

# Chapter Eighteen

### Birdie

B irdie entered the kitchen and took an apron down from one of the hooks. As she tied it into place over her dress, Mrs. Overly came in and crossed to the calendar hanging above the worktable. The woman put her finger on the last square for March and released a heavy sigh.

Birdie turned a worried look in her direction. "Are you feeling all right, ma'am?"

Mrs. Overly slipped her arm around Birdie's waist and gave a gentle squeeze. "As well as I generally do on a sunny Sunday morning." Her smile was teasing, but it didn't quite light her eyes. "But perhaps I'm a little melancholy." She tapped the calendar again. "Here we are at the end of another month. Time . . . it seems to slip by so quickly."

"Yes, ma'am. It does." Alone in the kitchen with the person she'd grown to trust as much as Aunt Sally, Birdie allowed her second thought to leave her mouth. "I thought by now I would be in Kansas City." But she was still at Hope Hill, singing at gravesides and with the choir for revivals, performing chores, and sewing items to trade with the mercantile owner in town. She did whatever she was asked to do without offering a word of complaint. But secretly, she battled aggravation. "When will I finally remember the street on which my aunt lives?"

Mrs. Overly patted Birdie's arm. "I'm sorry, dear. It must be disappointing that the information continues to elude you."

True concern glimmered in the woman's blue eyes. Birdie felt safe admitting, "Yes, ma'am. Sometimes it feels as if everyone is moving on in their lives except me."

Alberta worked for Mr. Fischer, seeing to his home and youngest children while the oldest ones attended school. She only resided at Hope Hill on the weekends. After a week of going back and forth from Hope Hill to Tulsey each morning and evening, Reverend Overly made arrangements for her to spend Sunday through Thursday nights with an elderly couple from the big church in Tulsey. A Speegleville rancher's son had asked the reverend's permission to call on Alberta. They hadn't yet announced a formal courtship, but Alberta spoke of little else than her beau from the time she arrived Friday evenings until she departed Sunday afternoons. She was nearly giddy at the thought of having her own home and family soon.

Reva had completed her studies in early March. Immediately afterward, Reverend Overly found her a job at the syrup mill in Nalley. They had a going-away party for her and surrounded her with prayers before Reverend Overly drove her to what he referred to as her new chapter in life.

Harriet, too, had been released to work away from Hope Hill. Dr. Paddock's wife decided her failing eyesight made it too difficult for her to keep accurate records for her husband and asked him to hire someone to do their books. Birdie had asked to help the Paddocks, but Reverend Overly said Harriet's keen number sense and neat handwriting made her a perfect fit for the position. So now Harriet resided with the Paddocks and worked for them. Birdie saw her on the Sundays they attended service in Tulsey, and she seemed content with her new chapter.

She wouldn't see Harriet today, though. Reverend Overly and the choir had led a revival in Ocee last Friday. Ephraim asked Birdie to sing "Oh, for a Faith That Will Not Shrink" as a solo, and it sent Iris into a jealous rage. Birdie didn't look forward to facing the spiteful young woman yet again across the breakfast table. Many things were changing, but Iris hadn't let go of her resentment toward Birdie, and Reverend Overly hadn't found a place for Birdie to work and earn money for her train ticket. But maybe it would be a waste of time. She couldn't remember Aunt Sally's address.

Mathilda scurried into the kitchen. Her flushed cheeks indicated embarrassment. "I'm sorry I'm late. I forgot it was my week to help with breakfast." She grabbed an apron. "What're we fixin' this morning?"

Mrs. Overly pointed to the weekly menu posted next to the calendar. "Scrambled eggs, biscuits, and jam." She gave Mathilda a gentle nudge toward the cellar stairs. "Fetch the eggs, please. And, Birdie?" She briefly rubbed Birdie's upper arm with her thin hand, her smile warm, as if trying to calm Birdie's internal storm. "Please mix the biscuit dough. I'll spoon jam into bowls."

The three worked together in companionable silence. After living with only Mama for several years, Birdie couldn't deny it was nice to be part of a large, family-like group. As eager as she was to reach Aunt Sally, she would miss Reverend and Mrs. Overly, little Ellie, and some of the girls. And Ephraim.

Her pulse stuttered, and her hands slowed in kneading the large lump of dough. Iris frequently accused Birdie of trying to steal Ephraim's attention from the rest of them. Maybe Iris wasn't completely wrong. Her hours with Ephraim were her most cherished ones. Because of the music. They took her back to the happy days of singing with Papa. Not that Ephraim sang with her, but he still shared music with her. He'd told her one day after music class that her voice was a gift from the Lord, and she should use it to praise His name. He even showed her a verse in the Bible—Psalm 100:2—that instructed people to come before His presence with singing.

An odd thought trailed through the far reaches of her mind. Had Papa used his singing to praise God? She couldn't remember going to church more than a few times with Papa. Mama had no use for church, Papa said. Yet several of the songs she recalled him singing reminded her of ones Ephraim taught the choir and the ones she sang with the congregation in Tulsey.

She patted the dough into a large rectangle and reached for the cutter. No matter where she was for the rest of her life, whether here in Texas or in Kansas with Aunt Sally, she would always sing. The way Papa had. The way Ephraim said she should.

Would God bless her with His presence if she sang His praise?

By seven o'clock, as always, everyone gathered around the table for breakfast. Since Harriet and Reva no longer lived with them, Reverend Overly had moved two chairs to corners of the dining room. Birdie missed the girls, but she liked having a little more space. And Olga needed it. Her belly had doubled in roundness since their arrival at Hope Hill. She often sat with her hands linked on top of the firm mound, her head low, and Birdie wondered what she was thinking at those times.

Mrs. Overly tucked a napkin into the neck of Ellie's dress. "Isaiah, please bless the food before it's cold."

Birdie frowned at the empty chair on Reverend Overly's right. One of the rules was no eating until everyone was seated and served. "Shouldn't we wait for Ephraim?"

Mrs. Overly laid her napkin across her lap. "He won't be joining us for breakfast, dear."

Iris's eyebrows shot up. "Why not? He ain't sick, is he?"

Birdie's chest fluttered in concern, too. "Will he be here for today's worship time?" Would they still sing hymns if he wasn't there to play the piano? The worship time wouldn't be the same without singing. Or Ephraim's presence.

Mrs. Overly bounced a smile from Iris to Birdie. "He isn't ill. He had an . . . errand . . . to attend to." Reverend and Mrs. Overly seemed to communicate silently across the length of the table for a few seconds. "He left early so he could be back before our Sunday worship begins." She laughed lightly, the sound strained. "But we might not be finished with breakfast by worship time if the reverend doesn't bless our food."

Reverend Overly folded his hands. "Let's pray."

### Ephraim

Ephraim glanced over his shoulder at Biscuit, so named by Mother for his coat color. The horse clopped steadily along behind the wagon at the end of the tether, his snow-white mane glistening under the early morning sun. Frustration tightened Ephraim's chest.

*Lord, it's not fair. I don't want to give him up.*

He knew he'd sent up a grumbly prayer. He'd offered quite a few of those over the past month after it became clear his prayers for enough money to pay for the horse weren't going to be answered affirmatively. When Ephraim was young, Mother had told him that a grumbly prayer was better than no prayer at all. *"God knows what you're thinking, so you might as well say it,"* she'd said with a smile. Then she'd smoothed his hair, the way she often did these days for little Ellie, and added, *"He wants you to talk to Him. And while you're talking to Him, ask Him to help you see your blessings. Because blessings are all around us, Ephraim."*

To take his mind off his heartache, Ephraim searched for some things Mother would call blessings. They'd had enough money to buy the lumber needed to fix the fence. Ted was all healed up, and no other acts of mischief had befallen them at Hope Hill, giving them hope that Ted's injury wasn't intentional. Two more girls were working in honest jobs, their lives on a better course than when Father had found them. All good things, for sure. But he didn't have the full amount needed to pay what they owed for Biscuit, and today was their deadline. Yesterday, Father told Ephraim to take the horse to Lida's Palace early, so he wouldn't have to talk to anyone, and leave him in the shack behind the hotel.

"Where he won't receive attention or care," Ephraim muttered under his breath. Whether childish or not, in his mind, that gross unfairness trampled the blessings. He flicked a glance skyward, imagining God in the heavens. "You say You care when a sparrow falls. Well, what about something bigger, like a horse? Like *this* beautiful horse?"

Biscuit blew his lips, making a snuffling noise. Ephraim sighed. "Yes, boy, I'm talking about you. I sure wish things were different. If I had the money, I'd—"

Biscuit whinnied. Red and Rusty lifted their noses. They snorted in unison, tossing their heads. Red stumbled a step, and the wagon jolted.

The hair on the back of Ephraim's neck stood up. "Easy there, big fella. What's the matter? What has you spooked?" He searched the grassy landscape for a predator. No wolves lurked in the tall grasses. No snakes slithered across or were coiled in the road. At least that he could see. Gooseflesh prickled his arms. He raised the reins, intending to deliver a flick that would hurry them to Lida's Palace. But before he brought down the reins, a suspicious smell met his nose.

Smoke.

"Whoa, boys!" He pulled back on the reins and the horses nickered as they stopped. They tapped the ground with their front feet, and behind him, Biscuit tugged at the tether. "Easy, easy . . ." The last thing he wanted was for the team to run away out of fear, but he didn't blame them for being nervous. The smell unsettled him, too.

Ephraim set the brake and stood, his pulse galloping faster than he'd ever ridden Biscuit across the pasture behind Hope

Hill. Had a grass fire started somewhere? He scanned the grounds clear to the southern horizon. Made a quarter turn and searched west. Then north. He could smell it, stronger than the smoke from someone's chimney or a trash pile. But where was it? What was burning?

One more turn and there, in the distance to the east, a white-gray plume writhed upward.

Ephraim stared at the spot for several seconds, trying to make sense of it. And all at once he knew. He sucked in a gasp. He plopped onto the seat, jerked the brake free, and grabbed up the reins. "Go, boys, go!" He urged the horses into a reckless dash up the road.

# Chapter Nineteen

## Ephraim

E phraim abandoned the wagon halfway up the lane from the fully engulfed building. If the grass caught fire, too, he wanted the horses to have a chance of escape. He leaped over the edge of the wagon and took off at a run for Lida's Palace.

Several girls stood in the front yard, none dressed appropriately, all either coughing or wailing. Ephraim caught the arm of the first one he encountered. "Is everyone out?"

She pushed aside her shaggy red braid, smearing the flecks of ash on her cheek. "All but Carrie and Lida." She choked out words between harsh hacks. "When we didn't find Carrie out here, Lida went after her. They ain't come out."

Ephraim gaped at the girl, uncertain he'd heard correctly. Lida Holland went in after one of the girls? He wouldn't expect her to try to save anyone but herself. He examined the building. Flames licked the windowsills, no doubt fed by the heavy draperies. Smoke poured from the windows, but also from the roof. If the fire had gone through the attic, the ceilings would soon collapse. Was there time to get both women out? Maybe, if they were in the same room.

He hollered over the roar of the fire, "Which is Carrie's room? Where should I look?"

The red-haired girl shook her head. "You can't go in there! It's too late!"

He grabbed her by her upper arms and yelled, "Which room?"

She waved one hand toward the hotel. "Up the stairs, second on the left."

He gave her a little nudge in the direction of the pump. "Get everybody gathered up and find as many buckets as you can. Splash water on the grass all around the building. We don't want this fire spreading across the prairie."

The girl darted off.

Ephraim clattered onto the porch and through the front door. Heat seared him from head to toe and nearly drove him back. He flung his arm up to shield his face. Smoke filled his lungs and stung his eyes. *Help me, Lord! I can't see!* Another grumbly prayer? Maybe. But there wasn't time to spare on a better one. The last time he'd been in the parlor, he'd noticed the staircase climbing the south wall. He shuffled in that direction, squinting through the dark fog.

His eyes burned. His chest ached from panting in the smoke-filled air. But hope ignited when he spotted a newel post. He pounded to the stairs and stumbled his way to the top, choking out, "Carrie! Lida!" He took two strides onto the upstairs landing and tripped over something large and soft. He fell flat. Here, close to the floor, the smoke wasn't as heavy. He'd fallen over a woman's body. He pushed himself upright, scooped the woman into his arms, and half walked, half skidded his way to the bottom of the stairs.

He burst onto the porch and fell again, dropping his load. The woman's thick, gray-streaked hair gave away her identity. He'd carried Lida Holland from the hotel.

Two girls dashed onto the porch. They dragged Lida to the yard. Ephraim pushed himself to his feet and turned again toward the door.

The red-haired girl raced up and grabbed his arm. "Don't!"

He struggled against her grip, coughing. "But Carrie—"

"She's out!" The girl yanked at him. "She was in the back! She'd already started dousin' the building with water!"

Ephraim's fear-clouded brain finally understood. He flung his arm around the girl and the two of them staggered off the porch. As they reached the yard, a frightening roar sounded behind him. He spun around and stared. The chimney toppled and the roof collapsed. A huge torrent of sparks and ash exploded upward and then rained down.

"Fire and brimstone," he rasped past his raw throat. He sank onto the grass right next to Lida Holland's inert frame and stared in horror as the old Bradford Hotel went up in flames. Had he really told his parents this was what he wanted? Watching the building burn brought not even an ounce of satisfaction.

Suddenly Lida writhed. She coughed—weak yet wracking.

Ephraim shifted to his knees and rolled her onto her back. He slipped his arm under her shoulders and supported her head. "Lida? Lida, can you hear me?"

Her eyelids quivered. Then they opened. Her bloodshot eyes met his gaze, and her jaw went slack. "You . . ." Her face contorted as a stronger coughing spell gripped her. "You . . . did you . . ."

The red-haired girl leaned over Lida. "He got you out, Lida. Carrie's out, too. We're all out."

Lida kept staring into Ephraim's face. "I . . . Now you . . . Why?"

Of course she'd wonder why he was there. He said, "I brought the horse back."

Lida's eyes closed. "Reckon we're square." She went limp in his arms.

Ephraim lowered her to the grass. Her face behind its smudges of ash was gray. Lifeless. Attired in a scorched gown, chapped lips bleeding, and graying hair frizzed from the heat, she was the most pitiable creature he'd ever seen.

He pushed upright and turned a stern look on the red-haired girl. "She needs a doctor. And I need to alert the sheriff about the fire." Didn't anyone from town see the smoke? By now, shouldn't someone be coming? But maybe they saw it, figured out what was burning, and didn't care. Guilt smote him. He was no better than any of them. "Round everyone up. I'll take you into town, and—"

The girl backed away, palms held up in a defensive gesture. "We can't go to town. Folks'll take one look at how we're dressed an' run us all out on a rail. Nuh-uh. Stayin' right here."

Ephraim swung his hand toward the still crackling building. "Where? There's no shelter except the shack. You can't stay in that." He hadn't even wanted to leave Biscuit in the sorry dwelling. But if Lida Holland meant what she'd said, Biscuit was now his, given in exchange for his rescuing her from burning to death.

The girl hugged herself, staring at the old hotel. "Better the shack than anyplace in town." Her tone was hard, unfeeling, but her chin quivered.

As much as Ephraim hated to admit it, she was probably right. He imagined how folks would react if he rode up Main Street on a Sunday morning with a dozen half-dressed prostitutes in his wagon. "All right, I won't take you to town. But you're not staying here, either. You'll come with me to Hope Hill."

## Ophelia

Isaiah led them in singing "O Day of Peace and Gladness" to open their worship time. He had a passable voice, but Ophelia keenly felt the absence of Ephraim's accompaniment. She sneaked a glance out the parlor window, hoping to see their wagon coming up the lane. Where was Ephraim? He'd left shortly after dawn's break, almost three hours ago. He should be back by now.

Ellie wriggled in her lap, and she absently kissed the child's temple, her thoughts on Ephraim. Her heart ached for him. He'd been so unhappy these past weeks. He credited his foul mood to not being able to pay for the horse, but she suspected the horse was only the surface issue. Long before they'd brought Biscuit to Hope Hill, she'd seen a restlessness in him. And who could blame him? With the exception of his years at college, he'd spent his entire life shuttered away with her and Isaiah. Schooled at home. Separated from others his age. They'd done it to protect him from ugly treatment, and she didn't regret shielding him. But he was a grown man now, able to fight his own battles. Was it fair of her and Isaiah to involve him in their ministry?

Yes, his skills were important and needed. But they intended to hire a housekeeper. Ephraim's responsibilities—groundskeeping and directing the choir—could also be done by a hired employee. He wasn't the only person who possessed such abilities. But God had yet to provide the funds even for a housekeeper. They would need twice as much in order to hire helpers for both housekeeping and groundskeeping. As for the music . . .

Ellie squirmed off Ophelia's lap and pattered to the window. She pointed, her face alight.

Iris stood and looked out. "It's Ephraim. And he ain't alone." The entire group stopped singing and turned their focus from Isaiah to the window. Chatter broke out.

Ophelia joined Ellie and scowled in confusion at the sight of a number of rumpled, distraught-looking women riding in their revival wagon. The black-and-white horse she and Isaiah had seen in Lida's shed was now tethered to the wagon on the opposite side from Biscuit.

She looked at Isaiah over her shoulder. "You'd better go check on Ephraim. I'll stay here with the girls."

Isaiah laid the hymnal aside and strode out the front door. The girls crowded in behind Ophelia, but she shook her head. "This is worship time. All of you, finish the hymn. Ellie, you, too." She urged Ellie into Lucretia's keeping. "Birdie, lead them in singing, please." A few girls muttered in protest and Iris's eyes spat fury, but they all moved to obey.

While the girls halfheartedly sang, Ophelia stared out the window. Isaiah reached the wagon. Ephraim jumped down, and the two men she loved most in the world engaged in a lively conversation involving waving arms and frequent glances into the wagon bed. Then Ephraim jogged to the wagon's rear, untied Biscuit, and mounted the horse's sleek back. He hunkered over the animal's neck and Biscuit galloped toward the road.

Isaiah climbed into the driver's seat and pulled the wagon clear up to the front porch. Ophelia had to sate her curiosity. She crossed to the front door and swung it wide. A chorus of coughs coming from the women in the wagon competed with the verse being sung in the parlor—" 'Today on weary nations, the heav'nly manna falls . . .' "

Ophelia closed the door on the song and hurried to Isaiah, who was unfolding the step. "What happened? Where is Ephraim going?"

His brow furrowed into lines of worry. "The old Bradford Hotel burned down."

She clapped her hands over her mouth. Could Ephraim have— She wouldn't allow herself to complete the thought.

Isaiah assisted the girls—Lida's girls, she now realized—from the wagon one by one. As they alighted, they gathered near the porch steps.

"Everyone escaped, thank the Lord," Isaiah went on, "but Lida hasn't regained consciousness since Ephraim put her in the wagon. He went to town to fetch Dr. Paddock." He heaved himself into the bed. Ophelia peered in. Lida lay in a crumbled heap on the bare wood floor, eyes closed, mouth slightly ajar. But her chest was rising and falling in shuddered heaves. Not normal breaths, but breaths all the same. She was alive. Which meant there was hope.

Ophelia clasped her folded hands beneath her chin, her heart sending up a wordless plea. "Bring her inside."

"I don't want to move her again until the doctor comes." Isaiah pulled the quilt they always carried from under the driver's seat and draped it over Lida's form, as tenderly as Ophelia had covered Ephraim or Ellie when they were babies. "Take her girls in, though. Have whoever is on bath-preparation duty fill the washbowls, and—"

Ophelia held up one hand, smiling past the tears distorting her vision. "I know what to do, Isaiah. I'll see to these girls. You . . ." She gulped, her gaze drifting to Lida's still, pale face. "Stay with Lida. And pray." She choked back a sob. After all these years of praying and hoping, they couldn't lose her. Not like this. Especially if Ephraim had set that fire. It would be hard enough to see him tried for arson. For murder? Her heart wouldn't take it.

The remainder of the day passed in a blur. Ophelia was at the center of it all. Between offering prayers for Lida and the displaced girls, she asked God to strengthen her heart. It pounded fiercely in her chest as she directed Hope Hill's residents in seeing to the girls' needs. Some kept the washtub filled with warm water so the new arrivals could bathe. Others located clothing. They fed twice as many people as normal, which meant cooking and cleaning took extra time and effort. There weren't enough beds for everyone, so they retrieved cots, sheets, blankets, and pillows from the attic and set them up in the bedrooms.

Amid all the activity, Dr. Paddock arrived with Ephraim. He

examined Lida first. Because she'd been in the burning structure longer than any of the others, who'd all gotten out shortly
after they realized the old hotel was on fire, she was in a serious
state. The doctor bandaged her many burns. Lida never wak-
ened during the ministrations. When he finished, he said Lida
needed quiet and much rest. They put her in Ellie's room and
moved Ellie in with Lucretia. This distressed the little girl, but
what else could they do? Ellie's room was the quietest place in
the house for Lida to recover. If she recovered.

Several of the girls had suffered minor burns. The doctor
spent more than two hours cleaning, applying salve, and ban-
daging their wounds. As the last girl walked away, Ephraim approached. To Ophelia's shock and concern, both of his arms at
his elbows, the knuckles of his hands, and his right shoulder,
knee, and ear bore raw patches. His hair above his ear was singed,
too. Clearly, he'd been very close to the fire. How had he suffered
so many injuries? She held the question inside.

Despite being hurt, he insisted on transporting Alberta into
Tulsey late that afternoon so she'd be where she was needed in
the morning. When he returned, he put the horses and wagon
away, then went to his cottage. He didn't come to the house for
supper. Ophelia wanted to go out and check on him, but Isaiah
insisted he was old enough to see to himself. She needed to attend their many guests.

Isaiah chose to skip their evening Bible reading and gathered
everyone for a simple prayer. He praised God for sparing the
girls' lives, for giving the Hope Hill residents the strength to
minister to the ones in need, and for providing the resources to
feed and clothe the newcomers. He asked God to grant them all
healing rest, then bid them good night.

As Lucretia led Ellie up the stairs that evening, Ophelia tried
not to weep at the silent tears rolling down the little girl's
cheeks. With everything else to do, Ophelia hadn't even read

Ellie a bedtime story. And now she was being tucked into a strange bed. So many changes in such a short amount of time. The child would need lots of hugs and assurance in the days ahead.

After the last person plodded up the stairs, Ophelia sank onto the parlor sofa in the spot she'd been when Isaiah began their morning worship service more than ten hours ago. She released a sad laugh. Never in her lifetime had she worked so hard on a Sunday. Never in all their years of ministry had they not formally worshipped the Lord on a Sunday. And never in all their years of ministry had so many been crowded into their home at once. The weight of exhaustion rested heavier on her than she could ever remember. But she didn't begrudge the overflow. Gratitude rose above all other emotions.

Miraculously, Lida's girls had all survived the fire. They were safely away from the brothel. Lida's Palace was no more. When she'd asked God to rescue Lida and close the brothel using whatever means He deemed necessary, she hadn't envisioned such an event. Yet she couldn't deny relief that the loathsome business was gone.

But what if—

Isaiah entered the room and sat beside her, blessedly closing down the thought she'd determinedly pushed aside all day. He took her hand, rested his head on the sofa's arched back, and sighed. "Such a day . . ."

Ophelia tipped her cheek against his shoulder. "Different from what we expected when we awakened this morning, yes?"

"Oh, my . . ." He heaved out the words as he sighed, and she chuckled softly.

They sat without moving or speaking. Was he enjoying the silence, too? Save the steady *tick* of the grandfather clock, the house was still. Peaceful. Then she gave a little jolt and sat up.

"Should someone sleep in Lida's room? Keep watch in case"—she swallowed—"something happens?"

Isaiah rolled his head without lifting it, turning his face toward her. "If something happens, there's very little anyone can do. Dr. Paddock said make sure she drinks water when she's awake, but otherwise let her rest."

Ophelia worried her lip between her teeth. "Even if we can't do anything for her, shouldn't someone at least be with her so she isn't alone if she releases her final breath?"

Isaiah drew her snug against him, pulling her head into the curve of his neck. He rested his temple against her crown and curled his arm around her. "I love your caring heart, my dear. You personify the very image of an angel of mercy. But you aren't going up there. Dr. Paddock said you shouldn't climb stairs, and especially after such a trying day, I insist you honor his instruction."

She couldn't have climbed those stairs if she wanted to. As weary as she felt, she might even need his help navigating the hallway to their bedroom. She toyed with a button on his suit coat. "Maybe Birdie would be willing to sleep on a cot next to Lida. Earlier today, Iris cut her finger while slicing carrots, and Birdie bandaged the wound even without being asked. She is quite compassionate toward others' pain."

"She is, and if I asked her, she would stay awake with Lida all night." Isaiah's warm breath stirred the hair near Ophelia's temple and tickled her. She smoothed it down as he added, "But I won't ask her."

Ophelia tipped her head and met Isaiah's gaze. "Why not?"

"I believe Birdie has suffered enough loss. Her father died, her mother abandoned her . . ." He ran his finger along Ophelia's jaw and then left it resting lightly on the little cleft in her chin. "The same compassionate nature that would prompt her to sit

at Lida's bedside would lead her to assume an unbearable burden if Lida passed away and Birdie was helpless against it. I can't
knowingly send her to a place of pain." He lowered his hand to
his lap.

Birdie's comment that morning when the two of them were
alone in the kitchen tiptoed through Ophelia's mind. "Isaiah,
I realize we can't contact Birdie's aunt about Birdie moving
to Kansas until God chooses to awaken Birdie's memory, but
could we not step out in faith and seek a job for her? Then she'll
have the money she needs to travel to Kansas City."

Isaiah laid his head back again and stared upward. His hand
on her hip slid up and down, the action keeping beat with the
clock's pendulum. He probably wasn't even aware he was doing it. "Believe me, my dear, I've contemplated that very thing.
But she's safe within these walls, buffered from influences that
could pull her astray." He shifted and smiled sadly at her. "The
ones with the most tender souls are often most easily misled.
Unwillingness to hurt or displease someone replaces discernment. From what she's said about her aunt, the woman wouldn't
lead her into harm. But no person, no matter how influential,
lives forever. Birdie can't rely on us, her aunt, or anyone else to
temporarily guide and direct her. She needs the Spirit's stead-
fast, eternal presence. And she has yet to receive Him."

Ophelia's exhaustion-muddled brain struggled to make sense
of what he'd said. Understanding dawned, but something still
puzzled her. "We've released other girls who hadn't committed
their lives to Jesus. Why are they different?"

"Because the Lord didn't prompt me to hold them near. He
prompted me to let them go so there was room for others to
come in."

She knew her husband's heart, so those decisions weren't uncaring. She still didn't completely comprehend his reasoning,
but perhaps tomorrow, after a night of rest, she would grasp it

better. Before she turned in, though, she had to ask him one more question. Even though the answer might tear her heart in two.

"Isaiah, the fire at Lida's Palace . . ." She gathered every bit of courage she possessed and forced her tight throat to release her concern. "How did it start?"

Isaiah's expression hardened. "I don't know. And I didn't ask. I think—" He closed his eyes for a moment. "I think, in this case, ignorance might truly be better than knowledge."

# Chapter Twenty

Birdie

The wake-up chimes sounded at six o'clock the morning of April 1, just as they had every morning since Birdie's arrival at Hope Hill almost two months ago. She stretched under her light quilt, urging her sore muscles awake. Mercy, they'd worked hard yesterday. The last Sunday of March had not been a day of rest. She sat up, sighing, and swung her feet to the floor. As she stood, her gaze landed on the cot pressed up against their bureau on the opposite wall. She blinked at it, confused. Where was Ernestine, the girl from Lida's who'd been assigned to their room? Neither Birdie nor Olga had risen with the chimes their first morning here. She expected Ernestine to still be on the cot, soundly sleeping.

Then she gave herself a little shake. The girl had probably gone to the outhouse. She'd be back. In the meantime, she and Olga should prepare for the day. She opened the wardrobe and took out a work dress. "Olga? Did you hear the chimes?"

"Ja, I heard them." Olga groaned in her bed and rolled over. She opened her eyes halfway and scowled at Birdie. "I can't believe you're wide awake after all the prowling you did last night."

Birdie paused in removing her gown. "Prowling?" She'd slept like a rock, worn out from the extra hours spent in the kitchen. With so many people to feed, they'd served two dinners and two suppers and washed all the dishes in between meals. "I didn't even wake up during the night."

Olga pushed up on her elbow and frowned. "Someone was

prowling around, opening and closing drawers. I thought it was you." She jerked her attention to the empty cot. "Oh. I forgot all about Ernestine being in here. It must have been her."

Birdie nodded. "Yesterday was an upsetting day. She might have had trouble settling down. Tonight should be better."

Olga sat on the edge of her bed and cupped her belly. "I hope so. This one wakes me enough each night. I don't need someone else waking me, too."

Curiosity drove Birdie to Olga's side. "The baby wakes you?"

Olga gazed at the mound. "It moves around. Lots of little bumps, and sometimes bigger ones." She lifted her head and gave Birdie a sheepish look. "It scared me at first. I thought something was wrong. But I asked Mrs. Overly, and she said it's normal for the baby to move and kick."

Birdie remembered that Olga had wanted God to take the baby away. He hadn't done so. But maybe by now Olga didn't mind. Birdie sat next to Olga. "If you were scared for it, you must care about it. Do you still . . . want it to go away?"

Olga lowered her head again. Her fingers twitched on her gown-draped belly. "I was seven when my last sister was born. I remember how little she was, how perfect and pretty. Mutter let me hold her and rock her, and it was fun. Like playing with a doll." She looked up again. Tears winked in Olga's blue eyes, and her hands flattened, as if a wind blew and she needed to hold her gown in place. "I feel it move inside me, and I think about my baby sister, and sometimes I imagine keeping it. But then I know I can't. Not by myself." She jerked her hands from her belly and grabbed fistfuls of the rumpled sheets. "I will send the baby to the orphanage Mrs. Overly told me about. It will be better that way."

Birdie put her hand over Olga's. "Are you sure?"

Olga slipped free of Birdie's light hold and stood. "We'll be late to morning chores if we don't get dressed." She opened the wardrobe and withdrew one of the maternity dresses Mrs. Overly had asked the reverend to bring down from a trunk in the attic. She draped it over her arm as she crossed to the door. "I will change in the washroom. I know you like your privacy." She opened the door and released a little yelp. Mathilda was standing on the other side of the threshold. Olga put her hand on her chest. "You scared me out of a year's growth."

Mathilda laughed. Then she leaned in and looked toward the cot. "Is yours missin', too?"

Birdie crossed to Olga, frowning at Mathilda. "What do you mean?"

"The one who slept in our room last night—the red-haired one, Minerva—was gone this morning. So were the two we put in with Myra." Mathilda rested her fists on her hips. "And they helped themselves to dresses, underclothes, shoes, hairbrushes, whatever else they could grab before they left." The girl huffed. "A fine way to show appreciation, I'd say."

Olga shoved the dress she'd selected at Birdie and moved Ernestine's cot away from their bureau. She opened the top drawer, grunted, and turned to Birdie. "The hairbrush and mirror I've been using since we got here is gone."

Birdie checked the wardrobe. At closer examination, she realized at least two dresses were missing from their hooks. "She took some clothes, too."

Mathilda nodded, her expression grim. "Who knows what else they pilfered before they sneaked off into the night. Better hurry and get dressed. I reckon Reverend Overly will have some things to say about it all." She took off down the hallway.

Birdie did as Mathilda suggested, then went downstairs to help with breakfast preparation. All the Hope Hill girls were already gathered in the dining room. Their chatter held the sharp tone of indignation. When they were all seated, Mrs. Overly crossed the hallway and beckoned the reverend from his study.

Birdie surmised he'd heard all the bitter complaints. She didn't blame the girls for fussing. After she and the others had taken in Lida's entire household, seen to their needs, and given them a shelter, the girls' choice to steal items and run away during the night seemed like a slap in the face. Reverend Overly would probably address the topic immediately.

He settled in his chair and glanced around the table. "Bow for prayer, please." He delivered his usual gratitude for the food and asked God to direct their paths during the day. At his "amen," they all looked up. A sense of expectation filled the room. He took two pieces of toasted bread from the platter at his end of the table. "Miss Long, pass the butter, please."

Surprise registered on each girl's face. Giving one another puzzled frowns, they passed the platters and bowls in silence. As soon as the plates were filled, Iris released a loud huff.

"Are you gonna send Ephraim into town when we've finished eating? Somebody ought to alert the sheriff." She glanced at Ephraim as she tore off a piece of toast, jammed it in her mouth, then spoke around it. "Those thieves need to be rounded up an' made to return every single thing they stole."

Agreements broke out from various places around the table. Myra said, "One of them who stayed in my room even took the quilt an' pillow!"

Mathilda snickered. "Bet she would have carried off the cot if it hadn't been too big."

More rumbling followed. Iris sent a smug look at Reverend Overly. "If it'll help, I'll write down all the things that've come up missing so Ephraim can tell it all to the sheriff."

Reverend Overly swallowed the bite in his mouth, wiped his mustache with his napkin, then laid the napkin beside his plate. He linked his fingers on the edge of the table—the pose Birdie recognized as his *I'm going to say something important, so listen* pose. Everyone, except Ellic who was busy eating jam directly from the small serving bowl with a spoon, shifted their full focus on him.

"We will not alert the sheriff."

A series of gasps echoed.

"We will be grateful that we had enough to share with these girls in need. They lost all their worldly possessions in the fire, and now they have some things to help them start anew."

A few mutters rumbled. Iris blasted, "But they didn't ask for any of the stuff! They just took it! That's stealing! It's wrong!"

The reverend shifted his serious gaze at Iris. "Yes, Miss Brown. It is wrong. They violated God's commandment 'Thou shalt not steal.' But they didn't sin against us. They sinned against God. He alone holds the right to sit in judgment of them."

Iris sat back, flinging her arms up in a gesture of frustration. "Then why do we even have sheriffs an' jails an' judges if God's the one to make everybody pay? We all worked like dogs yesterday makin' space for them an' settin' up beds an' such. An' now they're just gonna get away with stealin' us half blind in the middle of the night? That ain't fair."

Birdie drew back, her frame quivering. On her first morning at Hope Hill, Reverend Overly had shared his behavioral expectations for the residents. The very first rule concerning behavior was respectfulness. Iris had exhibited little respect or kindness toward Birdie, but Birdie wasn't important. The reverend, though, was a preacher. He owned Hope Hill. He decided who would come and go from this place of refuge. He was very important. Iris's tone and actions held contempt, the direct opposite of respect. Would Reverend Overly make Iris leave?

While Iris's chest heaved in angry huffs of breath, it seemed everyone else forgot how to breathe. They all sat still and silent, gazes flitting from Iris to Reverend Overly, back and forth.

The reverend's eyebrows lifted in mild curiosity. "Who remembers Paul's wise words in Romans three, the twenty-third verse? Would someone like to recite it for us?" He glanced at each of them in turn.

Birdie swallowed. She'd heard the reference before. Reverend Overly had probably read the verse during one of their daily Bible-reading times or at one of the revivals she'd attended. But she couldn't recall what it said. From the various expressions around the table, sheepish to sullen, she didn't expect anyone to recite the verse, whether they knew it or not.

" 'For all have sinned' "—Ephraim spoke so quietly, Birdie almost thought she imagined it—" 'and come short of the glory of God.' "

The reverend gave his son a nod. "Thank you." His serious gaze drifted from face to face around the table as he spoke. "Yes, all have sinned. Every single person ever born has sinned. We read in First John 1:8, 'If we say that we have no sin, we deceive ourselves, and the truth is not in us.' None of us can point a finger of condemnation at the girls who took advantage of our hospitality because their acts are no worse than any we, too, have committed."

He leaned forward slightly, and Birdie found herself leaning toward him, that odd pull drawing her toward . . . what was it? An invisible force she didn't yet recognize.

His eyes gleamed the way they did when he preached to crowds during a revival. "Yes, we've sinned. We have fallen short of God's glory, and we cannot save ourselves."

Birdie's chest went tight. She worked so hard here at Hope Hill. Obeying the rules, holding back the angry words she wanted to fling at Iris, doing everything she was asked to do. Even before coming here, she'd done her best to please Mama. Why bother if none of it mattered?

"God knew this. And He tells us in the next verse that if we confess our sins to Him, in His love and faithfulness to mankind, He forgives. He cleanses us from our unrighteousness.

Which means He removes the sin, restores us, as if the wrong had never even happened."

Birdie cringed, remembering what she'd done at Lida's Palace. She didn't want to admit those sins. Not even to God.

He zinged his attention to Iris, who sat with her lips in a resentful line. "This is the act of a just God, Miss Brown. When we ask, we are forgiven."

A flutter filled Birdie's breast. She wanted to clarify, *Even my sins?* But not here in front of everyone.

Reverend Overly went on in his powerful, confident voice. "Jesus, the One who died in our place to secure our righteousness—the greatest gift anyone could ever give!—commands us to love our enemies, to do good to them that hate us, and to pray for those who use us. If God, who is greater and more powerful and wiser than any created being, forgives us, who are we to withhold forgiveness from others? No, Miss Brown, we will not alert the sheriff. We will pray for those girls instead."

For several seconds, no one talked, although some of their eyes seemed to speak. No one took a bite of food, but most fidgeted with their napkins or silverware in self-conscious gestures. In the quiet of the moment, Birdie sought the courage to ask the reverend if God truly would forgive her sins if she asked. Her heart was beating as hard and fast as it did before she sang at a funeral. She pulled in a full breath, as Ephraim had told her to do, and let it ease slowly from her lungs.

She looked full in the reverend's face. "Reverend Overly, would—"

One of the girls from Lida's burst into the dining room. "Lida . . . she . . ." She waved her hand in the direction of the staircase. "Somebody needs to come." She darted off.

# Chapter Twenty-one

Ephraim

Ephraim stood so quickly he knocked his chair over. Father reached out and grabbed his arm, just above his bandaged burn. "Stay here, please."

Ephraim flicked a glance toward the second story. "But—"

Father rose, drawing Ephraim near at the same time. "Stay with your mother or she'll try to go up, too." He released Ephraim and turned to Birdie, who sat in the chair at his left. "Miss Clarkson, will you accompany me, please?"

Birdie shot Father a startled look, but she stood and followed him out of the dining room. The other girls put their heads together and began whispering, breakfast apparently forgotten.

Mother stood and moved to the hallway just outside the dining room, her gaze following Father and Birdie. Ephraim righted his chair, then rounded the table and stepped into her line of vision. "Mother, did the doctor say what time he was coming out today to inspect wounds and change bandages?"

Mother slowly met his gaze. "He said first thing, between eight o'clock and eight-thirty. I encouraged him to wait a bit, given that we took much of his time on Sunday. Now I'm grateful he insisted on the early arrival. The timing of his planned visit seems providential since Lida apparently is in need of . . . something." She glanced over her shoulder into the dining room, where the girls were clearing the table, still talking in hushed, secretive tones. "Obviously, at least one of our new guests is awake. Should I have Gladys and Mathilda awaken those who are still sleeping and tell them to dress and come down? They should be ready for the doctor's visit, and they'll be hungry. Should they eat breakfast before or after Dr. Paddock sees them?"

Was Mother asking his advice? Ordinarily she made the plans and doled out instructions in her always patient way. He wasn't sure if or how to respond.

"After that . . ." Her face pursed into a thoughtful scowl. "I won't know until your father has interviewed them which of the new arrivals haven't completed their education. For today, we will forgo schooltime. I would like them all to participate in music class, though. Unless . . ." She tapped her chin. "Will it be too much for you, given your injuries?"

Ephraim doubted he'd be able to direct or play piano. His burns weren't severe, the doctor said, for which he was grateful. But any slight movement brought pain. Drifting off to sleep last night proved difficult after driving Alberta to town and bending his arms so much in guiding the team. He preferred to cancel today's lessons. But if he held class, Mother would have an hour to rest. The dark circles under her eyes pained him more than his burns. Had she not slept last night? She would wear herself out taking care of everyone.

He dipped his head close to her and lowered his voice. "Mother, is it necessary to involve these new girls in our daily activities?"

Mother's brow puckered. "Do we not always get the new arrivals settled in our routine as quickly as possible?"

He straightened, startled. What was she saying? "You don't intend for Lida and her girls to stay at Hope Hill indefinitely, do you?"

She blinked at him as if she didn't understand the question. Then she folded her arms over her chest. "What did you intend when you brought them here? Did you think we would only see to their immediate needs and send them out the door?"

Ephraim didn't know what he'd intended. He'd only known they couldn't stay where they were and they wouldn't go to town. So he'd brought them home. In one night, they'd nearly doubled the number of people under this roof. Was there enough room for all of them to stay? "But there are so many of them."

Mother chuckled softly. "Better too many than none, considering what we do here."

Ephraim couldn't argue with her reasoning. Even so, this kind of busyness wasn't good for her ailing heart. His parents would likely be disappointed in such a thought, but he was glad that a few of the girls decided to leave. He would discuss with Father the wisdom of housing so many girls later. In the meantime, he should at least answer his mother's query concerning holding music class. "If they'll all fit in the music room, I will muddle through something."

"Thank you, Ephraim." She placed her fingertips on his upper arm. Lightly. A barely-touch. "When this current hubbub has quieted, your father and I need to sit down with you. There's much to discuss concerning your continued involvement in the ministry of Hope Hill."

Ephraim gaped at her. How could she say something like that with eleven—or was it only six now?—extra women in the house, Lida Holland lying sick—or dead?—in an upstairs bedroom, and her looking more weary at seven-thirty in the morning than many did at bedtime? Although he'd wanted to explore other possibilities for his future, now seemed an inappropriate time. Unless . . . Father sometimes made arrangements for a long-term resident to move elsewhere so they could minister to someone new. With all the extra people arriving, maybe they needed his cottage to house some of them.

Reva scurried to them and whispered something in Mother's ear, stealing his opportunity to ask Mother for the reasons.

Mother gave the girl a nod. "I'm coming." Reva returned to the kitchen. Mother offered Ephraim an apologetic look. "I see questions in your eyes, but I can't answer them now. I must attend to an issue and send some girls upstairs to awaken our newcomers. Please keep watch for the doctor and take him up to Lida's room as soon as he arrives." She disappeared around the corner.

Ephraim plodded to the front window. What were his parents going to tell him? And why, after so many months of feeling hemmed in by their ministry, did it worry him that they might tell him he was no longer needed?

### Birdie

Birdie didn't understand why Reverend Overly asked her to come with him to Miz Holland's room. When they'd arrived, he told her to stand aside while he lifted the woman from the floor and put her back in bed. According to Florence, who'd come to the dining room and alerted them to a problem, she'd found Miz Holland lying in the hallway, moaning. She wasn't making any sound by the time Birdie and the reverend came upstairs, and she hadn't even coughed since being put in the bed again.

Why, then, if Miz Holland was safe in her bed and seemingly fast asleep, did Reverend Overly remain seated on the edge of the mattress? And why didn't he tell her to go downstairs and help with the kitchen cleanup? She wasn't doing any good sitting on a chair in the corner of the room, watching him watch Miz Holland. But he'd instructed her to take a seat, so she had. And now she waited for him to say something else.

Or maybe she should say something. So many questions filled her mind. Why was the reverend so kind to this woman? Miz Holland had treated him very rudely when he came to Lida's Palace. He knew what she did for a living. He was a minister. Shouldn't he be disgusted by her? How did he find the means to treat this person—this enemy—with care and attention?

The directives he'd given Iris at the breakfast table concerning the girls who'd stolen items and sneaked away during the night repeated in her mind.

Love our enemies.

Do good to them that hate us.

Pray for those who use us.

During the short time she'd lived under Miz Holland's roof, she hadn't held one loving thought toward the woman. She'd done what she was told, but she never offered any other help—not in cleaning or cooking or anything else. And pray for her? Never. Not then, because she didn't know how. Not since, because of the resentment she harbored toward her.

Right after the reverend had put Lida in her bed, he knelt beside it and bowed his head. His lips moved, and even though no sound came out, Birdie knew he was praying. For Lida. An enemy. A sinner. How could he do it? Suddenly she thought she knew. Because he lived what he taught.

A lump filled her throat. Miz Holland was asleep. The door to the room was closed. No one would overhear. Birdie could ask any question and it would stay between Reverend Overly and her. She licked her lips, organizing the questions in her mind, and then asked, "How does God take our sins away?"

Reverend Overly shifted, angling his face in her direction. He didn't seem surprised that she'd spoken or even that she'd asked such an odd question. A slight smile lifted the corners of his lips, as if he'd been waiting for her to ask. "'For God so loved the world, that he gave his only begotten Son, that whosoever believeth in him should not perish, but have everlasting life.'"

Birdie had heard him recite the verse at the revivals. She searched her memory. "Is that . . . John 3:16?"

His smile grew. "You've been listening."

"Yes, sir. And thinking."

He nodded, as if he'd already known. He shifted a little more. The bed frame creaked, and he shot a quick look at Miz Holland's sleeping face before turning to Birdie again. "As I said at breakfast, we are all sinners in need of saving. So God, in His infinite love and mercy, sent Someone to save us. Have you ever heard the Christmas story about Mary, Joseph, and the baby Jesus?"

Lovely memories flooded her mind. "Oh, yes. My papa read it to me from the Bible on Christmas mornings when I was very young." Other memories, bitter ones, crowded in. Mama didn't approve him reading from the Bible. She said it was foolishness because God wasn't real. So Papa had stopped. But she hadn't forgotten those sweet moments of sitting on his lap, listening as he read.

"'For unto you is born this day in the city of David a Saviour, which is Christ the Lord.'" Reverend Overly said the words Papa had read.

She nodded eagerly. "Yes, I remember."

"Then you know that God sent Jesus to be the Savior. On the cross at Calvary, Jesus, the sinless Son of God, laid down His life in place of ours and took the penalty for our sins. We can be set free of the weight of our sins when we believe that He did, indeed, die for us, and we ask Him to save us." He angled his head. "Do you want to be set free of your sins?"

The heavy burden of shame seemed to press down on her, nearly crushing her. "I do. I want to be clean again. But . . ." She turned her face from him, a feeble attempt to shrink inside herself, the way a turtle hid in its shell. She rasped out, "I can hardly stand to look at myself. Why would a perfect God want to look at me?"

"Oh, Birdie . . ." Reverend Overly sounded so sad, she couldn't resist peeking at him. One quick peek, which revealed his sorrowful face and glittering eyes. Were those tears for her? He pointed. "On the table next to your chair, there's a Bible. Do you see it? Bring it to me, please."

Birdie looked. A small black leather-bound book with gold lettering spelling HOLY BIBLE lay on top of a stack of storybooks. She gingerly picked it up and carried it to him.

He flipped it open, his expression serious, and thumbed forward several pages. Then he turned it and handed it back to her. "Go sit down and read the first chapter of Ephesians through verse seven."

She returned to the chair, sat, and laid the open book in her lap. She read slowly, focusing on each word. A few stood out as boldly as if someone had drawn a circle around them. . . . *from God our Father . . . chosen us in him . . . holy . . . without blame . . . accepted . . . redemption . . . the forgiveness of sins . . .* A tremble filled her. Not a nervous quaking, but the way an egg quivered as a chick fought to peck its way free. Her chest ached with longing. She lifted her head.

Reverend Overly was smiling even while tears glistened in his blue-gray eyes. "God the Father formed you in your mother's womb. He knew you and He loved you even before time began. He knew you would fall into sin, and He sent a Savior to take those sins away. Jesus' blood, shed on that cross, can wash you clean. You only have to ask." He placed his hand on the mattress and leaned toward her, his eyes beseeching.

The pull she'd experienced so many times returned, nearly lifting her from her seat.

"Birdie, do you believe that Jesus died for you?"

Tears flooded her eyes. She didn't know why Jesus loved her, but she knew He did. His love coursed through her the way her blood filled her veins. She nodded, and warm tears spilled down her cheeks. "I do. I believe." All at once her chest seemed to burst open and release the throbbing ache she'd carried for so long. She clasped her hands to her thudding heart and closed her eyes, inwardly rejoicing. Jesus had taken her shame away.

# Chapter Twenty-two

Ophelia

Several minutes after Ephraim told Ophelia that Dr. Paddock was taking his bag of medicinal treatments up to Lida's room and would see all the patients there, Isaiah and Birdie entered the dining room. Ophelia looked up from guiding Ellie's hand in writing the letter *J* on her paper, intending to ask about Lida, but something in their expressions gave the answer. She said, "*J*, Ellie. *J* is for *joy*." Because that's what she saw shining in both pairs of tear-wet eyes.

She rounded the table, her gaze flitting back and forth between their faces. "Lida is better?"

Isaiah took her hand. "Lida is very weak. The doctor asked us to have someone remain in the room with her and see to her needs so she doesn't try to get out of bed on her own. He still can't say whether she will survive. All we can do is wait."

"And pray," Ophelia said.

He smiled. "Always." He glanced past her at the girls with open books on the table. "Can Ephraim oversee things here for a little while? Miss Clarkson and I have something important to tell you."

Ophelia suspected she already knew, but she wanted to hear the news. "Go to the study. I'll fetch Ephraim from the music room and join you there."

Isaiah escorted Birdie across the hall, and Ophelia headed up the hallway to the front of the house. Oh, how she wished for a strong heart that would allow her to run! But she knew her limits. She kept herself to a sedate pace. Ephraim readily agreed to take her place in the schoolroom, and he deposited a sweet kiss on her temple as he left her at Isaiah's study door.

Ophelia couldn't resist rushing to the open chair in front of Isaiah's desk. She sat, clasped the armrests, and turned an eager smile on the two of them. "All right. I'm here. What is your news?"

Isaiah held his hand to Birdie. "It is your news to share. Let Mrs. Overly rejoice with you."

Birdie fully faced Ophelia, her eyes shining bright. "I asked Jesus to forgive my sins, and He did. I . . ." A delight-filled bubble of laughter spilled from her throat. "I'm new."

Ophelia lunged from the chair and swept the girl into her arms. She laughed in Birdie's ear, unable to hold her happiness inside. "You are, my dear. I see it in your eyes. They are unburdened, no longer seeking."

Birdie drew back. "You could see it?"

Ophelia cupped the girl's cheek. "I could. But it's gone. The Light of the Lord shines in you now."

Tears swam, darkening her amber-colored irises. "Oh, I hope so. I've seen it in you and Reverend Overly, and I've wanted it so much."

Isaiah nodded wisely. "The Spirit has been calling you, Miss Clarkson. We've witnessed your struggle and prayed for you to receive Him. But He couldn't claim you as a child of God until you welcomed Him in. Now you have, and He will reside within you forever, guiding you to grow in Christlikeness day by day."

"Christlikeness . . ." Birdie whispered the term, wonder glowing on her sweet face. "I will do my best to please the One who took away my shame."

Ophelia gave Birdie another hug, then settled in her chair.

"And guess what else?" Birdie's voice quavered with suppressed excitement. "I remembered something. Aunt Sally owns a dress shop. It has the street in its name. She called it Fourth Street Fashionable Ladies' Frocks." A happy giggle escaped her lips. "Reverend Overly said we can send a letter to the shop."

Ophelia couldn't hold back a cry of delight. God had wisely waited for Birdie to release her burden before opening the door for her departure from Hope Hill. What a loving God they served.

Isaiah removed a writing pad from his desk and turned to a page. "Miss Sally Clarkson, Fourth Street Fashionable Ladies' Frocks, Kansas City, Kansas," he said as he wrote.

Birdie chewed her lip, watching his pen mark the paper. "I wish I still had her letters. Papa kept them all in a drawer of his bureau, but the landlord took a lot of our belongings as payment for past-due rent after Papa died. There wasn't much left for me to sell when Mama took off."

Ophelia's heart went out to the girl. So many of their rescues shared similar stories of abandonment and need. None they'd ever met over their years of ministry had desired to sell their bodies but, rather, were driven to it. If people understood, perhaps they'd refrain from judging these lost souls.

"I wonder . . ." Birdie glanced at Ophelia, then hung her head. "Will Aunt Sally want me now . . . after what I did?"

Isaiah rested his forearms on his desk and leaned toward the girl. "Miss Clarkson, listen to me."

Birdie faced Isaiah, her chin quivering.

"That sin debt is paid." Although he spoke forcefully, as he always did when sharing truths from God's Word, assurance softened his expression. "It's been cast away as far as east is from west. You are no longer the Birdie who worked in Lida's Palace. You are a new creature in Christ. I want you to remember this. There will be some who look at you and only see what you were. We cannot control what other people think. But we can control our own thoughts. From this moment forward, whenever the evil one tries to taunt you with reminders of your past, call on the name of Jesus. Bask in the truth of His love for you. Don't let anyone, even your beloved aunt, convince you that you are anything but a redeemed child of God. Will you remember?"

Birdie gazed at Isaiah wide-eyed and slack-jawed. Her body gave a slight jolt, and she sat upright, taking a princess-like bearing. "I will remember."

"Good." He stood and crossed slowly to the bookshelves lining the wall. "During the remainder of your time with us, Ophelia and I would like to carve some private minutes each day to answer questions about faith, guide you in Scripture reading, and pray with you." He removed a Bible from a stack donated by a church in San Antonio. He delivered it into Birdie's hands, but kept his hand on top of the leather cover while he looked intently into her eyes. "This isn't a mere book, Miss Clarkson. This is the inspired Word of God. Within its pages you will find all the guidance and wisdom you need to walk a pathway of faithfulness."

His hand slid away, and Birdie hugged the Bible to her breast. "Thank you, sir. I'll read it every day."

"Good." He perched on the edge of his desk and smoothed his mustache with one finger. "It will likely take time for the letter to reach your aunt and for her to send a reply. In the meantime, you will continue here as usual, singing in the choir and participating in the various activities and responsibilities with the other girls. Before you depart for Kansas, I would like you to consider being baptized. You can read about Jesus' baptism in Matthew chapter three."

Birdie's fingers moved to the Bible's endleaves, as if eager to find the passage.

"Jesus Himself was baptized," Isaiah went on in his preacher voice, "and we follow His example. If you are still here in June when we return to the Speegleville church for a mass baptism, you may join, if you choose."

Birdie's head shot up. "June? You think I might still be here then?"

Isaiah raised his eyebrows. "First, we must determine whether you will travel to Kansas City. Then, if your aunt isn't able to purchase your ticket, you must earn the train fare. These things take time."

She nodded, cringing. "Of course. In my excitement, I forgot about earning my ticket." Then she set her head at a regal angle. "I think you would tell me that if I'm meant to go to Kansas City, God will provide the way." A smile of contentment formed on her face. "I will wait and trust Him."

### Ephraim

It took nearly two weeks for Ephraim's burns to heal. During those days, three more of Lida's girls left Hope Hill. Margaret's sister from Dallas sent for her, which was cause for celebration. But Estelle and Lucy left on their own, and—not surprisingly, given her recent outbursts and obvious dissatisfaction—Iris went with them. Ephraim worried about what course Iris might take, but truthfully, he wasn't disappointed to see her go. Neither Mother nor Father was happy with the decision, yet, as they said after announcing the girls' departures, Hope Hill wasn't a prison. People could choose whether they stayed or not.

Including him.

He still couldn't believe that his parents had apologized for presuming he was as passionate about the ministry as they were. Father's eyes had welled when he put his hand on Ephraim's shoulder and said, "Forgive me for putting my desires above yours. I love you and, selfishly, want you near. But your mother and I agree, if God is carving a different pathway for you, then you must follow it or you'll never be content. So, please, son, pray and listen for His leading. Whatever you choose to do, we will support your decision."

He'd been relieved to know he wasn't being booted only to make room for the newcomers. Not that it turned out to be necessary. The remaining three girls from Lida's were settled in rooms—Anna with Myra, Ruth with Gladys, and Florence with Mathilda. Soon Alberta wouldn't come back on weekends. The Speegleville rancher's son had proposed, and the two were planning a late May wedding. Father and Mother were already praying for the girl who would fill Alberta's empty bed when the time came. Gladys asked to replace Alberta in caring for Mr. Fischer's children. Father hadn't yet approved it, but Ephraim suspected he would.

Even though they hadn't received a response from Birdie's aunt, Father arranged a wage-earning position for Birdie in Tulsey at the post office. Her first day was the upcoming Monday. This morning, Birdie was accompanying him, Mother, and Mathilda into town for their usual Saturday trading at the mercantile. While Mother and Mathilda shopped, he would transport Birdie to the post office, and the postmaster would apprise her of her responsibilities beforehand.

After breakfast, he hitched Red and Rusty to the wagon. Biscuit nickered from his stall, and Ephraim couldn't resist giving the horse a rub under his chin. "Hey, there, buddy. Sorry I haven't taken you out for a ride recently. Now that I'm healed up, I'll be able to ride you again soon." How comforting to know this horse would stay even when Lida left.

Lida had shown great improvement, and the doctor declared her recovery nothing short of a miracle. She was very weak, though, from so many days in bed. Mother and Father insisted she should stay until she was strong enough to see to her own needs. But her promise the day he pulled her from the fire, that they were square, meant Biscuit was his. When he left, he would take the horse with him.

Animals were peculiar. They chose their masters. Ted had chosen Ellie. There was no doubt in anyone's mind the dog would lay down his life for the little girl. Red and Rusty were most loyal to Father. Ephraim often drove the wagon, but when Father took the reins, the horses carried themselves differently. Prouder. And Biscuit had chosen Ephraim. He didn't take lightly the animal's trust. He'd be sure the horse was cared for the rest of its life.

He climbed up in the driver's seat and urged the horses to pull the wagon into the sun-splashed yard. Mother, Mathilda, and Birdie were already waiting beside the house, several crates and baskets stacked around them. He hopped down and helped them in, then put the goods at the rear of the wagon. As he slid the back gate into place, he smiled at them. "Ready?"

Mother nodded. "Ready."

He clambered back into his seat and gave the reins a slight flick. "Let's go, boys."

The women visited softly as the wagon rattled and jounced along the road. Not since her attack had Mother gone to town except to church. Ephraim hoped the outing wouldn't prove overwhelming. Especially given the stress of the past two weeks. He wouldn't have imagined how many changes would occur with the loss of Lida's Palace. He couldn't honestly say he rued the destruction of that place, but guilt sometimes nibbled at him about his adamant statements concerning burning down all the brothels.

What if one of the girls or Lida had died in the fire? Why hadn't he considered that a fire could do more than destroy a building? He'd apologized to God for his vindictive attitude. He hoped he'd never forget the sight of the building engulfed in flames, the feel of the heat against his skin, the smell of smoke, or the agony that rolled through him when that shower of sparks ignited against the morning sky. The memory would serve as a reminder to allow God and not man to enact judgment on the wicked.

In town, he carried their items for trade into the mercantile, then kissed Mother and returned to the wagon. Birdie looked so small and lonely in the wagon's bed by herself, he laughed.

She crinkled her nose at him, the way Ellie sometimes did to show puzzlement. "What?"

He couldn't invite her onto the driver's seat. It wasn't proper. But he wished he could. He curled his hands over the top edge of the bed and grinned at her. "You look lost in there all by yourself. Why don't you scoot from the end near the hatch and sit closer to the driver's seat? You can talk to me on the way to the post office."

Her bemused expression didn't clear. But she shrugged. "All right."

While he took his place, she rose and sat in the spot Iris had usually claimed for rides. Strange that it didn't bother him to have Birdie so near he could bump her with his elbow if he wanted to. The post office was only a short drive—four blocks' distance from the mercantile—and the street was noisy with an abundance of wagons and shoppers going about their business. They couldn't hear each other unless they shouted. But somehow it was nice just driving with Birdie sitting behind his left elbow.

She sharply angled her head and watched up the street, giving him a view of her sweet profile framed by a ruffled bonnet. Her delicate beauty had caught his attention within the first days of their meeting. Her lovely singing voice thrilled his music-loving heart. When he left Hope Hill to pursue his own calling, he'd no longer be bound by his parents' rules about forming friendships with the Hope Hill residents. He would be able to develop a relationship with Birdie. Assuming, of course, she was interested.

Then he trampled the thought. Birdie had other plans. She would leave for Kansas City as soon as she could buy her ticket. Only a fool would open his heart to a girl bent on leaving him behind. A relationship wasn't possible, but if he got the chance, maybe he would tell her how much he admired her. He wanted her to know she was special. It might give her a good memory to carry away with her.

A finger tapped his shoulder. "Ephraim?"

He jolted at the interruption and accidentally yanked on the reins. Red and Rusty snorted their disapproval. "Sorry, boys," he told them, then glanced back at Birdie. "Yes?"

She pointed behind them. "You drove past the post office."

He grimaced. So he had. He turned the team around at the end of the block, then parked in the street outside the brown brick building. He assisted her from the wagon and walked her to the door. "I'll wait for you out here," he said.

"Thank you." She went in.

He plopped onto the bench in front of the large plate glass window and resisted the temptation to peer through the dusty pane and ascertain she was all right. The protectiveness didn't surprise him. He'd experienced it numerous times already. But it was time to bring his—what, exactly . . . infatuation? fascination?—whatever he felt for her to an end. Mother always said talking things out helped. He hoped she was right. Because he would have that talk with Birdie. And then he'd be able to wish her well in her life's journey.

# Chapter Twenty-three

## Birdie

"Goodbye! Good luck in your job, Birdie!" Alberta waved over her shoulder as she ran toward the Fischer house.

Birdie waved and called, "Goodbye! Thank you!" Flutters filled her stomach. Was it wrong to want good luck? She hadn't encountered anything about luck in her Bible reading, and neither Reverend nor Mrs. Overly had referred to luck during their conversations about faith. God's Word and the Overlys had mentioned God's blessings, though. In her mind, she whispered, *Let this day be a blessing, Father, and let me be a blessing to those I serve.*

The nervous flutters ceased, and a sense of joy crept into their place. To think that she—a fatherless, abandoned former prostitute—could call God her Father was beyond comprehension. But she accepted it as truth. She was His forever and ever.

Ephraim sent a teasing grin into the wagon bed. "Are you going to stay there by the gate, or do you want to come up closer?"

A giggle threatened. Ephraim looked serious when he directed music. He looked serious at funerals when he played the organ. He looked serious when he helped the girls with their studies. He looked serious when Reverend Overly read from the Bible and shared with the group at breakfast and bedtime. But now, with a well-worn leather cowboy hat atop his wavy light-brown hair and that easy smile lighting his face, his countenance was relaxed. Happy. Inviting.

She toddled up the gently rocking wagon bed and perched on the bench close to his left shoulder, the same place she'd sat when he drove past the post office on Saturday. She swallowed another chortle, remembering his sheepish expression then. He was very cute when he wasn't so serious.

"Giddap," he said to the horses, and the wagon lurched forward. A wheel dropped into a pothole, jarring Birdie from her seat. She thumped shoulders with Ephraim. He looked at her, his serious face in place again. "Are you all right?"

She settled herself on the bench and straightened her bonnet. "I'm fine." She laughed to hide her embarrassment. "I'm glad I wasn't at the back. I might have gone over the edge."

He laughed, too, transforming his countenance. They left the Fischers' yard with its many holes—had the children been digging?—and rolled onto the road.

Birdie leaned against the wagon's high side, reviewing the list of duties Mr. Peterson, the postmaster, had assigned her. Sweeping, dusting, keeping the washroom clean, helping sort incoming mail, making coffee . . . Nothing seemed complicated. And she would be paid seventy cents a day! If she didn't spend any of her wages, she would have enough to buy a ticket in a little over a month. Sadness briefly pinched her. If she left before the end of May, she wouldn't be here for Alberta's wedding. Nor would she be baptized with the other new believers in Speegleville.

"What are you thinking about?" Ephraim's voice pulled her from her thoughts.

She turned his direction and squinted against the sun. She adjusted her brim so she could see his face clearly. "I was adding up how many days it will take to earn the money for my train ticket."

He nodded slowly, his lips pursed. "You're really going, aren't you?"

Had there ever been a question? "Oh, yes. I haven't seen Aunt

Sally since my papa died. She's the only family I have now with Mama gone, too." Where was Mama? Did she ever think about Birdie? Had she come back for her and found, instead, strangers in the little house they'd rented? And why did Birdie care? Aunt Sally would be a better mother to her than Mama ever had been. "I am very eager to be with her."

"I'm sure you are." He swallowed, his Adam's apple bobbing. His gloved fingers squeezed and relaxed on the reins. "Miss Clarkson, may I tell you something?"

His nervous actions made her hesitate. But she couldn't be rude to someone who'd always been considerate to her. "Of course."

Two more squeezes on the reins. He cleared his throat. Another swallow. "I want you to know . . . I like you." He glanced at her, then focused on the road. "From your first days at Hope Hill, I knew you were someone special. I admire many things about you."

She gaped at him. "You do?"

He chuckled softly. "Yes, I do."

"Like what?"

"Well . . . your singing voice, for one. It truly is a gift, and you use it to bless others. Then there's your patience with some of the more unpleasant residents." He lobbed a grin at her. "That was probably your biggest challenge, am I right?"

His fingers had stopped squeezing, and his voice gained strength. He'd cast aside his nervousness. But her stomach was quivering worse than it did the minutes before she had to sing. How often had he observed her to know how hard it was to hold her tongue around Iris?

He continued, "I think the thing I like best is your kindness to little Ellie. Most of the girls ignore her because she never says anything. But you . . . you notice her. You speak to her like she matters. It's a beautiful thing to see."

His praise raised a knot in her throat. She swallowed hard. "Th-thank you. But the things you said . . . they're not so much."

He shifted a bit on the seat and looked her full in the face. "Yes, Miss Clarkson, they are. You are a beautiful person, both in appearance and actions, and I want you to know—" The wagon shuddered. He jerked forward. He'd driven off the road into a pasture. He grimaced.

Birdie burst out laughing. She couldn't help it. He appeared so flustered. And she appreciated the interruption. His affirmation was reaching deep inside her, touching her heart and making her feel things she shouldn't feel for this man. Although her sins were forgiven and Jesus had forgotten what she'd been, people wouldn't forget. Even Reverend Overly said so. People would never accept a preacher's son joining his life with a former prostitute. Besides, would he leave his parents and travel to Kansas with her? Never.

Her laughter faded. She waited until he guided the horses back on the road, and then she put her hand on his shoulder and leaned forward. "Thank you for what you said. I will cherish your kind words for as long as I live. And . . ." Did she dare say the rest? Since she'd leave soon, she should. He ought to know. "You are special, too. I saw it from the beginning. You're a gentleman and a gentle man, like my papa was. I'm grateful to call you my friend."

They'd reached the edge of town. Birdie sat back and folded her hands in her lap. She'd said her piece, and it left her oddly at peace. She wished she'd told Papa how much he meant to her before he died. She'd been too young to know she wouldn't get another chance. She wouldn't have to carry that regret with Ephraim. And before she departed for Kansas City, she would find the time to tell Olga, Mrs. Overly, Reverend Overly, and Ellie how important they were to her, too. Then she could go to Aunt Sally with no regrets.

## Ephraim

*"You're a gentleman and a gentle man . . ."*

Birdie's statement repeated itself in Ephraim's mind all the way home. He drove into the barn, released the horses, and gave them fresh water. Then he took some time and rubbed Ted's belly, scratched Biscuit's chin, and even talked to the black-and-white horse from Lida's place. Smokey, as he'd dubbed the animal, wasn't nearly as personable as Ted and Biscuit, but he needed attention, too. So Ephraim provided it.

Then he ambled across the yard, a smile tugging at his lips. She saw him as a gentleman. As a gentle man. Some men might not accept such a description as a compliment, but he did. Because she'd favorably compared him to her papa, the man she loved so much. He'd never had higher praise.

He entered the house by the back door, careful not to let the screen door slam into its casing. It was study time, and some of the girls didn't need the distraction. He washed his hands and rid himself of the barn smell, then headed up the hallway toward Father's study. He wanted to browse Father's bookshelves for the copy of John Bunyan's *Pilgrim's Progress,* which his parents had given to him when he graduated from college. As he contemplated his future, the book could provide food for thought.

As he turned to enter the study, the sound of piano music drifted from the front of the house. He came to a stop, uncertain he'd really heard it. But it came again. Someone was playing one of Frederic Chopin's nocturnes—perhaps Nocturne in C-sharp minor, a complicated piece. None of their former residents played, so it must be one of the newest girls. Yet none had said anything during music class about the ability.

Curious, he strode up the hallway, slid the pocket doors to the music room open, and stepped in. He stared in shock. Lida

Holland sat on the stool, her head at a thoughtful angle, eyes closed while her fingers trailed up and down the keys.

Slowly, on tiptoe to avoid making even the slightest noise, Ephraim inched closer to the grand piano, his focus on the woman's long, chapped fingers. She missed notes here and there, but there was no mistaking the touch of a master pianist. Anyone could play notes, but a rare musician played the heart of the music. Even with the occasional sour note, the composer's heart came through. A shiver trembled through Ephraim's frame. Never would he have thought someone as hardened as Lida Holland would be capable of such beauty.

She came to the end of the piece, and her fingers lifted. Her head straightened, and she opened her eyes. With a gasp, she spun on the seat and glared at him. "What are you doin' in here?" The passage of time hadn't completely healed her throat. Her voice rasped as harshly as a steel file on iron. The accusation in her tone set him back for a moment.

*"You're a gentleman and a gentle man . . ."*

"I was listening." His answer emerged kindly. Patiently. Gently. He slipped his hands into his trouser pockets. "You play very well."

She stood quickly. Too quickly. She staggered and reached for the piano. Her palm landed on the keys in a discordant clash of sound. She winced and yanked her hand away. She sank onto the stool again and sighed. "That's a nice thing to say, but I think you might be fibbin'. Been a long time since I sat to a piano. I've lost most of what I knew."

"Then you must have been a genius."

She raised one eyebrow in obvious disbelief.

"I mean it." He pulled one of the chairs used during practice alongside the piano—close but not too close—and sat. "Did you study music when you were younger?"

She eyed him in silence, her expression unreadable. Wearing

a simple brown dress with long sleeves buttoned at the cuff, her braided gray-streaked hair wrapped around her head like a crown, she didn't resemble the woman in the sheeny red dress who'd taunted Father and him in the parlor of her brothel. Especially seated in front of a grand piano. At one time, she must have been something of a lady. What had happened to change her?

"I guess I ought to thank you."

The statement took him by surprise. Had he somehow hinted that he expected a thank-you? He didn't know what to say, so he lifted his shoulders in a weak shrug.

"I'd likely not be alive today if you hadn't brung me out." Her head tilted the way it had when she was playing. Her gaze narrowed. "Why'd you do that, anyway? Is it 'cause you know who I am an' you figured you owe me?"

She wasn't making any sense now.

"'Cause I have to tell you, it's a fool thing to go runnin' into a burning building. Seems like someone as smart as you should know that."

A chuckle built in his chest, and he couldn't hold it back. "That's an odd thing for you to say, given you went running in after Carrie."

She snorted, then coughed. The cough lasted awhile, and when it ended, she looked as worn out as if she'd run a mile-long race. She rasped, "I ain't been known for smartness. But you . . ." She pointed at him. "Don't do somethin' like that again. No sense in riskin' your life that way. You hear me?"

He doubted the opportunity would ever arise again. Uncertain what else to do, Ephraim nodded.

She stood. "Reckon I better get out o' your way. The girls'll be in to sing soon, am I right?"

Ephraim checked the clock. Music class was almost an hour

away. He started to tell her there was time for her to play another song if she wanted to, but she spoke first.

"Been listenin' every day. All that singin' . . . it comes up through the floorboards." She made a face, as if she found the sound unpleasant. "There's one song I ain't heard before. The words go somethin' like . . ." She closed her eyes. "Lead on, oh kingly turtle; we follow, not with fears," she sang in a growly, off-pitch voice, "for gladness breaks like mornin' where air your face-up hears." She popped her eyes open and raised one brow again in silent query.

How he hoped amusement didn't show in his expression. "Ah, yes. The title of the song is 'Lead On, O King Eternal.'"

She rolled her eyes. "King eternal. I should've figured that out." That brow rose again. "Reckon I messed up some of the other parts, too?"

"Um . . ." A chuckle escaped despite his best efforts. To his relief, a small smile pulled up one corner of her chapped lips. "The words were written by Ernest Shurtleff in 1887. An English composer, Henry Smart, wrote the music. We've only recently learned it."

"What do you like better, singin' the songs or playin' 'em?"

Ephraim shrugged with a sheepish grin. "I think most people would prefer I played them. I'm a passable singer, but not a soloist."

She nodded, the motion slow and deliberate, and he sensed his answer had pleased her somehow. "I like the hymn about King eternal. The words an' the melody go real nice together. Have the girls sing that again today, would you?"

Ephraim hadn't planned to work on it. Father was taking the choir to Bosqueville on Friday and had given Ephraim the songs he wanted sung at the revival. But for some reason he couldn't bring himself to deny her request. "All right."

She shuffled toward the door, and as he came alongside her, she paused. "Thank you, Ephraim Overly." Her fingers grazed his sleeve, and something in her eyes changed. A softness? A longing? Ephraim wasn't sure, because it happened fast and then her expression became shuttered again. "Tell 'em to speak clear. Can't have the audience think they're singin' about a crown-wearin' turtle." Mischief glinted in her eyes, and she left the room.

# Chapter Twenty-four

Ophelia

Ophelia had looked forward to Friday all week. She'd planned to accompany Isaiah, Ephraim, and the girls to the revival in Bosqueville. She nearly shouted with joy when Isaiah agreed she was recovered enough to make the trip. It seemed forever since she'd witnessed the Spirit move through a congregation, using her husband's words to stir hearts to repentance. But Friday morning, Ellie awakened with a fever. A spring cold, they concluded, nothing uncommon. The little girl would no doubt bounce back quickly. But given her fever, she needed to stay home.

To their surprise, Lida offered to keep watch over the little girl so Ophelia could go. Ophelia agreed. Until she looked into Ellie's begging eyes. The child was sick and she wanted Ophelia. Ophelia couldn't find the ability to leave her. So she stood on the porch and waved farewell to her husband, son, and the choir, then went inside.

She entered the parlor, assuming a cheerful tone as she asked, "Well, Ellie, would you like me to read to you?"

Ellie was curled at the end of the sofa, fast asleep. Ophelia's heart rolled over. How sweet the child looked with her tousled hair wild around her face and thick eyelashes casting a shadow on rosy cheeks. She bent down and placed a kiss on Ellie's warm, sweaty temple. The little girl didn't even stir. She would probably sleep for hours. Ophelia fetched a quilt and tucked it around Ellie's form, then stood and surveyed the quiet room.

The mending was caught up. Everything was dust-free and tidy from the morning's cleaning. She'd prepared a picnic supper to send along with the choir for them to eat on the way and held back a few sandwiches for her supper. So she didn't even need to cook. What should she do with herself?

She tapped her chin, thinking. Ah, tea and a book. She turned toward the hallway, but the creak of stair treads reached her ears. She crossed to the foyer and smiled up at Lida, who was descending the stairway slowly with her hand gripping the railing. "We have the evening to ourselves. You are welcome to play the piano for hours, if you like."

It had pleased her to see Lida sneak into the music room at various times during the past week. Every day, her playing became more fluid, more heartfelt, and Ophelia prayed she would find joy in rediscovering her former passion.

Lida reached the bottom and stopped. Her labored breathing calmed, and she glanced toward the closed pocket doors. "It's tempting, for sure, but I reckon it'd disturb the little one."

Ophelia doubted Ellie would be bothered, but Lida's concern for the child warmed her. Over her weeks at Hope Hill, Lida had largely kept her distance except at mealtimes. Rest was the best medicine, Dr. Paddock had told them, so they'd encouraged the seclusion and quiet. But Lida was gaining strength. Perhaps, soon, she'd follow the example of several of the girls who'd worked for her and leave Hope Hill. While she was here, though, they would lavish her with Jesus' love. Lida needed it.

Ophelia threw her arms wide. "Well, then, I was going to make a pot of tea. Would you like some?"

"Tea . . ." Lida seemed to sample the word, seeking its meaning. "Ain't drank tea with a lady in a good long while. But, yes." She gave a firm nod. "I think I'd enjoy it."

Delight exploded in Ophelia's chest. "Good! Settle yourself in the parlor. I'll bring the cups in there." She hurried off. While she waited for the water to boil, she prepared a tray with sugar and cream. Then she added napkins and plates of sandwiches and cookies. The choir and Isaiah were having a picnic. Why shouldn't she and Lida enjoy one, too?

The pot whistled its shrill signal, and she poured the tea. The tray proved heavier than she'd anticipated, but she sent up a prayer for God to strengthen her bones and headed down the hallway. She reached the parlor doorway, and Lida leapt from the opposite end of the sofa where Ellie slept. She took hold of the other side of the tray and together they placed it on the table in front of the sofa. They both straightened and sighed at the same time.

Lida swiped her hand across her brow. "Mercy. Didn't know how a body could wear down from so much layin' around. Might take me years to feel like myself again." She touched her throat. "And sound like me, too."

Ophelia reached across the tray and squeezed Lida's upper arm. "The rasp will go away and your strength will be restored in due time. For now, our tea is growing cold. Sit down and let's enjoy its curative powers."

Lida growled a chortle. "You always were a cheerful one. Never saw the bad side of anything. I remember that about you." She picked up one of the cups and slurped. She made a face, set the cup down, and added two spoons of sugar and a splash of cream. She sipped again, then nodded. "Mm. That's better."

Ophelia added the same to her tea and settled in the chair facing the sofa. She'd been hesitant to bring up the past with Lida, unwilling to open old wounds. But Lida had unlocked the door, so Ophelia walked through. "I remember you, too. Especially your talent, and the way you lit up when you sat at the piano."

Lida held the fragile cup between her palms and stared down

at it. "Reckon those days are long gone. Least for me." She glanced up. "But I'm glad you ain't changed. Good to know some things last." She sat straight and leaned against the sofa back, bringing the cup of tea beneath her chin. "You done real good with Ephraim—raised him right. He's a good boy. Well, he ain't hardly a boy, is he? A good man." For a moment, she stared to the side, her eyes glazing. She took a sip of the tea and faced Ophelia again. "Any man who'd go runnin' into a burning building to rescue somebody, especially somebody like me, who doesn't mean anything to him"—she winced, as if a pain gripped her—"is good. Real good."

What was Lida saying? Ophelia's hands trembled, rattling the cup on the saucer. She set the items down. "Do you mean to tell me that Ephraim . . . went into the hotel and brought you out . . . when it was on fire?"

Confusion marred the woman's face. "Didn't he tell you? Figured sure he'd let you know what he'd done. You had to've wondered about his burns."

Of course she'd wondered. She'd feared he'd injured himself while starting the fire. Remorse gripped her. No matter what he'd declared about setting fire to brothels, he wasn't a vengeful man. She should have known he wouldn't follow through with such a plan. "I did, but . . ." She shook her head. "He never said a word."

Lida took a longer draw of the tea, then placed the cup on the table beside the sofa. "At first I thought he'd done it because he knew"—a blush brightened her cheeks—"what you an' me know. But him doin' it for a stranger says even more about him, doesn't it? Yes, ma'am, you raised him right."

Ophelia's heart pounded fiercely, stealing her breath. Ephraim could have died. Even though he was fine, she couldn't set aside the fear of what might have been. Yet, at the same time, she was proud of his selflessness. She pressed her palm to her breastbone, willing her heart to calm. He was a good man, but she and Isaiah couldn't take full credit. "We taught him to follow God, but he made a personal choice to seek his Savior and live in service to Him. That isn't something we could decide for him or force him to do."

Lida's expression hardened. "You're right there. Some know about God, maybe even know everything about Him, an' still choose wrongly." She huffed. "Might even say I'm one of that sort." She grabbed the cup and drained it, then clanked it onto its saucer. "I probably should let you know, I'm fixin' to head out. Goin' to San Antonio. The miles'll put a little space between me an'—" She grimaced. "Here. Ain't been easy since you all moved so close. Might even be a good thing that I set the hotel on fire."

Ophelia had been formulating an argument about her leaving, but her final statement sent those thoughts scuttling. She gaped at the woman. "*You* set it on fire?"

Lida shrugged. "I don't know for sure, but I've been thinkin' on it. Remember when you an' Isaiah were out lookin' at the horses an' smelled cigar smoke? Well, that was because most every mornin' I had a smoke out behind the hotel after we'd closed down shop. It'd help me relax enough to fall off to sleep." She picked at a loose thread on her skirt. "Sometimes . . . I don't sleep so good." She grunted and gave up working it free. "The day of the fire, it was a little too chilly to be outside. So I smoked my cigar in the kitchen. Only smoked it halfway down an' decided I was too tired to finish it. I snubbed it in a little saucer on the dry sink, but, tired as I was, I might not've put it clear out. It could've started the fire."

Ophelia envisioned what Lida had described. Could a cigar bring down an entire hotel? If a small flame went unchecked, it might spread. Especially in an older building constructed completely of wood. "What's more important than how it started is that you all were able to get out. I'm so grateful everyone's lives were spared." Including Ephraim's. When the choir returned this evening, she would be waiting with a hug of both gratitude and apology.

"But spared for what?" The question rasped more raggedly than anything else Lida had said. She stared at Ophelia with narrowed eyes, her chin trembling. "Sure, my first thought when I came to in the yard was gladness I was still alive. But there's a part of me that wishes maybe I wasn't. That I'd died in the fire."

Ophelia clapped her hand over her mouth. "Oh, Lida, no . . ."

"Why not?" She barked the query. "The last thirty years've been more misery than pleasure. What good've I done in this world? I ain't had a day of peace in my soul since the first time he—" She shook her head and stood. "I told myself I wouldn't visit that place in my mind anymore. It doesn't do any good to look back."

Ophelia rose, too, and took a step toward Lida.

The woman raised both palms. "No."

Ophelia froze in place.

Lida smiled the saddest smile Ophelia had ever seen. "You're a kind woman, Ophelia Overly, an' I know you want to help me. But I'm not like the girls who come here. I'm an old woman already. Maybe not in years, but in livin'. There's nothin' anybody can do for me. Can you erase what's been? Can you make it so it never happened? Do you even want to, considerin' your son came about because of it all?"

Lida hung her head, her shoulders sagging. "I'm glad I met Ephraim. Glad I got to see for myself how he turned out. He's a man who'd make any mama proud. But stayin' here just ain't gonna work. As soon as I can walk up an' down them stairs without puffing like a steam engine, I'll go." Her gaze drifted to

Ellie, who still slept soundly, a peaceful smile curving her lips. "This little one'll be glad to get in her room again. Sometimes she stands outside the door an' looks in at me with those big, sad eyes of hers." She turned a determined look on Ophelia. "I've caused enough sadness for folks. Can't change it for none of the others, but my leavin' will at least bring a smile back to this little gal's face."

Without warning, she lunged forward and grabbed Ophelia in a breath-stealing embrace. The hug lasted for no longer than the minuscule time between heartbeats, and she let go as abruptly as she'd taken hold. She scuttled several feet away and peered at Ophelia over her shoulder. Tears winked her eyes. She whispered, "Thank you . . . for everything." Then she went upstairs without another backward glance.

Ophelia sank onto the chair. The sandwiches remained on the tray, untouched. She should have told Lida she needed food if she wanted to gain strength. She should have told her there were no lost causes as far as God was concerned. She should have told her to reach for hope. But the woman's heartbreaking questions had rendered her silent. The bitter utterances repeated in Ophelia's mind.

*"Can you erase what's been? Can you make it so it never happened? Do you even want to, considerin' your son came about because of it all?"*

Ephraim was the silver lining from the darkest period of her and Isaiah's lives. Doctors said because of her heart, she'd never enjoy motherhood. Yet she'd been gifted with a precious son. Watching him grow into a talented musician who loved the Lord and honored his mother and father had brought her more joy than she'd known a body could hold. Was it fair that she'd been so blissfully happy when poor Lida spent those same years in misery?

She bowed her head, battling a wave of guilt. She'd told Ephraim that he was proof God restored what the locusts had eaten, but she hadn't told him why. Maybe it wasn't her story to tell. She would pray about it. Until God gave clear direction, she must keep Lida here.

# Chapter Twenty-five

## Ephraim

Saturday morning, even before the sun had cleared the horizon, Ephraim exited his cottage and headed for the house. He generally didn't rise so early the morning following a revival. He doubted any of the girls would be up yet. The group hadn't gotten back to Hope Hill until almost eleven o'clock. But Father never slept in, no matter what time he went to bed. And Ephraim needed a few quiet words with him. He needed his father's counsel.

Father had considered yesterday evening's revival a glowing success. Nearly a hundred people had attended, with folks from all three of the town's churches joining together on the school's side yard. Although only four people made first-time proclamations of faith, more than a dozen committed to serving more faithfully. Eight of those were men. Father rejoiced over every soul won, but if a husband or father came forward, his joy multiplied. When the leader of the home served the Lord, Father always said, the next generations would be impacted for good. Sometimes Ephraim wondered why Father had chosen to devote his adult life to rescuing women when it was men who frequented the brothels. Wouldn't he do more good by going after them? But he'd never ask. There were some subjects a son didn't want to address with his father.

The large crowd had been generous when the offering bucket made its rounds. Ephraim couldn't ever recall a time when they received almost seventy-five dollars in a single night. Father had praised God the entire way home. He was probably still praising God upon waking. Ephraim didn't want to put a damper on his father's joy, but there was one part of the revival that, in his opinion, hadn't gone well at all. He thought he knew how to make sure the next one, which would take place in Robinson the first Friday in May, went better. In his mind, they needed to settle on his plan immediately. They had only two weeks to incorporate the change. But he valued Father's input. If Father didn't think it wise, Ephraim would squelch the idea.

Just as he reached the back stoop, the door flew open. He staggered backward, hands outstretched to keep his balance. "Whoa!" involuntarily left his lips.

Lida Holland came to a stop on the stoop, still holding the door wide. Her gaze lit on his, and a blush filled her face. She propped the door with her hip and crisscrossed her flannel robe over her nightgown. "I'm sure sorry. I didn't expect to see a soul out yet." Then she frowned. "Why're you up already? Seems like, late as you all rolled in last night, you'd still be snoring."

Ephraim swallowed a chortle. To his knowledge, he never snored. "I wanted to speak with Father before everyone else awakened. It's hard to find a quiet moment with him with so many other people around."

"I reckon so." She squinted at him, as if taking aim. "You've always had to share him an' your ma with a passel of others, haven't you? That ever bother you?"

Ephraim thought before he answered. He didn't want to tell an untruth. He scratched his temple. "Maybe some, when I was ten or so, but mostly it's just been the way it is. I haven't thought much about it."

"Never been jealous? Felt neglected?"

Was she interrogating him? Why was she so curious about his childhood? He shrugged. "I suppose I might have from time to time." What child didn't sometimes wish his parents did things differently? "But I can't complain. I've always been loved. My needs were always met. I've been treated well." As he said it, the accuracy of his words settled deep in his heart. "I'm more fortunate than many others."

She stared at him through narrowed eyes for several seconds, then gave a little huff. "Your pa's at the dining room table. He's got a pot of coffee right close an' his Bible open. But I don't reckon he'll see you as an intrusion." She stepped off the stoop and marched past him.

Ephraim chuckled to himself and went on. He never knew what to expect from the woman. He found Father exactly where Lida said he'd be. He hesitated in the doorway for a moment, wondering if he should interrupt. But already he heard stirring upstairs. If the girls were waking, his opportunity would escape.

He took a step into the dining room. "Father?"

Father looked up. His face lit. "Ephraim, come in." He gestured to his Bible. "I was reading Psalm 20, King David's psalm about deliverance in battle, and thinking of you."

"Oh?" Ephraim pulled out a chair and sat. "Have I been to battle?"

Father laughed. "Yes, and you still are, whether you know it or not." He shifted the book and pointed to verse four. "See? 'Grant thee according to thine own heart, and fulfil all thy counsel.' This is what I've been praying for you for the past weeks—that God would reveal His will to you and you would find fulfillment in following it." He closed the Bible and fixed Ephraim with a serious look. "Have you experienced any prompting in your soul concerning what you're to do next?"

Although he'd been praying about where he was to serve separate from Hope Hill's ministry, the Lord hadn't yet spoken loudly enough for him to hear. "Not about a new ministry, but I did receive a prompting concerning the current one."

Father folded his hands on top of the Bible. "Tell me about it."

Unexpectedly, tears pricked behind Ephraim's eyes. If only every child had a father so attentive, so willing to listen, what a different world it would be. "Last night, I was disappointed in the choir's performance." He cringed, remembering the faulty entrances and fumbled lyrics. "I realize we've recently lost several longtime members. The newest ones to join haven't had as much practice, and last night was their first time to perform. But even so, I would judge their performance as . . . clumsy. It was"—he hung his head—"embarrassing."

"Did you do your best, as unto the Lord?"

Ephraim's head came up in response to Father's somber query. "I think we did. And I can't decide if that makes things better or worse. Our best didn't bring Him the honor you expect. Nor the honor I want to give."

"Ah, but keep in mind the Lord can take even the most paltry of offerings and use them for His glory when they're given in sincerity of heart." Father angled his head and raised his brows in a thoughtful expression. "Was sincerity lacking?"

Ephraim scrunched his face the way Ellie did when she tasted something tart. "No. They were sincere. But woefully lacking in polish."

Father laughed and squeezed Ephraim's wrist. "You're too much a perfectionist sometimes. You come by that honestly. My father was a perfectionist. He wanted everything just right every time. It's not always realistic, though, especially when, as you said, some of these girls are very new to singing in a choir."

If only every girl sang like Birdie. What a choir he would have then. "I think it would be better if I didn't have to play the organ while they sang. They need someone giving direction, bringing them in at the right time, and mouthing the words to help them remember the lyrics."

"Well . . ." Father stroked his mustache. "I suppose we could send the music ahead to the minister sponsoring the revival. He could ask someone in his congregation to play for the choir and allow you to direct."

"I want to direct," Ephraim said, "but unless we practice beforehand with the accompanist, we'll have the same result. It will feel . . . unpolished. We all need to practice together multiple times for the performance to be its best. So I wondered if—"

The back door smacked into the casing. Lida Holland was returning from her morning visit to the outhouse . . . and possibly from smoking a morning cigar. He'd spotted a couple of butts in the rubbish bin. Slight splashing noises told Ephraim she was washing her hands. He turned sideways in his chair and watched the wide doorway. She passed by without glancing into the dining room. The thud of her plodding steps marched up the stairs. She was out of earshot.

He faced Father again. "I wondered if you would ask Lida to play for the choir and allow me to direct. At least until the Robinson revival. By then, hopefully, the new girls will have a better grasp of the music."

For a full minute, Father stroked his mustache, his gaze aimed somewhere beyond Ephraim's shoulder and his finger trembling slightly. Finally he lowered his hand and looked into Ephraim's face. "Son, I think it's a fine idea. But I'm not going to ask Lida. Until which time you move to your new vocation, you are the music director here at Hope Hill. If you want her to accompany the choir, you need to ask her yourself."

Ephraim watched all day for an opportunity to take Lida aside and ask her if she would accompany the choir. He anticipated possible reasons she'd refuse—she wasn't a good enough pianist, or she didn't plan to stay at Hope Hill, or she didn't think folks would appreciate a brothel owner helping at a revival. He planned his rebuttals—she was a better pianist than some with whom he'd attended college classes, he only wanted her to commit for preparation for the Robinson revival in two weeks, and what better place for a former brothel owner to be than a revival?

He hoped that last argument wouldn't come up. Unfortunately, there were people who would find fault with her participation. Some folks opposed the girls singing in churches because of where they'd worked. But he needed her if the new girls and the previous girls were to meld into a quality choir.

After supper, he observed her going out the front door. Was she planning to sit on the porch and watch the sunset? If so, the peaceful view might be the perfect setting for their talk. He paced back and forth in the music room for several minutes, allowing her time to settle, and then he followed. To his surprise, she wasn't alone. Birdie was there, too, with Ted lying at her feet. If it was anyone else, he would excuse himself, but he trusted Birdie not to run upstairs and repeat the conversation to the other girls.

Lida had taken Mother's rocker, and Birdie sat on the bench in front of the parlor window. He could sit beside Birdie. The bench accommodated two people. Wouldn't it be a fine way to end a day, sitting beside Birdie as the sun slipped below the horizon? But he didn't want Lida raising her eyebrows at them. He grabbed one of the chairs from the far end of the porch and brought it over, then sat.

"Do you ladies mind me joining you?" He hoped his smile looked relaxed.

Lida rocked, the chair squeaking against the porch board. "It doesn't bother me. I was just tellin' Birdie here some of the mischief her ma an' me got up to when we were no bigger'n Ellie. We were friends in school."

Ephraim shot a quick look at Birdie, then focused on Lida. "Is that right?"

"Mm-hm. Dorcas an' me were like this." She crossed her fingers and held them up. "We did everything together, including singin' in a young folks choir at the church. Well, that's to say, she sang. I played the piano for 'em."

Ephraim's ears perked up. This might go easier than he'd thought. "That's interesting."

"Back then," Lida went on, "we was both in church every Sunday mornin' an' every Sunday evenin' an' any other day there was something goin' on. I think I might've surprised Birdie when I told her that."

Birdie turned an uncertain look in Ephraim's direction. "For as far back as I can remember, Mama never went to church. Papa took me some when I was little. And he asked Mama to go, too, but she got so mad at him when he talked about it, he quit asking." She frowned. "She was always mad at church. Even at God, I think. Papa told me she lost several babies before I was born and that's why she never really let me get close. Out of fear of losing me, he said, and being hurt again. I always thought she blamed me for living when the others didn't. Maybe she blamed God for those lost babies, too." She shifted to Lida. "Do you know if that's why she was so angry?"

Lida glanced at Ephraim—an almost embarrassed glance. "I can't know for sure. By the time she married your papa, her an' me had parted company. But I can tell you, her bein' mad went back before she was married. She got mad about something that happened to me." She swallowed, and the rocking chair slowed. "Something that happened in the church. Something that shouldn't have happened. Her bein' my good friend, she took it hard, an' she turned her back on the church."

Birdie's eyes were wide. "What happened?"

Lida shook her head. "Nothin' that matters anymore. It was

a long time ago. But . . ." She paused and pointed at Birdie the way she'd pointed at Ephraim the morning he'd found her playing piano. A commanding gesture. "You remember that not every person who pretends to be good an' helpful *is* good an' helpful. Some people, they're just out to use you. You have to be wily an' figure out who. Don't trust folks right off. It can get you in trouble." Her hand dropped to her lap. "You might've already figured that, seeing as how you came to me for help an' didn't find what you were lookin' for." Her face contorted into a horrible grimace. "You're my best friend's little girl, an' I did you wrong. I regret that now."

It wasn't quite an apology, but the brokenness in her voice and her remorseful expression reflected true contrition. Ephraim watched Birdie from the corner of his eye, anticipating her response.

She sat for several seconds, quiet and almost withdrawn. Then she scooted to the edge of the bench, reached out, and put her hand on Lida's. "That's over and done. Like whatever happened to you and Mama, it's in the past. The Bible says if I want God to forgive me, I need to forgive others. God's already forgiven me for all the wrongs I've done. So how can I not forgive you?"

Ephraim wanted to shout hallelujah. What a kind soul she possessed, as kind and accepting as his mother's. If he searched the world over, he'd never find another woman like Birdie Clarkson.

Lida didn't say a word, but she gave a brusque nod and slipped her hand from beneath Birdie's. She sniffled and rubbed her nose, then set the rocker into motion again. "Well, Ephraim, when you came out here, I reckon you didn't expect to see a show such as that."

He chuckled at her lack of tact. At least he never had to wonder what she was thinking. "No, I didn't. But I'm glad to know a little something more about you—especially that you played piano for a choir."

She waved her hand. "Long time ago."

He internally organized his prepared responses. "But you clearly haven't forgotten what you learned. You proved it by playing the piano here at Hope Hill."

The rocker kept going, but she squinched her eyes. "What're you leadin' up to?"

She was wily, too, and suspicious. He might as well blurt it out. "I have several new girls in the choir who need more direction than I can give from my place at the piano. It would help me a great deal if you would accompany us during our practices."

She chewed the inside of her cheek, still skewering him with her squinted gaze. "I ain't planning on stayin' here much longer."

He laughed softly. "In truth, nor am I. But for as long as I'm here, I'll lead the choir. You don't have to commit to playing for them indefinitely, but let's say . . . for the next two weeks? Could you help that long?"

"What songs? Somethin' I might know?"

"The same ones you've heard coming up through the floorboards."

An amused grin briefly appeared on her lips. She flipped her hands in a gesture of *Why not?* "Considering you saved my life, I reckon I owe you a little somethin'. All right. I'll join your music class." She pointed at him. "Temporarily."

He smiled and leaned forward, propping his elbows on his widespread knees. "Thank you. The Robinson revival is May third. Father said it will be held outside, so we'll make use of the funeral organ. Playing it is a little different than playing the piano, so I'll bring it to the house tomorrow. You can practice on it whenever you like, not just during music class."

All humor fled her expression. "Why would I do that?"

Apparently he hadn't explained things well enough. "So you'll be prepared to play it the night of the revival."

She lurched from the chair as quickly as a frog from a pan of hot water. "No."

He sat up straight. "But—"

"Noooo." She drew the word out, shaking her head. "I vowed I'd never set foot in church again. Your pa's revivals are nothin' more'n fancified church. Not even for you, Ephraim Overly, will I play at a revival."

# Chapter Twenty-six

### Birdie

B irdie paid little attention during the Sunday morning worship at Hope Hill. Reverend Overly's powerful and heartfelt delivery always commanded full focus. Ordinarily, she wanted to listen, to learn, to grow in faith. But she couldn't push aside the odd statement Ephraim had made when speaking to Lida on the porch the evening before. He said he wouldn't stay here much longer. Where was he going? And why hadn't he told her he planned to leave?

They talked during the daily drives back and forth to Tulsey. Twice a day—taking her to work and picking her up from work—they rode for half an hour, just the two of them. And not once had he said anything about leaving Hope Hill. Maybe it was foolish, but it hurt her feelings to have found out about it in such a backhanded way. He told her he liked her. Didn't that mean they were friends? He should have told her. Would he leave before she had enough money for her train ticket? As much as she loved the Overlys and had grown accustomed to the other girls, Hope Hill wouldn't be the same without his piano playing. Without his cheerful whistle as he went about his outdoor duties. Without his presence across the dinner table. Without *him*.

Foolish, yes. Maybe even childish. But she didn't want him to go before she did. Somehow it would be all wrong.

Reverend Overly asked Ephraim to conclude the worship service by leading them in "Amazing Grace," one of Birdie's favorite hymns. She pushed all aggravation at Ephraim aside and allowed the beautiful words about grace's transforming power to speak to her heart. By the time they finished, she'd lost a bit of the hurt that had held her captive since Ephraim's flippant announcement, and she was even able to give him a genuine smile as she passed him on the way to the dining room.

Lida had stayed upstairs during the service, but she joined them for their simple Sunday dinner. She sat in Harriet's former place next to Ephraim, which put her across the table from Birdie. At first it had bothered her to have the brothel owner directly in her line of vision. The woman had taken her in and then abused her trust. But over the weeks, the Spirit's work in her took effect, softening her toward her former enemy. Now when Birdie looked at her, compassion rose above her resentment.

If Lida and Mama were the same age, then she was forty-two. Not a young woman anymore, but not old, either. Her hard life, though, had aged her. Streaks of gray decorated her thick, dark hair, and frown lines formed deep creases between her eyebrows and along her mouth. Yet, with a narrow thoughtful face, she wasn't an unattractive woman. In fact, when she relaxed and allowed herself to smile a little, she reminded Birdie of—

She jolted and dropped her fork. It clanked against the edge of her plate and bounced onto the table. Conversation ceased, and everyone looked her way. Gladys leaned forward and peered at her past Olga, her eyes dancing with laughter. "Did Olga goose you, Birdie?"

Olga shook her head, placing her hands on her belly. "Nein, I didn't, and neither did this one. I don't know what happened to her."

Birdie gaped across the table, first at Lida, then at Ephraim, then Lida again. Although one was clearly more masculine than the other, their similar features were uncanny. Why hadn't she noticed before? Maybe because she hadn't really examined them side by side, instead trying to avoid looking their way lest she inadvertently communicate bitterness or affection.

Heat filled her face. She picked up her fork and laid it right side up on her napkin, keeping her eyes averted. "I'm sorry for being so clumsy. I don't know what came over me." A bald fib. She did know. But everyone would laugh if she said what she was thinking—*Ephraim looks like Lida Holland.*

Reverend Overly patted Birdie's wrist. "No harm done. Ophelia, do I smell applesauce cake for dessert? Perhaps you and Miss Clarkson would like to serve it."

Bless the man for giving her an opportunity to collect herself. She rose, picking up her plate, and escaped to the kitchen. When Mrs. Overly joined her, Birdie kept the tip of her tongue clamped between her teeth to hold back the ridiculous question plaguing her mind. Were Ephraim and Lida Holland related? Could she be either the reverend's or Mrs. Overly's sister? If so, it would explain their deep concern for the woman. But neither had volunteered any kind of relationship, and it would be impolite to probe.

Birdie and Mrs. Overly placed saucers of cake in front of everyone. Birdie steadfastly avoided looking into either Ephraim's or Lida's faces as she served them. She had just settled in her chair again when a knock on the front door intruded.

The reverend made a mock scowl. "Someone comes now, when I've just been given the best part of the meal?" He chuckled and headed for the hallway. "I'll see who it is. Go ahead and enjoy your cake."

Moments later, the rumble of a man's voice carried into the room. Alberta turned sharply in the direction of the sound. "That's Mr. Fischer." She pushed away from the table. "I hope nothing happened to one of the children." She darted out of the room.

Several others began to rise, but Mrs. Overly waved her hands. "Everyone, stay put. If the reverend needs us, he'll let us know. Eat your cake."

They followed her instruction, but no one spoke above a whisper, and many tilted an ear toward the doorway, clearly trying to hear what was being discussed. After several minutes, the front door clicked closed. Reverend Overly and Alberta returned and took their seats.

"Well?" Gladys stared at Reverend Overly. "Was something wrong?" She glanced at Alberta. "I know I don't work for him yet, but Alberta talks all the time about the kids. It's almost like I already know 'em. Are they all right?"

The reverend put down the fork he'd just picked up. He shook his head, a teasing glint lighting his eyes behind his spectacles. "You won't be able to rest until you know what he wanted, will you?"

A murmur rolled through the room, and although some seemed sheepish, most girls shook their heads. Birdie understood their interest. Living out here away from town and activity, any kind of unusual happening stirred excitement. She was curious, too, what had brought Mr. Fischer to Hope Hill on a Sunday afternoon.

"First of all," Reverend Overly said, "the Fischer children are fine. Mr. Fischer is fine."

A chorus of relieved sighs, Gladys's the loudest, sounded.

"He only wanted me to know he is making some changes and won't have need much longer for the kind of help Miss Kearney's been providing."

Alberta sat up like a squirrel on a tree branch and sent a pert gaze around the table. "He's getting married!"

Gladys's mouth dropped open. "What? But I was going to work for him after you moved to Speegleville."

Alberta set her head at a proud angle. "I know. He said I've done a fine job caring for his house and children." Then she grinned. "But he's lonely. He decided to take a wife." She forked up a bite of cake.

Gladys pushed her plate aside. "Who's he marryin'?"

Alberta shrugged and swallowed. "I dunno. But whoever it is, she's gonna be real lucky. He's a nice man, so kind an' patient with all his kids. And a hard worker, too. That farm he bought was in bad shape, but he's got it fixed up real nice now. If he wasn't so old, I might've tried to woo him myself." She giggled. "And if Bertrand hadn't won my heart."

Bernice rolled her eyes. "Don't get her started talkin' about Bertrand." Everyone laughed, and Alberta popped another chunk of cake into her mouth with a broad grin.

The reverend cleared his throat. "I think we're getting carried away. Mr. Fischer wants to marry, but he hasn't yet found a bride. He intends to put a notice in the paper and asked me to pray for God to direct him to a local widow. Now that we know the details of the poor man's personal life"—titters rolled through the room—"we can set the topic aside, yes?"

Olga aimed a curious look across the table at Alberta. "How old is Mr. Fischer, do you think?"

Alberta swallowed her bite. "Well, his oldest girl is thirteen. She told me her folks got married when they were still young—sixteen and seventeen. They had their first child—you know, the son who died before they came here—pretty quick, too. So that'd make him . . ." She squinched her face in concentration. "Thirty-two or thirty-three, I reckon."

"That's not so old." Gladys sighed and poked a cake crumb with her finger. She looked hopefully at the reverend. "Do you figure he'll find a wife before Alberta gets married? Maybe he'll need some help, after all. I was lookin' forward to workin' there, earnin' some money."

Reverend Overly wiped his mustache with his napkin. "I assured him I would ask God to direct him to the woman intended for him. I won't presume to know God's timetable. But if it happens that your help isn't needed there, we will find a different placement for you." He gave the girl a warm smile. "I know you're eager for your next chapter, too, Miss Long. Be patient, my dear. God will lead you, too."

Some of the girls smirked in Gladys's direction, but Birdie wouldn't make fun of her impatience. Reverend Overly had sent the letter to Aunt Sally almost three weeks ago, and they still didn't have a reply. *When, Lord?* She pushed aside the fretful prayer. She hadn't worked at the post office on Friday. Quitting time was five o'clock, but the choir left for the revival midafternoon. Consequently, she'd not gone in. But Mr. Peterson paid her three dollars on Thursday for her first week's labor. The silver coins were safe under her stockings in the bureau drawer. She'd probably hear from Aunt Sally before she earned the $12.85 she still needed for her train ticket.

Alberta had said Mr. Fischer was patient with his children. Reverend Overly said God's timetable was best. She should be patient and wait.

The reverend laid his napkin aside and smiled down the length of the table to Mrs. Overly. "Thank you for dinner, dear, and most especially for the cake." She gave a gracious nod, and he turned his attention to the girls. "Ladies, please stack your plates in the dry sink, and then enjoy your afternoon."

They all rose, chatting softly, and worked together to clear the table. Birdie had begun the habit of taking her Bible to the second-floor balcony on Sunday afternoons and reading. She looked forward to becoming engrossed in the stories from the Old Testament or Jesus' teaching in the New Testament. Study would remove the worrisome thoughts concerning Ephraim's intentions to leave Hope Hill, the questions she held about the resemblance she'd glimpsed between him and Lida, and the delay in receiving word from Aunt Sally. She headed for the staircase.

Olga scurried up alongside her and caught her arm. "Birdie, can I talk to you?"

Although eager to open her Bible, Birdie couldn't ignore the pleading in Olga's face. "All right."

Olga pulled her into the music room and slid the doors closed behind them. She pressed her clasped hands beneath her chin. "Tell me the truth . . . do you think I would make a good wife?"

The question seemed to come from nowhere, and for some reason it tickled Birdie. She huffed a short laugh. "Why do you want to know?"

Tears flooded Olga's eyes. "Never mind." She took a step toward the doors.

Remorse stung Birdie. She grabbed Olga's wrist, bringing her to a halt. "I'm sorry. I didn't mean to hurt your feelings. Your question surprised me, that's all." She drew Olga to the folding chairs they sat in for choir practice and tugged her down beside her. "Tell me why you want to know."

Olga blinked several times. She cupped her belly, a habit she'd developed as the child within her rounded it more and more. "I think I want to keep my baby."

"Oh, Olga!" Birdie grabbed her in a hug. "I'm so happy. I've hoped you would."

Olga wriggled loose. "But I can't take care of it all by myself. I have been thinking and thinking about what to do . . . and then, when Mr. Fischer came, I wondered . . ." She bit her lip, her eyebrows tipping together. "Alberta said he's kind and patient with his children. Do you think he would be kind and patient with my child, too, and . . . with me?"

Birdie took Olga's hands. "I think he would if he's the kind of man Alberta described. But, Olga, do you not want to marry a man who loves you? Don't you want to love him first? I worry you might feel cheated if you marry only to be taken care of."

Her jaw jutted. "I would take care of him and his children, too. It wouldn't only be for me."

Birdie squeezed her hands and let go. "You're kind, too, and I know you'd take good care of him, his family, and his house. But you're also very young. Do you want to pledge yourself to a man who already has five children? Remember you told me you grew up in a crowded house and felt"—what were the words she'd used?—"crammed in. You'll surely feel crammed in at the Fischer house. I've seen it. It's not very big, and there are already a lot of people in it."

Olga cocked her head. "More people than here?" She sighed. "When the doctor came and took care of everyone who got burned, Mrs. Overly asked him to examine me, too. He predicts this baby will come sometime in late June or early July. If I keep it the way I . . . I want to . . ." Tears welled and slipped down her cheeks in silvery trails. "I have to get married."

Birdie sat quietly, uncertain how to advise her friend. Something else Olga had said their first night at Hope Hill tickled the back of her mind. She'd said maybe God orchestrated the timing of Reverend Overly's visit to Lida's Palace to save her baby. Had God sent Mr. Fischer at this time to provide Olga with a way to keep her baby? Excitement stirred within her. Hadn't she thought at Mrs. Fischer's funeral that Olga's German background would make her fit well in the Fischer household?

She stood. "Olga, let's go talk to Mrs. Overly."

"Now? She's probably resting."

Yes, she probably was, but if Olga's baby was coming so soon, there wasn't time to wait. "She won't mind. Come." She moved to the doors and hooked her fingers in the carved grooves, prepared to open them. Olga still sat on the chair, staring open-mouthed at Birdie. Birdie laughed again. "Do you want to get married or not?"

Olga hunched her shoulders and nodded.

"Then come."

Finally, Olga stood and crossed to the door. She wrapped Birdie in a short hug. "Thank you. If I do marry Mr. Fischer, I hope you will stand with me. We've come this far together. It wouldn't feel right to take that next step in my life without you."

Birdie had to be honest. "If I'm still here, I will gladly stand with you."

Hand in hand, they headed down the hallway toward the Overlys' room where Mrs. Overly often retired on Sunday afternoons. Birdie couldn't help thinking about how different it would be if Olga married right away. Olga wanted to leave, Ephraim said he was leaving, and even Lida planned to go soon. It shouldn't matter, because she was going to Kansas City, but somehow the thought of so many leaving—the way Mama had—made her sad. But now wasn't the time to think about herself. Olga was the important one.

They reached the door. Birdie looked at Olga. "Are you sure?"

Olga gave a firm nod. "I am."

Birdie knocked on the door. "Mrs. Overly? It's Birdie and Olga. May we come in?"

# Chapter Twenty-seven

### Ophelia

O phelia dabbed tears with her embroidered handkerchief. She always cried at weddings. Such a beautiful thing, witnessing two lives joined into one. Although the wedding was outdoors in Hope Hill's front yard instead of in a church, it was perfect. The day was calm and warm, with a few cottony clouds floating across the cerulean sky. Olga looked so at peace in a simple pale peach dress, a bouquet of bluebonnets dribbling over her hands and gracing the round mound of her growing babe. What a blessing that Arthur Fischer viewed the coming infant as a gift. He'd told Isaiah, "The Lord giveth, and the Lord taketh away. He took my Marta and our unborn *kind*, but now He fills the empty places they left behind." Yes, Ophelia had no doubt he would take good care of Olga and the baby.

Some of her tears today, though, weren't for Olga and Arthur Fischer. Her gaze drifted to Ephraim, seated at the funeral organ in readiness for Birdie's solo. He was already twenty-six years old, six years older than Isaiah had been when he pledged his life and love to Ophelia. When Ephraim left Hope Hill, would God lead him to the Christian woman for whom Ophelia had been praying from the time he was an infant? She wanted so much to see him fall in love, to witness him stand before God and those who loved him and pledge faithfulness to his wife, to watch the two grow together and become parents, to hold a grandchild before she went to her Maker. Would she live long enough to be part of her son's happy future?

During the week of preparing for Olga's marriage to Mr. Fischer, she'd suffered another attack. Not as severe as the one in February. She'd managed to hide this one from everyone, including Isaiah. Mainly because he was so busy counseling Olga and Arthur and preparing the message he was now sharing at their ceremony. But the pain had sent a strong message. She didn't have time to spare.

*Please, my loving and gracious Father, let me see my prayer for Ephraim fulfilled.*

As she listened to Arthur declare his promise to love, cherish, and keep Olga, she imagined Ephraim making such a vow. The mere thought brought a fresh rush of tears.

"Olga?"

Ophelia turned her focus to the bride and groom, but her Isaiah standing so proudly in front of them captured her attention. The tenderness in his eyes as he looked at the young woman reminded Ophelia why she loved her husband so much. He truly cared about the girls they rescued, as much as he would his own daughters had they been so blessed. She slid her arm around Ellie, who sat beside her swinging her bare feet. If Ellie's mother never returned, Isaiah might someday escort the daughter of her heart to her husband. But Ophelia didn't allow herself to imagine witnessing it.

"Do you take this man to be your husband, to love, comfort, honor, and keep him through sickness and health, to cleave only to him until death parts you?"

Olga pulled in a full breath, then said, "I do," on an airy sigh.

Isaiah offered a barely discernible nod, then glanced at Ephraim. Ephraim pumped the pedals on the funeral organ. The instrument wheezed in response, and his fingers played the opening notes of the song Olga had asked Birdie to sing.

Birdie remained beside her friend, looking at the bride and groom, as she sang, "*Führe uns, himmlischer Vater, führe uns . . .*"

Ophelia didn't understand German, but she recognized the tune. The choir had sung the hymn as written in English. The opening words, *Lead us, heavenly Father, lead us,* were perfect for a couple starting out on a new pathway together.

Birdie's beautiful soprano rang sweet and true. Ephraim's playing supported rather than overwhelmed her voice. Ophelia's gaze shifted back and forth between the singer and the accompanist, and she suddenly realized Ephraim wasn't watching the music score tied with twine to the organ's fold-up music desk or even his fingers on the keys. His gaze was locked on Birdie. And his expression . . . She'd seen that rapturous look before. On Isaiah's face the day they wed. Ophelia drew a sharp breath. Was Ephraim in love with Birdie?

The song ended. Isaiah introduced the couple to the small gathering as Mr. and Mrs. Arthur Fischer and invited the husband to kiss his wife. Their kiss was a mere peck, indicative of their fledgling relationship, but Olga's pink-splashed cheeks and Arthur's shy smile hinted that seeds of genuine affection had already been planted.

Ophelia and the girls had prepared a wedding dinner, which everyone enjoyed picnic-style at makeshift tables and benches under the midday sun. The Fischer children and Ellie chased Ted in the yard and gathered handfuls of wildflowers, which they delivered to Olga. By the time the Fischers were ready to leave, the children had collected almost a bushel basket of wilting flowers. Olga insisted on taking them all with her.

As a group, the residents of Hope Hill walked Olga and Arthur to his waiting wagon. He helped Olga up onto the driver's seat, then lifted each child by turn into the back. The smallest ones he swooped through the air, earning a cascade of giggles. He peered over the top rail, ascertaining all were accounted for, and then he pulled himself up on the driver's seat and settled next to Olga.

He sent a grateful look down at Isaiah. "*Danke* for the special day you make for us."

Isaiah reached up and shook the man's hand. "You're welcome. Bless you all."

Arthur nodded, then turned to Olga. "*Sind sie bereit?*"

Olga flicked a nervous look at Birdie, but the nod she gave Arthur held assurance. "*Ja*, I am ready."

They all waved as the wagon carried Olga away. Then, in pairs or trios, the girls ambled toward the house. Ellie trailed them, Ted prancing at her side. Ephraim picked up the organ. Birdie trotted over to him and took the stool. Side by side, they followed the girls.

Lida heaved a mighty sigh. "I guess that's that, then." She shuffled slowly across the lawn well behind the others. Soon only Ophelia and Isaiah remained on the trampled grass under the Texas sun.

He slid his arm around her waist and pressed a kiss on the crown of her head. "Are you tired?"

She emitted a rueful chuckle. "Immensely."

"Let's take you in and you can rest while the girls clean up the yard and prepare our supper." Isaiah urged her into motion.

They moved slowly, him tempering his strides to match her shorter ones, as he always did. So considerate was her dear Isaiah. She stopped and turned slightly, placing her hand on his jacket directly over his heart. "Isaiah, will you promise me something? Well, two somethings, I suppose." Another thought intruded. "Maybe three."

A slow smile pulled up the corners of his mustache. "Three, hmm? How about I withhold my agreements until I know for sure what you're scheming."

She laughed lightly. "No schemes, but . . ." She licked her dry lips. "Arthur needed a wife to help him raise his children. Obviously our situation is different, but we're responsible for guiding and directing young lives. When I'm gone—"

"Ophelia." His tone carried mild censure.

She curled her fingers around his suit lapel and gave a gentle tug. "Just listen, please. When I'm gone, you will need a partner for the continuation of this ministry. I saw you with Olga today. I know how much you care about these girls and what happens to them. Who will care for them and direct them to better pathways if Hope Hill closes for good? I couldn't bear it if this ministry dies because my heart wore out."

He gazed down at her with his thick brows tipped together and lips pressed tight.

"First, promise you'll keep the doors open. If that means taking another wife, promise you won't feel guilty about doing so." Her chest expanded as she smiled at his dear, stern, worried face. "You're a wonderful man, and any woman would be blessed to share her life with you."

His grim brow relaxed, but he still didn't speak.

She went on. "Second, please consider talking with Ephraim. I saw something in his eyes today when he was watching Birdie sing. I think he might be feeling more for her than he realizes."

Isaiah drew back slightly. "Would you disapprove if that's the case?"

"Of course not." Ophelia yanked his lapel for emphasis. "Birdie is a wonderful girl. But her desire to move to Kansas poses a mighty obstacle to formulating a relationship. Unless he's willing to go to Kansas with her." Her chest panged. Was it possible to miss someone even before they were gone?

"I'll have a talk with him," Isaiah said. "Now, let's get you inside."

She held her position. "There's one more thing."

Isaiah tilted his head, his concern evident. "Can it not wait?

The weariness shows in your eyes, my dear. You need to rest before you collapse."

"I'll rest soon enough." She hoped he didn't read her hidden meaning. "When you talk to Ephraim . . ." After all these years of carrying their secret, would it do more harm than good to divulge it now? But shouldn't he know before he pursued a marriage relationship?

"You think he should be told about his conception."

How well Isaiah knew her. She nodded, seeking his eyes for hints of his thoughts.

"I've been praying about that for weeks—years—already. Ever since we took up residence in this house." Pain laced his voice. "To tell him means sharing my greatest shame. I'm not worried about what he'll think of me. I deserve whatever rancor he might hold. But I don't want him to view himself differently afterward." He let his head drop back for a moment, then peered into her face again. Tears winked in his grayish-blue eyes. "Do you know what Birdie told me before she accepted Christ's forgiveness? She said she couldn't stand looking at herself in a mirror. It disgusted her to glimpse her own reflection. I saw the anguish in her face and heard it in her voice. Her view was skewed by someone else's sins." A tormented groan left his throat. "I don't want my son to bear that kind of burden. I don't want him buried beneath the weight of iniquities not his own."

Ophelia cupped Isaiah's cheeks, his thick whiskers creating a pleasant tickle against her palms. "He loves us. He might be surprised and upset for a while, but when he's had time to think and pray, he'll remember how much we love him. I believe that, Isaiah."

He gathered her against him and pressed his face into her hair. His mustache caught and pulled some tendrils, but she didn't mind. She clung to him, silently praying for God to guide his words, to prepare Ephraim's heart, to lay the foundation for healing in both men's lives.

He let go and set her gently in front of him, then lifted her chin with two fingers and placed a lingering kiss on her lips. "I love you, Ophelia Marker Overly. If I had the chance to start over and live my life anew, I would choose you. Again and again and again."

She rose on tiptoe and pecked his mouth. "I wouldn't let you choose otherwise. I love you, and I love our life together." She didn't want to leave him, but at least she could go without regrets.

He sucked in a long breath that expanded his chest. His gaze drifted to the house. "You asked me to promise three 'somethings.' I promise I will pray and then address 'somethings' two and three. But . . ." He tapped the cleft in her chin. "You, my dear, are irreplaceable. The second half of 'something' number one is not open for further discussion. Now, let's go in."

### Birdie

Birdie lay in her bed and stared out the window at the night sky. She had enjoyed the view since her first night at Hope Hill, but tonight it made her melancholy. How quiet and lonely the room seemed without Olga.

But she might not be lonely for long. Reverend Overly had announced at suppertime that he and Ephraim were planning an evening visit to a brothel in McGregor. "An empty bed at Hope Hill is an opportunity to impact another life," he'd said, his expression and tone as fervent as when he preached to an audience. He would wait until after the revival in Robinson, though, so Ephraim wouldn't miss a day of practice with the choir.

Birdie counted in her head the number of open beds. Olga, Reva, Harriet, and Iris were already gone. Ruth, Florence, and Anna from Lida's Palace had taken some of those places. But soon Alberta and Birdie would be gone, too—Alberta to Speegleville with her Bertrand, and Birdie to Kansas with Aunt Sally. That meant the reverend could rescue three girls. Or four, if Ellie returned to her own room. Then someone could share with Lucretia.

Mrs. Overly had asked the girls to pray for the upcoming revival, for souls to respond to the Spirit's call, and also for the girls living in the McGregor brothel, for them to choose freedom. Birdie spent several minutes in fervent prayer. She wanted every girl who worked in a brothel to find what she had—freedom from shame, freedom from sin, freedom to call God her Father and Jesus her Savior.

She rolled her gaze toward Olga's bed. Its quilt lying smooth over the mattress seemed odd after so many weeks of seeing the form made by Olga's frame beneath it. She heard in her memory Olga's breathy "I do" as she agreed to be Mr. Fischer's wife.

"I do," Birdie whispered in the quiet room. She'd said *I do* when Reverend Overly asked if anyone wanted to leave Lida's Palace for freedom. She'd said *I do* when he asked if she believed Jesus died for her. Two tiny words, but so life-impacting.

Her eyes slid closed, tiredness finally taking hold. *I do . . .* Would she ever use them to pledge herself in matrimony? An image of Ephraim danced in her mind's eye, and then sleep claimed her.

# Chapter Twenty-eight

## Ephraim

Ephraim held his cupped hand out at shoulder height, his eyes closed, and counted slowly to eight. Then he gave a brisk swish, pinching his fingers together, and the note the girls had been holding fell silent. Perfection . . .

He opened his eyes and clapped, smiling broadly. "Excellent, ladies, excellent." Having someone else accompany while he directed made such a difference. Being able to instruct them to swell their voices or lower to a gentle hush gave emotion to the songs. He slid his hands into his trouser pockets and bounced his smile at Lida before facing the girls again. "No offense to the former members who've gone on to other pursuits, but that was the best I've ever heard the Hope Hill choir sing."

The girls giggled and exchanged proud smiles.

It probably also helped that Birdie was in attendance today. Their need to depart by two o'clock for the Robinson revival meant she had to stay home from her job at the post office. Although she no longer attended the daily practice time, she and Lida met in the music room each evening so Birdie could learn the songs. Ephraim was torn between appreciation for the women's dedication and jealousy that he wasn't the one meeting with Birdie. But the two of them still had their daily drives to and from the Tulsey post office on her workdays. He savored those minutes, storing up little moments the way he used to collect pretty rocks in a discarded cigar box, so he could take them out and enjoy them at later times.

He glanced at the clock. Ten minutes remained before music time officially ended according to the schedule. He usually kept it, knowing how important structure was for these girls. But it wouldn't hurt to end a little early today since they'd be singing again this evening. And he needed a few minutes alone with Lida.

He strode to the door, speaking as he went. "Please remember to be on the lawn no later than one forty-five this afternoon. For now, you are dismissed." He slid the doors open, then moved aside while the girls exited the room. Birdie trailed out last, and he detained her with his extended hand. "Thank you for the extra time you've put in on your own, learning the new song."

She gave a tiny shrug, a shy smile forming. "I didn't mind. It's a lovely hymn." She sang, "'Rock of Ages, cleft for me, let me hide myself in thee . . .'" She sighed, her eyes briefly closing. "I am so glad I know the Rock of Ages and that He is ever with me. I'm never alone."

He sensed a bit of sadness beneath the admission. "You miss Olga."

She ducked her head for a moment, then met his gaze. "Yes."

He should probably ask Father before making plans, but at that moment bringing a smile to her face was more important than anything else. "When I drive Mother and some of the girls to Tulsey tomorrow for shopping, come along. I'll drop you at the Fischers' on the way. You can enjoy a visit with her."

Joy exploded on her sweet face. "Thank you, Ephraim!"

He chuckled, her happiness giving him joy. "You're welcome." She left, her steps light, and he watched after her, pleased at having brightened her countenance. The sound of a clearing throat startled him, and he turned toward the piano. Heat rose up his neck. How could he have forgotten Lida was in the room?

She stood and came from behind the piano, a knowing glint in her blue eyes. "You're fond of the girl, aren't you?"

Ephraim scuffed his toe against the floorboard. Two weeks ago, he might not have answered. But working together each day on music had guided them into an unusual yet oddly comfortable kind of friendship. Ephraim heard himself admit, "I reckon I am."

She laughed, the sound not as coarse as it had been the first weeks after the fire. Her throat was healing. "No need to hang your head about it. Birdie's a pretty girl, an' the way she sings . . . I can see why somebody who likes music as much as you do would like her."

Ephraim sheepishly nodded. He liked her too much, he was afraid. He'd told Father the same thing the Sunday evening after Olga's wedding when Father asked Ephraim about his feelings toward Birdie. Father's demeanor that evening had troubled him—he seemed more burdened than usual. When Ephraim questioned him, though, he said he needed more time in prayer before discussing the other topic. He ended their brief discussion by assuring Ephraim neither he nor Mother held any qualms about Birdie herself, but he should diligently seek the Lord's guidance concerning his future helpmeet. Ephraim promised he would. And he had. He'd also prayed for whatever grave concern Father carried. He hoped it didn't have to do with Mother's heart.

Lida released a soft huff, drawing Ephraim from his thoughts. "Almost seems a shame she doesn't plan on stayin' around here. I think you an' her could be real happy together, an' not only because of music. You two just seem to . . ." She rolled her eyes upward, as if seeking inspiration. "Fit."

He'd expected a more ostentatious word. But his curiosity was piqued. "Why?"

The wily smile he'd seen before—one corner of her lips lifting as her eyes narrowed slightly—returned. "Oh, it doesn't really matter what I think." Her forehead pinched, and her sly expression cleared. "What matters is what you an' Birdie think. But if you wanna know what I'm thinkin' right now . . . that choir o' yours is gonna miss Birdie as much as you will when she leaves for Kansas. Her singin' in it makes a heap o' difference."

Ephraim wouldn't argue that point. "Let me tell you what else makes a heap of difference." He'd never touched Lida, but he wanted her to fully grasp the truth behind what he was about to say. He placed his hand on her shoulder, not to keep her in place but to connect with her. "Having you at the piano."

She rolled her eyes and muttered, "Pshaw," but she didn't move away.

Ephraim lightly squeezed her bony shoulder and lowered his hand. "Don't belittle yourself. I knew I wasn't giving enough direction from my place at the keys, but not until the past two weeks did I realize how much *heart* these girls were capable of bringing to life through song." He swallowed, aware his next words could bring a burst of anger. "Mother and Ellie are going along with us to Robinson today. Will you please come, too, and play for the choir?"

Her expression hardened.

He pretended not to notice. "The girls need you. *I* need you." He pulled in a breath of fortification and added, "Please?"

Indecision danced in her eyes. She chewed the inside of her lip, and her chest rose and fell the way it had when she'd lain in the grass the morning of the fire. She opened her mouth, and he prepared himself for a denial.

"All right. I'll come."

Ephraim's mouth fell open. He tried to close it, but he ended up flapping his lips like a fish gasping for air. Finally, he squeaked out, "You will?"

She gave him a withering glare. "If you're gonna act like a ninny about it, I might change my mind."

He laughed. "I'm sorry. I just— You—" He shook his head.

He'd witnessed a miracle. He smiled so big his cheeks hurt. "Thank you."

"You're welcome," she grumbled. She started skirting past him, but he put out his hand and she stopped. "What?" The barked query didn't invite conversation, but Ephraim had to tell her.

"You said Birdie and I fit together in part because of music." She offered a slow nod, her eyes slipping into a squint.

"Well, the same could be said for you and me. Thank you for playing for the choir." His voice caught, an expected wave of emotion sweeping over him. "It means a lot to me."

She stared at him for several seconds, expressionless, then a strange sound left her throat. A sob? She pushed past him and ran out of the music room. Her slippered feet slid as she careened around the corner, and for a moment he feared she might fall. But she caught herself and threw the front door open. She exited, then yanked the door closed behind her with a resounding *bang!*

Bernice hurried to the parlor doorway, a feather duster gripped in her hand. She gaped at the door. "What was that all about?"

Ephraim shook his head. He didn't know. And he didn't know how to fix it.


Ophelia

Ophelia jolted, nearly knocking herself from her rocking chair. The lap quilt she'd draped over her legs when she'd settled in the chair a half hour ago slid to the dusty porch floor, and she released a little grunt of aggravation. She grabbed it up, then turned her frown in the direction of the person who'd rudely disturbed her nap.

Lida Holland stood at the edge of the porch glaring across the grounds with her arms wrapped around herself. Agony pulsed from the woman's tense frame.

Ophelia's annoyance faded in a heartbeat. She pushed from the chair, crossed to Lida, and placed the quilt around her shoulders like a mantle. "What's wrong?"

Lida's jaw muscles quivered. She blinked rapidly. "I . . ." She spoke through gritted teeth. "I can't stay here another day."

Ophelia guided Lida to the rocking chair and urged her onto the seat. She pulled the bench closer and sat, then placed her hand on Lida's knee. "Tell me why."

Lida flung an accusatory glower at her. "You know why."

*Ah. Ephraim.* Ophelia sighed. "It must be hard for you."

"Hard?" The word blasted out on a harsh note. "Oh, lady, *hard* doesn't even come close."

Ophelia hung her head. She'd hoped playing the piano again would be healing for Lida, but maybe it had only raised ugly, long-buried memories to the fore. "I'm sorry."

Lida grasped the edges of the quilt and pulled them tight against her chest. "As soon as I woke up an' saw him next to me in the yard at the old hotel, I should've saddled a horse an' rode for San Antonio. No, as soon as the three o' you moved back to Tulsey an' took up residence not three miles from the old hotel, I should've hightailed it out o' here." She glared at Ophelia, but hurt shone behind the fury. "Why'd you all have to come back?"

"We didn't have a choice." Ophelia sat upright. "Citizens in Gatesville came to our front door one evening with torches and threatened to burn us out if we didn't leave. We left that very night. In Waco, people did more than threaten. Merchants there refused to do business with us. Townsfolk threw rocks through our windows, painted horrible messages on the side of our home, even attacked Isaiah on the street. We couldn't stay when faced with such opposition."

Lida flopped against the rocker's back and groaned. "So you had to leave. But why'd you come here?"

A sad smile pulled at Ophelia's lips. "Because this is where God planted us."

Lida angled her head slightly and glared with slitted eyes.

Ophelia nodded. "It's true. This wonderful, big property safely outside of any town but near to many towns was the perfect place for girls to recover, relax, and be reborn. We didn't come here to torment you, Lida, but I believe God used the people in Gatesville and Waco to propel us to the place we were always meant to be. And . . ." Maybe Lida wasn't ready to hear it, but Ophelia might not have another chance to share what she'd been thinking for the past month. "Maybe He used the fire at the old Bradford Hotel to bring you where you needed to be to recover, relax, and be reborn."

Lida snorted. "Those're real pretty words, Ophelia, an' I don't doubt a bit God has His hand on you. But He let loose o' me a long time ago." She shrugged, assuming a flippant air that Ophelia didn't believe for one moment. "Or I flung Him loose. Either way, like lots o' other things, that's long past. Can't do anything about it now."

Tears stung Ophelia's eyes. "There are many things that can't be changed. What happened to you when you were young is one. What you've done in the years since then is another. But, Lida, God isn't bound by minutes and hours and years. He is eternal. He remembers the decision you made to follow Jesus when you were a girl. He's been waiting all this time for you to turn around and take one step in His direction. He will run with open arms and embrace you again. You only need to ask."

Ophelia closed her eyes and implored the God she and Isaiah had asked persistently—even insistently—for the past twenty-six years to draw Lida to Him. She'd once served Him, faithfully attending church and using her God-given skill as a pianist to bless the congregation. God did not forsake His own. Ophelia's Bible told her so, and she believed it. She'd seen His redemption fall on countless broken souls over the years. So many victories. But she couldn't rest until this one bitter woman sitting next to her found her way to Him again. She begged God to help Lida see that He wept, too, over the selfish choice made by a fallen man and the heartache it had caused her.

The chair rungs creaked. Something soft and warm drooped across Ophelia's legs. She opened her eyes. Her quilt lay rumpled in her lap, and Lida was at the edge of the porch, staring across the grounds again. Ophelia put the quilt aside and crossed to Lida.

Lida glanced at her with watery eyes. "Ephraim asked me to play that little organ he carries from place to place at tonight's revival. I'd already told him a while back that I wouldn't do it, but he asked me again. He's got some stubborn in him. Kinda like the mama who raised him." She glanced at Ophelia again, and Ophelia met the brief peek with a smile. Lida faced forward and sighed. "I'm gonna play tonight. I want him to remember me fondly when I'm gone. But what I said about leavin'?" She turned her head and looked sternly into Ophelia's eyes. "It's time."

Ophelia opened her mouth to protest, but the steady beat of horses' hooves on the road interrupted. The rider was bent low over the horse's neck, and the animal pounded at a full gallop.

Lida pointed. "Must be an emergency of some kind."

The rider turned the horse at their lane, and the animal galloped clear up to the porch. Ophelia pattered down the steps and greeted him. "Is something wrong? Can we help you?"

"No, ma'am." The young man pulled an envelope from inside his jacket and held it out. "My pa sent me with this. He said that girl of yours who cleans at the post office has been watchin' for it. He didn't want her to hafta wait clear 'til Monday to get it."

Ophelia's heart gave a little leap. Finally. Birdie's aunt had sent a reply. "Oh, yes, Birdie will be so happy. Please thank your father for her."

"Will do, ma'am." He tipped his hat, then yanked the reins, whirling the horse toward the road. He left at the same speed he'd arrived.

Ophelia shook her head as she climbed the steps. "I hope he doesn't spill that poor animal." She gently waved the envelope. "I'm sorry to leave you right now, Lida. There's much more I'd like to discuss with you, but Birdie has been so eager to hear from her aunt. Can we talk a little later?"

Lida shrugged. "Talk all you want. You won't change my mind."

Despite herself, a little laugh escaped. "From where did Ephraim get his stubborn bent?"

Lida rolled her eyes and thumped off the porch.

Ophelia crossed to the door. As she went, she glanced down at the envelope she held. Her feet stumbled to a stop. She pressed her fingers to her quivering lips. *Dear Lord, no . . .*

# Chapter Twenty-nine

Birdie

Birdie entered the parlor, seeking Florence. The girl was supposed to help set the table, but she had a tendency to disappear when it was time for chores. Ellie was in the parlor, sitting on the middle of the sofa bouncing her rag doll on her lap. "Ellie, have you seen Florence?"

The little girl went on playing as if Birdie hadn't spoken.

Bernice came down the stairs, and Birdie asked her the same question. Bernice huffed. "No. But if you can't find her inside, she might have gone out. I heard the door slam a little while ago."

"Thank you." Birdie crossed to the door, opened it, and started onto the porch. She nearly collided with Mrs. Overly. Birdie took one look at the woman's wan face and pain-furrowed brow and forgot all about Florence. "Ma'am! Are you all right?" She pulled Mrs. Overly into the house and guided her to the parlor. "Please, sit down."

Ellie scooted to the other end of the sofa, staring wide-eyed with her doll clutched to her chest the way Mrs. Overly clutched the envelope. Birdie pressed Mrs. Overly onto the sofa cushion. "Would you like me to fetch you a cup of water?"

"No. No, I'm fine."

But clearly she wasn't. Birdie crouched before her and bobbed her head toward the envelope. "Did you receive bad news?"

The woman's eyes slid closed. Her lips quivered. She nodded.

Birdie patted her knee. "I'm going to get you some water." She started to rise.

Mrs. Overly grabbed her hand. "It is bad news, Birdie, but it isn't *my* bad news."

Birdie slunk back down and sat on the edge of the low table in front of the sofa. "What do you mean?"

"A young man just delivered this." She turned the envelope. "The post office in Kansas City returned the letter we sent to your aunt."

Birdie lowered her gaze to the envelope. *DECEASED—Return to Sender* was scrawled across the bottom. For a moment the room spun. She grabbed the missive and held it closer, hoping she'd misread the note. But no, she'd seen correctly. Aunt Sally was dead. She let the envelope drop to the floor and buried her face in Mrs. Overly's lap. Sobs shuddered through her.

Gentle hands stroked her head, and she heard Mrs. Overly murmur, "Shhh, shhh, dear Birdie."

Then another voice added a soft, "Shhhh . . ." Small hands took hold of Birdie's head and lifted it. Tears made her vision blurry, but she recognized Ellie gazing at her with her little face puckered in sympathy. "Shhhh," she said again.

Mrs. Overly put her shaking hand on Ellie's tousled curls. "Are you sad for Birdie? Do you want to comfort her?"

Ellie nodded and wrapped her arms around Birdie's head and gently rocked her to and fro. Birdie rested her cheek against the child's chest and allowed the ministrations, sorrow for her loss and joy at the slight sound Ellie had uttered mingling into a tumult of emotion. She brought her tears under control and gently extracted herself from Ellie's thin arms. She cupped the little girl's sad face between her palms and placed a kiss on her forehead.

"Thank you, Ellie. That's exactly what I needed. I feel better now."

Ellie seemed to search her face, then scooped up her doll, placed it in Birdie's hands, and scampered out of the room. Birdie, with the doll cradled in the crook of her elbow, shifted from the floor to the sofa. She stared at the envelope lying on the carpet.

Mrs. Overly slipped her arm around Birdie's waist. "I'm so sorry, my dear."

Birdie sniffed hard. "I am, too." For so many reasons. She didn't even know when Aunt Sally had died. Where was she laid to rest? What had happened to her shop? What was Birdie to do now? She had no family. She whispered raggedly, "I'm truly alone."

Ellie returned to the parlor, pulling Ephraim by the hand. She drew him to the end of the sofa, then let go of him and pointed at Birdie. He sent a puzzled look from Ellie to his mother, and then to Birdie. It lingered on Birdie. "Father told Ellie to fetch you all for dinner, but she dragged me out here instead. What's wrong?"

Mrs. Overly shooed Ellie with her fingers. "Go and have your dinner, sweetheart. We'll be in soon." Ellie obeyed, but she scuffed her feet as she went. Mrs. Overly looked up at Ephraim. "The letter we sent to Birdie's aunt was returned. According to the note written on the envelope, the woman passed away."

Ephraim hurried to the other side of the sofa. He sat and gazed at her with such sorrow, tears filled Birdie's eyes again. "I'm so sorry. Do you want to stay here this evening instead of going to Robinson? If so, I understand."

She'd forgotten about the revival. Would she be able to sing "While I draw this fleeting breath, when mine eyes shall close in death" without breaking down? But everyone from Hope Hill was going. Except Lida Holland. "I . . ." She swallowed. "Maybe I'll stay here with Lida."

"Lida is going with us. She said she would play for the choir.

*Tonight.*" He glanced at his mother, his eyebrows briefly rising in a silent message. "But maybe an evening to yourself would help."

How? The question screamed in her brain, but she didn't voice it. She hugged Ellie's doll to her chest. "I don't want to stay alone."

"Then you want to come?"

Mrs. Overly reached past Birdie and touched Ephraim's knee. "I think Birdie is still in shock. She needs a little time to accept what's happened. Let's go to dinner and give her some quiet now." She kissed Birdie's cheek and stood. "We'll let the reverend and the others know about your aunt. I'll save a plate for you. You can eat when you're ready."

Birdie nodded, the lump in her throat stealing her ability to thank her.

Ephraim rose slowly, his sympathetic gaze pinned on her. "I'm very sorry for your loss. I will ask God to comfort you."

They left, and Birdie sat with Ellie's doll, her thoughts reeling. Grief pressed down on her, but also anger. A fierce anger that frightened her. Wasn't it enough that all her siblings died at birth, that Papa died, that Mama ran off? Why did God take Aunt Sally, too? Only an hour ago she'd told Ephraim how grateful she was for the Rock of Ages because it meant she'd never be alone. Had God decided to test her commitment by delivering the news of Aunt Sally's passing? Oh, if only she still had her dream of going to Kansas to sustain her.

She curled on her side on the sofa and pulled Ellie's doll beneath her chin. The child's scent was caught in the doll's fabric. She inhaled, reliving the feel of Ellie's arms holding her close, remembered her soft *Shhhh* . . . A fleeting thought formed in the far reaches of her numb mind. Maybe God was using Birdie's sadness to draw Ellie from her self-imposed bubble of silence. If so, would losing Aunt Sally be worth it?

\* \* \*

As he'd promised, Ephraim dropped Birdie at the Fischer farm on his way to Tulsey on Saturday morning. She stood in the yard and watched the wagon roll away. Nearby, two barefooted little boys busily carved in the dirt with garden trowels. Beside the house in a patch of sunshine, the Fischer girls pulled wet clothes from a basket and draped them over a line strung between wobbly poles. None seemed a bit interested in Birdie's arrival.

She turned toward the house. A little face peered at her from the other side of a windowpane. Birdie waved, and the face disappeared. Moments later, Olga waddled out of the house directly to Birdie with her arms open wide. Birdie dodged holes and ran to meet her. Olga rocked back and forth as she hugged tight, reminding Birdie of Ellie's sweet comfort. Hugs felt so good.

Olga pulled loose and pushed a strand of hair away from her round face. "I'm surprised to see you. Don't you have work to do?"

The girls looped arms and ambled toward the house. "I do, but the Overlys are being very kind to me right now because"— her throat went tight—"we found out my aunt died."

Olga stopped and gaped at Birdie. "Oh . . ." She grabbed Birdie in another hug, then led her into the house. She pulled out a chair at a crumb-spattered table and invited Birdie to sit. She sat in another chair. "How did it happen?"

The child who had peeked out at Birdie toddled to Olga and lifted his arms. Olga pulled him into her lap. He sucked his middle fingers and stared at Birdie. Birdie stared back. How quickly Olga had adapted to motherhood. For reasons Birdie didn't understand, seeing Olga and the littlest Fischer boy so at ease together gave her hope for herself.

She cleared her throat. "I don't really know. Reverend Overly sent a letter to Aunt Sally's shop. The letter came back, un-opened, and someone had written *deceased* on the envelope. So I don't know when she died, how, or anything else."

Olga smoothed the tuft of hair poking up on the child's crown, clicking her tongue on her teeth. "Will you still go to Kansas and run her shop?"

Birdie drew back. "Run her shop?"

Olga frowned. "Is there someone else in the family who will run it?"

"There is no other family."

The little boy squirmed. Olga set him on the floor and deliv-ered a light pat on his backside. "Go play with your blocks." She watched him patter to the corner and crouch in front of a pile of wood pieces, then turned to Birdie again. "Did she own her shop or rent it?"

Birdie recalled snippets from the letters Aunt Sally had sent Papa. "She owned it. Aunt Sally lived above the shop. The whole building was hers."

"Well, then, it has to be bequeathed to someone. Did she be-queath it to you?"

Birdie shrugged. "I don't know."

"You need to find out." Olga sounded so sure of herself. "It could very well be the shop is now in your name. If that's so, you could live there. Or you could sell it and use the money however you please."

Birdie released a huff of disbelief. "How do you know about these things?"

Olga flicked crumbs from the table. "My oldest sister mar-ried a man who worked at a bank. He helped people establish trusts. She married him because she figured someone so smart about money would have lots of it. We had very little when we were growing up." She wiped her hands on her apron. "But I didn't like him. He talked to her like she was stupid. No amount of money is worth being treated that way."

Birdie hoped Olga wasn't giving a hint about her own situation. "Are you treated well here?"

A smile brightened Olga's face. "Ach, ja, Arthur is good to me. There's always a lot of work to do, but the children help. I am content with my decision." She sat back. "So tell me what is happening at Hope Hill. Have any new girls come yet?"

Birdie told her about the revival in Robinson last night, how Lida had played piano for the choir and how the audience clapped louder than she'd heard before. "I didn't think I'd be able to sing, I was so sad about Aunt Sally. But somehow the words comforted me. Aunt Sally is at peace now, with God and with Papa." She shared Reverend Overly's plan to visit a brothel in McGregor and invite girls to leave that life behind. "So there might be some new girls coming next week. I hope some do." She teasingly poked Olga on the arm. "It's very quiet and lonely in my room now without you."

Olga laughed. "But what if you get a girl like Iris moving in with you? Then what will you think?"

"I better find out if I can go live in Aunt Sally's building in Kansas City."

They laughed together. The children came in, and Olga asked if they remembered Birdie from the wedding day. Although shy at first, they warmed up quickly, and Birdie enjoyed becoming better acquainted with Olga's new family. She wanted to get to know Arthur, too, but by the time the Overlys' wagon returned, he still hadn't come in from the field.

Olga walked Birdie to the wagon and exchanged a few words with Mrs. Overly, Ephraim, Bernice, and Gladys. Then she hugged Birdie again. "Please come see me whenever you can. If you're still here in July, you'll want to meet the newest little

Fischer. Arthur says he hopes this one is a *Mädchen*. If it is, I will name her Elizabeth, for you, Birdie."

Birdie gasped. "For me? But why?"

Tears winked Olga's eyes as she rubbed her belly. "If you hadn't been brave enough to leave Lida's Palace that night, I wouldn't have gone. This baby wouldn't be born. I am grateful to you, Birdie. I wanted you to know." They hugged again, long and hard. Olga whispered in her ear, "Ask Reverend Overly about your aunt's shop. Find out if she left it to you."

"I will."

Ephraim unfolded the step to the bed and helped her in. As he slid the gate into place, he sent her a hopeful half smile. "Did you have a good visit?"

Birdie nodded.

"And you feel a little better now?"

It would take a while for her heart to heal from the unexpected loss, but she did feel better. Olga had given her hope that maybe there was still something waiting for her. Not a person, as she'd wanted for so long, but an honest way to provide for herself. She could still hold on to her dream about going to Kansas.

# Chapter Thirty

Ephraim

S unday morning, Father led the Hope Hill residents in a worship service. Ephraim led the singing, as he always did, but he missed being able to simply direct. As much as he enjoyed playing piano, the weeks with Lida accompanying the choir had shown him his real passion lay in directing singers' voices to bring life to the words of the song. A hazy idea had begun taking shape in the back of his mind. Though the concept was far from fully developed, he trusted God would bring it to life, just as his hands did with a song when he stood before a group of singers.

Father had mentioned before the service started that he'd like to speak with him in his study after dinner. Ephraim presumed it had to do with their planned trip to McGregor. But when Father closed the door behind him, signaling the desire for privacy, his stomach quivered in unnamed trepidation. He remembered their last private conversation in Ephraim's cottage concerning his feelings about Birdie, and the odd sadness Father seemed to carry. He sensed he would soon know what troubled his father, and he sent up a silent prayer for God to bolster him, whatever the news might be.

"Have a seat, Ephraim." Father gestured to one of the side chairs in front of his desk.

Ephraim sat, and Father took the second one instead of sitting in his desk chair. Ephraim couldn't recall a time, ever, when

Father didn't take his position behind the desk. His pulse skittered. He blurted, "You have bad news."

Father's mustache twitched in a sad smile. "I have news, yes."

"Is it about Mother?" Myriad emotions danced in Father's eyes, increasing Ephraim's angst. "Father, please, just say whatever it is."

Father hung his head. "I wish it were that simple." He sighed, then straightened and met Ephraim's gaze. "But for you to understand, I must first tell a story. Will you be patient and listen?"

So often during Ephraim's growing-up years, when Father wanted to tell him something important—why people were unkind to them, why they had to move to another town, why their family continued in a ministry so many opposed—he had presented the situation in story form. The practice reminded him of Jesus telling parables. Ephraim settled into his chair as he'd done when he was a boy, ready to listen.

"You already know that your mother and I grew up in Tulsey. We went to school and church together. We were good friends long before we became sweethearts."

Ephraim nodded. He'd heard this before. "And you both sang in the church choir under your father's direction." He'd always known his love for and talent in music came from his grandfather.

"Yes, that is right." Father lifted one finger. "But there is more to this story." He linked his hands in his lap, his grip tight. Tense. "For a time, a very young accompanist played for our choir. A girl only thirteen years old. You know her—her name is Lida Holland."

Ephraim jolted, his spine connecting with the back of his chair. Lida had played for his grandfather's choir? Why hadn't she told him this?

Father nodded, as if Ephraim had spoken. "My father called her a prodigy. Never a lesson, yet at that young age she could play anything by ear. He took it upon himself to teach her to read the notes, and she blossomed under his tutelage. Her reputation spread, and the townsfolk speculated that she would one day be a famous pianist, comparable to well-known composers such as Chopin or Liszt."

Was this a true story, or was Father spinning a tale? Ephraim didn't doubt Lida's ability. He'd heard it for himself. But how could someone with such potential end up owning a brothel? He wanted to ask, but Father went on without pause.

"Suddenly, when Lida was sixteen, she stopped coming to church. She stopped coming to choir practice. She even stopped going to school. Before long, rumor spread . . . she was expecting a child outside of wedlock." Father's chin began to quiver, and his knuckles glowed white. "Our minister visited her, insisted she confess with whom she'd lain, but she refused. Her name was stricken from the church membership list, and she became a social outcast."

Ephraim had always known his parents had personal reasons for opening their home to prostitutes and women pregnant outside of wedlock. But he hadn't known until that moment where it all began. Lida Holland's plight had launched their ministry. He also understood why Father had visited Lida's Palace more often than any other brothel in McLennan County. He'd hoped to rescue Lida. And now, because of the fire, Lida resided under their roof. Beauty from ashes, Mother would say.

A smile grew in his heart, and he couldn't stay silent. "How you and Mother must praise God that, after all these years, she is no longer selling herself."

Father gave a solemn nod. "We do. We've prayed unceasingly for Lida's heart to be restored to the Father. But there is more to this story, and I ask you to listen." He unlinked his fingers and placed a trembling hand on Ephraim's wrist. "Listen, Ephraim, with your ears and with your heart." He closed his eyes.

Ephraim waited quietly. He was sure Father was praying. For himself? For Ephraim? Maybe for Lida. Father's eyes opened, and the love shining there nearly took Ephraim's breath away.

"Mere weeks before Lida's child would make its entry into the world, she knocked at our back door. The hardness in her face both frightened and saddened me. How much the girl whose eyes had shone with joy when she played piano had changed. She told us that the person who'd fathered her child was familiar to us. He was"—Father drew a shuddering breath— "my father."

Ephraim's heart seemed to skip a beat.

"She gave no details of the relationship, and I didn't ask for any. I didn't want those pictures in my head." Father's face contorted into a horrible mask of agony. "But, deep inside, I knew it was true. I'd seen things, little things I'd dismissed as an instructor's affection for a prized pupil. Those things rushed back in that moment, and I knew Lida was carrying my father's child." A ragged sigh nearly doubled him forward. "Until my dying breath, I will carry regret for my inaction. Had I spoken up, maybe . . ."

Ephraim couldn't sit quiet and do nothing to ease his father's pain. He shifted to the edge of his chair and put his hands on Father's knees. To his surprise, they were quivering. His always strong father was falling apart in front of him. Such a burden of guilt he bore. He choked out, "Father, you—"

Father shook his head, the motion desperate. "Listen. Listen."

Ephraim pressed his hands more firmly, stilling his father's tremble, and listened.

Father laid his hands on top of Ephraim's, bringing his face near. "She wanted money." His voice lowered to a raspy half whisper. "If we paid her what she asked, she wouldn't tell anyone else what m-my father had done. The entire town knew that Ophelia's parents had recently died and left a large plot of land to her, which we'd sold to a rancher. So Lida knew we had money. She also knew I was training to be a preacher. The scandal could affect my reputation, end my ministry before it even started. Despite her young age, she wasn't a fool. She knew to come to me."

Ephraim's chest swelled with compassion for the mistreated girl Lida had been, thrust into a heartbreaking place not of her own making. But to bribe Father? Threaten him? Father hadn't deserved to be held accountable for someone else's foul choices, and Ephraim started to say so.

"She wanted something else, too."

The shift in Father's tone—a hesitance coupled with pain—silenced Ephraim's planned words of defense.

"She wanted us to find a home for her baby. It was, after all, my half sibling." Father swallowed. "I had no responsibility toward *her,* she told me. But given my relationship to its father, I had a responsibility toward *it.* I told her I would give her the money, and I would see to the child, too."

Long ago, Ephraim's parents had developed a relationship with an orphans' and foundlings' asylum in Austin. Many of the babies born to girls who'd come to them over the years were adopted out of that asylum. Had Ephraim's aunt or uncle been the first child his parents took there? Maybe Father had recently reconnected with the child and wanted Ephraim to meet him or her.

"At the time Lida came to us, Ophelia and I had been married for almost four years. I knew even before I asked her to be my wife that she had a weak heart. She'd told me about the family curse and that doctors said her heart wouldn't survive the stress of pregnancy and childbirth. She begged me to court someone else who was strong enough to bear my children."

Ephraim frowned. This part of the story didn't seem to connect with the previous part. Then a chill attacked his scalp. Or did it?

"But I loved her, and I assured her I would be happy the rest of my days as her husband and God's servant. I didn't need fatherhood. I meant it, but . . ." Wonder seemed to bloom in Father's moist eyes. "God had a different plan for us."

Ephraim bolted backward, yanking his hands from Father's and grasping the chair's armrests to keep himself in place. "Am I . . . I . . ." He couldn't ask it. Did he even want to know?

Father sat up, too. Slowly, by increments, as if his spine had grown rusty and stiff. "Ophelia had accepted her plight, yet at the same time she held to hope that one day she would cradle a child in her arms."

Ephraim wished he could plug his ears, but his fingers seemed glued to the chair, refusing to release their hold.

Father's soft, gentle, pleading voice seemed to screech into Ephraim's ears. "Lida gave birth to a baby boy. She brought him to us, and the moment your dear mother laid eyes on him, I knew I wouldn't take him to an orphans' home. We would keep him, raise him as our own. He would be our beloved son." Tears swam in Father's eyes—his beseeching, love-filled eyes. "And he has been."

Mother's comment the day of her attack returned, and Ephraim finally understood what she'd meant when she said he was proof of God's ability to restore what the locusts had eaten. He wanted to take comfort in her words. He wanted to take comfort in the knowledge of their love and devotion to him. Not once in all his growing up had he ever questioned how much they loved him. But knowing now that they'd lied to him by calling him their son created a stab of pain he couldn't process.

He bolted to his feet, pushing the chair backward. "I . . . I need to . . ." What? He didn't know.

Father stood and gripped Ephraim's shoulders. "I'm sorry for not telling you before. We should have. I see the accusation and confusion in your eyes, and it breaks my heart to know how much I've disappointed you. But please understand . . . neither of us have ever seen you as someone else's child. Not even as my half brother. You're our son, Ephraim, in every way that matters, and you always have been."

Ephraim very gently grasped Father's wrists and lifted his hands from their light hold. He moved a few feet away and pulled in a deep breath. "I know you love me. You've proved it every day of my life. But right now . . ." He stifled a groan. "I don't like feeling this way."

"How do you feel?"

Ephraim searched himself. Two words came to mind. "Betrayed. And foolish." He grated out, "Does *Lida* know who I am?"

Father grimaced. "We took the remainder of your mother's money and moved to Waco the same week you were born. We never told Lida we kept you. So she didn't know then. But she knows now, even though we haven't openly talked with her about it. The night we rescued Birdie and Olga, she stared at you. I think she saw herself in you."

Ephraim gaped at his father. "Is that why you had me go in with you that night?"

Father looked aside for a moment. "I suppose a part of me felt it was time she knew. That she saw what a fine person you'd grown up to be. That perhaps you would be the driving force to take her out of that life and seek something better. If not for her own sake, for yours."

Father had tried to use him? The idea didn't sit well. And the accusation she'd screeched at them as they drove away—*Ain't you stole enough from me already?*—finally made sense. As did Father's reluctance to explain it. Suddenly something else occurred to him, and a bitter laugh spilled from him. "I told her we fit together because of music. And she stormed out of the house as if I'd called her a dirty name." He shook his head, anger swelling again. "I must have looked like such a fool."

Father moved toward him, arms outstretched. "Son, I—"

Ephraim flung his hands up. "No." Father stopped, pain furrowing his brow. The expression pierced Ephraim, but he balled his hands into fists and took another step backward. "Not now. I need . . . time."

Father gave a sad nod. "I understand. Take as much time as you need. Ask any questions you want to ask. We will tell you whatever you want to know."

*It's a little late for transparency, Father.* Long-held respect for his parents kept him from uttering the bitter statement. He moved stiltedly to the door. With effort, he opened it quietly, walked down the hallway in a normal stride, and let himself out the back door. He took a dozen steps into the yard, and then the tangle of emotions whirling within him took control. With a strangled cry of anger, pain, and confusion, he broke into a run.

# Chapter Thirty-one

Ophelia

From her bedroom window, Ophelia watched Ephraim race toward his cottage as if the neighbor's prize bull was chasing him. While he and Isaiah met, she'd prayed for Ephraim's acceptance and understanding. But that mad dash from the house spoke clearly. He'd resisted the truth. He didn't understand. Her heart throbbed in self-recrimination and empathy.

The door clicked open, and Isaiah entered. His drawn face and tear-wet eyes stirred another rush of compassion. She hurried to him and wrapped him in an embrace. "I should have been with you when you told him."

Isaiah shook his head against her temple. "No. It was my father's shame. It was my story to tell."

She nestled her cheek against his shoulder. "He's angry?"

His arms tightened around her. "Angry. Hurt. Embarrassed."

She drew back. "Embarrassed?"

"Because Lida knew and he didn't." He sighed, his breath stirring her hair. "Apparently he made a comment to her about their mutual love of music, that it connected them. Lida didn't respond to it well."

Ophelia nodded slowly, recalling Lida bursting onto the porch Friday. "Ah. No, she didn't." She slipped her arms from around his waist and rested her palms on his chest. "She took an empty flour sack from the pantry after dinner. She's upstairs packing the few items we gave her. She intends to leave tomorrow morning."

He frowned. "Where is she going?"

"She said San Antonio."

"How? Her business burned down. She has no means to support herself, does she?"

Ophelia offered a sad smile. "Isaiah, she has never been a foolish person. Do you think she kept her profits in her home with men coming and going at night? I'm sure she has an account at the bank."

Isaiah stepped away from her and paced back and forth, running his hand through his steel-colored hair. "She can't go. Not yet. Not until Ephraim's had a chance to sort through his feelings about his conception. Only she can answer some of the questions he'll have. He needs those answers." He stopped and stared at her for a moment, determination filling his eyes. "We've waited too long, prayed too long, for Lida's recovery from what my father did to her. We can't let her go until she reaches a place of healing. We can't let her go until we know for sure Ephraim is at peace."

Ophelia held out her hands in defeat. "We can't hog-tie her. We've always said people are free to come to and to leave Hope Hill as they choose."

"But—"

She closed the short distance between them and took his hands. "Isaiah, before you speak to Lida, come here." She sat on the edge of the bed, drawing him down beside her. "Let's pray together for both Ephraim and Lida. We want Lida to reconcile with the Lord, and we want them to reconcile with each other before they go separate ways. Let's ask Him, who loves them even more than we do, to work His plan. He knows best how to bring about their reconciliation—with each other, with us, and with Him."

Isaiah cupped her cheek, his expression tender. "You are a wise woman, Ophelia Overly. Yes. Let's pray."

Birdie

Birdie had hoped to speak to Reverend and Mrs. Overly after dinner concerning her aunt's property. But before she had a chance, the reverend closed himself in his study with Ephraim. Then he closed himself in the bedroom with his wife. Unwilling to disturb them, she went to the front porch and settled in Mrs. Overly's rocking chair. Nearly every Sunday afternoon, Mrs. Overly spent time on the porch. Surely she would come out before suppertime. Birdie would talk to her then.

As she'd come to expect, Ellie was wandering in the yard with Ted. Bluebonnets bloomed in profusion, and the little girl had a full fist of them already. Still, she bent and broke off another stem while Ted nosed her hand. She straightened, searching the area as if seeking another perfect bloom, and her gaze met Birdie's.

A rare smile lit the child's face. With Ted at her side, she crossed the grassy grounds and climbed the porch steps. She moved to the chair and thrust out the bouquet.

Birdie placed her fingers on her collarbones and feigned surprise. "For me?"

Ellie bobbed the flowers, her eyes shining.

"Are you sure you don't want to give them to Mrs. Overly?"

Her smile turned into a frown. She pulled back her elbow and then jammed the flowers at Birdie.

Birdie swallowed a laugh. "All right, then." She took the wilting blooms with as much care as she would take a bouquet of greenhouse roses. "Thank you, Ellie. They're lovely." The little girl hunched her shoulders and shook in a silent giggle, her happiness restored. Birdie smiled at the child, and suddenly sadness struck her. She smoothed Ellie's ever-tousled hair and sighed. "You're a very special little girl. I am going to miss you when I go to Kansas."

Ellie jerked away so quickly Birdie wondered if she'd accidentally pulled her hair. Ted skittered sideways, a whine leaving his throat, his dark eyes fixed on the child. Ellie scowled fiercely at Birdie, her eyes spitting fire. Then she snatched the flowers from Birdie's arms, turned, and ran off the porch.

Birdie stood. "Ellie? What's the matter? Where are you going?" The child didn't pause. She darted around the corner with Ted close behind her. Concerned and confused, Birdie followed. She didn't spot Ellie, but she glimpsed Ted's fluffy tail disappearing through the barn's doorway. She lifted the hem of her skirt and trotted after them. She entered the barn and immediately spotted Ephraim saddling Biscuit.

She dropped her skirt into place and moved to Biscuit's stall. "Ephraim, did you see Ellie come in here?"

He nodded in the direction of the deeply shadowed back corner and went on adjusting the saddle strap.

Uneasiness struck. He had the ability to speak, so why use gestures? She examined the stern set of his jaw, his stiff motions, and concern rose within her. "What's the matter?"

He swung himself into the saddle.

She caught the horse's chin strap and looked up at him, her worry increasing. "Ephraim?"

He gritted his teeth. "I'm all right. I just need to get out of here for a while. To come to . . . grips."

She'd never seen him so distraught. Had something happened to Mrs. Overly? "Tell me what's wrong."

"Not now." He leaned forward and bumped her hand. "Please move aside so I can leave."

At that moment, Ellie flew from the shadows and wrapped her hands around Ephraim's boot shaft.

He frowned down at her. "Ellie, let go."

The child grunted and yanked at him.

Birdie stared at Ellie in amazement. Had she just made another sound? She bent down. "Ellie, are you upset with Ephraim?"

The little girl shifted her glare on Birdie.

"Are you upset with me, too?"

Ellie made a near growl in the back of her throat. She smacked first at Ephraim's boot, then at Birdie's arm.

Ephraim swung down from the horse and took the child by the shoulders. "Ellie, you know better than to hit. Shame on you."

Ellie wriggled free. Tears flooded her eyes. She rubbed them dry with her fists and glowered at each of them in turn.

Ephraim put his hands on his hips and aimed his frown at Birdie. "What started all this?"

Birdie thought back to the minutes on the porch. "She gave me some flowers, I thanked her, and then I told her I would miss her when I went to Kansas." She shifted her focus to the angry child. "Then just now, you said you were leaving." Birdie thought she understood. She propped her hands on her knees again, bringing her face to Ellie's level. "Is that why you're upset, Ellie? Because we both said we were going away?"

The child's chin quivered and tears rolled. Birdie reached for her, but Ephraim scooped her up first. She clung to him like a baby bear to a tree trunk, her face pressed into the curve of his neck. He patted her back. "Ellie, sometimes people go away, but it doesn't mean we're leaving *you*."

Birdie couldn't resist touching Ellie's mop of curls. "That's right, Ellie. And no matter where I go, my love for you won't change. You'll always be special to me."

Ellie lifted her head. She seemed to search Ephraim's face, then she looked down at Birdie. Uncertainty pursed her little face.

Birdie nodded, smiling. "It's true. I'll always carry you right here." She placed her palm over her heart. "And you can remember me in your heart, too."

Ellie wriggled, and Ephraim set her on the ground. She scuffed slowly to the corner where Ted lay panting, his watchful gaze never wavering from her. As soon as she flopped down with the dog, Birdie sighed. Her gaze on the child, she said softly, "I feel so bad for her. I know how it feels to have a mother leave you."

Ephraim huffed. "Yes. So do I."

Birdie abruptly faced him, fear flooding her mouth with the bitter taste of bile. "Did Mrs. Overly—"

He grimaced and shook his head. "No. Mother is fine." He blew out a breath. "Well, as fine as she can be given her heart condition. But she didn't die, if that's what you're thinking."

Birdie's knees went weak, her relief was so intense. She staggered to a nail keg and sat. "Thank the Lord." Then she frowned at Ephraim. "If Mrs. Overly is fine, how can you know what it feels like to be left by your mother?"

His expression hardened. He stared toward the barn's wide doorway. "I got left the day I was born. I just didn't know until now."

Birdie slowly rose. "Lida's your mother, not your aunt . . ." She hadn't realized she'd spoken aloud until he jerked his frown at her.

"How did you know?"

Birdie drew back, startled by his angry tone. "I . . . I didn't. But I thought you must be related somehow. You look alike. And then, of course, there's the—"

He snorted. "Music."

She nodded. "Yes."

Ephraim toyed with the reins falling from Biscuit's chin. "I'm such a fool, not seeing it for myself. The truth was right there in front of me, and I didn't see it. Now that I know . . ." He pressed his fist to his forehead, the thin leather strap drooping over his shoulder. "How can I ever face her again? I'm the reason she became a prostitute."

Birdie gasped. "Ephraim, no!"

He flung his hand downward and whirled on her. "It's true. She could have been a concert pianist. She had an amazing gift, evident even in childhood. My father told me about it." He blasted a snort. "My half brother told me, I mean."

She gaped at him, and he nodded, his eyebrows high.

"My grandfather made her with child. Then my half brother and his wife took me in."

Birdie sagged back onto the nail keg, reeling.

He absently stroked Biscuit's neck as he spoke. "The one I've called Father my whole life told me that everyone in town expected her to become someone special. But then she got pregnant with me, and you know what happened from there. Her life changed." He sent her a remorseful frown. "And yours did, too, when your mother's faith was shattered by my grandfather's decision to abuse Lida's trust."

He stepped away from the horse, his movements jerky. "In these past weeks as I've asked God to direct my path, I began seeing myself using music to minister to men." He shifted and faced her, his brow creased. "Think about the hymns we sing in choir, Birdie. The words inspire us to seek Him, obey Him, honor Him, grow in grace and compassion. They invite us to take a closer look at ourselves and the way we think and behave."

He jammed his hands into his trouser pockets and scuffed up bits of hay and dust with the toe of his boot. "Father rescues women who sell their bodies. I've always admired that. But I've also pondered why no one addresses the men who make the purchases? Even the woman caught in adultery was dragged in front of a mob for the purpose of stoning her to death. Why wasn't the man dragged there, too? Wasn't he equally guilty?"

He planted his boot against the ground and drew a breath that expanded his chest. "If the men are convicted about the wrongness of their actions, they won't seek illicit relationships with women. And prostitution will come to an end. Won't it?"

In theory, he was right. But, as much as it pained her to admit it, she doubted it would happen. According to what she'd read in her Bible, the practice dated all the way back to the earliest civilizations. But that didn't mean it should be ignored. Someone should try to change it.

Ephraim took up digging his toe into the dirt again. "I had the idea of starting a men's choir, using music to soften their hearts and awaken them to their true purpose—honoring God and valuing those crafted in His image. I believed the idea was God-inspired, a worthwhile ministry. I still believe it's worthwhile. But how can I do it now?"

Birdie stood and stepped close. "Why can't you?"

He laughed. "Have you not heard anything I've said? Who would take me seriously? I'm the illegitimate son of a prostitute and fallen church leader. Who am I to tell men they need to change?"

"Who better to tell men they need to change than someone personally impacted by the act of adultery?"

He stared at her as if she'd lost her mind. Then he sighed, his shoulders slumping. "I appreciate your efforts to make me feel better." A small smile pulled at the corners of his lips. "You're a good friend. I'd hoped you might be something more someday. But now, I . . ." He swallowed and turned aside. "I know who I am, and yet I don't know who I am."

She curled her hand around his arm, gazing directly into his confused face. "You are Ephraim Overly, the cherished child of Isaiah and Ophelia Overly, a man who loves God, who uses his gifts to glorify God, and who has no reason to hang his head in shame." She squeezed hard, silently praying the truths she'd come to accept could somehow be passed to him through her fingertips. "You can't blame yourself for someone else's sins, Ephraim. You didn't ask to be conceived in such a way. You aren't responsible for the circumstances of your birth."

"I know you're right." The anguish in his eyes made her want to weep for him. "But I can't help how I feel. And I feel . . . tainted. Unworthy." He swept his fingers beneath his eyes, and then his expression changed. "Did you tell Ellie you would miss her when you went to Kansas?"

Surprised by the sudden change in topic, she gave a puzzled nod.

"But your aunt is gone. Why would you go there now?"

She shared Olga's advice about discovering who was taking possession of Aunt Sally's shop. "If she bequeathed it to me, I'll have a way to provide for myself."

"You need to talk to a lawyer. A lawyer can uncover the details of your aunt's will, if she had one. And even if she didn't, it seems to me that if you can prove you're her only heir, a lawyer could claim the property for you." His tone was flat, almost uncaring, but Birdie didn't hold it against him. He was grieving a loss. "Let me unsaddle Biscuit and I'll walk you to the house. You can talk to F-Father about it."

She stood by while he removed the saddle, put it away, and gave Biscuit some gentle strokes. Then he turned toward the corner. "Ellie, come with us to the house." The child didn't stir. He walked closer. "Ellie?" Then he sent a sad smile over his shoulder. He beckoned Birdie with his finger.

She tiptoed over. Ellie had fallen asleep, her arm draped across Ted's furry form. The dog, however, was awake, his bright eyes flicking back and forth between Birdie and Ephraim.

"He's such a good friend to Ellie," Birdie whispered.

Ephraim nodded. "Yes. He can be trusted to keep her safe." He put his hand on Birdie's lower back and turned her toward the door. "Let's go in. Mother will see to her later."

As they headed to the house, Birdie lifted a hopeful gaze to him and asked what he'd asked her when he retrieved her from the Fischer farm. "Are you feeling a little better now?"

His lips formed a grim line. He didn't answer.

# Chapter Thirty-two

Ephraim

Monday morning after breakfast, Lida asked Ephraim to take her along to town when he drove Birdie in for her job. She needed to empty her bank account. Both Mother and Father asked her to stay. They looked at him with expectancy, silently begging him to make the same request, but he pretended not to notice. The tension hovering over them was palpable. Maybe he would be at ease again when she left.

During the drive to town, Lida and Birdie talked together. As much as he'd enjoyed morning chats with Birdie, he didn't contribute. He dropped Birdie at the post office without giving her his customary wish for a good day. Then he aimed the team for the bank. He parked outside the ostentatious limestone building, set the brake, and hopped down. His soles met the ground and sent a shock up his legs. They felt wobbly as he moved to the back and helped Lida out.

He grabbed the flour sack holding her belongings and held it out, looking everywhere except at her. He didn't want to see a reminder of himself looking back. When he was sure she'd taken a grip on the sack, he let go and started toward the driver's seat.

Her hand landed on his arm. "Wait."

He looked at her hand. His fingers unconsciously curled into a fist.

"I want you to come in with me."

Startled, he lifted his head and met her gaze despite himself. If she planned to give him some money, he'd refuse it. "Why?"

"Birdie said she's gonna hire herself a lawyer to find out if she's got an inheritance waiting in Kansas." She spoke so softly, he had to strain to hear her over the noise of others on the street. "Gettin' a lawyer to take up on her side'll cost dear, an' she doesn't have a lot saved up yet. The longer she waits, the more likely it'll be the courts take control of her aunt's property. I wanna give you some money to pay for the lawyer."

The gesture was kind even if, in Ephraim's opinion, the money she offered was ill-gotten. He should acknowledge the heart behind the gift. He tried, but the words wouldn't form. "I'll wait out here."

Her gaze narrowed, as if she intended to argue. But then she huffed. "All right. Hold this for me, then." She gave him the sack and entered the building.

He sat on the wagon's fold-down step and watched the activity on the street while he waited. Strange how people all went about their business, caught up in their own little worlds. Did any of them sense that his secure world had been shattered? If they knew, would they care? He'd always felt a bit like a misfit by virtue of his parents' associations with former prostitutes, so maybe it was foolish to worry he'd be viewed differently when folks found out he was the product of an adulterous relationship and not born to the reverend and his wife after all. But why shouldn't others see him differently when the truth of his birth had altered the way he viewed himself?

He pushed aside the uncomfortable thoughts and idly drew circles in the dirt with his finger, a way he'd entertained himself when he was a boy. The way Jesus had when the men wanted to stone the woman caught in adultery. He sat up straight, folded his arms over his chest, and watched the door for Lida's return.

When Lida emerged from the bank, she carried a thick leather pouch with a wide flap folded over and tied with string. As she approached him, she sent a nervous look up and down the boardwalk. "I don't wanna open this out here where anybody can see. There's always a few ne'er-do-wells loitering, an' I don't have my pistol anymore."

Ephraim stood and glanced around. He didn't see anyone suspicious, but she was probably better versed in spotting ne'er-do-wells than he was. "Where, then?"

"At the lawyer's office. I'll ask him how much he thinks he's gonna need, an' I'll give it to him. Then"—she pointed at him, the familiar gesture tempting him to grin—"you ain't gonna tell Birdie I done it. She's a proud girl, wants to see to it herself. But I figure I owe her somethin' after the pain I caused her." Tears momentarily winked in her blue eyes, but she blinked fast and they disappeared. She stuck out her elbow. "Help me in."

Too surprised to do otherwise, Ephraim gripped her arm and helped her into the bed. He pushed her sack of belongings farther from the edge, then settled on the driver's seat. As he unlocked the brake and picked up the reins, she called, "Go to the firm on Sixth Street—Turner & Gallagher. Way back when, they helped me buy the ol' Bradford Hotel. I trust 'em to do Birdie right."

Heat climbed Ephraim's neck at the mention of the former brothel, but he gave a stiff nod and drove to the law firm. There, he helped her down and escorted her inside. She insisted he go in with her. He felt conspicuous walking her through the lobby and sitting next to her in the lawyer's wood-paneled office. He sat quietly as she questioned the man about what would be needed to secure Birdie's inheritance, the expected amount of time it would take, and how much it would cost. Despite her lack of formal education and questionable choice of career, she proved herself capable of business dealings. Admiration for her formed in his chest, coupled with the agonizing pondering of what she might have accomplished if she'd never been violated.

Money exchanged hands, she signed an agreement to pay any outstanding balance owed, and then she stood. "I'll be in touch about a further bill, but if it turns out there's somethin' left from what I gave you today, make sure it goes to Elizabeth Clarkson. Don't keep it in your pocket, you hear?"

The lawyer reached across the desk and shook Lida's hand. "Yes, ma'am."

Out on the boardwalk, Lida put her hands on her hips and turned a penetrating look on Ephraim. "I reckon this is good-bye now."

A lump of emotion he couldn't define filled his throat. "I reckon so."

She stuck her hand out, the way the lawyer had done. He took hold, expecting her to shake it, but she gripped it hard. "I didn't figure I'd ever see you again after I gave you to Isaiah all those years ago. Honestly, I wasn't sure I wanted to. Not because of anything you done, but 'cause it'd remind me of what I done."

Didn't she mean what had been done to her? Or maybe she couldn't see it that way.

"But now," she went on, "I'm grateful. Grateful to you for riskin' your life to save mine. Grateful I've had a chance to see how fine you turned out." She blinked some more and sniffed loudly, then let go of his hand. "You take care o' yourself an' stay on the narrow path like your ma an' pa taught you. Don't be straying on that path of destruction. There's a lot of regret to be found there."

Her advice sounded like something Father had told him when he went off to college. But how odd to hear it from her lips. Or was it? She certainly understood the path of destruction. She must care about him at least a little to want to spare him burdens of regret. He nodded. "Yes, ma'am." He glanced over his shoulder. They were in the middle of town, a good distance from the train station. "Can I drop you at the station?"

"Nah." She pulled the flour sack from the wagon bed. "I ain't gonna board a train totin' this. I'll do some shoppin' first, buy me a decent travel bag." She looked up at the sky and sighed. "It's a pretty day. It'll do me good to walk." She pinned her gaze on him for several seconds, her lips pursed and eyes squinted, as if she was taking aim. Or memorizing him. Then she gave a little jolt. "Bye now, Ephraim Overly." She turned and ambled off, the sun glinting on her crown of braids.

That evening after supper, for the first time since he returned from college, Ephraim didn't go with Father on a rescue mission. Guilt smote him as he watched the wagon roll away with Father all alone on the driver's seat, but he feared the hours on the road. Father wouldn't be able to stay silent. And Ephraim didn't want to talk. His guilt increased when Father came to the breakfast table Tuesday morning with a swollen eye and his spectacles missing.

The girls gasped, and Bernice said, "Gracious sake, Reverend, how'd you get that?"

Father touched his cheek and grimaced. "A fellow did not take kindly to me coaxing girls to leave the McGregor brothel. But I shall not be deterred. My eye, given time, will heal. Those girls will not unless they're removed from that den of iniquity."

After breakfast, Ephraim overheard Father tell Mother he wanted to go back as quickly as possible. "Two girls seemed ready to leave," he said, "but the man's behavior frightened them into staying." Ephraim couldn't bear to look at his father the rest of the day. If he'd been along, maybe the man would have thought better about attacking him. But then, maybe not. Both he and Father had been accosted at Lida's Palace. Still, the idea that he'd let Father be injured by his refusal to go weighed heavily on him.

On Wednesday, when he took Birdie to town for work, the postmaster was waiting on the bench outside the building, reading a newspaper. He gestured Birdie inside, then jogged to the side of the wagon and squinted up at Ephraim. "I've got a message for you from the preacher of the Methodist church. A family in the congregation lost their twelve-year-old son to fever. He wondered if you would do a hymn or two at the funeral on Friday. It'll be at the church cemetery, ten in the mornin'."

He'd need to switch music time to the afternoon, but he'd done it before when funerals were in the morning. He shook his head sadly, thinking of the family's tremendous loss. Although playing didn't bring him as much pleasure as it had before he knew from where he'd inherited his skill, he couldn't refuse such a request. "Please tell him we'd be happy to, if you'll let Birdie take the morning off from work."

Mr. Peterson looked aside. "Well, now . . ." He rolled the paper and bounced it against the top edge of the wagon bed. "They didn't ask for the singer. Only the organ player." He aimed a sheepish look at Ephraim. "Seems the folks didn't want someone who'd . . . er . . . worked where she worked to sing at their boy's service."

Indignation rolled in Ephraim's chest. What would the boy's parents say about him if he told them about his illegitimate beginnings? Would they tell him not to play? "That's absurd." On both counts.

"It chaps my hide, too, Ephraim." Mr. Peterson gave the wagon one more solid smack with the paper, then tossed it into the bed. "She's a good worker. I knew her pa's family way back when, an' she comes from good stock."

Ephraim winced.

"But you know how folks can be."

Yes, he did.

"An' since they're grievin', we gotta give 'em some extra grace."

Even though they offered no grace to Birdie? *Love thy neighbor as thyself.* The biblical reminder helped him hold the question inside. He gave a quick nod. "Please let the minister know I'll be there. I'll choose something comforting for the family."

Mr. Peterson reached up and shook Ephraim's hand. "You're a good man. God'll bless you for your kindness." He went inside.

Ephraim flicked the reins and called, "Giddap there, boys." As he drove toward Hope Hill, Mr. Peterson's final comment—*God'll bless you for your kindness*—rang in his mind. Would He bless Ephraim even after his less-than-charitable thoughts concerning the parents' feelings toward Birdie?

He'd left his hat behind this morning, and the sun heated his head and shoulders. The breeze teased his hair. The wildflowers dotting the landscape drew his eye. The scents of spring on the prairie filled his nostrils. He'd been taught that his ability to enjoy his senses was a gift from God—a blessing. He'd always believed in God's blessings thanks to his parents' teaching and example. What would he believe if he'd been raised by Lida? What if Father had delivered him to the orphans' asylum, as they'd originally planned? Would he have been adopted into a good family, or would he have languished there?

There was no way to know what could have been, but he did know what was. He was loved by Isaiah and Ophelia Overly. Shouldn't that be blessing enough to overcome the ugly feelings the truth of his birth had planted in him?

Alone on the prairie with no ears to overhear save Red's and Rusty's, Ephraim looked skyward. "God, I've been taught my whole life that You are good. That You are love. That You have a purpose for every life born, and that purpose is to be in fellowship with You. I knew my purpose when I thought I knew who I was—the son of Isaiah and Ophelia Overly. But I'm not their son. I don't reckon it should change my purpose or who I am, deep down, but it does. And I don't know how to get me back. I don't know if I can do what I felt called to do when I'm not me."

Tears blurred his vision. He swiped his hand over his eyes. "You're the God of miracles. I've seen You change the hearts and lives of girls who were on, as Lida called it, paths of destruction. So I know You can change these feelings inside of me. Will You do it, God? Will You help me be Ephraim Overly again?"

# Chapter Thirty-three

## Ophelia

Ophelia donned her formal black dress and rode to Tulsey with Ephraim and Birdie on Friday morning. She had always attended the services when Ephraim played at the graveside. When he said he would be playing for the Burke boy's service, she didn't ask if he wanted her to go. She told him she was going. To his credit, he didn't even bat an eye.

Given the distance between Hope Hill and the Methodist church, she'd suggested the evening before that it made more sense for her to go along when Ephraim delivered Birdie to work and stay in town until the funeral. Isaiah asked what they would do with themselves in the two hours between Birdie's work time and the service, and after a bit of discussion they decided she and Ephraim could do the usual Saturday shopping and trading a day early.

So now she sat in the back of the wagon with Birdie, enjoying the morning breeze and anticipating some precious only-the-two-of-them minutes with Ephraim. Ever since Isaiah told him the truth of his conception, he had kept his distance except for meals, not even coming to the house for their evening Bible reading. She'd prayed for him. Had given him time to think. Now it was time to talk. Just as she hadn't given him an opportunity to deny her presence today, she wouldn't give him a chance to shut her out. Time was fleeting. She wouldn't waste it.

They left Birdie at the post office, and then Ephraim drove to the mercantile. He helped her out, then told her very politely to stand aside while he carried in their items for trade. The comment stirred her ire, and she caught hold of his jacket sleeve and yanked.

He stared at her, his eyebrows high.

"Ephraim James Overly, if you talk to me like that again, I don't care how old you are, I'll wash your mouth out with soap."

His jaw dropped open. "What did I say?"

" 'Please step aside, ma'am, so I may access the goods.' " She imitated his formal tone as she quoted him. She glared at him. "Is that any way to speak to your mother? As if I were nothing more than a stranger on the street?"

A grin twitched at the corners of his lips, the first sign of humor she'd seen in days.

"I won't tolerate it, young man." She shook her finger at him, then winked.

His shoulders slumped. "I'm sorry, Mother."

Her heart warmed. Her son was still inside this standoffish shell who'd been masquerading as Ephraim over the past couple weeks. She gave him a quick hug. "All's forgiven. Now, hand me the basket of embroidered linens. I'm certainly capable of carrying it in."

He gave her the basket, offering a charming half grin as he did so, then picked up the crate of plum jam and followed her into the store. Ophelia put the basket of linens on the counter and turned to ask Ephraim to place the crate on the floor where she could more easily reach the jars. A motion near the door caught her eye, and she gaped with as much surprise as Ephraim had shown when she scolded him. She grabbed Ephraim's sleeve again and pointed.

He looked, and he gave a start. "What is she doing here?"

Lida's gaze drifted their way, and sheepishness crept across her expression. She advanced toward them slowly. "I didn't think y'all did your trading on Fridays or I wouldn't've come in today."

Ophelia admired Lida's ivory blouse and dove gray skirt. She'd pinned a cameo at her throat and topped her braided hair with a black silk hat adorned with feathers. Ophelia took hold of the woman's upper arms and smiled. "Lida, you look as if you stepped out of the pages of *The Ladies' World* magazine."

Lida blushed. She toyed with the tip of a black-dyed feather. "Thank you. I hope I look"—she glanced at Ephraim—"respectable."

"You do." Ophelia released her and folded her arms. "But I thought you'd left town. Where are you staying?"

Lida shrugged. "I took a room at the Delaney Hotel. I got to thinking about goin' all the way to San Antonio. I don't know anybody there, which might be a blessing in some ways, but I reckon I wasn't ready to leave . . ." Another glance in Ephraim's direction. "Yet."

Ophelia couldn't resist delivering another hug. "I'm glad you've decided to remain in Tulsey."

"Don't know if I will for good, though." Her gaze skittered back and forth between Ophelia and Ephraim as she spoke. "I need a job an' someplace besides a hotel room to live. I can't rent a place, though, 'til I'm workin' somewhere. I've already been to most businesses in town. None o' them want to hire a—" She clamped her lips together and turned her face aside.

From the corner of her eye, Ophelia witnessed Ephraim's jaw muscles tense. She caught his attention. "Would you bring the rest of our items inside, please?"

He nodded and strode out without a word. With his departure, Ophelia felt safe asking, "Do you want to stay in Tulsey so you have the opportunity to truly get to know your son?"

Lida flung one hand in the air as if blocking a thrown rock.

"He ain't my son. He's your son." Then her hand dropped, and her expression softened. "But it'd be fine to get to know him as a friend, as someone who likes piano-playing as much as I do." She fiddled with the feather again. "It'd be nice if folks who knew me clear back before I opened Lida's Palace would see me as that girl again. Maybe it's foolhardy to think it could happen, so many years've passed. But I want to at least try to . . ." She scowled. "I don't know what to call it. Maybe . . . redeem myself."

Sympathy stung Ophelia's heart. "Dear Lida, no matter how hard we try, we cannot redeem ourselves. Only God can redeem and restore. But He is always willing to do so when we ask Him." She sent a quick look around the store. Only a few customers browsed the aisles with baskets on their arms, much less activity than on Saturday mornings. "Let's find a quiet corner while Ephraim gathers up the items on our shopping list. We can pray together. Yes?"

Indecision clouded Lida's blue eyes. "I haven't talked to God in a good long while. He might've forgot me by now."

Ophelia squeezed Lida's wrist. "He hasn't. He couldn't. You've wandered a bit, Lida, pushed from His pathway by a mighty storm, but His Word tells us He will not leave nor forsake us. He's waiting for you to return." Hope beat like a bird's wings in her breast. "Would you like to talk to Him now?"

Lida swallowed. Moisture brightened her eyes. She nodded. Ophelia looped arms with her and headed for the corner where men's boots were displayed. The shoppers were all women. Hopefully none would visit that corner. Perhaps the boot corner in a Texas town's mercantile was an unlikely location for a prayer meeting, but God wasn't choosy about where He met people.

As they stepped around the end of the last aisle, Lida said, "Since we'll be prayin' anyway, can we ask Him about finding me a job? I can't stay around here if somebody doesn't hire me."

Ophelia slid her arm around Lida's waist. "Of course. We will ask for your open door."

## Ephraim

Ephraim loaded the organ into the back of the wagon, sliding it between the baskets and crates of goods they'd selected at the mercantile. He accepted his token of payment from the minister with a polite thank-you, then helped Mother onto the driver's seat. He sat quietly beside her while he drove the wagon from the cemetery to the road. Ephraim presumed Mother was too tired to talk. These days, after only a bit of exertion, she wore fatigue like a cape. It troubled him, and he decided not to tax her by engaging her in conversation. Besides, he needed to sort his mixed feelings concerning the Burkes.

He listened to the crunch of the wagon wheels on the dirt road and fixed his gaze beyond the horses' bobbing heads. The couple's intense sorrow as he'd played "All the Way My Savior Leads Me," knowing He'd led their son all the way to perfect rest in heaven, had bruised his soul. His compassion in those moments had trampled the resentment he'd held toward them for not seeing Birdie as good enough to sing at the service. The scriptures they'd chosen for the minister to read were all beautiful, encouraging passages about God's openness to receiving His own. They obviously believed in God's grace. Then why wouldn't they extend it to Birdie?

They reached the edge of town, and Ephraim guided the team to the far right to accommodate wagons traveling the opposite direction. As the wagon rolled onto Main Street, Mother touched Ephraim's arm.

"Park in front of the Delaney Hotel."

He shot her a brief frown. "For what purpose?"

She angled one brow at him. "To pick up Lida Holland."

He thought for a moment. "Are we transporting her to the railroad station?"

"No, we're transporting her to Hope Hill." Triumph glowed behind Mother's weary smile. "I hired her as our housekeeper."

Ephraim's jaw went slack.

Mother's expression quickly changed to chagrin. "Oh, my. Should I have asked you before offering her the position?"

He shook his head although he wanted to nod. But he had no right to dictate who should or shouldn't work at Hope Hill. He was, after all, only a worker there, not the owner. And how much longer would he reside there? If he secured the position he'd read about in Mr. Peterson's discarded newspaper, he'd be gone by summer's end.

Mother's smile returned, although not as brightly as before. She patted his arm and remained quiet until Ephraim pulled up in front of the Delaney. Lida was on the boardwalk, sitting on a trunk. Several new bags lay at her feet. Clearly, she'd been shopping.

She stood and walked to the edge of the wagon. "Ophelia, are you sure this is the right thing to do?" Her gaze flitted to Ephraim and then away. "I don't wanna cause trouble for y'all."

Mother whisked her hand as if shooing a fly. "I'm sure. Ephraim, help Lida with her bags, please."

Ephraim did as she asked. With his organ and stool, the goods they'd picked up at the mercantile, and Lida's belongings, the floor of the bed filled up. Mother had sat sideways on the seat, observing him. When he put the last bag in, she clicked her tongue on her teeth.

"There's not even room for Lida's feet back there. Come up here with me." She patted the driver's seat. "We can sit three abreast, and your feet won't be crunched."

Lida and Ephraim exchanged a glance. He read the same consternation in her eyes that rolled in his chest. But he wouldn't argue with Mother. He led Lida to the right side of the wagon and helped her onto the seat. Then he took his time folding up the step and sliding the gate into place, allowing a few needed minutes to collect himself.

Once on the seat again, he took up the reins and unlocked the brake. "Are we ready?" His attempt at a lighthearted tone fell flat, but neither Mother nor Lida seemed to notice. They both nodded. He urged the team into motion, and the wagon rolled forward.

Mother bumped Ephraim's arm with each rocking motion of the wagon. From the corner of his eye, he observed Lida's tightly clenched hands in the lap of her skirt. The little feathers on her hat fluttered in the breeze, as if trying to take flight. Now and then she reached up and smoothed them. They left Tulsey behind and headed toward home. Mother leaned slightly against Ephraim's frame, and a sigh eased from her chest.

He glanced at her. "Are you all right?"

She lifted a weak smile to him. "Yes, I'm fine."

Lida huffed. "I'm not. Stop the wagon."

Ephraim drew the team to a stop without conscious thought. Mother's head turned in Lida's direction, and Ephraim leaned forward to look past her. Lida's face was blotched pink, her lips in a stern line. Was she getting sick? He set the brake, prepared to help her down.

Mother patted Lida's folded hands. "What's wrong?"

"I shouldn't have listened to you. This is a crazy notion, me working at Hope Hill." She shook her head hard, and one of the feathers drifted from her hat. The breeze swirled it away. "Y'all are *ministers*. An' me? I'm"—she gulped—"nothin' compared to you."

"Lida Holland." Mother used the same tone Ephraim remembered from his boyhood when he'd misbehaved. "Do not ever call yourself *nothing*. You are formed in God's image, one of His priceless creations." She leaned against Ephraim as if in need of bolstering, and he automatically put his arm around her. Despite her physical frailty, her voice held strength. "He sent Jesus to die on the cross for you! This means you are equal in value to the life of His very own Son. Is Jesus nothing? No! And neither are you."

Lida stared at her hands. "Maybe once I was somethin'. Someone with somethin' of value to offer. But now?" She barely raised her head and peered at them from the corners of her watery eyes. "I'm what one of the folks I asked for a job called me—an old, worn-out prostitute. No wonder they laughed me out of their shops."

An unexpected flame of indignation burned in Ephraim's chest. How dare they sit in judgment of her? Were they so perfect? A splash of guilt extinguished the flame. Had he viewed her any differently than those who'd sent her away in humiliation?

She shook her head, the sadness in her eyes stinging Ephraim's soul. "I came with you 'cause when we were prayin' back there at the mercantile for me to find a job, you said God told you I was the one to take the housekeeper position at your place. But, Ophelia, you must've heard wrong. He's big an' mighty an' wise. Wise enough to see I got nothin' of worth to offer. Not anymore."

Mother rested fully against Ephraim. Although Ephraim couldn't see her face, he sensed by her stillness she was seeking God's counsel. He caught himself joining her in a silent plea for God to give Mother the words Lida needed to hear. For those words to comfort him, too, because he understood Lida's feelings all too well.

Suddenly Mother sat up. "Lida, I have only one word for you right now."

Ephraim held his breath, anticipation tingling through his frame.

"Rahab." She slumped against Ephraim again. "Son, take us home."

# Chapter Thirty-four

### Birdie

Birdie watched out the post office window for the revival wagon. She twitched, nervousness and eagerness warring for victory in her mind. A messenger from the Turner & Gallagher Law Firm had delivered a note from Mr. Turner only an hour ago. She hadn't opened it yet. Whatever it said, she wanted to be in the presence of Reverend and Mrs. Overly when she read the message. She wished she felt equally eager about sharing it with Ephraim. But the friend she'd come to cherish had turned into an unsmiling, withdrawn stranger. She missed him.

The wagon rolled up, and she hurried onto the boardwalk. She went to the rear of the wagon, as always, and waited for Ephraim to unfold the little step for her. To her shock, as he approached, he was whistling. She drew back and stared at him. What had happened to the solemn Ephraim who'd been moping around Hope Hill?

She stammered out, "You . . . you're happy."

He stopped whistling, and a bashful grin gave him a boyish appearance. "I reckon I am."

Delight blossomed in her chest. A giggle formed and spilled. Her Ephraim had returned. And just in time to share in her news. He would either celebrate with her or commiserate with her. But having him as part of her support system again brought eagerness above the anxiousness. She clambered to the front of the wagon and perched at the end of the bench close to the driver's seat.

Ephraim settled onto the seat and called, "Giddap, boys!" The wagon rolled up the street.

Birdie held the envelope flat in her lap, debating whether to tell Ephraim about it during the drive to Hope Hill. But by the time they'd left town behind, curiosity about his change in demeanor had gotten the best of her. She tapped his shoulder. "Ephraim, why are you so happy?"

He chuckled, the sound self-conscious. "I guess you could say the joy of the Lord got ahold of me again."

"How?"

His shoulders lifted and fell in a sheepish shrug. "Rahab."

Had she heard correctly? She leaned closer. "What?"

"Rahab." He sent a glance over his shoulder. "Do you know who she is?"

Birdie searched her memory. She'd read a Bible story about someone named Rahab. Wasn't she the woman who— Awareness bloomed through her, sending chills up and down her spine. She nodded. "I know who she is."

"Me, too." Ephraim tugged the reins a bit, and the horses pulled the wagon around a gentle curve up the middle of the road. "I reckon quite a lot of people in her town didn't think she was worth very much. But God called her to service. He didn't even wait until she was no longer a prostitute before He prompted her to act for His people's good." Wonder tinged his tone. "And she became one generation in the lineage of Christ. Think of it, Birdie. In the lineage of God's own Son."

Unexpectedly, tears pricked Birdie's eyes. "I'm so glad He sees what we can be instead of what we are."

Ephraim sent a brief smile over his shoulder. Then he released a heavy sigh. "For my entire life, I've heard my father counsel the girls who've come to us to see themselves through God's eyes of love and compassion. He's told them again and again that God made good plans for every soul conceived. That

He redeems those who've gone astray. That He restores what's been broken. I always believed it because I spent my whole life watching Him redeem and restore broken lives." He sent her another glance, a blush streaking his cheeks. "One of His most beautiful restorations is you, Birdie."

Her heart swelled, and she started to thank him. But he went on.

"Mother told me months ago that no child is a mistake in heaven's eyes. We were talking about Ellie at the time, and I fully agreed that, regardless of its conception, a child is a blessing. Yet somehow I couldn't see how those truths—redemption, restoration, being a blessing—applied to me. I felt useless because of my lineage." His voice cracked. He raised one gloved hand and rubbed his nose. "How belittling to God. How short-sighted." His Adam's apple bobbed in a swallow. "How hypo-critical."

The wagon wheel slipped into a rut, jarring the wagon. The jolt seemed to knock Ephraim's bitter reflections aside. He glanced at her again, his lips forming a soft curve. "But I spent some time on my knees this afternoon, and I'm seeing things a little differently now. God forgave me, and He even brought Lida back to Hope Hill. She doesn't expect to be my mother—she told me so. She said God gave me the best mother on earth, and I won't argue with her."

Birdie nodded. She wished she'd had a mother like Ophelia Overly. But at least, thanks to Lida, she understood her own mother better. She'd forgiven Mama, and she prayed they'd someday be reunited.

"But she wants us to be friends." He sighed, the expression one of satisfaction. "I want that, too."

Suddenly one of his comments sunk in. "Did you say Lida is back?"

He chuckled. "Yes. Mother and I encountered her in the mercantile this morning. She decided not to go to San Antonio where she didn't know anyone."

For a moment, uncertainty gripped her. What if this missive said the dress shop building was hers? Did she want to go someplace where she didn't know anyone?

"But she needed a job in order to stay. No one in town would hire her." Ephraim rubbed his nose again. "So Mother hired her to be the housekeeper at Hope Hill." He released a boyish snicker heavy with mischief. "As long as I'm there, too, I'll coax her into playing for the choir."

Birdie shot his profile a startled look. "As long as you're there . . ." She blinked several times, gathering her courage to ask. "Have you made plans to leave?"

"Not yet."

She sagged in relief. Maybe it was selfish, but if she was going to Kansas, she wanted everyone she loved at Hope Hill to be part of her going-away celebration.

"But I'm praying and listening. God will make clear my pathway when the time is right."

The horses snorted, a signal Birdie had come to recognize as their *almost home* warning. She peered past Ephraim's shoulder as the wagon turned in the lane and rolled toward the big house. She'd never forget her first night here, coming up the lane and seeing the candles in the windows. Their welcoming glow had ignited hope in the center of her breast. God had fanned that hope into a flame of healing. She'd changed here. Grown here. Discovered her worth in God's eyes here. She swallowed a knot of sadness. It would be hard to leave.

Ephraim drew the wagon to a stop near the back door, set the brake, then hopped down. He helped her from the wagon, and he held her hand for a few seconds, smiling down at her in a way that made her pulse flutter. Finally he gave a little squeeze and let go. "I'll see you at supper, Birdie." He climbed up on the driver's seat and flicked the reins. "Giddap, Red and Rusty!" He drove off, whistling.

Birdie went inside and searched out Mrs. Overly. She was in the kitchen helping with supper preparations. Birdie fiddled with the envelope. Maybe she shouldn't interrupt the routine. But how could she wait any longer? She tapped Mrs. Overly's shoulder. "Ma'am? I got a message from the lawyer in Tulsey. I . . . I haven't looked at it yet. I wanted . . ."

Understanding bloomed in the dear woman's expression. She put her arm around Birdie's waist and drew her to the hallway. "Let's go to the reverend's study. We'll read it together."

Reverend Overly was at his desk with a book open in front of him. He set it aside the moment the women entered, concern glimmering in his expression. "Is something wrong?"

Birdie rushed forward and pushed the missive into his hand. "This came today. It's from the lawyer in Tulsey." She wrung her hands together, staring at the envelope. "W-would you read it, please?"

He gave her a kind smile and retrieved the silver letter opener from a little box on the corner of the desk. As he slit the flap and removed the contents, Birdie and Mrs. Overly sat in the chairs. Mrs. Overly took Birdie's hand, and they waited in silence while the reverend unfolded the pages and scanned them. Birdie bit her lip, staring at his face for hints of what the letter contained. But his countenance was unreadable.

Finally, he returned the pages to the envelope. He laid the missive on the desk, within Birdie's reach, and turned his attention on her. "According to the information the lawyer uncovered, your aunt married a widower named Burton Steigle five years ago."

Birdie's mouth fell open. Aunt Sally had married? An unexpected flicker of joy lit in her breast. Part of her sorrow when she'd learned about Aunt Sally's passing was thinking of the poor woman dying all alone. But she hadn't been alone after all.

"She passed away almost a year and a half ago of pneumonia. Because he is your aunt's husband, Mr. Steigle is the heir to her property."

Little puzzle pieces began dropping into place in Birdie's mind, creating a picture of what had transpired in Kansas.

"He was aware Sally had a niece, but since the letters she'd sent to your house in Waco were returned, he didn't know how to contact you about your aunt's death. He's actually grateful to have located you. Apparently your aunt spoke of you often and expressed her desire for you to come to Kansas and work with her." A small smile lifted the corners of the reverend's lips. "She must have cared for you a great deal."

Tears clouded Birdie's vision. She blinked them away, nodding. "I cared a great deal for her, too. I'm sorry I didn't have the opportunity to see her again, but it brings me comfort to know she didn't spend her final years alone." But Birdie was alone. And now she had no inheritance. Maybe it was just as well. She'd wanted to go to Aunt Sally even more than she'd wanted to go to Kansas. Even so, it stung to release the briefly held dream. She reached for the envelope.

"There's one more thing."

Birdie's fingers lit on the envelope but she didn't pick it up. She met Reverend Overly's gaze.

"Mr. Steigle told the lawyer that Sally always hoped you'd come to Kansas. Thus, to honor her memory, he shared an offer. Apparently he and Sally resided in his house after their marriage and rented out her apartment. It is currently vacant. You could live there and work in the shop."

Birdie drew back. "The dress shop is still in operation?"

The reverend shook his head. "Mr. Steigle has turned it into a clock repair shop. But even if you don't have a job waiting in

Kansas, there is a home available. You could seek employment, and your uncle would be close at hand to provide guidance as needed."

An uncle she didn't know. But if Aunt Sally had loved him, he must be a good man. Maybe even as kind as Papa. If he'd been a widower before he married Aunt Sally, he might even have children. Her cousins. Might they become friends?

She stacked her hands over the envelope and pressed down hard. "I . . . I have much to think about."

Mrs. Overly placed her hand on Birdie's arm. "And pray about."

Birdie nodded. Then she shot a hopeful look from the reverend to Mrs. Overly. "Olga's baby is due to arrive in early July. I would like to be here when it comes, to help welcome it into the Fischer family."

Mrs. Overly nodded, her eyes shining with understanding.

Birdie shifted her imploring gaze to the reverend. "And I want to be baptized, the way you said I should. In Speegleville, where I sang with the choir for the very first time." She'd never forget that revival or the man named Dan who'd made her question whether she could ever be clean again. Yet here she sat, secure in God's grace, forgiven and whole. The uncertainty of her future couldn't change what had already transpired within her soul.

Reverend Overly reached across the desk and patted her hands. "That's a fine plan."

"So is it all right if I stay until Olga's baby is born?"

The reverend sat back. "My dear, we would be delighted to keep you with us for the rest of your life. But God's will is always best, and we must always go where He leads us. While we wait for Him to instruct you, we will enjoy your company and your lovely voice in the choir, and we will pray for the next chapter in your life's story."

Birdie sighed. A part of her hoped God would wait until she'd met Olga's baby. "Thank you, sir."

"You're welcome. Now, I believe it's suppertime and I smell something sweet."

Mrs. Overly smiled. "Applesauce cake."

He rubbed his stomach. "Mm . . . Shall we eat?"

The ornery twinkle in his eyes cheered Birdie more than the prospect of a waiting apartment in Kansas. She laughed and looped arms with Mrs. Overly as they crossed the hallway to the dining room. She ate and visited with the other residents, and she tried to memorize the moments. She'd grown to love this big, boisterous group and its noisy meals and serious Bible-study times and even the spats that led to compromise and reconciliation. It might take time, years even, until she had a family of her own. But she wanted what she'd discovered here—a home with lots of people around the table, lots of bedrooms with homemade quilts on the beds, and lots of laughter, hugs, and shared tears. *Please, God?*

May melted away and June sneaked in. Birdie worked every weekday at the post office, but she no longer saved her money in the bureau drawer. Lida had advised her to open an account at the bank instead. On Fridays, Birdie deposited her pay. The teller wrote down the amount in a little book with her name on it. It heartened her to see the dollars add up. She had enough for her train ticket plus more. She was tempted to spend some of it, but Mrs. Overly reminded her she might need the money to fund her next life chapter. So she left the money in the bank.

She and Ephraim were called upon twice the first week of June to sing at gravesides. She wasn't able to leave work for both of them, so Lida went in her stead for one. But Lida played and Ephraim sang. According to Lida, he sang better than he'd led anyone to believe. Birdie was grateful God had sent someone who would help at the services. Ephraim had confided during one of their drives that providing comfort through music at funerals was a blessing but also a burden. He keenly felt the families' sorrow. Now, even if she left for Kansas, he wouldn't have to carry that emotion alone.

Every evening after Bible-reading and prayer time with the other residents in the parlor, she spent a few more minutes on her own in prayer before going to sleep. Frequently, she asked God to lead her to friends in Kansas City. She didn't want to revisit the loneliness she'd often experienced as an only child. Her Bible said to make her requests known before God, so she felt confident asking Him for the things she wanted. But she remained mindful of seeking His will above her own. She grew increasingly grateful that He was always with her. Even if she didn't make a single friend in Kansas, she wouldn't be alone.

On June 22, the Saturday before Birdie's eighteenth birthday, all the residents of Hope Hill traveled to Speegleville for a joint baptism. Birdie stood on the creek bank with the others who'd professed faith in Christ while the reverend waded out to water as high as his hips. He faced the group, his expression both joyous and somber.

"Today is a special day." His powerful voice boomed louder outdoors than it had in the church. "Today you each will follow our Lord's example. Jesus Himself was baptized by His forerunner, John. Baptism is a symbol of what has taken place within your hearts. You have cast aside your old, selfish, sinful life, and have been raised to new life in Christ. No longer dead in sin, but alive in Christ forevermore! Hallelujah!" He raised his hands to the heavens, and those on the bank and the crowd of folks who'd gathered to witness the baptisms all cheered.

The reverend stretched one hand toward the group waiting to be baptized. "Who will come first?"

Birdie had never been one to push ahead, but she couldn't wait a moment longer. She splashed into the greenish, cold water. Her simple calico dress ballooned around her knees. She fought the wet tangle of fabric and the gentle flow of the current, her bare feet sinking into the soft, muddy bottom, and reached the reverend. The joy shining in his eyes brought a rush of tears.

He placed one hand on her shoulder and held the other skyward. "Birdie Clarkson, do you believe Jesus Christ died for you?"

She blinked against tears of wonder. "I do."

"Have you asked Him to forgive your sins and be your Savior?"

She clasped her hands over her thrumming heart. "I have."

"Do you vow to seek His ways and follow His will for the remainder of your earthly life?"

Birdie drew in a full breath. "I do." Her promise exploded as loudly as he preached.

His smile grew. "Then, my dear sister, I baptize you in the name of the Father, the Son, and the Holy Spirit!" He dipped her backward into the creek. The water flowed over her, washing away the tears that had already begun raining down her cheeks. He lifted her up, and a spray of droplets flew in a rainbow-like arc in front of her. Each little drop glittered like a diamond in the sunlight, and she imagined God tossing a handful of confetti gems to celebrate with her.

The reverend captured her in a big hug, whispering in her ear, "I'm so proud of you," and Birdie felt like Papa was bestowing his blessing on her.

She waded out of the creek and stepped directly into Mrs. Overly's embrace. The woman wrapped a blanket around her shoulders and took her into the church, where she changed into dry clothes. By the time the last person who wanted to be baptized came out of the creek, the sun had nearly dried Birdie's hair.

They'd planned a picnic dinner afterward, but Birdie was too excited to eat. She gathered her hair into a tail and deftly plaited a braid as she crossed the grass to the Overlys, who were sharing a blanket in the shade of a tall, scraggly oak. She knelt on the edge of the blanket and tied a bit of string around the end of her braid. "Reverend Overly, could we please stop by the Fischers' farm on our way home? I'd like to tell Olga what I did today."

The reverend wiped his mouth. "I think that's a fine idea. She will be pleased to hear your news, and we'd be pleased to see how she is faring in her new role as wife and mother."

"And we should invite the Fischers to join us for dinner at Hope Hill tomorrow." Mrs. Overly's eyes sparkled impishly. "Olga will want to help celebrate your birthday."

Birdie wheezed a happy sigh. "Oh, that would be grand. Thank you."

"You're welcome." The woman picked up a sandwich and gave it to Birdie. "Now eat."

Laughing, Birdie accepted the sandwich and took a bite. As she chatted with the reverend, Mrs. Overly, and Ephraim in the dappled shade of the oak tree, she paid attention to every tiny detail. She wanted to remember this day. The scent and coolness of the creek water as the reverend baptized her. The witnesses' raucous laughter and applause as she came up out of the water. The warmth of the sun on her head and the touch of the breeze on her cheek. And this simple, happy picnic.

If she never married and had a family of her own, she would have these remembered moments of being part of the Overly family. She examined their faces one by one, imprinting their images on her mind. She met Ephraim's gaze across the blanket, and he smiled. She lingered on his dear face the longest. She would remember forever.

# Chapter Thirty-five

Ephraim

F̲ather opted for an at-home worship service instead of driving into Tulsey on Sunday morning. Although yesterday's event in Speegleville wasn't a revival, everyone—especially Mother—was tired from the drive and long day under the sun. A service at home would be less wearing. Ephraim didn't mind. He had the choir sing what was fast becoming Mother's favorite hymn, "Lead On, O King Eternal," which sounded better than ever with Lida at the piano. Daily, her skills improved, and Ephraim's admiration for all she'd overcome increased.

Just as Father was setting aside his Bible to deliver a closing prayer, the sound of a wagon's approach drifted through the open windows. Mother sat up and looked out. "Oh. The Fischers are here a little early."

Father nodded. "That's fine. Let's pray, and—"

Someone pounded on the front door. "Reverend? Reverend?" Mr. Fischer's voice carried over the thuds.

Father strode to the door and swung it open. Mr. Fischer caught Father's sleeve. "Olga . . . her water breaks this morning. Come."

Ephraim followed Father and Mr. Fischer to the wagon. Olga sat on the floor of the wagon bed surrounded by the bewildered Fischer children. Mr. Fischer opened the hatch. *"Kinder, kommt da raus."* The biggest girl picked up the toddler boy, and the children clambered out of the bed. Mr. Fischer pulled himself in and crouched next to Olga. *"Du wirst in Ordnung sein."*

"Ja, I know I will be fine. And the baby will be, too." Olga's face reflected fear, but her voice held confidence.

Father climbed in, too. "Mr. Fischer, let's get your wife into the house."

Mr. Fischer and Father helped Olga to her feet. They guided her to the end of the bed, and Ephraim scooped her into his arms. He headed for the porch, the cluster of children jogging alongside him like a pack of puppies. Mr. Fischer shooed them back, barking in German. He must have commanded them to stay outside, because they all stopped near the porch.

Father put his hand on Mr. Fischer's arm. "Let them come in and have their dinner."

The man nodded. He said something else to his children, and they trooped into the house, then stood in a little group at the base of the stairs.

Mother scurried over the moment Ephraim crossed the threshold. She stroked Olga's hair. "Are you ready to meet your little one?"

"Nein." Olga coughed a short laugh. "But I don't suppose I have any choice." She held her hand to Mrs. Overly. "You will be with me?"

"Every minute," Mother said, cradling Olga's hand between her palms. "Ephraim, take her to my room."

Ephraim frowned. They'd always used Ellie's—now Lida's— room for births. But Mother couldn't climb the stairs anymore. Hers and Father's was the only bedroom on the main floor. But it was across from the dining room, where they planned to have Birdie's birthday dinner. He'd been in the house for enough births to know it wasn't always a quiet event. If Olga got noisy, it could alarm the children. "What if we go to my cottage? You and Olga will have privacy"—he used his eyes to indicate the children's presence—"and quiet there."

Mother pursed her lips for a moment, but she finally nodded.

She turned to Father. "Fetch the bag we use when a baby comes and bring it to Ephraim's cottage. We're taking Olga there."

Father headed down the hallway, his arms swinging, and Ephraim carried Olga out of the house. Mother and Mr. Fischer followed. At the edge of the porch, Mother said, "Mr. Fischer, you stay here with your children. I've helped deliver more than a dozen babies over the years. I know what to do for Olga."

The man yanked off his hat and twisted it, indecision marring his features. "You take good care of her?" His heavy accent made his plea sound even more desperate. But why wouldn't he worry? Only a few months ago, he'd buried his wife and their newborn child. His fear must be great.

"I promise." Mother patted his arm.

The man entered the house as Father exited. Father escorted Mother and Ephraim to Ephraim's little cottage. Midway across the yard, Olga grimaced. "Ephraim, you can put me down. I'm able to walk."

Ephraim wouldn't be sad to put her down. With her expanded belly, she weighed more than he'd expected. But he'd come this far. He might as well carry her all the way. "I'll put you down in the bed."

"Not yet." Mother panted, stumbling a bit. Father gripped her arm. "I'll need to ready it. Put her on your sofa for now."

Father opened the door and Ephraim turned sideways. He'd always imagined carrying his bride over a threshold, and suddenly Birdie's face flashed in his mind's eye. He blinked hard to clear the image. Now wasn't the time for fanciful thoughts. He bent down and gingerly placed Olga on his hay-stuffed sofa cushions. "There you are."

She sighed and leaned back, cupping the underside of her belly. "Thank you."

"Yes," Mother said, "thank you. But now shoo, both of you. Olga and I have work to do."

Father tipped his head. "Are you sure you don't want me to stay?"

"Or me?" Ephraim could at least direct Mother to extra linens and run for the doctor, if necessary.

"Send Lida out. She's been through childbirth and will be more help than either of you will be."

Father exchanged a look with Ephraim, then shrugged. "All right." He kissed Mother's forehead. "We will pray for Olga and her baby." Out in the yard, Father released a heavy sigh. "I hope Lida is willing to help. I worry it will be too much for your mother, although it would break her heart not to assist Olga's baby into the world. She's always loved babies."

Ephraim wasn't surprised by Father's comment. He'd seen his mother with little ones at church, with the babies born at Hope Hill, and with Ellie. "It's too bad she didn't have a dozen of her own."

Father lobbed a sad smile at Ephraim. "I've always thought so, too. But, son, she's likely impacted more children in her years of ministry than she would have if she'd borne her own. By helping young women find freedom and teaching them to carve a different pathway, she's impacted not only those lives, but the lives of the children born to them." He clamped his arm across Ephraim's shoulders. "God's ways aren't our ways, but—"

"His ways are always better." Ephraim finished the statement. He envisioned a pebble dropped into a pond and the circles that spread from it. Mother's life was the pebble. Heaven only knew how many people her ministrations had touched. Ephraim hoped to make a similar impact on others' lives.

At the back door of the house, Father paused and gave Ephraim's shoulder a squeeze. "While Olga labors, we will make our Birdie's birthday a joyous one, yes?"

"Yes."

"Eighteen years old today . . ." Father's voice turned pensive.

"Your mother was just-turned eighteen when I told her I was in love with her. I loved her before, but I wouldn't let myself admit it. Seventeen sounded too young." He chuckled. "But another day marks a year, and suddenly she didn't seem too young at all." He winked at Ephraim. "Let's go in."

Lida hurried out as soon as Father whispered to her. He invited everyone else into the dining room, and they had Birdie sit in his place at the head of the table—the place of honor, Father called it. They enjoyed the simple dinner of rolls, meat and cheese, pickles, dried apples, and a rich spice cake for dessert.

A few of the girls presented Birdie with gifts—embroidered handkerchiefs from Lucretia and Gladys, hair ribbons from Mathilda, and a battered copy of Victor Hugo's *Les Misérables* from one of the newest girls, Florence. After Birdie thanked them, Florence shrugged and said, "I found the book in the bottom of the wardrobe. I think maybe Iris left it behind. But as many times as it's been read, it must be good."

Ephraim couldn't imagine Iris choosing to read. She hated doing classwork. But Birdie would probably enjoy the story.

Birdie held the book up, smiling. "I'll read this on the train when I travel to Kansas."

The mention of Kansas dropped a boulder in Ephraim's stomach. Birdie hadn't wanted to leave until she was baptized and Olga had her baby. After today, there'd be no reason to remain in Texas. Except . . . He gave himself an internal shake. He couldn't be selfish. At least he had something to send with her that might help her remember him fondly. But he'd left the gift in his cottage, thinking he'd have time to get it between service and dinner. The Fischers' arrival and Olga's situation stole the opportunity.

He would give it to her tomorrow morning when he drove her to town for work. She wouldn't mind a belated present, and it might be better to give it to her when they were alone. He'd never purchased a gift for any of the other girls' birthdays. They might be jealous. Or they might speculate, the way Iris had, that his feelings for Birdie were more than friendship. Of course, they'd be right. But he still didn't want to raise their suspicions and make Birdie's last few days at Hope Hill uncomfortable.

Her last few days . . . and maybe his, too.


### Birdie

The other girls assured Birdie they would see to the cleanup. She should go enjoy herself on her birthday. "But tomorrow," Lucille said, laughing, "your birthday will be over an' you'll be back to chores as usual." Birdie decided to accept their generosity. If she couldn't use cleanup chores as the means to distract herself from Olga's laboring, her new book would make a pleasant diversion. She carried the book to the upstairs balcony.

She settled in the chair where she'd read her Bible many times before and opened the copy of *Les Misérables*. She turned to a page titled "Book One—An Upright Man" and began to read about Monseigneur Myriel. She'd only made it to the end of the second paragraph when the ruckus of children's voices and a dog's wild barking below stole her focus. She stood and peered over the spindled railing. The Fischer children and Ellie romped on the yard with Ted. Giggles rang, and Ted leaped at the children by turn, barking with every lunge.

Birdie couldn't hold back a smile while watching them. How carefree they seemed, even Ellie. The child was usually reserved, but when part of a group of children, she came alive. Maybe spending all her time with adults was hindering her from truly being a child. Seeing her smile and laugh and— Birdie gripped the top of the railing and stared hard at Ellie. Was she truly laughing or only making a happy face?

Suddenly the little girl dropped on the grass. Ted swiped at her face with his tongue, his tail twirling in joy. A squeal erupted, and Birdie was certain Ellie had released it. She laid her book aside and pattered down the stairs in search of Reverend Overly. Neither he nor Mr. Fischer was in the parlor anymore, but Ephraim was there, bent over the table in front of the sofa, writing something.

She grabbed his wrist. "Come with me." He dropped the pen and it rolled onto the carpet. He leaned down, reaching for it, but she yanked his arm. "Ephraim, do that later! Come with me!"

He trotted alongside her, uncomplaining but shooting looks of confusion at her. She led him out to the balcony, then pointed down at the children. "Look. And listen."

His face puckered with concentration and he peered in the children's direction. They'd all settled into a circle on the grass, Ted panting beside Ellie, the raucousness of the previous minutes seemingly over. He aimed a puzzled frown at her. "What am I supposed to look at?"

Birdie groaned. "We took too long. They must have worn out." She plopped into the chair and folded her arms.

Ephraim's lips twitched into a half smile. "All right, then. What did I miss?"

Birdie sat forward. "I heard Ellie squeal. A happy squeal."

His eyebrows shot up. "Are you sure?"

"I am." She recounted the child's wrestling match with Ted and her excited exclamation. "That's three times I know about that Ellie has made sounds. First, when I was crying and she comforted me. She said, 'Sh.' Then, in the barn when she was frustrated with you—remember? She grunted. I heard her."

He nodded. "Yes, I heard her, too."

"And just now, she squealed. She might have been laughing, too. With so many children giggling at the same time, I can't be sure about the laughter, but I know she squealed." She hugged herself, trying to hold on to her joy. "Ellie can make sound, as your mother suspected. She just chooses not to. Until she forgets herself, apparently." Birdie tilted her head, her gaze locked on Ephraim's. "Why do you suppose she chooses to stay quiet?"

Ephraim leaned back in his chair and crossed his legs, as if settling in for a long chat. "If it isn't a physical problem, it's likely emotional. It could be related to being abandoned by her mother. She got angry and grunted when we talked about leaving."

Birdie nodded slowly. "That makes sense. Abandonment hurts. I've forgiven my mother for running off and leaving me behind, but it still hurts when I think about it. She must not care about me at all to walk away without a word." At least Aunt Sally had made an effort to contact Birdie over the years.

Sympathy glinted in his eyes. "Your mother made a terrible mistake, Birdie. I don't understand why she did it either, but unhappy people don't always make wise decisions."

Mama was the most unhappy person Birdie knew. Was she happier now, away from Tulsey and with the man with whom she'd gone? Deep down, Birdie hoped so, even though the rejection stung. She sighed. "I still find it strange, though, that of all the things Ellie could do to express anger or confusion or sadness, she stays quiet."

She glanced down at the group of children. Ellie had rolled onto her back, bare feet propped on Ted's stomach, her eyes aimed at the sky. It was too early to search for falling stars, something Birdie had done when she was little so she could make a wish. Was Ellie cloud-watching, perhaps? Her gaze on the child, she said, "It delights me to see her become so lively when other children are around. She chased and played and acted like a little girl with the Fischer children the day of Olga's wedding, and then again today. I think being around others her own age is good for her. It's too bad she can't go to school with the children in town."

Ephraim tapped his chin, the way she'd seen Ophelia do when she was thinking. "Maybe she'll get to . . . someday."

The cryptic statement piqued her interest. "How?"

Ephraim rolled his eyes upward, as if contemplating something. Then he looked at her. "I haven't said anything to anyone yet. Not even my parents. But it's possible I might take a teaching position in Tulsey this coming fall."

"Really?"

A slow smile curved his lips. "I saw an article in the newspaper announcing the man who has been teaching music resigned his position and is moving to Waco to teach at the college level. After I dropped you at work last Thursday, I visited the school superintendent. I have the credentials to teach. He's going to present my résumé to the school board. If they approve me, I will move to Tulsey and work at the school. I think Mother and Father might allow Ellie to go if I'm there."

Two emotions struck simultaneously—happiness for him and Ellie, and disappointment for her. But why should she be disappointed? Even if she didn't go to Kansas City, she couldn't stay at Hope Hill forever. Eventually, the two of them would go their separate ways. She focused on happiness. "That's wonderful, Ephraim. I've watched you with Ellie. You're always so patient with her. You'll make a wonderful teacher."

He uncrossed his legs and leaned forward, resting his elbows on his knees. "And you'd make a wonderful dressmaker. You're very bright and creative. I hope you'll have the opportunity to work in a dress shop someday, the way you'd wanted to with your aunt."

His words were so kind. Why did a hint of sadness linger in

his blue eyes? "Thank you, Ephraim. Your encouragement means a lot to me. I will"—she gathered her courage—"miss you when I go away. You've become a very good friend."

He smiled but didn't say anything, leaving her oddly deflated.

On the lawn, the children suddenly came to life. Birdie moved to the railing and looked over, hoping to catch Ellie laughing or squealing or—better—talking. They were all running in the direction of Ephraim's cottage. She turned quickly. "Ephraim—"

He took her hand. "I see them. Let's go."

# Chapter Thirty-six

### Ophelia

"I'm so proud of you, Olga." Ophelia pushed the girl's sweat-dampened hair from her face. "You worked hard to bring your little one into the world."

Wrapped in a blanket and nestled in the crook of its mother's arm, the babe had given up its weak cries and slept, rosebud mouth puckered and swollen eyes pinched shut. Olga tipped her head sharply downward and squinted at the cap of dark hair. "What is it? A boy or a girl?"

Ophelia adjusted the edge of the blanket, tucking it under the baby's chin to better show the sweet, wrinkled face. "Wait until Arthur is here. Then you can find out together."

Olga flopped her head onto the pillow and closed her eyes.

Ophelia rose and crossed to the sitting room of Ephraim's little cottage. She'd sent Lida to fetch Mr. Fischer. She should have told her to bring Birdie, too. Such a gift for the girl, that Olga's child made its entrance on her birthday. But Birdie might come running even if she wasn't invited.

While she waited, she carried the rags she'd put on the bed to protect the sheets to the waste bin and used a damp cloth to wipe Olga's face and the baby's head. Both mama and baby looked more presentable after a quick wash. Arthur had seen newborns before, but this was different. This was not a child of his flesh. Whatever she could do to help him fall in love upon sight would be beneficial to the child, to Olga, and to the stepfather himself.

The front door opened, and Mr. Fischer peeked in. "I can come?" Eagerness showed in his wide eyes and quavering voice.

Ophelia smiled, holding out her hand in welcome. "Please come." As she'd suspected, Birdie hovered on the stoop, wringing her hands and trying to peer past the man's shoulder. The Fischer children were also there in a wriggling, excited group. Ophelia laughed. "And the rest of you, too." They all rushed in, but Ophelia held up a hand of caution. "Let the papa go first. I'll call you when Olga is ready for the rest of you."

Birdie's brow pinched with consternation, but she remained on the rug with the children while Ophelia led Mr. Fischer into the bedroom. At their entrance, Olga's eyes opened and lit on her husband. She slipped her hand from beneath the light covering and held it toward him.

He rushed forward and gripped it, his gaze bouncing from Olga to the babe. "You are fine? Baby is fine?"

Olga nodded weakly, a soft smile forming on her weary face. "Ja, we are fine, Arthur. But I don't yet know whether we have a boy or girl. Mrs. Overly wouldn't tell me."

The man scowled. "Ja, well, it must be one or the other." He faced Ophelia. "Ma'am? Do we have Elizabeth or Eli?"

Ophelia thought her heart might explode for joy. God couldn't have chosen a better father for this baby than Arthur Fischer. She clasped her hands and pressed her knuckles to her chin. "Elizabeth would be more appropriate, because you have a little girl."

"A girl . . ." Mr. Fischer sank down on the edge of the bed and touched the baby's cheek with his work-roughened finger. "She is *schön* . . . like her mama."

Olga laughed softly. "Oh, Arthur, I'm not beautiful. I am sweaty and more tired than I can ever remember being."

He placed his palms on either side of her head and leaned in. "But you are *froh*?"

Olga sighed. "Ja. Very happy."

Ophelia turned aside when the husband delivered a kiss on his wife's mouth. Then she said, "Is the little one ready to greet some admirers? Birdie would like to see her, and I'm sure your other children are quite eager to meet their new baby sister."

Mr. Fischer stood and rocked on his heels, his chest puffed in pride. "Bring them in."

Birdie, bless her heart, allowed the children to crowd past her. She waited in the doorway while the Fischer children oohed and aahed over the new baby.

Ophelia moved close to Birdie and rubbed her back. "She's a perfect little girl, and named for a very kind young lady."

Birdie smiled, but her eyes were moist. "She should be named Ophelia, because no one is kinder than you."

Ophelia briefly tipped her temple to Birdie's. "Thank you, dear one. But Elizabeth is appropriate. Especially since she arrived on your birthday. Not everyone receives a namesake as a gift."

Birdie's expression turned dreamy. "I know. It makes me feel . . . accountable to her somehow. As if I should always be here for her. Does that make sense?"

"It does." Ophelia turned slightly and fully faced Birdie. "What else are you thinking?"

Birdie laughed softly. "Oh, nothing important. I was only wondering how much longer it will take for God to tell me what I'm to do . . . go to Kansas or find a place to live in Tulsey. I . . ." Her gaze drifted in the direction of the family members gathered around the new mama and baby. "I confess I'm not as eager to go so far away as I once was. Because I have reasons to stay here."

"Ah." Ophelia nodded, examining Birdie's profile. "To get to know little Elizabeth, perhaps to help Olga a bit, and . . . what else?"

The girl's cheeks went pink. "Nothing else."

Ophelia didn't believe her, but she chose not to pursue the subject. "You are welcome to stay until you know for sure what you're to do."

Birdie peeked at her from the corner of her eye. "But what if the bed is needed for another young woman who's lost and hurting? Reverend Overly doesn't go to the brothels and rescue someone new if all the beds are filled." She hung her head. "I feel guilty staying when I'm strong enough now to be on my own. And thanks to Aunt Sally's kind husband, I have somewhere to go. I'd be where she wanted me to be." She lifted her head, squaring her shoulders. "I should move on and give my place to another girl. It's selfish to stay."

Ophelia started to ask again if there was another reason she wanted to stay in Tulsey, but Olga called Birdie's name.

Birdie touched Ophelia's arm. "Excuse me, ma'am. I would like to meet my little namesake." The Fischer children moved aside and allowed Birdie close to the bed.

Ophelia watched for a moment, smiling at the sweet way Birdie touched Olga's cheek before reaching for the baby. Then she went to the sitting room and sat on Ephraim's lumpy sofa. Her chest panged, and she absently rubbed her collarbone in response. She rested her head on the sofa back and smiled at the ceiling, imagining God smiling back from the floor of heaven. "Thank You, Lord, for the safe delivery of a perfect little baby." She whispered, unwilling to tax herself too much by speaking aloud. "Thank You for the loving mama and papa who welcomed her into the world. Guide and direct little Elizabeth all the days of her life, and may those days be long and healthy. Bless the entire family, my dear Father, and let them grow ever closer to each other and ever closer to You."

My, she was tired. But there was work to do. Olga needed to stay at least through tomorrow before she took a rattling wagon ride to the Fischer farm. Arthur wouldn't want to leave her, so they should make pallets on the floor for the children. That meant Ephraim would have to sleep somewhere in the house— the music room? It would work with a cot for his bed.

She pushed herself to her feet. She wished Lida was still at the cottage. She could ask Birdie to help, but she hated to pull the girl away from Olga when her time in Tulsey was limited. "Well, Lord," she said on a sigh, "You promise we can do all things with Christ's strength. I need it now." She moved resolutely to the chest where Ephraim's extra linens were stored.

## Birdie

Birdie climbed into the back of the wagon Monday morning for the drive in to work and found a small box tied shut with a blue ribbon in the spot where she usually sat. She picked it up and showed it to Ephraim. "What is this?"

He glanced over the edge of the bed, his eyebrows high in a mock show of innocence. "Well, look at that. The birthday fairy must have been late delivering your gift."

Birdie put her hand on her hip and scowled at him as he pulled himself onto the driver's seat. "There's no such thing as a birthday fairy."

He shrugged. "There must be, because he left you a present." He winked.

Birdie laughed. She turned the box this way and that, trying to guess what might be inside. "Is it really for me?"

"Who else had a birthday yesterday?"

"Elizabeth Ophelia Fischer," she said.

He laughed. "Sit down so we can get going, or you'll be late to work. Open that and then tell me if it belongs to you or the baby."

Birdie sat and cradled the box in her lap. Until her birthday celebration yesterday, she hadn't had any real presents since Papa died. Mama didn't celebrate birthdays or Christmases. And this gift was wrapped so sweetly, she wanted to enjoy it. By the time the wagon reached the end of the lane, though, curiosity won over contemplation. She untied the ribbon, lifted the lid, and gasped. "Ephraim!"

He glanced over his shoulder. "What?"

"Ohhh . . ." She covered her lips with her fingers and gaped at the delicately painted, round brass box. A Victorian couple in their finest clothes, posed in the midst of a waltz, decorated the lid. "It's beautiful."

"Take it out." Ephraim sounded as excited as she felt. "It plays music."

Birdie smiled so widely her cheeks hurt. "Truly? Oh!" The wagon bed rocked gently. She gingerly lifted it from the box, biting her lower lip. She didn't want to drop it. A tiny lever stuck out from a hole in the side. Curious, she cranked it. A tinkling melody emerged from the box. She cocked her head and listened. "It's a waltz, but who wrote it?"

"Franz Joseph Haydn. He was an Austrian composer well known for writing music meant to be performed by stringed instruments. But his piano pieces are lovely, too."

Birdie gaped at the back of his head. "You know so much about music, Ephraim. You're going to make a wonderful teacher."

He chuckled and shot a quick grin over his shoulder. "Thank you. But I haven't been hired yet."

"You will be." She returned the music box to its case and then held it in her lap. "They would be foolish to turn away someone with your talent and love for music. But . . ." Maybe she shouldn't ask if he'd given up on the calling he'd shared with her. She didn't want to rub salt in a wound.

He leaned sideways slightly, turning his ear in her direction. "But what?"

She might as well ask. "But if you teach all day, will there be time to start the men's choir you talked about?"

"Yes." He nodded so enthusiastically, she couldn't help smiling. "And if I'm living in town, it will be easier for me to bring the men together for practices. It's much more likely that I'll be able to establish a men's choir if I'm teaching than if I remain at Hope Hill."

Birdie couldn't imagine Hope Hill without him. But she hadn't been able to imagine it without Olga, either, and somehow she survived. She supposed the same would prove true when Ephraim wasn't there anymore. But what was she thinking? She wouldn't be there, either. The thought brought a feeling of loss. She squelched it and assumed a cheery tone. "I love my music box. Please tell the birthday fairy thank you when you see him. And I hope I'll be in town long enough to hear your men's choir perform at least once."

"I will pass your message to the birthday fairy, but as for the choir . . ." He glanced at her, and the disappointment she glimpsed in his eyes brought her sadness to the fore again. "It will take time to bring the men together. More time to prepare for a performance. And more time, still, to find a venue for performing. It could be a full year before it all comes together. I doubt you'll be here that long."

"No, I suppose not." She didn't sound sure, even to her own ears. "Whether I'm here or not, I will pray for your choir. I will pray that the words from the songs impact hearts. And I will pray that you find joy in your calling."

He turned clear around and pinned her with a grateful look. "Thank you, Birdie. That means a lot to me." He faced forward again. "So many things seem to be lining up for me to do what God placed on my heart. But . . ." He drew a deep breath and whooshed it out. "There's one thing that doesn't seem attainable. I'm going to have to pray about that one and trust God to work His will."

She waited, but he didn't say what the one thing was. Although Birdie was curious, she held the question inside, and he remained quiet the remainder of the drive.

He dropped her off at the post office and called his usual "Have a good day." His smile seemed a little sad as he waved farewell.

She entered the post office, the strange cloud of sadness that had descended following her. He'd said many good things were falling into place for him. The same could be said for her given her invitation to come to Kansas and start anew. Why, then, this lingering feeling of dread?

# Chapter Thirty-seven

Ephraim

Ephraim left the school superintendent's house, a song of joy playing in his heart. He urged Red and Rusty into motion and aimed them in the direction of the post office. He couldn't wait to tell Birdie his news.

After her confident statement that morning about him being hired to teach in Tulsey, he hadn't been able to set the thought aside. So he came into town a little early and visited Mr. Boulder. To his delight, the man assured him the school board was very interested in his application and he should expect to receive a contract soon. Maybe he shouldn't celebrate yet since he hadn't put his signature on an agreement, but he felt in his bones God was paving his way. He wanted to celebrate each step, and he wanted Birdie to celebrate with him.

He pulled up in front of the post office a few minutes before five o'clock. While he waited for her to emerge, he sent his gaze slowly up and down the street. Tulsey was a little smaller than either Waco or Gatesville, the other two cities in which he'd lived. How many children resided within this town's limits? He hadn't attended school after his first year in Waco. The children weren't kind to him, no doubt influenced by their parents' opinion about Father's ministry. Mother had given him a fine education, and his training at the university and his experience with the Hope Hill choir left him confident he could teach. But it would be a little strange entering a classroom for the first time since he was six years old. He would be learning along with the students.

The post office door opened and Birdie came out. She cradled the box he'd given her. His heart rolled over at the protective way she held his gift. She treasured it. And—his pulse stuttered—he treasured her. *Easy, Ephraim* . . .

He hopped down and reached for the box. "Here, let me take that for you while you get in." She kept a grip on the little box and pinned an uncertain gaze on him, seeming even to cease breathing with her intense focus. Trepidation tiptoed up his spine. "Is something wrong?"

"No." She blinked twice. "Yes." A tiny sigh escaped her parted lips. "I don't know."

He glanced up and down the street. "Did someone say or do something unkind to you?" At least in Kansas no one would know about her brief time as one of Lida's girls. She could start with a fresh slate, free of the judgmental attitudes of some in Tulsey.

"No. Nothing like that." She continued to stare at him as if trying to see beneath his surface. "I've just been pondering something all day. Well, even before today, I suppose, and . . . I don't know . . ." She bowed her head.

"Are you feeling burdened?"

She nodded.

He wanted to see her sweet face. He put his finger under her chin and lifted her gaze to his. "Whatever you're seeking, God will be with you every step of the way. Remember what my father read during our home church yesterday?" He recited from Isaiah 43, " 'When thou passest through the waters, I will be with thee; and through the rivers, they shall not overflow thee: when thou walkest through the fire, thou shalt not be burned; neither shall the flame kindle upon thee.' " He tilted his head. "Do you remember why?"

A soft smile lifted the corners of her rosy lips. "Because He, the Lord, is with us."

"Yes, He is." The last few weeks had tested his belief, but he'd emerged stronger and surer of God's presence than before. "He's with us here in Tulsey. And He will be with you in Kansas."

A fierce scowl marred her brow. "Please don't mention Kansas as if you want to send me there this very moment."

Send her? Hadn't she already made the choice to go? If he'd not been promised the position at school, he might have pushed past his apprehensions and asked to accompany her. To build a life with her there. But God had made it clear his ministry was to be here in Tulsey, and God had paved the way for her to leave. Her comment didn't make any sense.

He slid his hand into his pocket and frowned at her. "I'm not sending you there." If it were up to him, he'd keep her in sight forever. "I thought you wanted to go."

"So did I."

Clearly she was confused. But the main street in Tulsey wasn't the place for a lengthy conversation or prayer. "Come on. Let's get you to Hope Hill." To his relief, she gave him the box. He placed it on one of the benches in the wagon, then helped her into the bed. She picked up the box on her way to her usual spot. Even though she didn't speak a word the entire drive home, he was very aware of her presence behind his left shoulder.

At the house, she kept hold of the box while he helped her alight. When her feet met the ground, a little sigh eased from her throat, and a rueful chuckle followed it.

Ephraim couldn't stay silent any longer. "Birdie, please tell me what's troubling you. I'll help if I can."

Birdie

So many emotions rolled through Birdie's frame she marveled that she didn't burst. Ever since Papa died, she'd longed to be loved. She'd dreamed of being part of a real family. Aunt Sally, who would have welcomed her with open arms, was gone, but her husband offered refuge. He was her uncle. In time, wouldn't she feel as if she was part of his family? The things she'd wanted to do before she left—be baptized, see Olga's baby enter the world—were done. She had the money to go. Why, then, did she delay purchasing her ticket and going to the place where her dreams could come true? What held her here?

Ephraim stood before her, his concerned gaze pinned on her face. He wanted to help. Should she let him? Could he sort through this tumult of confusion and point to God's path for her? Holding the music box he'd given her snug against her breast, she opened her mouth and allowed the torrent to spill out.

"If I go to Kansas, I won't get to watch little Elizabeth grow up. I won't have the chance to hear Ellie speak her first words. I'll never watch you direct the men's choir. I won't be where Mama could find me if . . ." She gulped, her deep yearning for a reunion with her only remaining relative making itself known. "If she comes back someday."

Did she really want Mama to return? Mama's abandonment had propelled Birdie to Lida's Palace. She inwardly winced as her mind trailed to her first night in that awful place. Then, blessedly, her thoughts leapt to the night Reverend Overly and Ephraim had come. A new awareness began to dawn. She wouldn't have met them and been brought to Hope Hill if she hadn't been at Lida's. Tears threatened, making her eyes sting. What if Mama hadn't run off with the drummer? Would she still know Jesus? The most painful events in her life had served a purpose in sending her into the Father's loving embrace.

Ephraim grazed her elbow with his fingertips. "Birdie, may I ask you something?"

Still caught up in the wonder of where her thoughts had taken her, she nodded.

"Are you saying you don't want to go to Kansas City?"

She blinked several times, battling the urge to dissolve into tears of gratitude. God in His great mercy and love hadn't given up on her but had, instead, drawn her to Him. She didn't need to go to Kansas to find love. She already had it, right here in Tulsey, Texas. "Yes. That's what I'm saying." The peace that flooded her as she made the concession told her more than anything else she'd made the right choice.

"Then"—he sucked in a breath—"may I tell you something?"

Something glimmering in his blue eyes warned that whatever he said might inspire her to lose her tenuous hold on her emotions. "Only if it won't make me cry."

His lips twitched. "Well, I can't guarantee it won't. But I'll tell you anyway." He took the box from her and laid it in the wagon bed. Then he slipped his hands under hers and linked fingers with her. "I'm glad you won't be going to Kansas after all. I'm glad you're staying in Tulsey. Because if you stay in Tulsey, maybe I'll be able to spend more time with you. And if I spend more time with you, maybe you'll come to care about me as much as I already care about you. And if you come to care about me, maybe . . ." One side of his lips rose in the sweetest, most bashful, boyish, appealing grin she'd ever seen. "We will build a life and ministry together."

"You . . . and me?" Birdie gulped, her chest fluttering with hope. Her forehead pinched with a painful thought. "Are you saying this because you feel sorry for me? You're a kind person and a very good friend. But you don't need to feel obligated to take care of me now that my plans all fell apart."

His fingers closed more firmly around hers. "Maybe *your* plans fell apart. But I see *God's* plans falling into place." He glanced around, then guided her to the front porch. He sat on the bench and urged her next to him. "Birdie, from the first time I saw you and heard your sweet singing voice rising above the others in the choir, I was drawn to you. I remember thinking then what a difference one voice made. Well, it's made a huge difference in my life. It's opened me to loving you."

Her pulse thrummed, and the sting behind her eyes intensified. She blinked hard.

"I fought it. You were one of Hope Hill's residents, and my parents cautioned me about getting too close to any of the girls because of the problems it could cause." He tapped the end of her nose. "You know what I'm talking about. You suffered as a result of Iris's jealousy, and I hadn't even proclaimed affection for you."

Birdie grimaced. "Sometimes I was jealous of her because she stole so much of your attention with her antics."

He raised one eyebrow, his expression smug. "Ah. So you liked me, too."

She more than liked him. She loved him. But she held the words inside. They were too precious to squander. Until she knew for sure where he was leading, she wouldn't expose the most tender place in her heart. "I suppose so."

His grin grew. "My parents guessed how I feel about you."

Birdie's chest fluttered again. "They did? What did they say?"

He leaned forward and touched foreheads with her. She saw her reflection in his blue eyes. She didn't want to look away. "They approved. They love you, too."

Warmth flooded her. "I love them."

He gave her a sweet smile, then sat up. "But they advised me to seek God's will because we all thought you were going to Kansas. I spent a lot of hours in prayer, but I never received real peace about going so far away. I made myself give up envisioning a life with you. But the desire never left me." His gaze softened. "I love you, Birdie. I want to spend every day of the rest of my life with you."

She met his unwavering gaze, licked her dry lips, and asked, "Why?"

"Because you are the harmony to my life's song."

The poetic words delivered in his husky voice while his eyes glowed with love overwhelmed her. Tears filled her eyes, and she laughingly batted at the moisture. "Ephraim, I told you not to make me cry."

He laughed and swept her into his arms. "My sweet little songbird . . ." His warm breath kissed her cheek and stirred the little tendrils of hair coiling near her ear. "How I love you."

She smiled against his shoulder, amazed at how perfectly she fit in his embrace. "I love you, Ephraim."

He pulled back and clasped her hands. "Do you want to be my wife, my partner in ministry, the mother of my children, the one who fills my heart with song for the rest of my life?"

Birdie gazed into his honest, precious eyes. Everything he wanted, she wanted, too. Had wanted for so long but thought could never be. Might never have been if not for God extending His hand of rescue. There was no answer she could give Ephraim, save one.

She laced her fingers with his and said, "I do."

# Epilogue

Five years later

"Come along now, Cornelia. Don't dawdle." Birdie gave a gentle tug on her three-year-old daughter's hand and waddled up the winding brick sidewalk, her free hand resting on her rounded belly.

Did the builders of the Tulsey Opera House have to set it so far from the road? Yet she couldn't deny the lengthy walk gave her an opportunity to admire the ostentatious limestone building towering two stories tall. Her favorite details were the plaster roses and swirls decorating the arched heads of the window frames. Reflecting the early evening sun, the plaster glowed as white as a full moon against a black velvet sky. Surely the building's appearance rivaled that of opera houses in much larger cities. And building it on the site of the old Bradford Hotel helped chase all memories of Lida's Palace from people's minds. Such a blessing.

On both sides of the sidewalk, wagons filled the mowed fields. The opera house seated two hundred guests, and Ephraim had told her that every seat was sold. Apparently all the other attendees had already arrived. What time was it? Ephraim had said she needn't come early—he'd saved seats for them. But if they didn't hurry, they might miss the opening number.

She released Cornelia's hand and cupped the back of her head, hoping to propel her along. Ahead, in the shade of the building's columned portico, Ophelia, Isaiah, and Ellie waited next to the large framed poster stating the title of the evening's event. Even from this distance, Birdie made out the words.

## Tulsey's Men's Choir in Concert—
## Songs of Faith & Commitment

Her heart thrummed in excitement. Ephraim's photograph was prominently featured in the upper left-hand corner of the poster, and three-inch-tall block letters proclaimed his name and title.

## Mr. Ephraim Overly
## Featured Conductor

Despite the sun warming her head, she experienced a delight-inspired shiver. While it wasn't the men's choir's first public performance, this was their first not held in a park or a church. Birdie's heart expanded with pride in her husband's accomplishment. How hard he'd worked, diligently striving to bring glory to the One who'd called him to this ministry. He deserved every bit of recognition he received.

Cornelia suddenly jerked away from Birdie's light hold, her lower lip poking out. "I tired of walking, Mama."

Birdie stroked her daughter's dark, silky hair. Ephraim declared Cornelia was a mini replica of Birdie, but Birdie didn't think she'd been as strong-willed. "I know, sweetheart, but we're almost there. Papa reserved seats for Grandmother, Grandfather, Ellie, and us right in front of the stage. He said you could wave at him if you wanted to. We have a nice place waiting for us to sit when we get inside."

Cornelia was definitely her papa's girl, just as Birdie had been, and Birdie didn't begrudge their special closeness. But she secretly hoped the baby due next month might be a little boy who would be as close to her as Ephraim was to his beloved mother.

She extended her hand to Cornelia. "Come now."

Cornelia folded her arms and plopped onto the sun-warmed bricks. "I sit now."

Birdie aimed a hopeful look at the waiting trio, and without a moment's pause, Ellie raced to them. At nearly twelve years of age, she was losing her little girl looks and growing into a willowy young lady. Tonight she wore her nicest dress and her red-gold curls were corralled by a big satin bow, giving her a grown-up appearance. But the mad dash proved there was still quite a bit of child within her.

She scooped up Cornelia and perched the little girl on her hip, bouncing her a bit. She sent Birdie a crinkled-nose grin.

"Yes, she's getting big," Birdie said with a nod. "Which is why I don't carry her anymore."

Ellie's eyebrows rose in silent query.

Birdie smiled. "You may carry her if you wish. We might get inside faster if you do."

Ellie broke into a huge smile, and she jogged up the sidewalk, her arms wrapped tightly around the little girl. Cornelia's giggles rang with every jouncing step.

Birdie followed as quickly as her legs would carry her, and as she stepped beneath the portico's shade, she swept her hand across her forehead. "Phew. I hope Ephraim arranged to have the fans running inside. It's quite warm for mid-May."

Ophelia wrapped her in a hug, laughing softly. "You should have done what we did—hired a dray to carry us to the front doors."

Birdie gloried that Ophelia was able to attend tonight's concert. She rarely ventured far from Hope Hill anymore, saving her limited energy to pour out on the girls who found refuge within the sturdy walls of the old house. Every day with her was a blessing none of them took for granted.

Birdie noted Ophelia's pale face and slumped shoulders. She gently chastised, "Why didn't you go on in?"

The woman's frame straightened. "All of Ephraim's family should go in together, showing our great pride and support for him."

All his family except Lida. But only because Lida was already inside, seated at the grand piano. In tiny letters beneath Ephraim's name and title, the poster declared, **Accompanist, Miss Lida Holland.** Birdie would never admit it, but she found more pleasure in Lida's recognition than Ephraim's. The woman had come so far to regain the path God had intended for her when she was a girl. Her willingness to perform, as well as people's willingness to purchase tickets to hear her play, proved God's ability to redeem and restore.

Isaiah offered Birdie a sympathetic frown. "I'm sorry your mother isn't here to attend tonight's concert with all of us."

No, Mama wasn't there, but at least Birdie had heard from her. After years of praying, hoping, and wondering, she had received a letter last month from California. Mama was well, working as a clerk in a large department store, and saving her money for a train ticket with hopes of visiting near the end of the year. By then, the new baby would be almost six months old, the perfect age to enchant its grandmother.

"The men are doing a Christmas concert at the Presbyterian church." Birdie sighed, holding on to hope. "Maybe she'll be here for that one." She gave a little jolt. "But we will miss tonight's if we don't go inside. Is everyone ready?"

Isaiah held out his elbow to Ophelia, and she took hold. Ellie put Cornelia on the floor and took her hand. She offered the other one to Birdie. Her heart swelling with gratitude, Birdie caught hold. She entered the performance hall with the family God had gifted her just as Lida played the opening bars of "Amazing Grace."

The blend of men's voices accompanied Birdie up the aisle. "Amazing grace, how sweet the sound that saved a wretch like me . . ."

She sighed, smiling. Yes, indeed it had. She once was lost, but now she was found and forever free, thanks to God's amazing grace.

# Readers Guide

1. Alone and abandoned, Birdie went to Lida in search of food and shelter. She got caught in something she didn't want to do. When has desperation driven you to make a decision you later regretted, if ever? How did you find your way out of the situation?

2. Prostitution has been in practice since the earliest civilizations. As Ophelia and Ephraim discussed, it results in harmful consequences for all involved parties. Since it is a harmful practice, why do you think it continues to flourish? What can we do as a society to bring the institution to a close? How can we help people who are trapped in the industry?

3. Ephraim was an integral part of his parents' ministry, using his talents for good. Yet he didn't feel as if he was doing what God intended for him. How can we know if we're serving as God wills or merely serving? Does it really matter if it's God's will as long as we're doing good?

4. When Isaiah invited girls from Lida's Palace to leave and discover freedom, Birdie found the courage to go. Because of her courage, Olga went, too. Why do you think Birdie chose to leave when the others didn't? How would Olga's story be different if Birdie's shame had kept her from walking out the door?

5. Lida went into prostitution after being assaulted by some-one she trusted. Why do you think she chose that path? If people had known what happened to her, do you think they would have treated her differently? Why or why not?

6. Isaiah kept secret what his father did for fear of it dam-aging his ministry. Then he blamed himself for Lida's plummet into prostitution. Is it fair to hold one person accountable for another person's choices? If someone had spoken up and told the truth, how might the story be dif-ferent?

7. Little Ellie has the ability to speak but doesn't do so. How would you feel if someone you loved never spoke to you? What do you think causes some people to live in silence? By the close of the story, Ellie still hasn't chosen to use her voice. What do you think needs to happen for her to finally decide to talk to the people who love her?

8. Ophelia is suffering a health challenge that will shorten her life. She muses that time is fleeting and tries not to waste a single minute. How can we be more cognizant of the hours we have and better use our time for others' good? Have you taken the time to tell the people in your life that they mat-ter to you? If not, why not do so while you can?

9. The overarching theme of this story is that no one is a "lost cause" in God's eyes. How have you found this to be true in your life? How has God reached you? Do we sometimes write people off as too far gone? How can we hold on to hope even when the situation seems impossible?

# Acknowledgments

I always thank family first, so sincerest gratitude to Mom and Dad for guiding me through word and example to love and serve Jesus. I can't imagine better parents than the ones God gave me. Thanks to my husband (forty years together . . . can you believe it?) for your faithfulness to God and me. Thanks to my beautiful daughters for being all-around amazing people and giving me ten amazing granddarlings. Thanks to those granddarlings for delighting Gramma's heart.

To my Texas tornado pal, Eileen, thank you for always scoping out historical story ideas for me. I miss your emails, texts, calls, and visits, but I'm so grateful that you're breathing heaven's glory. Give Mom a hug for me. I'll see you soon, my friend.

Thanks to my writing friend, Connie, for answering my frantic plea for a what-if session. Those imaginative meanderings settled the story plot in my mind. You're the best brainstormer I know!

To Jamie and the amazing team at WaterBrook, thank you for your efforts on my behalf to make the stories shine. I'm glad I don't travel this publishing journey alone.

To Tamela, my agent extraordinaire, thanks for your support and encouragement over the years. God blessed me big-time when He let my path cross yours.

Thanks to my Sunday school and Lit & Latte ladies for your

prayers and encouragement. Y'all mean more to me than you'll ever know.

Finally, and most importantly, thank You, God, for Your hand of grace and healing in my life. I once was lost, but my hope is forever found in my relationship with You. May any praise or glory be reflected directly to You.

# About the Author

KIM VOGEL SAWYER is a highly acclaimed, bestselling author with more than 1.5 million books in print in seven different languages. Her titles have earned numerous accolades including the ACFW Carol Award, the Inspirational Readers' Choice Award, and the Gayle Wilson Award of Excellence. Kim lives in central Kansas with her retired military husband, Don, where she continues to write gentle stories of hope. When she isn't writing, you'll find her petting cats, packing Operation Christmas Child boxes, or spending time with her daughters and grandchildren.

## About the Type

This book was set in Legacy, a typeface family designed by Ronald Arnholm (b. 1939) and issued in digital form by ITC in 1992. Both its serifed and unserifed versions are based on an original type created by the French punchcutter Nicholas Jenson in the late fifteenth century. While Legacy tends to differ from Jenson's original in its proportions, it maintains much of the latter's characteristic modulations in stroke.